WELCOME
TO THE
TIZOC
RESORT

**WE HOPE YOU
ENJOY YOUR STAY.**

ZERO STARS

DO NOT RECOMMEND

A Novel

MJ WASSMER

sourcebooks
landmark

Copyright © 2024 by MJ Wassmer
Cover and internal design © 2024 by Sourcebooks
Cover illustration © Mallory Heyer
Internal design by Laura Boren/Sourcebooks
Internal illustrations © VikiVector/Getty Images

Published by Sourcebooks Landmark, an imprint of Sourcebooks
P.O. Box 4410, Naperville, Illinois 60567-4410
(630) 961-3900
sourcebooks.com

Cataloging-in-Publication Data is on file with the Library of Congress.

Printed and bound in Canada.
MBP 10 9 8 7 6 5 4 3 2 1

to Linda and Bill, for telling me I could
to Leslie, for making sure I did

I

D an Foster was on his fifth Miller Lite when the sun exploded. Or maybe his sixth—that familiar fog floated between his ears and the hair on his head felt heavy and he was talking more than normal, which meant he was talking a lot, because Dan Foster wasn't the strong, silent type. It was the perfect temperature, he pegged it around eighty-two degrees, give or take, and the waves were big enough for people exiting the water to say, "Rough out there!" but not so big that you actually felt helpless. His girlfriend, Mara, was looking at all the girls in bikinis, which Dan liked to watch her do, and the guy two umbrellas over was just *blasting* his Bluetooth speaker. Dan normally hated guys who brought their speakers to the beach—like, How self-centered do you have to be to assume we'd rather listen to your shitty playlist over the sound of seagulls or water crashing or, you know, our loved ones—but the dude was playing eighties yacht rock, and something about it was hitting *just right*. Dan swayed to the rhythm and pointed at Mara, and soon she joined him, dancing and touching and laughing and stumbling in the sand, not a thought about who might be watching because everyone was making their own moments.

But then there was this soft, low rumble, a flicker, and the sun exploded.

It was upsetting.

You'd think the sun exploding would be dramatic, like the Death Star at the end of *A New Hope* or, you know, the bigger Death Stars at the end of the other ones. It's the *sun*. A gaseous ball of fire a million times the size of Earth, Dan remembered from third grade. A red dwarf. Or was it yellow? Either way, it was big—and when it exploded, one would reasonably expect a hell of a light show.

Instead, it was like someone had pelted Earth with an egg. The yolk dripped down the side of the sky and was gone.

Then it was dark.

Not scary dark, not I-need-to-walk-with-my-hands-out-so-I-don't-hit-a-credenza dark, but normal dark. Nighttime dark. The lights of the resort clicked on—must've been on autodimmers—and Dan put his hands on his hips and thought, Huh. As a man, he knew it was important to appear unshakable in the face of an emergency, even if his insides were melting. He'd learned that from his dad, who had learned it from his. It was a fake-it-till-you-make-it tradition passed down through generations of Foster men, who, at their core, had no idea what they were doing. Dan's instinct was to do that here too. To contort his face in a way that indicated someone should be along to fix this shortly, must've tripped a breaker, seen it a million times. But who would believe he'd experienced a cosmic event with galaxy-altering implications before? He was only twenty-nine.

So he just stood there dumbfounded for a while.

The worst part, really, was the screaming. Mara, God bless her, felt no burden to pretend she was in control, and screamed so loud that it shot the beer fog straight from Dan's head and into the night. Well, the day. The day-night. Mara tugged his arm, collapsed in the sand, wept. She pounded her phone with her index finger but cellular was down.

It probably wasn't a good time to bring it up, but Mara did have a flair for dramatics. Dan once used dish soap on her grandma's cast-iron skillet, which apparently you're not supposed to do because it ruins the flavor or something, and she'd performed monologues about that for three weeks. It was anyone's guess how long she'd go on about the sun exploding.

People kicked up sand as they sprinted to their rooms, like they could outrun the dark, and once Dan got Mara to her feet, they ran too. There might've been a tsunami coming, for all they knew, because the sun controls the oceans' waves. Or was that the moon? Whatever. The beach felt like the worst place to be when the sun exploded, and so soon they were on the wooden beach access ramp, and then they were on the textured cement pathway, and then they were wedged in with the crowd trying to squeeze into the breezeway of Building B.

"We can't take the elevator!" Mara screamed, and Dan realized those were the first real words she'd said since the explosion. "You're not supposed to take the elevator in an emergency!"

Dan said, "That's for a fire," as he shouldered a man next to him trying to cut in line.

"No, Danny. It's for all emergencies."

"I think it's just fires, actually, but okay. Okay. It's three floors up. We can take the stairs."

They veered right and joined the crowd of half-dressed people climbing the stairs outside of Building B, facing the resort court-yard and overlooking three pools and a couple lazy rivers. Some shriveled old folks were still enjoying a dip, sitting at swim-up bars, stirring their mai tais as guests shrieked by.

"You know," one guy on the stairs said to his trembling wife, "the sun's so far away that it takes eight and a half minutes for its rays to reach Earth." He was a real know-it-all type, and he had his towel tied under his armpits like a woman stepping from the shower, and he spoke loudly enough to ensure everyone on the staircase heard. "So we saw it explode two minutes ago. But really it happened *ten* minutes ago."

Awesome, dude. Super impressive. We'll be sure to swing by room brainiac on the second floor after Earth defrosts so you can tell us that this wasn't actually the second ice age, but the twelfth, because you didn't sleep through freshman science like everyone else here.

Dan and Mara made it to the third floor, where the crowd thinned out, and raced down the walkway to their room. It occurred to Dan that he wasn't sure what they were racing *toward*, because what protection would their queen, nonsmok-ing room provide? If phones weren't working—and they weren't, people had been trying to post pictures of the apocalypse—then what was there to do, really? They were on a remote island in the middle of the Bahamas.

Shots?

He opened the door for Mara, who leapt inside as though

spring-loaded. Their next-door neighbor, a man in his fifties with graying temples and a TV soap actor face, had just opened his door. Dan and the man locked eyes for a moment, and the older man blew air from the side of his mouth and threw a hand up, like, Can you believe we gotta deal with this? Dan scoffed, like, Unbelievable, and the two entered their respective rooms, Dan grateful that at least his tomb had a minibar.

2

Their first date was Chili's.

Or TGI Fridays—he always got them confused.

He was nervous and overdressed, unsure about his top button. Was it too much chest if he left it unbuttoned? He was too buttoned-up if he buttoned it…

She was relaxed. Unflappable. She repeated the waitress's name back to her and used it throughout dinner, saying things like, *Thanks, Sarah,* and *It's delicious, Sarah,* and *No problem, Sarah, I'll just take the vinaigrette then.*

When the bill came, she offered to pay. Not pretend-offered like a lot of the other girls, who rooted around in their purses like their debit cards had slipped through a side pocket and into the Mariana Trench. She *really* offered, slapped her card down before Dan could even pry his wallet from his pants. He didn't let her. He said he was a feminist, but not an asshole, and that made her laugh, and he laughed too. She threw her head back when she laughed, like a Pez dispenser.

He used the opportunity to unbutton his top button.

After dinner they went to the park. The same park he'd taken girls to since sophomore year of high school because he never moved away, the one with the wooden dock that split through the lake like it was slicing a cake. They ate cake, actually. Sarah the waitress had slipped them a free dessert to go. It was really dry and really carroty—Dan hated carrot—but he ate it because, you know, free cake. He'd never been given anything free in over two decades of visiting restaurants, so this was something. He could tell it was a regular occurrence for Mara though. She had the type of face you wanted to feed things.

He wanted to draw her face. It was a weird thought, probably, but the way the moonlight stretched across the woods and then the lake and then rested on her face—like it'd traveled 240,000 miles just to illuminate her—made him want to draw it. He was terrible at drawing. His houses looked like fire trucks, and his fire trucks looked like dogs. But that night, staring at that olive face framed by that raven hair, he thought maybe all these years, he'd just lacked the proper muse. He drew her on a blue sticky note the next day at work, using a picture from Instagram for reference. The tiny profile picture—he hadn't worked up the guts to follow her. When he finished, it was grotesque, more Crypt Keeper than Priyanka Chopra, and he threw it away and never mentioned it to anyone.

After the cake she wanted to skip rocks. Her dad had taught her how to skip rocks, she said, growing up camping, and she missed that and him. Her eyes grew when Dan told her he'd never skipped rocks before. They didn't go camping, he explained, they had an aboveground pool, and he once got in trouble for tossing rocks in it. She was excited to teach him and screamed and hugged him when he made one bounce three times—three times!—because that was awesome for a beginner, dude. She called him dude. Was that a good sign or a bad sign? Dan called the cashier at the gas station dude. He did like him though.

Then he picked up another rock, confident now, and just as he was prepared to unleash the Foster fury, she lunged forward and caught him. The rock fell to the ground and she scooped it up. No, she said, you can't throw this one. Look at the wavy pattern on it. See? Means this rock has seen some shit. Probably worked really hard to get to where it is, on this shore, tonight, with us, so you can't just throw it back in. It's really good luck to find a rock like that.

Dan felt the smoothness of that rock in his swim trunks and stood over Mara while she cried into the recess between the pillows in their resort room. He looked for the moon through the sliding glass door, but it was pointless. You only see the moon because it reflects light from the sun, so that might as well have disappeared too. He'd never again see the moonlight on Mara's face, and that made him feel worse than anything so far.

He tried to fix it, because that's what men do—fix things that break, even if what breaks is the universe. He pounded his laptop awhile, but Wi-Fi was still out. He went out on the balcony and shouted to some guys down in the garden, but they didn't know either. They just squinted up at the black sky, said, "We must be missing something here," and then eventually threw their arms up like, Yup, well, the sun exploded, I guess. Dan said to Mara they could get a flight out early, get home to her mom, who he was sure was fine, but then he stopped talking when he realized he didn't know how to book a flight without the internet. Do planes still fly when the sun explodes?

He sat on the edge of the bed and listened to Mara weep. Then he reached out and held her hand, something he knew how to do without internet access. They stayed that way for a while, and she quieted down, and it was quiet. Somehow even quieter without the sun, though Dan was pretty sure it never made any noise.

Mara sniffed, her voice muffled by the mattress. "Danny?"

"Yeah, babe."

"Did you get the travel insurance?"

"What?"

"The travel insurance." Mara tugged her hand free from his and rolled over, sat up. She wiped her eyes with the insides of her wrists. Women always use the inside. "On travel sites, when you book the trip, there's a little box at the bottom where it asks you if you want to protect your trip with travel insurance. Did you do that?"

Dan racked his brain. It'd been months since he booked the trip. "I don't remember seeing a box."

"There's always a box. It's, like, a little extra money, but it protects your trip in case the flights get messed up, or you get sick, or if the nearest star blows up." She shook her head. "You *really* didn't get the travel insurance, Danny?"

Was she serious? Life as they knew it had just been fundamentally altered, or even canceled, and she was worried about whether they'd recoup twenty-five hundred—oh. She was smiling now, because Mara had a good poker face, but there was a timer on it. She could only hold it for a little while before whatever she was feeling burst through the surface like it'd been holding its breath. She laughed, he laughed, and that was Mara for you. Devastated one second, cracking jokes the next, a slideshow of emotion that Dan loved scrolling through. They laughed for a while and then held each other in bed.

"I'm worried about my mom," Mara said, her eyes closed. She didn't need to say it, Dan knew she was. She always was. Mara's mom, Ami, had a pair of no-good kidneys, just real deadbeats, and she was on dialysis three times a week back home in Memphis. Mara's older sister, Raveena, was in charge of getting her to appointments while Mara was away in the Bahamas, but Mara already didn't like that because Raveena once tried to microwave her phone after she read online that it charged the battery faster. Raveena wasn't smart like Mara, or responsible like Mara, or pretty like Mara, though Dan could never say that part aloud.

But she could handle taking Ami back and forth to the hospital for *two weeks*, Dan had said, and finally Mara had agreed. But then half an hour ago everything changed, or thirty-eight minutes ago if the guy on the stairs knew what he was talking about, and they both knew Raveena couldn't handle the apocalypse *and* getting her mom to the hospital on time.

"Her kidneys can fail in a couple weeks," Mara said, squeezing the sheets. "If she doesn't get to dialysis, Danny, she—"

"We're going to figure this out," Dan said, because that's what a man says in emergencies, even if it doesn't mean anything. He'd been the one to push this trip, the one who saw the ads on Facebook during his lunch break, the one to say Building

B would be nice. It's not Building A, of course, because we're not Kardashians, but it's certainly not Building C either, because we're not vagrants. If Mara's mom died while they were on *this* trip, on *Dan's* trip, then Mara's hand might not fit inside his the same way ever again.

"We're going to figure this out," Mara repeated, and she slid from the bed and went to the mirror above the vanity and looked at her face, puffed her cheeks, and sighed. She put on eyeshadow. She didn't need it, but Dan knew better than to stop her, because Mara liked to feel like she was in control, and she could totally control a smoky eye.

There was a pounding on the door, and they both jumped, but Dan played off his jump like he happened to be hopping from the bed at that exact moment, what a coincidence. He cautiously peered through the peephole first. Could have been NASA rounding up brave young men to shoot into space to poke around. But it was only Julio, the kid with the flat nose and white teeth who was working the Sola Pool yesterday. Julio loved Dan. Dan was so generous with him, tipping singles because he was quick with the drinks and because weren't dollars in the Bahamas worth a lot more than back home? And after a few coconut rum and pineapple juices Dan started tipping Julio *two* singles per drink, because what the hell, and he kind of felt like Oprah.

"My man!" Dan said as he swung open the door, but Julio's expression was vacant. Dan pushed his thumb into his chest, then over his shoulder back at Mara, and said, "Coconut rum and pineapple juice!…Sola Pool?"

"Alright now, hey," Julio said, but his eyes were cloudy, and Dan thought, What a waste of some perfectly good singles.

Mara joined him. "Do they know what happened?"

"Mr. Sheridan wants all guests to meet at the Adobe Amphitheater on the Great Lawn in ten minutes." Dan noticed Julio was sweating now and short of breath, like he'd sprinted the length of the resort. He was gone as quickly as he appeared, banging on the next door and the next, and soon people congregated outside their rooms, murmuring and worrying and saying "This is ridiculous, isn't it?" like somehow the resort was responsible for a supernova. Dan and Mara were swept up in it, washed from their room and pushed downriver like rocks with waves on them.

Neither knew who Mr. Sheridan was. They knew it sounded official though, so Dan shrugged at Mara, and his face said, Well, if Mr. Sheridan wishes to see us, my goodness, we better get a move on, hadn't we.

3

The Great Lawn was west of Building B and west of the gardens, a big patch of manicured grass that Dan mistakenly assumed was a golf course. It rolled down south to some jagged cliffs that loomed over the beach like sentries, and the Adobe Amphitheatre cut into it up north, away from the crashing of the waves, a giant crater with concrete stadium seating carved with Aztec symbols and a stage at the bottom center. Dan and Mara took seats near the aisle—Dan preferred the aisle, wasn't so claustrophobic—and they watched as more panicked faces poured into the hole.

It would have been a pretty night if it wasn't four in the afternoon. Dan could see stars in the sky now, just not the one that mattered. There were no clouds, which he was thankful for. Imagine if the sun exploded but you missed it because a cumulus was parked in front. Mara held his hand in her lap and idly tapped the top of it, which she only did when she was nervous, and she was singing "Linger" by the Cranberries under her breath, which she only did when she was *really* nervous.

It was getting full. Some folks resigned themselves to standing on the Great Lawn because they couldn't find nice seats for a party of two. Staff members, dressed like Julio in white linen shirts and pants, ushered them as best as they could, requesting guests scoot toward the center, please, thank you, and Dan was pissed he had to give up his aisle seat to someone late to the apocalypse explanation show. The staff eventually signaled they were at capacity, and the crowd adopted a collective hum of anticipation.

"Got that Bahamas beard coming in, huh, man?"

Oh, no. There was a stranger talking to Dan, a guy one row down had turned to make friends, and that was the last thing Dan wanted to do right now and most of the time, really. The guy had a heavy but immaculately shaped beard, and the girl with him didn't bother turning around, which made Dan think he must do this a lot.

Dan heard him fine, but still leaned forward and said, "What's that?"

The guy laughed. "Oh, no, I'm just saying you've got the stubble of a man who's been in the Bahamas a few days." He pointed to Dan's face, and Dan rubbed it. Yeah. He hadn't shaved in a couple days. He needed a haircut too, come to think of it, the dark brown thicket on his head was starting to do that wavy thing on the sides.

"We got here yesterday," Dan said. Everyone got here yesterday, of course, because that was the resort's grand opening. Dan averted his eyes in a way that indicated, Okay, man, nice talking to you, but I've got some other stuff going on right now, if you don't mi—

"Man, that's exactly how mine started."

Dan closed his eyes and hung his head. The rhythm of Mara's tapping on his hand changed. It was Morse code for *Be nice.*

"Oh, yeah?" Dan muttered.

The dude lit up like a Christmas tree, like no other human had ever followed a statement of his with an oh, yeah?

"Yeah, man. We were in Cali for a couple weeks two summers ago visiting my cousin, and I thought, like, Okay, I'm just gonna let this thing go because I'm in Cali, right?" He slapped Dan's leg and Dan hated him. "And so, I'm like, looking in the mirror, thinking, Okay, this thing's looking pretty good, fuller than I thought. And so I just went with it, man. And what you see before you today is after two years. The ladies love it. Don't you love it, babe? You should go for it, dude."

Dan's wandering eyes settled on the guy's tank top. There was a silhouette of a beard in the middle and it said, WITH GREAT BEARD COMES GREAT RESPONSIBILITY, and Dan wondered if it was possible for eyes to roll 360 degrees, just back and around and back up again like cherries in a slot machine.

Dan asked, "Would I have to wear stupid fucking shirts if I did?" and Mara's nails pierced his skin, and the guy mumbled something and spun back around, like, what an asshole, but at least it ended the interaction.

Dan hated guys whose whole personality was having a stupid beard.

Mara whispered, "Real nice, Danny," and she sounded actually annoyed, not playfully annoyed, but now there was music playing from the stage—was that Stone Temple Pilots?—and the crowd took a communal gasp of air like they were being dunked in the ocean.

A tall skinny man resembling a cornstalk appeared onstage, just ambled out there like one of the brooms in *Fantasia,* and the music stopped abruptly. He was in his midtwenties, probably, or maybe a bit younger, and he swayed like three children stacked on top of each other, like something masquerading as a man but definitely not really a man at all. And he had a man bun, Jesus, like that settled it. My bun is a man, see, so that means I am too.

But he wasn't.

There was some feedback on the mic, which made him wince, but eventually he spoke. "Good evening," he said, but it wasn't either of those things. His voice cracked. "I-I-I'm Brody Sheridan, owner, general manager, and CPO at Tizoc Grand Islands Resort and Spa. *CPO* stands for *chief party officer.*"

Dan deflated. This is the guy in charge?

"And, well, I guess first of all, I want to thank everyone for joining us for the grand opening here at Tizoc. Isn't this place beautiful?" He raised his hand for applause but only heard from confused cicadas. Brody cleared his throat. "Hard to believe, but when I bought this island four years ago, there wasn't anything on it. Well, besides the old airstrip and the observatory."

Dan glanced at Mara. Observatory? Mara pulled the resort map from her shorts pocket. It wasn't listed. Dan studied the map more closely, hoping that maybe he missed some emergency exits. There were four large buildings on the island, each creatively named, surrounding a massive courtyard and pool deck. Building A, designed for the hoity-toity, had the best location on the island. Beachfront, steps away from the sand. Building B had views of the gardens, which were okay, and Building C, to the north, was like an hourly motel in a parking lot riddled with hypodermic needles. Okay, there weren't really needles, but Building C *was* near the lot where they kept golf carts, Jeeps, and buses. Think third class on the *Titanic* without the fiddles. The Main Building, which housed the ballroom, gym, spa, and other shared amenities, was straddled between B and C.

Brody rubbed his arm and continued. "And I think, ah, that we can all agree that everyone was having a really tight time up until, well, this afternoon. No cap. Like, I saw you guys lookin' pretty chill, really vibin' with the place, and then. You know. Womp, womp." The crowd shifted. He was losing them.

A man a few rows up stood. He was wearing long shorts and an AC/DC shirt—definitely a Building C guest. "Tell us what the fuck happened!"

There were calls of agreement. Another man near the stage shouted something and pointed aggressively, someone somewhere shrieked about flights home. Brody trembled. He looked offstage at somebody, like, help me out, here, then slowly returned the mic to his mouth and gulped.

"So. Okay. Uh. We think the sun is…actually gone."

It was the crowd's turn to explode. Asses shot from seats, the pointing became pointier, several guests dragged their partners toward the exit like they could stomp their way across the Atlantic. The cries became more desperate.

"You have to get us off this island!"

"We have children!"

"Why can't we connect to the internet?"

"We'll freeze to death!"

Mara squeezed Dan's fingers so tight that they almost snapped like pencils. His chest tightened. He'd seen the sun

explode with his own eyes—why'd it take this asshole's confir-
mation to make it feel real?

Brody's head whipped back and forth as if he was watching
a violent tennis match, and his face grew paler and his mouth
gaped and he had the general appearance of wetness. He took a
big step backward, then another, and he almost fell off the stage,
but a small man shaped like a church bell appeared and grabbed
him. He politely took the microphone from Brody, patted his back
a few times for reassurance, and ushered him safely off the side.
As the new man—and this *was* a man, just a small balding one—
approached the front of the stage, a hush rolled over the amphitheater. This guy was wearing a bow tie. He had to know something.

"Hello. Yes, please. Please sit. My name is Dr. Terry Shae. I
live and work at the observatory on the northeast cliffs that Mr.
Sheridan just mentioned. My observatory is part of the Space
Telescope Science Institute network." He paced the stage with
small measured steps, the kind that Dan associated with learned
men somehow. His eyes were tiny and black like the dark side of
a moon, and his dimpled skin was like the surface of one. "I've
been stationed on this island, on and off, for almost thirty years,
observing the small-body population of our solar system while
searching and identifying exoplanets in our greater galaxy. When
Mr. Sheridan says he purchased this island four years ago, he is
mostly correct. He purchased one hundred ninety acres of a two-
hundred-twenty-acre island. The observatory and the airstrip
still belong to me."

He paused, looking up at the stars that remained.

"What happened today is, without question, the most signif-
icant natural event in the history of our species. In the history of

our planet, truly, dating back billions of years." He said it like he was in awe, like he'd met God himself, and there was fear in his voice but also great reverence.

"Like you, I have many questions. Also like you, unfortunately, I currently possess very few answers. Mr. Sheridan requested I take a short break from my duties at the observatory to come here to address you all, to shed light—excuse my choice of words—on the situation." Even the cicadas were quiet now, because Shae was a man who commanded attention, a shout if Brody was a whisper.

The man in the AC/DC shirt stood again, but his hand was raised this time and he waited to be acknowledged. Shae pointed to him and nodded.

"Sir, do we know why it blew up?"

Someone near Dan whispered that it blew up because Jesus had returned. Another cursed ISIS. The thought of terrorism had briefly entered Dan's mind, but blowing up the sun felt like a poorly thought-out jihad.

"I am afraid I do not," Shae said, "not at this time. Others may, but as you know, whatever happened also cut off communication to and from the island. I understand that Mr. Sheridan and his team are working diligently to get systems back online, but it may take some time." He inhaled, trapping the history in his lungs. "You inquired, sir, how it *blew up*, and I would like to make a note on that. An explosion implies that something has ceased to exist or is structurally unrecognizable, and current evidence does not suggest that."

Another hand up, this time closer to the stage. "Dr. Shae, I saw it blow up. It looked like butter on a hot pan."

Yeah, others agreed, *me too, definitely.* As noted, Dan thought it looked more like an egg, but okay, butter. Definitely a breakfast ingredient.

Shae nodded slowly. "Yet here we are." He promptly walked to the back of the stage and hopped off, disappeared down and out of view. People stood, trying to get a look at him. What was he doing? Then he was back, helped onstage by a member of the security team—had there always been a security team?—and he clutched a black stone. He turned it in his hand, presented it to the audience. He raised his eyebrows and cocked his head like a magician, as if to say, This is a stone, no tricks here, just a normal stone—wouldn't you agree? No one spoke. Shae really had them. The guests on the Great Lawn stepped down into the aisles, uncrossed their arms, leaned in.

Shae sifted through his khaki pockets, produced some twine, and tied it around the stone. He allowed the stone to fall to the stage, and when it landed with a thud, several women in the audience leapt. There was nervous laughter. Even Shae smiled. He had the grin of a boy who was getting away with something, a boy playing with toys after all the lights in the house had been switched off. He signaled to someone offstage, and another member of the security staff appeared. The man held the microphone to Shae's mouth so both hands were free.

"Let us put aside the fact that if the sun were to explode, we would be liquefied. Instead, pretend the sun disappeared completely. Vanished into thin air without a cosmic trace." He tested that the stone was secure at the end of the twine once more. Then he began to swing it above his head in a wide orbit, slowly at first, but then faster and faster, like David preparing to pummel Goliath. At a certain speed, it reached an equilibrium, and Dan barely saw the twine anymore, just a hunk of rock hurtling through space.

"Due to the sun's extreme gravitational force, Earth orbits it at thirty kilometers per second, or sixty-seven thousand miles per hour. Even at this blistering speed, in order to completely orbit the sun, it takes Earth…" He paused, prompting the class for answers.

Dan knew this one. "One year," he said with several others.

"One year. Imagine each rotation of this stone around my head being one year in the history of time. Earth has completed this journey four and a half billion times, give or take, though for the purpose of this demonstration, I may stop around a million or so."

Polite laughter.

"So now, the sun disappears, as you say. What happens to Earth? Well, depending on our precise location in orbit…" Without warning, he released the string and the stone flew off stage left and out of sight.

A woman near Dan gasped, and Dan thought, Okay, lady, calm down.

"We would be slingshot through space at our original speed of sixty-seven thousand miles per hour. Earth would be an uncontrollable spaceship on a crash course with whatever poor celestial mass stood in our way, flying through the cosmos with little indication of where—or when—we might settle."

Several guests around Dan gripped their cement amphitheater seats, knuckles white. Mara's hand dug into his leg. Her eyes said, I agreed to go on a trip, Danny, but this isn't what I had in mind.

But the stars weren't moving. They looked the same as normal. A little ahead of schedule, maybe, but still reporting for duty. If Earth was shooting through space, wouldn't it look like entering hyperdrive?

"No," Shae said, as though answering Dan personally. But it was more of a general no. Shae thanked the security guy, signaled him offstage, and took back the mic. "Everything I've observed since the incident this afternoon suggests Earth remains firmly in its planetary neighborhood, right at home in orbit where it belongs. The same applies to other planets in our solar system."

There was a communal exhale, because it's nice to be home, isn't it, but then the murmuring started back up. Shae's explanation only begged more questions. Soon people shouted again, the cicadas screamed.

"So then, what *happened*?"

"Are we going to freeze to death?"

"What next, Professor Shae? Dr. Shae. Whatever!"

"Is tonight's pig roast still happening?"

"What can we do?"

Shae raised his hand, which lowered the volume.

"I do not know—please, listen. I do not know what it means, besides that we should take comfort that Earth is precisely where it should be. However, I will not lie to you. I have grave concerns. Photosynthesis cannot occur without the sun, as you know, so small plant life and crops will suffer. This will have worldwide effects on our food chain. My other concern, at the moment, is Earth's average temperature. Our planet will retain heat for some time, but not in perpetuity. I predict we will reach temperatures near freezing by the end of the week. By the end of the year, models suggest Earth's average temperature could fall to negative one hundred fifty degrees."

He may have imagined it, but Dan felt a cool breeze sweep over the Great Lawn and funnel into the amphitheater, and he and Mara huddled even closer, goose bumps riddling their exposed arms and legs.

"At this time," Shae said, "our primary focus should be remaining calm. We are on an isolated island in the middle of the Bahamas. We need one another. Our other focus should be getting to the mainland. Barring mass panic, riots, general chaos—the government will likely implement heating stations, scramble the military to provide aid. Nuclear fuel may be a viable option for keeping underground communities warm, and geothermal areas—like Yellowstone—will produce heat for the foreseeable future. There are options, though limited, and none existing in the long term on this island."

Many members of the audience stood, tugged their loved ones up. Let's go, their faces said, Come on. How we doing this?

"On that note, I will bring back Mr. Sheridan to discuss evacuation plans. I must return to the observatory. Terrifying though it may be, my job is to record my observations so that future astronomers—God willing, there will be future astronomers—better understand what we may not today. Good luck to you all."

And with that, he was gone, hopped off the side of the stage and disappeared among the gathered staff and security. Dan felt immediately worse once he left. Brody Sheridan, the steaming pile of a human being, practically had to be poured onstage. He fumbled the microphone like it might burn him.

"O-okay, so let's give it up for my man Dr. Shae. Love that

dude. When he talks, my mind's like, *BOOM*." He mimed his head exploding, the fractured pieces shooting every which way. The imagery was perhaps too soon, a little too fresh, and people booed.

"Alright, alright, yeah, no, I get it. This situation is definitely not chill. And I want to address that, um…presently. As Dr. Shae said, we need to get off the island. The thing is, though, the problem is, the planes you flew on here from Nassau? Those planes aren't scheduled to be back to pick people up until two weeks from yesterday, when everyone was scheduled to go home. And, like, sure, you might say, Why don't you just call them, tell them to come early? I would love nothing more than to do that, guys, for real. But communication is down, so—"

Brody dodged a beer bottle that shattered at his feet. Then another. Security flanked him. Women screamed about their babies back home, and the amphitheater shook so violently that it might've dug itself farther into the earth. Mara signaled, Come on, Danny, it's time to go, and just as Dan was about to make a run for it, Brody miraculously quelled the noise.

This was his last chance.

Please, kid. Say something smart.

"Listen! Listen. Please, listen. Remember what Dr. Shae said about being calm. Obviously, we are going to keep trying to reach the plane people, and, like, whoever else we can reach. The Coast Guard, maybe. Trust me on that. And we have food and water. Plenty for the next two weeks and…a little extra. We are going to work so hard to get y'all off this island, believe that, okay? But getting all, like, psycho about it isn't going to help. We have a badass IT staff, and they're trying to get communication back as we speak, okay? So uh…let's just let them do their thing and stay calm. Like, enjoy the island, maybe."

He was so stupid. So, so stupid, but also kind of right, which was aggravating. They'd arrived on the island after a connection in Nassau—the planes barely sat a hundred each—and afterward Dan watched as they became dots on the horizon, and he remembered the faintest feeling of being trapped, of being stuck on this postage stamp in the ocean for two weeks, no matter what. But then he was handed a fruity drink with a little umbrella and that feeling was gone, sputtered away the same as those planes.

It was back now, with a vengeance, and not even an aisle seat could've kept him from feeling claustrophobic.

The crowd finally lost its fight. Guests sat quietly, buried their faces into each other, shoulders trembling. Brody remained onstage, in his sandals, his lips petrified against the microphone.

Mara whispered it first this time.

"We're going to figure this out."

"We're going to figure this out," Dan repeated.

A slender woman in her midfifties with flowing blond hair and a symmetrical face stood a few rows back from Dan. Her voice carried as though she'd had a miniature bullhorn injected during one of her neck's many Botox appointments.

"When the planes *do* come, Mr. Sheridan, is it safe to assume that guests of Building A will receive priority boarding?"

4

The pig roast was canceled.

Julio, pool boy extraordinaire, guided Dan, Mara, and the rest of Building B's stupefied guests back to their rooms with instructions to, well, await further instruction.

Around seven, a staff member delivered dinner—cold tortillas with dry taco beef and clumps of gloopy rice. As Dan and Mara ate in bed, they wondered aloud if the food had been better before the sun exploded or if they'd just been in better moods. After they ate, they had sex because what if it was their last chance. Like the food, though, it was lukewarm, and afterward Mara cried and Dan felt a stinging in the corner of his eyes too, but he disguised it. Mara seized his wrists and told him it was okay, babe, it's okay to cry when the sun explodes, but men don't cry, so he held Mara while she did. They showered—what else was there to do?—and Dan told Mara he was sure Raveena was taking care of Ami, and Mara told Dan that his parents and sister would be okay too.

Usually they watched *Disappearance Report* on Netflix before bed. It was their show, their guilty pleasure, and it was a documentary series about people disappearing under mysterious circumstances. That felt a little too raw now, and the internet was still out anyway.

So they played cards. Mara found a deck above the closet next to the iron, it was missing an ace, and Dan won because Mara's poker face kept shattering. They drank what was left in the minibar, the airplane bottles of rum collecting on the dresser faster with each hand, and they ate the candy bars to wash the taste of dinner away. When the room began to spin—not spin out of control, more like a lazy carousel—Dan noticed how thin the walls actually were. He could hear their neighbors on either side and down below. He heard the stress-fueled screaming matches and the optimistic packing of suitcases and the thud of something heavy against the wall, hopefully a piece of furniture and not somebody's head. He heard the wails of a mother crying out for her children, so muffled that it may have been two rooms over, but then he slid open the heavy balcony door and also heard drunken, unrestrained laughter, and someone playing a ukulele in the garden. Whoever it was didn't know more than four chords, and even those were suspect, but still it was nice.

They lay down, switched off the lamps, and Mara's breathing became heavy. She was a good sleeper. One of the best. If there was an Olympic sport for sleeping, for drifting off while being subjected to increasingly flamboyant distractions—a marching band, a reanimated tyrannosaurus rex, a bombing—Mara would take home gold for her country so long as there was a pillow on which to prop her legs. And when Dan, proud as could be, was interviewed afterward, he'd say, Well, Bob, she's been training tirelessly for years, in cars and in planes and in movie theaters and doctors' waiting rooms. She never gave up the dream, he'd say, and they'd laugh together at his little joke.

Dan wasn't sure how long he lay there unable to sleep, it must've been hours, because the thin walls quit talking and the only sound from the garden was the breeze in the shrubbery. He thought another drink might do it, just one more to cap the end of a fine day—the last day—but he glanced at Mara, and the thought of leaving her alone without the sun made him feel guilty.

She snorted and turned over.

She'd be fine.

He climbed from bed, pulled on some clothes in the dark— he'd have to get used to doing a lot of things in the dark—and slid outside.

He stumbled north along the walkway, staring out at the pools, the lazy rivers, the water blue green under the resort lights and still like ice. It *would* be ice. Soon. He found the staircase and descended, clutching the railing for balance, careful that his flip-flops didn't do too much flipping or flopping. Normal people needed their sleep.

He reached the small tiki bar carved into the northern end of the ground floor of Building B, facing the Main Building. No one was there, just as he hoped, and he hopped the bar, flicked the cap off a bottle of rum, and poured himself a generous serving. He knocked it back, felt it ooze down inside of him, pooling in the crevices that needed filling.

This isn't stealing, right? Tizoc Grand Islands is an all-inclusive resort. So…

Another?

Oh, thank you. Sure.

He poured another, clutched the glass, and just as he was about to slam it back—

"Well, if you're pouring, what the hell, I'll take one."

Dan almost dropped the bottle. It was the man from earlier, his next-door neighbor, the one with graying temples and soap opera face. The man grinned, straddled a stool, folded his hands on the bar. He nodded at the glass in Dan's hand.

"Take mine on the rocks if we've got 'em."

Dan was the right amount of drunk and the exact right amount of wistful to make friends, a rare occurrence, so he snatched another glass from under the bar, scooped some ice from the machine with his bare hands, and poured the man a drink. The man raised his glass in a toast.

"To the sun. We hardly knew ya."

"The sun," Dan said, and they clinked glasses.

Dan shot his back, the man nursed his. He chuckled as Dan steadied himself against the bar.

"Drinking the pain away, kid?"

"I see no reason to disrupt my routine."

The man laughed and offered his hand. "I'm Alan Ferris."

Dan shook it. "Ferris? Of wheel fame?"

Dan was entering the silly stage of drunk now, but not so drunk that he didn't recognize it. Upon hearing his own stupid joke, he forced a mental adjustment, stood up straight. There was something about Alan that made Dan feel young, and he didn't want Alan to think him young. He had the eyes of a capable man, a man who always knew the next right thing to do. When he was little, Dan thought every adult had those eyes. He knew now that wasn't true. Those certainly weren't the eyes that stared back in the mirror.

"I'm Dan Foster. You and your buddy have the room next to us, right?"

"Me and my husband, yeah."

Wow. Nice one, idiot.

"Where you from?" Dan asked.

"Michigan. Upper Peninsula."

"Christ. You're used to cold. You'll outlive us all."

"Not in these fucking sandals. You?"

"Memphis."

Alan nodded, sipped. "Heard nice things about Memphis."

Dan laughed. "No, you haven't."

Alan grinned and shook his head. "You're right. I haven't."

"That's okay. We like it that way." Dan sipped his rum now, matched Alan's pace. "So, Alan from Michigan, we gonna die on this island?"

Alan scratched his stubble, gave the question the consideration it deserved. "I'll die swimming across the Atlantic before I die on this island, Dan from Memphis."

"Family back home?"

"Two high school boys. My husband's sister's, before she died."

"Worried about them?" What a stupid question.

Alan raised the glass to his lips, took a longer pull. Just before he placed the glass back on the bar, he paused, smiled at Dan in a way that said, Hey, maybe you have the right idea. He threw his head back and the rest of the drink along with it.

Dan poured him another.

"When I left the military, I swore I was done traveling." Alan stared into the fresh rum like he might fall in. "But Charles loves the beach. And Facebook knows that, obviously, so they just *bombarded* him with ads about this place."

Dan snorted. He could still see the ads now. RELAX, DINE, AND STAY WHERE THE ELITES COME TO PLAY. And ATTN THOSE WHO SET TRENDS: TIZOC'S GATES OPEN SOON. Or his personal favorite, NEW RESORT, NEW YOU. MAKE YOUR DEBUT WITH TIZOC GRAND ISLANDS RESORT AND SPA.

"That Brody guy," Alan said, rubbing his brow. "You know his deal? Trust-fund baby. Mom was some bigwig. Charles told me all about it. There's talks of a reality show starring him."

Brody Sheridan? The sentient lamppost? He wasn't charismatic enough to carry someone's luggage, much less a TV show.

Alan sighed. "But, shit, I want to make Charles happy, so I cave. We left the boys home alone for the first time in their lives." He patted his chest pocket, then his shorts, feeling for something. "Wife drag you here too?"

Dan exhaled. "Girlfriend. And it was my idea. Facebook got me too."

"Shit." Alan abandoned his search. "Hats off to the social team. You smoke, Dan from Memphis?"

"Nope." Should he?

"Me either. Not officially. I bought an overpriced pack from the lounge after the sun exploded. Must've left it in the room. I'm out of practice." He shrugged, drummed his fingers against the bar. "What's your story? What illustrious career back home in Memphis allows you to enjoy the breathtaking amenities of Tizoc Building B?"

Against better judgment, Dan downed another drink. He burped. He felt it bubbling in his gut, the molecules sloshing to and fro as they morphed into the slurred words he was about to vomit. Dan was talkative—to Mara, to friends, to his steering wheel on the lonely drive to work—but never this talkative with strangers.

"You know, they put me in gifted classes."

Alan raised his eyebrows, like, oh, yeah?

"Yeah. Starting in, what, third grade. Teacher thought I was quick in class or something, and then they tested me, this small little room with puzzles on the table. Word association. What shape should come next, the opposite of *servile* is blank, that kind of thing."

"What's the opposite of *servile*?"

"*Dominant*." Dan poured another, just stared at it. "They meant well, but shit goes to your head, man. When you're told you're reading at a tenth-grade level in elementary school, that doesn't give you much incentive to practice, you know? College hit me hard. I go from this kid who's expected to do something amazing with his life to a C student who wakes up at noon and can't read three paragraphs in succession."

"Smart but lazy."

Dan waved that away. "That's a veneer. Something worthless people say to hide from their worthlessness. Turns out I'm the total package, Alan: dumb *and* lazy. Even dumber than the other kids too because it took me longer to realize it. All because I circled the right fish on a sheet of paper in third grade." He dialed his glass against the bar top. "The word *gifted* implies you were given something, so you grow up thinking you owe the world in return. Took me twenty-nine years to realize I don't have anything to offer."

He was embarrassed now, because the question had been *What you do for a living?* not *Why are you a useless piece of shit?* The end of the world will make a man reflective. Dan pushed the remaining rum away, suddenly disgusted with it.

Alan smacked his lips, clearly uncomfortable. "Don't score a girlfriend who looks like yours without something going on."

"Lucked out there." Dan clutched the bar and leaned backward, stretched his spine. "So I do digital marketing for a midsize regional in-home maid service. I sit in a cubicle all day." The words felt barbed as they rolled over his tongue.

"Maid company?"

"Marvel Maids. Ever heard of 'em?"

Alan chuckled, shook his head, took a sip.

"'Marvel Maids. A home so spotless—you'll *marvel*.'"

"Oof."

"*Oof* is right."

They laughed together, Dan grateful that Alan hadn't feigned interest. His job *did* suck, no use pretending otherwise. On the rare occasion that Dan shared something about his work at home, Mara acted interested. She was convincing, actually, but she was only being polite. Dan knew deep down she wanted him to quit, move on to something she was prouder to tell her friends about. Maybe actually start writing, something Dan pretended was a passion.

Mara was a nurse. She saved lives. Dan calculated baseboard-cleaning discounts by average zip code income.

A figure appeared on the far-right stool as if by teleportation.

Brody Sheridan. He wrapped over the bar like a vine, the messy man bun bobbing atop his head. He sniffed loudly.

"Don't have to stop 'cause of me, dudes." Sniff. "I'm just, ah, making my way to Building A, thought I'd stop and sit 'cause, well." That was the end of the sentence, apparently.

Dan poured him a glass of water from the hose nozzle thing, feeling like a real bartender now, thinking maybe he'd trade the plastic cubicle for a mahogany bar top if it paid well enough. Yeah, that's it. People respect thirty-year-old bartenders.

Brody downed the glass of water in one gulp, his Adam's apple working overtime. He examined the glass afterward, like, What'd you just make me, it tastes great, can I get the recipe?

Dan felt compelled to explain why they were there. "We just wanted one more drink, the minibar was—"

Brody leaned over the bar and pressed his praying mantis finger against Dan's lips. "Shh," he said, eyelids heavy. Sniff. "What's mine is yours, dudes. Drink the whole ocean if you want to."

Alan said, "Nice to see you hard at work restoring communication to the island. Any update on that front, *Brody*?" Alan spit out his name like it was something dirty.

Brody pushed from the stool, stood on wobbly legs. "My men"—sniff—"are on it, guy. You rest easy tonight, 'cause I think tomorrow…w-we'll figure this whole thing out. You know— you know, my mom, she had melanoma. So—so when the sun exploded for like, just like a second, I was like, Yeah. Fuck you, sun!" Sniff. "But no, yeah, I know we gotta get off this island." He displayed his palms. "You're in good hands, my dudes. Good hands. But I gotta go to Building A now."

He turned north. Alan stood, seized Brody's shoulders, and faced him south, toward the shore and Building A. Brody tapped Alan's hand as a sign of thanks, sniffed, and lurched away.

"That fucknut is our only ticket off this island," Alan said, nostrils flared. "And he's high as shit."

Dan lost his short-lived aversion to rum. He took a sip and felt like breaking something. "What can we do?"

Alan leaned across the bar, whispered like they weren't alone. "We can get the fuck out of here."

Dan furrowed his brow, but Alan only leaned in closer, his eyes even clearer and more capable than they'd been before the drinks.

"Three hangars on that airstrip. You see that when you flew in? Three hangars. You mean to tell me there's not a plane in one of them? That Dr. Shae. How's he been coming and going for so many years?"

"I don't know," Dan said, honestly not knowing. Does the presence of hangars indicate the presence of planes? That's not information to which dumb and lazy guys are privy.

"And we *won't* know until we look for ourselves. I'm going to the airstrip tomorrow night. Checking it out."

"Wait for the cover of nightfall," Dan said, tapping his temple. "Good thinking."

Alan didn't appreciate the joke. He looked through Dan now, seeing only his plan, only what he thought needed to be done. Here was a man. Here was a guy who always knew the next right thing to do.

"Come with me. I could use your youth."

Alan might've had twenty-five years on Dan, but he looked

like he could bench-press John Goodman. *Before* the weight loss. He needed Dan?

Dan said, "Say you find a plane. Then what?"

"Air Force engineer for ten years, kid. I'll figure it out."

Huh. Still. Felt risky. If they were caught, they'd lose favor with Brody, and what if the planes eventually *did* come, and Brody decides who boards and who has to wait behind and eat dry tacos, and meanwhile it's getting colder and colder...

"Man," Dan said, "I don't—"

"You *just* said you spent twenty-nine years of your life not giving anything back to the world. Well, here's your chance. Help me get home to my boys. And get your girl home too."

It was a cheap shot.

But it landed.

"I'm drunk," Dan announced to the ocean, alone, twenty minutes later. Alan had gone back to his room to try and sleep, and Dan said that was where he was going, too, but first he wanted to stop by the vending machines to see if they'd been looted. He liked Crunch bars when he was drinking. He forgot about the candy though and lurched past palatial Building A, ignoring the peculiar amount of activity there. Dan ended up at the edge of the world, sand between his toes, water crashing down like the universe was shouting at him.

He shouldn't have said all those things to Alan, a stranger. Hell, he hadn't told most of those things to Mara. About how lately he'd felt worthless and listless and other adjectives that end with *-less* that he couldn't think of right now. That wasn't even the worst of it. The sun had exploded that afternoon. He was going to *die* knowing he was *-less* of what he could've been, a frozen heap of wasted potential and bad decisions for some alien species to discover in a billion years, a petrified corpse they'd excavate and place in their space museum with a plaque inscribed Unimpressius Doughy Heinous.

There'd always been time to turn things around. Not anymore.

Dan reached into his pocket, seized the rock from his first date with Mara, screamed, and flung it into the ocean. It didn't skip once, it just hit the water, barely made a dent, and disappeared. He didn't need a fucking rock with waves on it, he lived on one, and it may have worked really hard to get where it was but pretty soon that wouldn't mean anything.

He shouldn't have thrown it though, because, Christ, that was the first thing Mara ever gave him. Dan dove into the water, desperately sifting the seabed through his fingers, but it was already gone, gone, gone.

He sat under the water for a moment, thinking maybe he'd stay gone too, but the ocean spit him back onto the beach and said, Not yet, Daniel Foster. Not just yet.

At least get the girl home to her mother, loser.

5

Bang, bang, bang.

Oh, God. The door. Dan distinctly remembered placing the Do Not Disturb placard on the handle before succumbing to his blackout. Maybe it'd stop. Maybe if he just rolled over, nuzzled his head into this…ooh, newly discovered pillow divot, very nice…maybe whatever it was would go awa—

Bang, bang, bang.

"Dan! Dan, it's Alan Ferris. From next door. We've got a situation out here, partner."

Mara was stirring now, groaning. Dan liked Alan very much, but he hated everyone before a certain hour, and—he poked open one eye—it wasn't even *light* out. Who bangs on someone's door before the—

Oh.

Right.

He begrudgingly spun from under the covers and into a pair of resort-branded slippers. The room continued to spin after he stopped. He slammed his eyes shut and clutched the mattress for dear life. A hangover. That's perfect. Just *once*, Dan said to God, can I not experience the consequences of my own actions.

"Ugh," Mara said, now fully awake. "Why do you smell like sushi."

Dan sniffed his pits. "Took a dip last night."

"Last night? After we went to bed?"

"Yeah, I—"

Bang, bang, bang.

"Dan! It's Alan! The guy from the bar last night. The one you opened up to about how you've been feeling kind of—"

In a flash, Dan rolled across the bed, over Mara's legs, and unlatched the door. Yup, there was Alan. Handsome as ever, clear eyes. He stood beside his partner, Charles, a chubby, pale man in a bright Hawaiian shirt and yellow shorts cuffed at the thigh. It was comforting to know that, without the sun, Charles's wardrobe existed as a source of light.

Alan looked Dan over. "Oh. You're not dressed."

"He is *not*," Charles said, each syllable basted in Southern twang. He had a softness about him, like a favorite armchair come to life.

Mara, wrapped in a robe, joined Dan at the door.

"Hello." She smiled. How did her hellos always sound so kind? Her voice was warm like it was preheated overnight.

"Why, hello," Charles said.

"This is Alan," Dan said, his voice a tire atop gravel. "And this—"

"I'm Charles Ferris, an absolute pleasure." Charles stuck out his hand, Dan and Mara took it.

"I'm Mara. Nice to meet you, Alan and Charles."

Charles waved his hand. "Oh, we know you, Ms. Tropic of C Lira two-piece in Mama Africa print."

Dan didn't know what any of those words meant when strung together in that particular order, but Mara was astonished.

A devilish grin spilled over Charles's face. "I'm a *big* fan of her stuff."

"It's all so cute!" Mara said. "But so—"

"*Expensive!*" they said together.

"I wasn't even sure if I should splurge on it, Charles, but I haven't taken a vacation in so long, and I just loved the, you know, twist rope, so I thought—"

"What time is it?" Dan asked Alan.

"Just after seven."

This personally offended Dan. "Okay. Wow. I don't discuss bikinis until at least eight, so if you fellas don't mind." He began to shut the door, but Alan's forearm didn't budge.

"Dan, there's a situation." His eyes did that serious thing again, and Charles quieted down too, looked at his boat shoes like, Oh, right, we're not here to chat swimwear.

"Yeah," Dan said. "The sun. I remember."

"Building A took all the food overnight."

"What?" Mara said.

Yeah. What? Dan stepped outside in his boxers, between Alan and Charles, and peered over the railing at Building A. There was a crowd gathered just past the pools—he hesitated to call it a mob, but it hummed with the collective unease characteristic of mobs—and it was growing by the second. Armed guards stood at the entrances of Building A's breezeways, pistols strapped at their waists, shaking their heads, holding out their palms.

Not only is there a security force, there's an *armed* security force?

Alan joined Dan at the railing. "Must've been after we went to bed. Charles and I were looking for grub this morning—a lot of people were—and there's nothing. The fuckers paid off the guards and most of the staff members. Stole all the supplies from the restaurants, the main kitchen, the bars. Infirmary. Pallets of shit. They've got it all."

"We're sure?" Dan asked.

"Julio told us. I guess they couldn't buy him."

Three doors down, a sweaty man in a cabana hat hurriedly exited his room, his rolling suitcase skipping along the cement walkway. Where was he possibly planning to go?

Alan shook his head. "People are panicked."

Dan hugged himself and squeezed back inside. It was already cooler than yesterday. Not cold, not yet, but low sixties?

Christ, it was really happening.

"They paid the guards?" Mara asked. She tossed Dan a T-shirt from his suitcase and then a pair of sweatpants he wore around the house when he didn't care what he looked like. Mara called them his fart pants.

"Well, you know they've got deep pockets over there," Charles said, having invited himself in. "We sat next to a couple from Building A at dinner the other night, right, Alan? And she had a Chanel bag. The Maxi Flap. Oh, and it was real, I could tell. But she got it with the tweed? Like, if you have five grand to spend on a bag like that, you're really gonna get *tweed*, honey?"

Guests in Building A—they didn't even call them guests, they called them visitants—could afford Chanel Maxi Flaps in tweed or silk or mongoose skin or any other type of fabric, because Building A was designed for upper society. They also enjoyed upgraded amenities, an exclusive restaurant named after some Aztec goddess, a premier cigar lounge, butler service, first choice of cabanas on the shoreline. Their balconies were larger, their drinks stronger, and rumor had it their elevators were faster, the bastards. Simon Cowell was supposedly staying in Building A. Dan hadn't seen him, but a drunk man at the Sola swim-up bar swore that he had. Said his boobs weren't as big as they appeared on TV.

By the time Dan, Mara, and their neighbors joined the crowd amassing outside Building A, tensions were rising. Tiki torches plucked from the beach were lit and shaking overhead. Empty airplane bottles of liquor shattered against the stucco. Residents of Buildings B and C shouted up at the balconies, demanded explanation, breakfast. Guards pointed their pistols into the crowd now, which marked the first time Dan had ever been in the sights of a gun without NERF printed on the side.

Mara became part of the resistance almost instantly, chanting, "Dude, dude, where's our food?" which was kind of catchy, and Charles soon joined. As they forced their way toward the center of the increasingly irritated crowd, Dan spotted a familiar figure and grabbed his shoulder. Julio. The kid had a lousy memory for good tippers, but maybe he could do something about all this.

"Julio! What the hell's going on?" Dan's question was almost completely drowned out.

"They took the food!" Julio replied, and Dan wasn't sure what else he was expecting. Where was Brody? Had he really lost control of everything this quickly? And big picture here: If their small Bahamian island had already collapsed into anarchy, what did that mean for back home?

Memphis would burn.

Mara tossed a hair tie at Building A, like that would do anything but get hair in her eyes, and then she turned to Julio. "How'd they do it?"

"The resort has a series of underground tunnels for workers!" he said. "The bastards paid off the guards, most of the staff and transported the supplies underground overnight!" He spit on the ground, which was so tightly packed with sandaled feet that Dan was sure it never reached cement.

Mara said, "Tunnels?" and then she lost her balance when a man brandishing a luggage rack above his head bumped into them. Dan steadied her. A few other unbribed staff members weaved through the mob—Dan was officially calling it that, a mob—and were conversing with Julio now, and one of them held a megaphone in his hand. Julio nodded and turned back.

"We need someone to address the crowd!"

Okay, Dan thought. Go ahead.

Alan and Charles reappeared. Alan pointed Julio toward a wrought-iron table. "Get up there and demand they release the fucking food!"

Julio nodded. He wrung his wrist. He was sweating, but not from body heat. He looked faint.

"Well, what are you waiting for?" Charles said. He leaned in and whispered to Dan. "If I don't eat by eight, I am a *zombie*."

Julio pushed the megaphone into Alan's chest. "I can't! I have…terrible stage fright! My heart starts pounding and I get lightheaded, and my throat clogs up!"

This was Brody Sheridan's job. Where *was* he?

Alan shrugged, like, fuck it, but as he climbed onto the table, Charles seized his collar and yanked him back into the masses.

"Honey, I love you, but you ain't the man for this." Charles squeezed Alan's shoulder and turned to Mara. "He'll get hotheaded. Cuss. If he had negotiated with Patty Hearst's captors, honey, her head would've come home in a Kroger sack. Come on, Alan, you know it."

Alan's face conveyed that yes, he knew it. He held the megaphone out to Charles, who pushed it away.

"Oh, hell no. Uh-uh."

Mara snatched the megaphone, and now it was against Dan's chest.

"Danny should do it," she said, and she smiled at him in that way that made him believe he could do anything. And for the briefest of seconds he thought, Yeah, you know, I kicked ass in my public speaking course in college, and that was a lot more pressure because the topic was wage gaps in the public sector and the room was full of women's studies majors. Maybe I could—

He shook free of her gaze and put his hands up. "I can't. I'm not—I'm not the guy."

"He was a political science major," Mara said to Alan and Charles. "And he writes so well. It's his talent. You should hear him talk when he's drunk. He can talk."

"Oh, I know," Alan said. He nodded at Dan, and Charles smiled, and Dan felt the group come to a consensus without him, and his hangover was suddenly worse. He wanted to go back to his room and draw the shades, sleep this whole nightmare away.

Draw the shades from what?

"Time to be the guy," Alan said, and he hoisted Dan onto the wrought-iron table as effortlessly as he would a kitten.

The mob saw Dan, megaphone in hand, and there was a hush. The last thrown chair landed somewhere with a clatter. Then came applause, Dan's heart keeping pace with each clap.

You stupid assholes, he thought. I just happened to be standing near the table.

He raised the megaphone to his lips—why was it so heavy?—but before he pressed the button, the crowd did an about-face. Brody Sheridan had appeared on one of the top balconies of Building A, had a megaphone of his own, and was shirtless for some reason. People booed, others hissed—Dan had never heard people hiss in real life—before Brody was able to calm them down.

"Wow," Brody said, and his tone was way too sarcastic right off the bat. "Angry much?"

It was impressive, really. Brody might've said the single worst thing you can say to a hungry group of people whose star had blown up less than twenty-four hours ago. The guy with the luggage rack hurled it, and then people took off their flip-flops and threw those too. The guards got aggressive with their guns, dimpling the chests of people nearest the breezeway.

This was on the brink of becoming ugly.

Brody and Dan locked eyes for a moment, and Dan glared at him, but then Brody dodged a Yeezy slide. Whoever threw that must've been super pissed because those are expensive.

"Okay, okay, whoa. Point made. I just want to, ah, explain everything. First of all, obviously everyone here is gonna have food to eat. I mean, it's not like we're douchebags or something. We're making breakfast right now."

That probably should've been his opener. The guests who still had their flip-flops slid them back on.

"But, like—" He gulped. His Adam's apple was more of an Adam's pineapple. "You should know I put Building A in charge. So okay, they're going to decide how things go from now on. They're rich, and so obviously they're supersmart, and we need to make sure their needs are met first, and then—"

The flip-flops again took flight. But something was different this time, Brody had run out of chances. No more stuttering, no more explanations, the crowd wanted blood. Brody dipped out of sight, clearly sensing his head might soon be perched atop something even skinnier than his body.

Dan watched from above as Julio and the other unbought members of the staff, now near the front of the crowd, charged. There was screaming, like the screaming yesterday on the beach, and the mob moved as one, a battering ram against the breeze-way of Building A, and Dan snatched Mara's wrist and pulled her up onto the table to avoid being trampled. A sharp crack pierced the black morning air—Dan had played enough *Call of Duty* in his time to know it came from a rifle—and the forward march abruptly halted. The screaming changed octaves, from disgust to anguish, and Mara buried her face into Dan's chest. Dan located the guard who fired the bullet, some big son of a bitch who was immediately insulated by his colleagues. Their faces were stricken, like, oh, shit, what just happened, but their pistols remained rigid.

Dan nearly puked up last night's rum when he saw that the man who had been shot was dressed in white. Julio. His shirt was now red and becoming redder, and the crowd surfed him backward because forward clearly wasn't an option. He ended up somewhere by Alan and Charles, and Mara hopped from the table before Dan could stop her, leading a small group who placed Julio in a lounge chair and carried him off.

Dan's face felt wobbly, his legs were flushed. No, wait. Reverse that. His systems weren't working, the wires were crossed. He was in bed ten minutes ago. Did he just see a man—a *kid*—actually get shot? Over breakfast? Yesterday morning Mara was carrying pool towels. Now she was carrying a pool boy with a hole in his chest.

Earth would freeze in a week. Humans wouldn't make it that long.

Alan looked at Dan, and Dan looked at him, and his eyes said, Airstrip, tonight, and Dan, mouth agape, nodded. Please, God, let there be a plane at the airstrip. A canoe. Anything.

Dan's systems began to click back on. Half the crowd had scattered and the other was rearing for a second charge. This was going to get worse, and soon, unless somebody did something.

The megaphone throbbed in his hand. He didn't want to do this, he wasn't the guy who did things like this, but no one else was doing anything, and that big guard with the rifle was back out front again, and Mara had said Dan was a good talker, so maybe he was, and he was already up on the table so—

Dan lifted the megaphone, pulled the trigger, and returned fire.

First he shouted some nonsense—something between "hey!" and "wait!" that came out like "hwaey!" But it worked. At once, everyone's attention turned to him. He sucked in an unsteady breath.

"Julio's one of your *own!*" he screamed, his voice cracking. It was the first thing that came to mind. There were cries of concurrence. Yeah. Okay. Appeal to the paid-off guards, Dan, and the staff. This was all fresh, maybe they could still be reasoned with.

"Look—look around. What are you doing?" He lifted his arms in an exaggerated shrug. They were sore with adrenaline. "What are we *doing?* Last night, Dr. Shae told us the only chance of survival is *getting off this island.* We have to work together! Tizoc security team, staff—I don't know what the assholes in Building A are paying you. But it cannot be worth a man's life. It can't be worth"—he motioned to the chaos—"this!"

Dan laughed, realizing something. "We don't even know if money is still a thing!"

That registered with some folks, he could feel it. A few pistols sagged, some guards exchanged whispers. "Yeah," Dan said, feeding off the vibe shift and taking another dry breath. "Yeah! Listen. It doesn't have to be like this. There—we still have time. We all have family back home. The only way we're going to see them again is if we work together."

This was already getting redundant, and hypocritical, actually, since Dan was planning on running away with Alan later. But it was landing. No one else had been shot yet. The guests who had fled were returning to listen, a few pistols were now fully holstered. Even though most of the crowd still looked horrified, maybe Dan had a kumbaya moment cooking.

"Here's—uh—my proposal!" he said, waving a finger in the air, having never submitted a proposal in his life. "We form a committee *without* Brody Sheridan. Representatives from Buildings B and C—and maybe, like, someone in Building A who wasn't involved in all this—working together to make sure everyone has what they need until we figure out a way home. What do you say, security team? That way, we—"

A thunderous roar from the heavens nearly blew Dan off his feet. He didn't know what hit him at first, but his ears adjusted, and he realized it was music, the booming chorus of Rachel Platten's "Fight Song." It reverberated from speakers atop the balcony Brody had abandoned. Just like that, he'd lost the crowd again. No mere mortal can hope to compete with the infectious melodies of multiplatinum recording artist Rachel Platten.

After a dramatic moment, a new figure stepped onto the balcony, her gaunt hands in the air and her tan face solemn. Dan recognized her. It was the blond woman from the amphitheater yesterday, the one who'd asked about priority boarding if planes ever reached the island. She was in immaculate shape for her age, her skin like leather stretched over a drum, but not gross leather, full-grain leather. She was in yoga pants and a snug tank top, and Dan was pretty sure he wasn't supposed to be attracted to visitants from Building A anymore, but goddamn she looked like she stepped from the back third of a JCPenney catalog, which is the hottest part of a JCPenney catalog.

The music faded. She spoke without need for a megaphone.

"Y'all," she said, her voice real folksy, like she was addressing a PTA meeting, "I cannot believe what's happened here this morning. Please join me in praying for that young man who was hurt. Please, y'all, before we do anything, let's just have a moment of silence and ask for God to heal that man through His grace. Please."

To Dan's astonishment, the crowd fell silent, bowed their

heads. What the hell, people? He'd been in the middle of a proposal. The megaphone flopped to his side. Dan tried to find Alan's eyes again, but even his were buried in the pavement.

"Thank you," she said after a minute. When she raised her head, her gaze briefly met Dan's.

The prayer calmed things. Her presence calmed things. Just like that, folks seemed ready to listen again, more so than when Dan was talking, and all it took was a middle-aged woman with a bangin' bod endorsed by the Lord. Dan crossed his arms, having decided he didn't like all this.

"I'm Lilyanna Collins," she said, "CEO of BeachBod by Lilyanna. Do I have any BeachBod boss babes out there?"

A dozen or so women in the crowd *woo*ed, igniting a neuron in Dan's head. *That's* who she was. *BeachBod by Lilyanna.* BeachBod was the fitness pyramid scheme moms from Dan's graduating class hocked on social media with promises that they could transform other women's lives spiritually, physically, and financially, because look how they transformed their own. Pay no attention to the fact that most of the boss babes hadn't lost that baby weight, and Dan just *knew* they were shopping at Dollar General at 3 p.m. because there was less chance of being seen. And a lot of times they used pictures of Lilyanna Collins in their posts because Lilyanna had an eight-pack under that snug tank top, and she had a bone structure that would make you stop scrolling for about three seconds before saying, Ugh, more of this pyramid scheme bullshit, and moving on.

That was Lilyanna Collins.

"Y'all," Lilyanna said, "I got a question for ya. Which voice are you gonna listen to?" She let that linger for a moment, like it was real poignant, real deep. "When the sun *exploded* yesterday, you know what I did? I screamed. I cried. Okay, I'm not afraid to admit it—ladies, I ugly cried. You'll learn this about me. I overshare!" And she was laughing at herself, trying to appear humble, self-degrading, relatable. And shit was *working* too, because people in the crowd didn't see Julio's bloodstained uniform anymore, they just saw Lilyanna Collins, of BeachBod by Lilyanna, and God, she looked amazing for having had two kids.

"So my hubby, Pete, he's dragging me through the sand and I'm like, Pete, honey, can I have just one second to overreact, please? By the way, Pete, come out here!" A handsome man with a Cheshire cat smile joined her, dressed in a full suit. Who brings a suit to the Bahamas? Pete lifted a megaphone to address the crowd, but Lilyanna pushed it down.

"That's my man. You'll get to know him over the next few days. He's a preacher, believe it or not. Hey, shout-out to all the handsome hubbies out there, because I think I speak on behalf of the mommy warriors when I say we can be absolute *pills* to live with sometimes. But by the grace of God, they support us, don't they? Big hand for our men, they deserve it!" People clapped. After an awkward moment, Pete stepped out of sight with a wave. She added, "And let's not forget the *single* mommies out there! They have the hardest job in the world, and somehow they make it look so easy!"

More *woo*ing. Dan wished the sun would be reborn angrier and consume them all.

"Okay, so, like I said—I'm upset, y'all. Makeup's runnin', can't find my Chanel bag anywhere, and we get back up to our suite in Building A, and I sit on the chaise on the balcony, and

I look into that dark black afternoon sky awhile. Worried about my babies, my vacation home in Salinas, my independent fitness consultants around the world who I love like family. And then it hit me. *I* might not have a plan right now. But you know who does?" She pointed up. "*God* has a plan."

She paused for applause, and she got it.

"Because listen, ladies, I remember a time when I prayed for the things I have now. And God delivered. He always does, doesn't he, though it may not be exactly when or where we thought. Hey, Amazon's got guaranteed two-day delivery, why can't God?" She paced the balcony, the eyes of the crowd like marbles on a string.

"So I put on my big-girl Lululemons, and I listened for God, like I do every time I need to make a decision. And He told me I was on this island for a reason. Just like when He told me to found BeachBod by Lilyanna, He told me I was here to help people. And I was humbled by His message. So I stood up tall, straightened my crown, and I got to *work*. Building A didn't collect all this food to keep it for ourselves, y'all. Come on, now! You know I live for tacos and pizza, but even *I* can't eat pallets of it!"

She looked like she hadn't sniffed a carb since 2002.

The guards in the breezeway parted, and out marched men and women dressed in sleek black uniforms, balancing silver platters stacked with deviled eggs, chicken and waffle hors d'oeuvres, quiches. Others had what looked like mimosas, Bloody Marys. They floated through the stunned crowd, hopped over Julio's puddle, offered everyone their fill. There was a murmur now, but it was happy murmur, a mouth-full-of-breakfast murmur. Even Dan forgot about Julio for a moment, leapt from the table and snatched enough for himself and Mara, piled the food against his chest like a gorilla picking berries.

"Now, I'm sorry breakfast was a little late," Lilyanna said with a giggle, "but it's our first day, y'all. We'll work the kinks out. And hello! How delish is that chicken?" She smiled real big, flashed a thumbs-up at some folks. "Okay, y'all are probably wondering why *we're* cooking the food instead of Brody and his crew. Well, y'all have met Brody. And he's a sweet boy, Lord knows he's doing his best, truly he is, but he's in a bit over his head, ain't he? I'm here to help. We don't know how long we'll be on this island, so we'll be needing some structure. It's like I tell my ladies: ain't no profit without a little polish. Right, girls?"

A few more *woo*s, chunks of deviled egg spit onto the backs of people's heads.

"So Building A has come up with a system. Just like back home, everyone pitches in, everyone eats. Tomorrow morning, our fabulous staff members are gonna be passin' out pitch-in cards for y'all. Nothing hard, nothin' backbreaking, just stuff we need to get done if we hope to make it without freezin' to death out here. That would *not* be cute. And no moaning!" She laughed. "I picked my pitch-in card just before, and I got laundry duty. Anyone who watches my Insta story knows how I feel about laundry!"

Mandatory work assignments. Dissenters shot. Would they complete the tyranny trifecta with ration cards too?

But the chicken *was* good. *Fuck.*

6

Julio Martinez—they learned his last name was Martinez—
bled out on a lounge chair near the Maize Pool south of
Building C. By the time Dan got there with all the food, Julio
was covered with a towel, and there were runny spots of yellow and
red swirling toward the drain. The six folks who tried to save him
just stood there silently, shoulders sunken. When Mara saw Dan,
she shattered, wept into him, and said they did everything they
could, and Dan said, "Of course you did, babe, of course you did."

No one from Building A—the building most likely to house
doctors—was there.

They weren't sure what do with the body.

The guy who slept in the bunk above Julio said he had had
family in Atlanta—or maybe Miami—and that Julio would call
his grandma every Sunday to talk about the Falcons, so yeah, it
must've been Atlanta. And he said Julio only wanted to work at
Tizoc for a year, because that was enough time for him to save

some money and finally buy his girl back home a ring. He had at least had a couple people somewhere in the world who cared about him, people who'd want to be there for his funeral, who might have a few things to say about him beyond that he was real quick with the coconut rum and pineapple juices at the pool.

In the end, the decision was made to bury him in the garden behind Building B, but not too deep in case they needed to retrieve him. Alan called it a battlefield grave, but Charles hushed him and said it was a pop-up grave, like a boutique at the mall that could pack up and leave any day, so everything felt more special. The grave was only three feet deep, if even, and the ground was harder than anyone thought it would be, so they took turns digging.

Nobody from Building A attended the afternoon ceremony, probably worried what might happen to them if they did, but Lilyanna Collins sent trays of finger sandwiches and a letter of condolence, and Dan heard some of the B and C women saying, Actually, you know what, despite everything, you have to admit she is a class act. Mara read aloud a passage from the Bible, and Dan, who everyone turned to because he'd been the one with the megaphone earlier, felt obligated to say something. He and Alan had found a bottle of rum before the service.

"How do you bury a friend you've only just met?" he asked those gathered. "You do so with a promise that you will seek them again in the next life, to create the memories you were robbed of on Earth." He wasn't sure it made sense, not really, but everyone said, hear, hear, and Mara squeezed his hand the way she did when she loved him a lot, and the guy whose beard was his whole personality played "Bubble Toes" by Jack Johnson on the ukulele because it was the only song he knew the whole way through.

7

Lilyanna said the 9 p.m. curfew was for the good of everyone. At 8:59 she cut the power, and the resort plunged into darkness as if dipped in ink.

People screamed.

The island was running on generators now that solar power had gone kaput, Lilyanna explained, and why waste precious fuel lighting common areas or keeping the air-conditioning running when it was a comfortable sixty degrees. That might've been sound reasoning, maybe, if it weren't for Building A shining like a casino long after the men with pistols motioned guests of B and C toward their gloomy rooms. Dan thought surely this was it, that Lilyanna had pushed too hard, too fast, that guests would rise up and end the regime spreading across the island like a weed.

But at 9:01 it was quiet.

Dan's phone had good battery life because he always closed his background apps, so he turned on the flashlight and slid it under a water bottle as a makeshift lamp. After pulling the shades, Mara unlatched the interior door that connected Alan and Charles's room to theirs.

"I just—" Charles's jowls trembled as he shook his head. "I just don't think it's a good idea, y'all. I won't bury you next to that boy in the garden."

"He's right," Mara said, pacing because she couldn't sit still when she was thinking. "I understand why you'd want to check out the airstrip, Alan, and that was a good idea *before* Building A took over and shot someone. But now..." She covered her trembling bottom lip with a hand.

Alan's eyes appealed to Dan, who shrugged, feigning bravery. Charles sat in the vanity chair and tore open a Snickers. "Ugh, Lilyanna. Like, pick a name, sweetie. Lily or Anna? They're both horrible. Struttin' around with two names like you deserve more than the rest of us."

Alan said, "Your mother's name was Rosemary."

Charles's head whipped around. "And she was a *saint*. She deserved twenty names, that woman, she wasn't a stack of bones selling diet pills to fat Midwesterners like *Li-ly-an-na*." He slammed the candy on the vanity. "I can't think about that woman."

"Okay."

"I hate her whole face."

"Okay."

Charles huffed and meticulously separated the candy bar into fours, passing a piece to each of them. Dan would've usually preferred an endpiece, but he popped it in anyway. "We're already here?" he asked, working through the nougat. "Rationing candy bars?"

"The fuckers emptied the vending machines this afternoon," Alan said. "What do you bet they turn off the water next, start rationing that?"

Huh. Dan stepped into the bathroom, plugged the bath drain, and filled the tub. He'd seen Viggo Mortensen do that in *The Road*. When he stepped back into the bedroom, Alan looked impressed and shuffled off to do the same.

Alan, a *man*, impressed with something Dan thought of. He felt taller.

"Building C doesn't have separate bathtubs," Mara said. "I remember looking at the pictures when we were deciding where to stay."

"We were never going to stay in Building C," Dan clarified. Charles waved him off, like, Of course. We know what type of people you are.

"Fuck Building C," Alan said, reemerging. "Not our problem."

Mara scoffed. "Don't you think that's a little harsh?"

"There's probably a thousand people on this island. Not even a rounding error in total U.S. population. No one back home's thinking about us. Those planes aren't coming."

"We don't know that," Mara said. "But even if it's true, that just means everyone has to work together, Alan. If Building C needs our—"

"You're not getting me," Alan snapped, probably sharper than he'd intended.

Charles scolded him.

Alan took another deep breath, silently apologizing.

"Help me get you," Mara said.

Damn. *Help me get you.* With a thousand years to workshop different responses to someone snapping at him, Dan never would've thought of that. She could be dramatic sometimes, yeah, but Mara was never flippant about people's feelings, even when they were flippant about hers.

"What I mean," Alan said, "is that Dan's speech earlier was nice. But wrong." He cocked his head at Dan. "No offense."

Dan shrugged that off. He wasn't sure he believed what he had said either. He just didn't want anyone else to get shot.

Alan continued. "We're on our own. And when I say *we*, I don't mean the whole island. I mean the people splitting this Snickers." He ate his piece. "Charles and I have your backs if you have ours. But we can't save everyone."

"What if we can?" Mara asked.

"We can't. And believe me." He twirled his finger. "Conversations just like this are happening all over."

Dan stepped in. "Look, none of this means anything if there's no way out of here." He pushed his fear as far down as it would fit. "Alan and I are doing this. Tonight." He said the next part before Mara could object. "We'll be careful."

"So, what?" Charles said, his arms crossed across his ample chest, his face a broken sneer. "You think y'all're just gonna find a 757 with drink service and Wi-Fi parked on a runway they conveniently forgot about? Oh, woops, you're telling me the very thing we needed to escape this postapocalyptic hell-scape was sitting in the one place it could conceivably be this entire time? How silly of us not to check! Okay, yeah, you boys go. Wonderful idea. Go get torn to pieces like poor Julio, you macho a-holes."

Lenny Fava had seen Bruce Springsteen in concert at least four times. He didn't tell Dan that, not yet, but Dan was sure of it from the second he opened his mouth. Dan tried not to stereotype anyone—he was a middle-class white guy who blasted Matchbox Twenty in his Dodge Caliber, so who was he to talk—but Lenny Fava was North Jersey personified. Even in the nearly pitch-black parking lot north of Building C, Dan could make out the gold cross under his Affliction tank top, the barbwire tattoo etched into his bicep. He was shaped like a meatball and probably ordered meatball subs at his favorite diner next to some parkway exit, and his wife was Connie or Coleen or Vickie. But if Dan was sure of *any* of these things, it was that Lenny loved The Boss. No doubt about it. Lenny Fava was Born to Run.

Cwoffee was the word that gave him away. When Alan and Dan, panting from their sprint through the bushes and past the Main Building, plopped down behind the tire of a bus in the resort parking lot, Lenny offered them two piping hot cups of cwoffee. It was one of the few beverages guests still had in their rooms. Dan refused—he didn't drink the stuff—but Alan gulped it down without any regard for its temperature, then snatched the cup meant for Dan.

"This is Lenny," Alan whispered, peering past their shoulders for any sign of guards. "He's from C. We met at the Maize Pool before everything."

"How you doin'?" Lenny's handshake was like a vise grip. "We was doin' the limbo out there. You wouldn't believe how low this guy's boyfriend can get, Jesus Christ. Never seen a guy that flexible."

"Husband," Alan said, his breath returning.

"Right, yeah, husband. I still forget sometimes you guys can do that now."

Dan nodded at Lenny. Alan hadn't mentioned meeting anyone else during this covert operation. What happened to looking out for themselves? And "Fuck Building C"?

"Airstrip's about a mile through there," Lenny said, pointing at the dense woods hugging the north side of the parking lot. The trees danced and screeched as if alive. "We could take the road they used to bus us here, but they're still lighting it. Better chance they'd spot us. Hope you two ain't scared of the dark."

"What about east along the beach?" Dan offered. "Circle around the top of the island and make our way in?"

"They're all over the beach. And that Shae guy's place is northeast, that's fenced off real good. We'd have to scale some cliffs if we came at the airstrip from the north. Don't know about you two, but I don't scale fuckin' cliffs." That looked accurate. Dan placed Lenny in his early sixties at least, though the salt-and-pepper stubble on his face betrayed the jet-black hair up top. Looked like he was wearing a motorcycle helmet.

Dan asked, "How do you know so much about the island?"

"Found some maps in the boiler room of our building, down near the staff quarters. They're old. From like, the fifties, so none of this Tizoc resort shit's on 'em. The observatory either, but I got a feel for things. I was a surveyor back in the eighties, so I know maps."

There it was, the reason Alan invited him along. Alan finished the second cup of coffee, crushed and tossed it on the asphalt. "Through the woods then."

Through the woods, Dan thought, and just as he was about

to stand to assist his geriatric companions, a flashlight beam slinked along the windows of the bus. Dan felt his heart in his throat—it tasted like the middle of a Snickers—and Alan snatched his shirt and yanked him under the bus, out of sight. Lenny, astonishingly, wasn't as nimble, so they both grabbed hold of one of his hairy wrists and tugged. He grunted as his stomach scraped along the tarmac. Dan hoped whoever owned that flashlight was hard of hearing. And seeing. Smelling too, because someone had forgotten deodorant.

Alan hissed, "Fuck," as the flashlight steadied on Lenny's flailing legs. Lenny's face sunk into the tar as he began the laborious process of backing out. Dan crawled out next, standing with his hands above his head, followed by Alan, snarling like a trapped raccoon.

Caught already. *Dead* already. They hadn't even stepped foot off the property. Way to go, Danny boy. Stopped before making even an ounce of progress. Typical.

The guard clicked off his light. Now, the word *guard* implies some sort of sentinel, a barrel-chested defender of life and property, and this wasn't that. It was a kid playing dress-up, a boy with a pistol he could barely wrap his hand around. A pathetic attempt at a mustache quivered above his lip. When Alan got a good look at him, he relaxed.

"What—what are you doing out here?" the kid said. He couldn't have been older than Julio. When no one said anything, he shook the gun at Lenny. "Answer me!"

"Listen, kid," Lenny said, his scraped palms pointed outward, "how much is that bitch paying you? You don't want to—"

"We were told to shoot trespassers on sight," the boy confessed, like he couldn't process it either.

"On sight?" Dan said. His tongue was sandpaper. "Jesus Christ. Lilyanna said that?"

"Hey, hands up!" He wildly swung the gun at Alan, whose hands shot back up.

Dan took a baby step forward. "Listen. Hey, man, listen. What's your name?"

"David," David said. The gun was in Dan's face now, and Dan was glad he didn't drink coffee because it'd be trickling down the side of his leg.

"David. Okay, David. I can tell you don't want to shoot us. Do you know why we're out here?"

"The food. You want to steal the food back."

"No! No, no way. David, we were—well, you know how you found us under the *bus*?" Dan was stalling, he couldn't think of a reason they'd be out. Why do people leave their hotel rooms at night? To get ice? "Well, man, it's a funny story." Dan laughed and put a hand on Lenny's shoulder, who laughed like, heh, yeah, heh. "What we were *actually* doing, David, and trust me, you're going to love this one, because you look to me like a guy with a sense of humor. Doesn't he? Actually, you know who you really look like? I do. Doesn't he look like that comedian? Lenny, who does he—"

"Carrot Top," Lenny said.

Dan closed his eyes. Come on, Lenny. The kid's Bahamian.

"No!" Dan said. "No, that's not it. Well, anyway, David, like I said—"

Alan lunged forward and punched David in the jaw. His

whole body buckled, just like in the movies, like Henchman #2 stumbling across James Bond on his way to the death ray. But David wasn't Henchman #2, he was David, and Dan felt a little sorry for him when his head bounced off the blacktop.

Alan snatched the pistol and struck David one more time. Dan pushed him away.

"Christ, Alan. I think you got him."

Alan checked David's pulse. "He'll be fine. Kid was going to shoot us. Take his radio."

After stripping him of his equipment, they carried David into the bus, placed him in the driver's seat, and handcuffed him to the steering wheel. Dan adjusted the driver's seat all the way up and positioned David's head delicately between the spokes.

Waking up with a sore neck is the worst.

8

A razor-sharp branch had torn Dan's shirt open, Alan's knees were acting up, and Lenny wheezed like Darth Vader training for a 5K, but an hour later they made it through the woods north of Building C alive. They used the flashlights on their phones to illuminate the way—Dan had to give Lenny a tutorial on where to find his—but they hardly helped. The woods were a nearly impenetrable maze of trees. And not just normal trees. These were *trees*, hulking sons of bitches standing shoulder to shoulder like riot police, smacking their limbs against their trunks. The thought of returning the same way made Dan weary.

But thanks to Lenny's sense of direction, they'd made it. They scampered across the desolate airstrip and against the tin siding on the first of three hangars. The plane-sized door was shut tight, and the human-sized door was locked. After taking one final look around, Alan shattered the glass above the door handle, reached through the blinds, and they were in.

God, he was impressive.

The hangar, however, was not. It was cavernous, save for a

stack of empty cardboard boxes against the back wall and the skeletal frames of several ATVs from the late seventies or eighties. It smelt of stale air and mildew. Lenny sifted through the boxes, looking for any paperwork he could get his hands on, and Alan inspected the four-wheelers. Dan tapped his foot and watched the door, positive David's comrades would rain down on them any second.

"Eighty-three Suzuki QuadRunner," Alan said, and Dan said that's what he thought too, but really he had no idea. Alan flicked a wheel. "One of the original four-wheel, all-terrain vehicles. There's a shop back home that restores them. These have been here a while."

"Nothing," Lenny said, flinging a final box. "Not a thing here. Bunch of fuckin' cardboard. Why they need three hangars on an island this size?"

Alan abandoned the Suzuki whatever. "Well, we can't ride these home. Keep moving."

"Maybe we split up," Lenny said. "More quick that way."

"Ever seen any movie ever?" Dan asked. "Let's stick together. I can hide behind you when the shooting starts."

The second hangar wasn't exactly a treasure trove either, just some old tools in a side office. Dan and Alan were disappointed, but Lenny took a particular interest. "These are farming tools," he said, confused.

Alan picked caked dirt from a spading fork. "So what?"

"Someone made 'em," Lenny said.

"Someone makes everything," Dan said.

"Nah, like, someone *made* these. Like hand-made 'em. Weird."

Handmade or not, they were little help. The party moved on.

The final hangar was unlocked. That was the first surprise. The second?

There was a plane in it.

Alan whooped and hollered, and Lenny shook Dan so hard he thought his head might pop off. They circled the plane like banshees, running their hands along the doors, the wings, the propeller, Dan keeping at least one finger on it at all times so it wouldn't vanish. It was a small plane with a cool red stripe up the side.

"Single engine," Alan said, scoffing. It was the first time Dan had seen him lose his cool. "I can fly this in my sleep. And it seats—yeah. It seats six. It's perfect."

Dan stood on his toes and peered inside a window. Six would be snug, yeah, they weren't talking ample legroom here, but it would work. He could get Mara home.

The plane was in rough shape—Alan said he wasn't sure when it'd last seen the sky. He placed David's pistol on a tool bench and went inside to poke and prod and do whatever it is men do when they know what they're doing.

Dan couldn't believe it. A *plane*. A fucking plane!

"Will she fly?" Lenny asked, kicking the deflated landing gear.

Alan's head popped out from one of the windows. "She's a project." He scanned along the wing, clicked his tongue. "I'm pretty sure she's a Piper Cherokee. Pretty sure."

"Could she get us to Nassau?" Dan asked.

Alan laughed. "Nassau? This thing could get us to the mainland. The tip of Florida, at least, any farther might be stretching it. Once we land, we can get up to Miami and, assuming the whole country hasn't gone to shit, find a way home."

Any more good news and Dan would take flight himself. "How long?"

Alan's head reemerged. "What's that?"

"How long till you can get her running?"

"It depends. A week, tops." Alan looked out into the hangar. Lenny was poking around, singing to himself. "I bet a lot of what I need is here."

The hangar was packed with rows of crates and toolboxes and workbenches and other machinery. Dan could hardly take it all in next to the headliner, the plane, their carriage off this godforsaken island.

A week. That's a long time, but it could work. Lay low for just a week under Princess Lilyanna's rule. Then Mara could see her mom, Dan could see his family, Alan and Charles could see their boys, and Lenny could see—well, Lenny could see Springsteen at the Garden again. After that? Who knows? Freeze to death, probably. But at least Dan will have done this. Before the end, he'll have done *something*.

He navigated the aisles of hangar junk to join Lenny in the back office, leaving Alan to ogle plane guts. Lenny was bent over a folding desk, his phone light scouring unrolled paperwork.

"Get a look at this, kid. All the island's tunnels, laid out right here. We're in the money, baby." Lenny slapped the maps with the back of his hand. "Laundry, food service, storage area, pool pumps, armory, you name it, bro. All right here. Matter o' fact—"

Armory? "Sorry. Did you say armory?"

Lenny glanced up. "Yeah, well. *Armory* might be a strong

word, that's what's written here. Guard barracks, ya know. Where they sleep. That's underground too."

"Why does a resort need an armory?"

"This Sheridan guy, he's like, uh—he's like—"

"A cokehead."

"Well, yeah." Lenny scratched his temple. "But no, see, he's a—prepper! Guy's a prepper. Someone told me 'bout it at the pool. But he's a gun nut too, ya know, he likes guns. And he's got all of Mommy's money, so he bought an island, built a playground for himself, and hired these goons to be his friends. And now they're working for Lilyanna. Heh."

Dan sighed. Of all the islands in the world to be stranded on after the sun explodes, he and Mara chose the one with assault weapons. He glanced at the files over Lenny's shoulder.

"What're you gonna do with these?"

"Get our food back."

"Get the food back? Lenny, we just found a way out of here. Mounting an underground invasion of Building A isn't exactly laying low."

Lenny folded the diagrams and stuffed them in the lower pocket of his cargo shorts. "I don't care if we got a ferry outta here this second," he said. "You don't ever let someone take something of yours that don't belong to 'em. Nevah. Those pricks up in Building A been stealing from people all their lives. Not my dinner. No way."

Dan sensed he would need Alan's help to convince Lenny, so for now he changed the subject. "You said you were a land surveyor in the eighties. You retired?"

"Me and the missus own a deli in Jersey City." Of course they did. "Fava Deli, corner of Second and Brunswick. Best pepperoni bread in the city. Opened her ten years ago."

"Ten years, huh? Late career change."

"Never too late to follow a dream, kid. Nevah." He kicked a bolt on the ground. "Got my nephew running the shop up there while we're out. First time we ever left him in charge, ya believe it? Knowing him, he's letting the neighborhood eat for free, with everything going on with the sky and all that. Real softie, my nephew. Liberal, you know, these kids. Heart gets him in trouble." There was a streak of pride across his face. "Anyway, so yeah, gotta get back to the deli."

Dan almost leapt into Lenny's arms as a furious *clack, clack, clack* roared from inside the hangar. His first thought was Alan had somehow already got the plane started, but he and Lenny shot from the office to find the whole place doused in blinding light.

Headlights. Security Jeep. *Shit.* They'd opened the bay door. Dan's fight-or-flight response immediately kicked in and ordered the regular—flight. As the driver clicked on the low beam, Dan shoved Lenny behind a steel toolbox. The way Lenny folded to the floor made Dan uncomfortable. Men in their sixties aren't meant to fold, especially not ones shaped like Lenny. Dan's quivering fingers switched off his phone light and Lenny struggled to do the same but couldn't remember how. He settled for stuffing the entire thing under his Affliction shirt.

The Jeep's engine cut off, and multiple doors slammed. Dan inched sideways to find a narrow unobstructed view of the front of the plane, near the propeller. His heart pummeled against the floor. The first thing he saw was sensible pair of pink flats. He scanned up. Toned calves. Pink swimsuit cover-up.

Lilyanna Collins.

She wasn't alone. Looked like two or three guards. And—

"So this is it," Brody Sheridan said. He placed his hand on the propeller, sniffed. "Like I told you, it doesn't work, like, at all. Dr. Shae said it's been here since the seventies or something. Shit's busted." He rubbed the back of his neck. Twenty-four hours with Lilyanna had curved Brody's spine, turned him into a walking question mark.

Lilyanna circled the plane, her hands on her hips, out of Dan's sight and then back again. Dan tried not to breathe, prayed that Alan remained perfectly still.

"'Shit's busted,'" Lilyanna repeated, her Dolly Parton drawl ricocheting off the corrugated ceiling. "That your opinion, Mr. Sheridan, or the opinion of someone who knows their way around a plane?"

Brody gulped. "Dr. Shae said so too, and he's a supersmart dude. Like, crazy smart. I know he's a space scientist or whatever, but he actually knows about a lot of other things."

Lilyanna laughed, but it wasn't a real laugh, no way, and she placed a condescending hand on Brody's shoulder. "Don't exactly sound conclusive, though, does it? We got any engineers in Building A?"

"I dunno."

"My Lord," she said. "She's a pretty little thing, though, ain't she? Bit of paint…" She got on her tippy-toes and looked in a window. Dan winced. "Some seat covers… I'd fly around in this thing. Not to Coachella or anything, but around." She clapped her hands together and squealed. "Would you just look at this! This is God, Mr. Sheridan,. This is God saying, Here you go,

Lilyanna. I know it's not exactly what you wanted, but when is it ever?" She booped Brody's nose. "God's always writing our stories, but He lets *us* choose the endings."

She tapped her foot, said, "Hmm."

"I need to find me someone who knows planes. This is it. This is my way back to my babies in Nashville."

She *would* live in fucking Nashville.

"You can't wait for the other planes to come get us?"

Lilyanna stared at Brody, blinked. "Mr. Sheridan. Now, you really think those planes are coming? Sun's exploded, whole world's gone dark, chaos everywhere. You think they're worried about a little ol' island in the Bahamas? Oh, honey. *Honey.*"

Brody studied the floor. "But everyone can't fit on this plane."

"Aw, listen to you! I love your heart."

Suddenly, a muffled voice sprung forth from Dan's shorts, sending Dan and Lenny into a flailing panic. Dan swiped David's radio from his pocket. He hadn't switched it off. *Shit!* Before Dan could figure out how to silence it, the voice continued. "David. Where you at, dude? They want us to check out the docks. Something—"

Dan turned the knob on top and the voice cut out. He pushed Lenny away, thinking maybe there was time for him to hide so only Dan got caught, but the big man wouldn't budge. Lenny's phone fell from under his shirt and clattered against the epoxy floor. Lenny scooped it up, and his fingers bounced against the screen as he tried in vain to turn his flashlight off, but all he managed to do was start his music app, so now a song was blaring from the phone's speakers, and to Dan's absolute shock, it was Barry Manilow.

They were caught. Again. The worst covert operation in the history of covert operations.

Dan assumed the position, stood with hands above his head, guns pointed at him *again*, and Lenny used Dan's waist to hoist himself up, almost yanking down his shorts in the process. Lenny could hardly get his hands above his head, but he did his best.

Dan recognized one of the guards. It was the one who shot Julio, the only one with a rifle. He had a block head, a buzz cut, and he was the size of a shipping container. Dan got a good look at his eyes. Like the sky, there was no light in there.

"Hey, y'all," Lilyanna said, stepping through her men like they were background dancers. "It's the boy with the megaphone from earlier! I recognize the big guy too."

At least that's what Dan thought she said—"Copacabana" was still pulsating from Lenny's phone. Lilyanna snatched it and silenced Barry with a dainty swipe. "I wonder what these boys are doing all the way out here after curfew."

"Fuck you and your curfew," Lenny said, and Dan grimaced because that's a tough place to start a negotiation for your life.

Lilyanna feigned offense. "My, my. Is that any way to address a lady?"

Dan knew he'd better start talking, because the big guard's trigger finger definitely twitched when Lenny did. "Hey, he doesn't mean it. He—"

"Yeah, I do. Ya fuckin' c—"

"No, he *doesn't*." Dan elbowed him. "Listen. Can we just—can we lower the guns for a second? My name's Dan Foster. This is Lenny. We're only out here because—"

"What's this?" Lilyanna bent slowly at the waist and retrieved David's radio. She waved it in Dan's face and said, "Tsk, tsk, tsk. Y'all hurt one of my boys? Lord, tell me you didn't hurt one of my boys."

Lenny pointed to the man with the rifle. "This motherfucker shot a pool boy."

Dan's chin flattened into his chest. When they did his autopsy, under cause of death it would say, JERSEY CITY DELI OWNER W/ VERY BIG MOUTH.

Lilyanna paused. "What happened to that boy has been weighing heavily on me all day, sir. He shouldn't have rushed us, he really shouldn't've, but I take no pleasure in what happened. Pains me to think he might still be alive if he'd worked with us. Just pains me."

Okay, the hypocrisy was becoming too much even for Dan and even at gunpoint. Lilyanna closed her eyes in silent prayer, but Dan interrupted.

"You say that, Lilyanna, but tonight you ordered your guards to shoot on sight."

Lilyanna cocked an eyebrow before her lids opened. "I did no such thing." She turned to the guard with the rifle. "What's he talking about, Rico?"

Rico—God, what a perfect name for this guy, *Rico*—thought over his answer a minute. He eventually lowered the rifle, and the other guards lowered their guns too. "You told us to keep them in line."

Lilyanna gasped and said, "Oh, hun, *no*! Not like that." She shook her head, pitying him like a puppy in a window. "We just started working together, so we're still learning each other's styles. But we *barely* squeaked past what happened to that waiter. What's that they say, y'all? Speak softly and carry a big stick?" She winked at Dan, but all he saw was Julio under that beach towel, and he seethed. Lilyanna sagged against a toolbox and equipped one of her more empathetic tones. "Y'all think I'm being too tough? That it?"

"You stole our food," Lenny said. "Killed the power. You got the medical supplies, the linens, the—"

"You know, y'all, through BeachBod by Lilyanna, I have speaking engagements all over the world. And afterward, these ladies, these mompreneurs who want to escape those nine-to-fives, they always ask me how I did it. How I became who I am today. You know what I tell 'em?"

"Botox," Dan said, having fully accepted his fate.

Lilyanna pinched his cheek. "Bless your heart. No. I tell 'em to remember the three *D*s! Decision, determination, and, most important, discipline."

Oh, no. A business lecture from Lilyanna Collins. Rico could just get it over with.

Dan tried to catch Brody's eye, tried to appeal to the kid's humanity, something, but Brody was intentionally avoiding him. He rubbed his arm and looked at the ceiling.

"Now, how's that apply here?" she asked, pacing. "I made the *decision* to keep as many people safe on this island as I could. I have the *determination* to see that decision through. But without the big *D*, *discipline*, it wouldn't be possible! And discipline means doing things you should do, even when you don't feel like doing 'em."

"Like killing people," Dan said.

"Like keeping this island *safe*," she corrected. "And keeping everyone fed. And warm. You boys put that at risk, running around after curfew, hurtin' my guards, disturbing the peace. Don't you think I'd rather be up in my room right now, drinking champagne and getting my nails done? I saw a need and I acted. In the interest of everyone. Y'all're just acting for yourselves."

"Cut the act, lady," Lenny said. "We heard you. You're here for the same reason we are."

"Forgive them, Father, they know not what they do. I believe in second chances, really, I do." She giggled and threw her hands in the air. "But y'all got me in a tough spot!"

"Ma'am," Rico said, stepping forward. "People don't have to know. I could just, you know, do it quiet." He raised his rifle, and Dan felt two things at the same time: the cold steel of the barrel against his ear and the knocking of his knees. He was positive this guy would do it. "We could get their wives too, so there's no one to miss 'em. It'd be easy. We could—"

Dan's brain hemorrhaged at the thought of this man anywhere near Mara. His fight-or-flight was back, but something was different this time. He wasn't flying. He felt his body subtly shift toward Rico, felt the hairs on his neck stand at attention, the creases in his knuckles tighten. Rico only needed to move his finger a quarter of an inch to blow Dan away, to seal his fate as a nobody, but there was a reason Rachel Platten's Billboard Hot 100 hit wasn't called "Flight Song," it was called "Fight Song," and Dan was getting Mara on that plane even if he died trying.

The door on the plane squeaked open, momentarily distracting Rico. Dan leapt atop his back, swinging wildly at his face, pulling at his ears, poking his eyes. He had no chance, Rico was built like a Thwomp from Super Mario World, but Dan wouldn't let him get to Mara. While Lilyanna screamed, Rico effortlessly swung Dan over his shoulder and cratered him into the hangar floor. Dan couldn't breathe, but he could still move, so he just kept kicking, kicking, kicking, waiting for the sound of the rifle.

But what he heard next wasn't a gun—it was a familiar voice crying out.

"Stop! Stop! Get off him. I can fix it! Hey! *Stop.* I can fix the plane."

9

Dan cracked one eye open, prepared to hit St. Peter with some Foster charm, but he wasn't in Heaven and that definitely wasn't St. Peter. He was in a dingy airplane hangar, and that was Rico pushing a rifle into his chest, raging hunger in his eyes.

"Cut it out, Rico," Lilyanna said. She clutched his boulder of a shoulder and attempted to pull him back. "That's *enough*."

"He attacked me," Rico said, the rifle sinking further into Dan.

Dan had never attacked anyone before. It was hard. His lungs were burning, he panted like a Doberman. And—Jesus—his back.

"I think you got the better of him, hun," Lilyanna said. "It's over."

Alan appeared and offered a hand to Dan, who lumbered to his feet, leaning on Alan for support. Rico's rifle remained trained on him.

"I can fix it," Alan repeated to Lilyanna.

"Good Lord," Lilyanna said, amused. "We sure kicked a nest, didn't we, Mr. Sheridan?"

"I don't think you should shoot them, Rico," Brody said, a sentiment that would've been appreciated a little earlier.

"My name's Alan Ferris. I'm an engineer. I was with the Air Force for more than ten years. I can get her running." He pointed at Dan and Lenny. "But if you hurt either of them, you won't get any help from me. Can we lower the fucking guns?"

Lilyanna waved for her guards to comply. Everyone did except Rico.

Lilyanna chewed the inside of her cheek, thought a second. "You can fix it."

Alan nodded.

"How long?"

"It needs some work. A week and a half."

She laughed. "Whole world might be frozen by then."

"Planes fly in the winter."

"Reckon you'll want a seat on the first flight out."

"Unless you intend to fly it yourself."

She crossed her arms, tapped her foot, considered Alan more closely. Lilyanna had a way of looking at a person like she was slicing open a Thanksgiving turkey, rummaging through the inside to see what their stuffing consisted of. Alan's stuffing was probably mostly scrap metal and engine parts, hot diesel, shell casings. Dan's stuffing was probably—well, just that. Stuffing. Kraft Stove Top, $2.99 a box. Flour and onions and high-fructose corn syrup.

Lilyanna turned to Rico. "Rico, handcuff Mr. Foster and Mr.—what was it?"

"Fuck you," Lenny said. He was consistent, Dan had to give him that.

"Mr. Foster and Mr. Fuck You"—she chuckled—"and take them on back to their rooms unharmed. They have jobs in the morning, just like everyone else."

"Thanks, warden," Dan said.

"Let me just do this one," Rico said, his rifle buzzing. "Just this one. He attacked me, ma'am."

It was the first time Dan heard Lilyanna truly be stern. "*Rico.* You and I have an agreement. I won't say it again."

As Dan's hands were forcibly secured behind his back, Alan took a step from the hangar to join his fellow dissenters. Lilyanna placed a hand on his chest. "Nuh-uh. Where you going?"

Alan blinked.

"You've got a plane to work on, Mr. Ferris."

"I'm beat. I'll be a lot more effective in—"

"I'm sure breaking curfew and sneaking around the island after hours is *exhausting*, Mr. Ferris, but it's like I tell my BeachBod girls: you can't get much done in life if you only work on the days you feel good." She squeezed the shoulders of another guard. "You'll get started now. Hunter here is gonna keep you company. Who knows? Maybe you'll have this girl up and running in a week. We call that a stretch goal."

Alan shot Dan a look, like, Nice job with the radio, dummy, and Dan gave him a look back, like, Well, maybe you should've held on to David's gun.

Rico shoved Dan between his shoulder blades as he and Lenny were led toward the Jeep. "I'll tell him," Dan said to Alan before being tossed in the back seat.

Alan waved a wrench.

Rico uncuffed Dan outside his room.

"You know, Foster, next time I won't wait for the order. I'll put a bullet in your ass without hesitation."

"You're a monster, got it." Dan reached for the door handle but turned back to Rico and sized him up once more. Maybe it was the waning effects of the adrenaline—maybe it was the way Rico had threatened Mara—but Dan still very much wanted to hurt the man. "When Brody hired you to be head of security, did the contract specifically state you'd be murdering guests? Or is that out of scope?"

Rico smiled. He had a gold tooth in the back. "Killing you will be one of the only perks of this job."

Dan tilted his head. "Oh, no. One of the *only* perks? You don't like your job? I can actually relate. Hey, what'd you want to be when you grew up?"

The briefest of frowns from Rico told Dan he'd struck a nerve, so like an idiot, he drilled.

"Wait, don't say it." Dan snapped and pointed. "A luchador. No? Okay, I'm looking at you, and I'm seeing...artisanal cheese-maker. Wait. A dictator. That's it. Small economy, somewhere tropical, with one of those little berets that—"

Rico slapped Dan so hard that he thought he might need his own gold tooth. He slunk into the wall and clutched the side of his face. *Shit.* Rarely were Dan's jokes worth it, but that one definitely wasn't.

Rico waved a finger. "Don't fucking play with me, Foster. I'll bury you like I buried that pool boy."

Dan barreled inside and slammed the door before Rico could swing again. Then he remembered something and shouted into the peephole, "David is handcuffed to the bus in the parking lot, but he's fine. Bye!"

When he was sure Rico was gone, Dan collapsed into bed—it was curiously free of Mara-sized lumps—and tried to steady the spinning room. When he opened his eyes, Mara and Charles hovered over him, their cell phone lights bearing down. Mara hugged him, squealed. She reeked of tequila.

"What happened to your shirt?" Mara asked.

"Alan," Charles said, panicked. "Where's Al—"

Dan sat up and explained everything, which was more embarrassing when reconsidered aloud. They'd been caught. Twice. They'd found a means of escape and lost it within the span of ten minutes. Alan was captured. Dan was open-hand-slapped by a Neanderthal. He was a little vague on having been almost executed—for Mara's benefit.

Charles paced the room, his feet leaving little puddles atop the tile. Mara's legs were slick too, come to think of it.

"Why are you two wet?"

"We were soaking our feet in the jacuzzi tub and drinking tequila from Alan and Charles's minibar," Mara said. "Do you want some?"

Dan blinked. "That water was for drinking."

"Y'all, I'm so anxious about Alan. What if they hurt him? He gets so grumpy when he doesn't sleep. She can't have him working all night." Charles paused. "So, say he fixes the plane, and then…well, what then?"

"Lilyanna and Simon Cowell or whoever her rich friends are fly to Miami, I guess." Exhaustion engulfed Dan. "I don't know. I think we need to keep our heads down for a bit. Pray Alan can fix the plane more quickly than he promised Lilyanna, and we can slip out of here."

"And leave everyone else to fend for themselves," Mara said.

Dan stared at her, the familiar pit of disappointment just inside his belly. "I don't know what you want me to do, Mara."

She bit her thumbnail. She didn't know either.

"I'm going to get him," Charles said, marching toward the door.

Dan and Mara shouted, "No!" simultaneously, and Mara snatched his arm. This broke him somehow, and now a man they'd only met that morning was sitting on the edge of their bed weeping, fanning his eyes with his hands, saying, "I'm okay, I'm okay, I'm okay," while Mara wrapped her arm around his back and said, "Shh, shh." There was something unnatural about Charles crying. It was like watching Mickey Mouse sob on the steps of the castle or something—he was just so big and lovable and soft that he wasn't supposed to be sad. Dan found a box of tissues in the bathroom, and Charles mouthed Thanks while dabbing his face.

"Tequila tears," he said with a chuckle. "Y'all, I'm just so worried."

Mara raised her eyebrows at Dan, like, Say something, and Dan raised his eyebrows back, like, I've been doing a lot of talking lately, but then she blew air from her nose, which meant she insisted. After a moment, Dan sat next to Charles. His hands fidgeted.

"It's alright, man. Alan's going to be okay. They need him. We just—we just need to lay low for a while." Then, an old faithful: "We're going to figure this out."

"We're going to figure this out," Charles repeated.

Right. That's what men say in emergencies, even if it doesn't mean anything.

10

If there was one thing Dan Foster could do, it was lay low.

Back home, 90 percent of his existence was spent meandering between the same two physical spaces, completing mindless tasks in each, and then waking up grumpy and doing it all over again. He'd enjoyed eight years of this soul-crushing lifestyle so far, and he had expected to devote an additional thirty or so before inevitably succumbing to heart disease, or lung cancer, or choking on a Funyun or similar snack.

Then, while on his first vacation in a decade, the sun exploded, resulting in a substantial deviation in Dan's schedule. But that's the thing about schedules—once you fall out of one, you slip into another, and Lilyanna Collins had a few ideas on how to pass the time.

The next morning—Wednesday morning—the resort's new daily schedule was printed on Tizoc stationery and slid under guests' doors along with a note from the woman herself. Dan was awoken from his existential night's rest by the soulful sounds of Rico driving a Jeep haphazardly over the pool deck, shouting muffled commands into a megaphone. He groaned and rolled over, searched for an authoritarian snooze button. His head pulsed like a nightclub as he tapped the bedside table for his phone.

Assuming clocks could still be trusted, 5:30 a.m. on the dot.

Mara was sitting straight up in bed like one of Dracula's brides, her hair wrapped in a messy bun. She placed the schedule on Dan's lap. "They're really doing it," she said.

Dan was furious as he read through it, and the bruise over his left eye throbbed, swollen and black. He took a deep breath though and steadied himself. It was routine. Dan could do routine, especially if it was his best hope of saving Mara. He could hide in the ho-hum, tiptoe through the tedium. Just avoid Rico, do whatever they say, and keep your mouth shut. For one week.

He crumpled the schedule and threw it across the room.

He was made for this.

Mara, on the other hand, sprung from the bed like a boxer beating the ten count. Dan knew that look—she wanted to fight. Plan a sit-in, lead a march, lie in front of some golf carts like a low-stakes Tiananmen Square. He rolled from under the covers and clutched her shoulders just as guards began banging on their door.

"Hey. *Hey*. Look at me."

Mara squirmed in place, her fists clenched, eyes wild.

"We stick to the plan," Dan said, giving her a little shake. He crouched down, forced her to look at him. "When the plane's ready, Alan will come for us. He will. Until then, we lay low. Keep our heads down. Model prisoners. Okay?"

"I don't like it," she said, and the banging outside was louder.

"I don't either." Dan pulled her in for a hug. "But I'm getting you home to your mom."

She deflated in his arms.

Wednesday, June 7

Morning, y'all! Hope you got some shut-eye 'cause we got a BIG week ahead of us. You can expect a note from me each morning—even if it's just to say howdy! ☺ The following schedule is in immediate effect for all Building B and C guests.

I can't think of a team I'd rather be on this journey with. See y'all out there!

♥ Lilyanna

P.S.: As a friendly reminder, anyone caught outside their rooms after lights out will face severe punishment. It's for everyone's safety!

TIZOC GRAND ISLANDS RESORT AND SPA
MANDATORY SCHEDULE—EFFECTIVE IMMEDIATELY

5:30 a.m. :	Wake Up
6:00 a.m. :	Sunrise Yoga Hosted by Lilyanna Collins—Great Lawn
6:30 a.m. :	Worship Service Hosted by Pete Collins—Great Lawn
6:55 a.m. :	Grab 'n' Grow Breakfast—Great Lawn

7:00 a.m.	:	Morning Pitch-In Assignments
11:30 a.m.	:	Lunch—Tlaloc Restaurant, Building B
12:00 p.m.	:	Afternoon Pitch-In Assignments
5:00 p.m.	:	Sweat the Day Away Hosted by Lilyanna Collins—Main Building Ballroom
6:00 p.m.	:	Building B Showers (30 Minutes)—Guest Rooms
6:30 p.m.	:	Building C Showers (15 Minutes)—Guest Rooms
6:45 p.m.	:	Guest Count—Pool Deck
7:00 p.m.	:	Dinner and Devotional Hosted by Pete Collins—Tlaloc Restaurant, Building B
8:00 p.m.	:	Tizoc Entertainment—Main Building Ballroom
8:30 p.m.	:	Individual Enrichment Time—Guest Rooms
9:00 p.m.	:	LIGHTS OUT

Dan and Mara were forced into some clothes and out into the dark. They sleepwalked shoulder to shoulder with fellow guests, moths bouncing off carriage lights, down three flights of stairs, past the breezy gardens, and onto the Great Lawn, where Rachel Platten's "Fight Song" roared from some speakers like the entrance music to hell.

Dan spotted Charles and Lenny—of course the old men beat the morning rush—and he wordlessly lined up beside them. He swayed in place as hundreds of other guests filtered onto the lawn. Mara's hand occasionally brushed against his, and when it did, he grinned at her like everything was going to be fine, like You must not have read the brochure as closely as me, like This is all just part of Bahamian culture and we should try to be respectful.

Lilyanna Collins stood atop a Jeep, and the music died down. She was wearing a pair of denim overalls that had never seen a day of work in their lives, and her smile put the resort lights to shame. She had her hands on her hips and a bandana wrapped around her head, Rosie the Riveter live and in the flesh.

"Good morning, y'all, good morning!" After a lukewarm reception, she pursed her lips and clapped her hands together. "Now, I know y'all can do better than that. Come on, Tizoc. I said, 'Good morning!'"

Some folks bellowed "good morning" like their lives depended on it. Maybe they did.

"We got a big day ahead of us, y'all. A big week! Now, I know I might look a little worse for wear up here, I know I look like a raccoon with these dark circles under my eyes." She was literally glowing. "But that's 'cause I've been up most the night finalizin' this week's schedule, which I hope you've already read. In a moment, we're going to get started with some Sunrise Yoga." Moans. "Oh, come on, y'all. Just cause the sun won't rise and shine, doesn't mean we shouldn't!" She giggled. "But first, we're gonna pass out pitch-in cards so we all know what we're responsible for this week, okay?"

Staff members floated through the crowd, assignments were written in pen on Tizoc-branded sticky notes. Charles received laundry. Lenny was ordered along with other Building C men to chop down trees for firewood. Dan and Mara lucked out and received an assignment together.

"Inventorying shops in the Main Building," Dan said, comparing his note to Mara's.

"That's a plum job," Lenny said, looking over their shoulders and huffing. He glanced at his card again and then into the northeastern woods. "Whaddya know, the Building B people got all the plum jobs."

Lilyanna returned to the Jeep and held her hands up for quiet. "Alright, y'all, who's ready to rock their pitch-in assignment?" She didn't wait for an answer. "Now, I know we've got Worship Service in a bit—can't wait for y'all to hear from my hubby—but before all that, would you join me in a teeny-tiny little prayer? Lord knows I could use the extra blessing. I have a good heart, y'all, but this mouth!"

She bowed her head. "Lord, I give You all that I am this week. Please brush away my weariness, so that I may be inspired in my work. Teach me to make good use of the time You give me for working. And Lord, please help us to do good work so that we may all earn full ration cards for the nourishment of our bodies. Amen!"

Dan locked eyes with Mara.

Yep. Fucking ration cards.

Thursday, June 8

Tizoc family: I loved seeing the passion everyone brought to their pitch-in assignments yesterday. And how about that mariachi band last night? I'm still tapping my foot!

If you received decreased rations as a result of your output, today's your day to turn things around! Rations are evaluated at the end of every workday. Think of it like life—you get what you put in. You got this!

♥ Lilyanna

"Hey, Mara. Mara—look."

The following day, Dan and Mara sifted through inventory inside the disheveled Tommy Bahama in the Main Building. Shoulder-height stacks of brightly colored shirts and dresses and blouses lined the walls. Dan wore a straw hat he found in the dressing room.

Mara glanced up from her clipboard, and Dan laughed. He had removed a mannequin's shorts and bent him into an inappropriate position. "It looks like"—Dan adjusted the mannequin's hand a little bit—"it looks like he's banging the Adirondack chair."

She blinked at him and then returned to scribbling. "Did you count all the chinos, Danny? We need a count of chinos for—"

"Seventeen," he said. "And there was a water bottle in the minifridge behind the register."

He had been trying to get a smile out of Mara all morning, but she'd fallen into an even deeper funk since yesterday's ration cards were distributed. They both received full rations—which they deserved, by the way, Tommy Bahama was the fourth store they'd inventoried—but several older guests' rations had been cut in half or three-quarters because they couldn't keep up.

Dan was about to add some locomotion to the mannequin because surely that would get her, but then a young guard appeared at the entrance of the store. "Lunch is in five," he said, his hand resting on his pistol. That's not something one needs to say with their hand resting on a pistol, but okay, we get it, you're in charge.

Five minutes later, they were queued up along with everyone else working in the Main Building and then ordered outside toward B. The temperature had dropped again, a cool breeze nibbled at Dan's legs and weaved its way through the marching guests. The sun had only retired three days ago, but Tizoc had already transformed from a tropical paradise to an inhospitable work camp. Guests shuffled in single-file lines between buildings, fires burned in steel drums and reflected off pools. Plants, like people, were beginning to wither. Palms fell from their trees. Ahead of them on the sidewalk was a twitching overturned iguana.

Mara stopped in her tracks. "That poor thing," she said. "Do you think—maybe it just needs…" Before Dan could stop her, she broke from the group, which was a huge no-no, and she folded onto her knees and pulled the water bottle from her pocket. She filled the cap with water and placed it near the iguana's head, but it didn't seem to notice.

"Hey," the young guard said, his gun unholstered. "*Hey!* You! Back in line!"

"Whoa, whoa, whoa," Dan said. He seized Mara, pulled her away, guided her back to the line. "Sorry," Dan said, his grip tight. He frowned at the guard. "Sorry, man. Soft spot for animals. We're good. She's good."

The guard grunted as they turned near the lazy river.

"What are you *doing*?" Dan hissed once they were out of earshot.

Mara rubbed her wrist. "It was dying, Danny."

Friday, June 9

Y'all, I wanted to address some of the feedback we received yesterday afternoon during Sweat the Day Away. Now, I know some of y'all think you're too exhausted for a fitness class following your pitch-in assignments, but remember: the best project you'll ever work on is you. We need healthy minds, bodies, and spirits if we're going to make it through this thing together. Give it your all today!

♥ Lilyanna

P.S.: Rico Flores, head of security, has reported a pistol missing from the armory. This is a serious offense. Any guests that provide tips leading to the recovery of the weapon will be rewarded with full ration cards, no questions asked. Thx!

Mara used a pair of fabric scissors to slice open a weight bench.

On Friday afternoon, Dan and Mara were given a new assignment in the fitness center. There were tons of soft surfaces in there—weight benches, recumbent bikes, foam rollers—and their task, along with several other guests, was to collect the insulation contained within and bag it for winter clothing. Dan had to give it to Lilyanna—it was a smart idea. If he had been put in charge of the postapocalyptic dictatorship, he probably wouldn't have thought of it.

They had entered the second full day of rationing, and the effects were starting to show on some of the sixty-five-and-older crowd. The man working alongside Dan, with droopy eyes and a face shaped like a crescent moon, nodded off every few minutes. Dan repeatedly nudged him awake before the guards could spot him, because that wouldn't be good news for anyone.

It seemed as though guard cruelty had an inverse relationship with the temperature. As it got colder, they got meaner, and a swift boot from Rico or one of his men was now a constant threat. Just that morning, during Pete's Worship Service, Rico had dragged a man by his hair into the gardens. The man had interrupted the sermon, shouting something about the regime needing God's forgiveness, and, well, that was that. The remainder of the service was punctuated by the man's indistinct wailing. Dan held Mara's hand and sang "Our God Is an Awesome God" loudly enough to drown him out.

"Mara," Dan said, grabbing a yellow yoga mat and draping it over his head and shoulders. He double-checked that the guards had stepped out and then equipped a ridiculous Southern accent. "Welcome to Sweat Your Life Away, y'all! The temperature may be dropping outside, but in here, all we're dropping is stubborn belly fat! Teamwork makes the regime work!"

The man with the crescent face laughed, and even Mara cracked a smile, which was a massive win. "You better cut it out before they see you," she said, scooping up her insulation and dumping it into a pile next to the row machine. "They're in a particularly bad mood tod—"

"Whose is this?"

From the front of the gym, a mustachioed guard reached into a trash bin and plucked something out. He studied it and then shook it above his head, the object catching the fluorescent lights. Looked like a candy wrapper. Dan prided himself on being able to identify any candy wrapper up to a football field away, but even he couldn't place it.

"Whose is this?" the guard repeated.

No one spoke. No one moved.

"This is an unauthorized snack," the guard said, stepping between some treadmills, waving it in terrified guests' faces. "This wasn't here this morning. I'll ask nicely one more time: Whose is this?"

A woman near the front pointed to the man with the crescent face. Dan's heart dropped.

"I—" the man stammered. "I found a protein bar under one of the bikes. I'm on half rations. I didn't think—"

The guard grasped the man's shirt and dragged him to the stretching mat, he yelped as he was thrown to the ground. Another guard pinned his shoulders, screamed for him to stop resisting.

Mara instinctively stepped forward, but Dan blocked her.

"Please—please," the man begged, "I didn't think it was a big deal. I didn't—"

"We are on a ration system," the mustachioed guard said.

"I know," the man said. "I just—"

"Quarter rations until further notice."

The room gasped. Over a *protein bar*? The guard turned to them.

"All food is eaten with permission from Building A. Anyone caught—"

"I didn't know," the man said, writhing. "It's just a protein bar!"

"I don't think he gets it," the other guard said.

The mustachioed guard snorted his concurrence and stomped to the free weights section. Oh, no. Dan's pulse quickened. The guard slid a forty-five-pound plate from a barbell, and Dan reached backward, securing Mara in place. He wasn't really going to—was he? Dan clamped his eyes shut and turned his head as the weight fell atop the man's foot with a nauseating crunch. The man squealed, and several people cried out, and Mara pulsated with rage in Dan's grasp.

"Now he gets it," the mustachioed man said. He barked for everyone to get back to work, and they complied. Dan turned from the whimpering man as he was dragged from the room. Before slicing open another seat, Dan caught his reflection in one of the gym mirrors. His bruise had turned a yellowish green.

Saturday, June 10

Lights out means LIGHTS OUT, y'all. And before anyone goes fussin' about the power to Building A after 9 p.m., please know that we'd much rather be asleep. A lot of work goes into making sure this place runs smoothly!

I will ask Brody to turn down the bass in his music though. That's fair.

 ♥ Lilyanna

"Not a peep," Charles said, pulling his face from Mara's shoulder. He sniffed loudly and rubbed the tears from his eyes. He sounded like a baby elephant when he blew his nose. "Not one. I keep asking the guards in the laundry about him every day, twice a day, but they insist they don't know anything. I just— what if he's hurt?"

"He's not hurt," Dan said, sitting on the bed next to them.

Dan was beginning to wish there wasn't a door that connected the Ferrises' room with theirs. He liked Charles, quite a bit, actually, but he liked sleep more. This was becoming a nightly thing. The lights would power off, he and Mara would settle into bed, and just as Dan felt the warm embrace of sleep, footsteps atop the tile. There was Charles, a child with a monster under his bed.

"If something happened to him—and I didn't go—"

"I understand," Mara said, rubbing his back. "But imagine he *is* fine—which he is—and then *you* get hurt trying to reach him. Alan would never forgive himself."

He'd never forgive us either, Dan thought.

Mara's last point seemed to hit home. Charles closed his eyes and nodded, which usually indicated he was all cried out. Finally. Just as Dan was about to say, "Welp, good night," the sound of something sweet came from the gardens. They shared a puzzled look. Dan tiptoed to the balcony and cracked the sliding door.

Ukulele.

It was beard man, standing out in the gardens after lights out, softly playing ukulele over Julio's grave.

"What is he *doing*?" Dan whispered. Charles and Mara's heads stacked atop his like a sitcom trope. Beard man played the only song he knew the whole way through, his back to Building B, and a cool breeze swept through his hair, disrupted the shrubbery, and carried the tune downwind. "He's insane."

Dan felt Charles's hand on his back. "Shh. It's nice."

"It *is* nice," Mara said, and none of them spoke the whole rest of the song, they just stood there quietly, cheeks pressed to the doorframe, listening. And then when it was over, there was a smattering of applause from other Building B rooms, because they must have been listening too, and beard man turned around, shocked, thinking this whole time he was alone. He waved to everyone, laughed, and then started the song from the top. Halfway through though, Dan heard several balcony doors seal shut, one after another, and then it was evident why. A flashlight illuminated beard man, and it belonged to Rico Flores, who was trudging across the gardens, rifle strapped to his chest.

"Oh, no," Charles said, pushing himself inside. "I can't watch this."

Dan couldn't make out all of what was said, but it ended with Rico snatching the ukulele and slamming it over the man's head, its splintered pieces falling to rest besides Julio's plot.

Mara, outraged, yanked their door wide open and screamed. "Hey, you can't—"

Dan covered his girlfriend's mouth and pulled her back into the room, her feet kicking out from under her, her ferocious cries muffled beneath his quaking hand. He tossed her on the bed next to Charles and swung the door shut behind them.

Mara curled into herself, and now it was her turn to cry on Charles's shoulder.

Sunday, June 11

This ain't going to be popular, but sometimes leading means making the tough calls.

Starting today, water will be rationed. We're going through it too quickly, y'all. I barely had enough to fill my hot tub last night. (That's a joke—trying to keep things light!)

Water will be available during designated bathing times per our schedule.

Let's have fun today!
Best, Lilyanna

"Mara—I just—I don't know how to explain it any simpler to you. It's like—am I doing something wrong, here? What don't you *get*?"

Dan had walked a tight figure eight in front of their bed so many times that his feet threatened to carve a trail. At dinner earlier that night, he had caught Mara sneaking a portion of her meal to an elderly couple who stayed on the floor below them. She was slick about it too, sliding her turkey sandwich onto the husband's tray just as Pete asked everyone to bow their heads in prayer. Dan's head was up of course, his head was always up, and he saw it.

Mara sat on the edge of the bed, her knees rubbing against each other. She hadn't spoken in several minutes.

"These guards—they're not fucking around, Mara. Rico is insane, that's well established. You've seen what he can do.

What his men can do. Why—" Dan realized he was shouting. He rubbed his face in his hands and sat down next to her. Somewhere outside, glass shattered, and guards howled with laughter.

Dan lowered his voice. "What if they'd caught you?"

Mara shrugged, her body loose like a rag doll. She collapsed backward onto the bed, the fire in her eyes extinguished. "They're hungry, Danny. And desperate."

"So are we," he said. "And if you'd been spotted, they would've cut *your* rations. Or worse. Do I need to remind you about the guy in the gym?"

"No," Mara said. She crawled away.

"And who's to say the old people won't rat? What if they start rewarding people who rat? That's Fascism 101, Mara." Dan could go on for another half an hour, but his anger was melting into weariness. He tugged off his shirt, closed the door that connected their room to Charles's. He flipped on the faucet to brush his teeth and then threw his hands up in frustration.

The building's power cut as he crawled into bed beside her.

They lay quietly for some time.

"I'm sorry," he finally said. "I just need you to be more careful, okay? Just a few more days. Then, when the plane's ready, Alan will come for us, and I'll get you back home to your mom, and we can forget this place and everything that happened here. Okay?"

"Okay," Mara said.

Dan searched for her hand in the dark, but it wasn't there.

He slept on his left side. The bruise only hurt if he thought about it.

II

Some guests from Building C escaped in a boat overnight. Well, tried their best to, anyway. It was the talk of the resort. Tizoc Grand Islands Resort and Spa wasn't known for its impressive fleet, having only six vessels to its name, and the boats they did have were mostly for parasailing and snorkeling right along the shore. Alan had called them prawn mowers on account of their small engines, the way they coughed up diesel, and the fact that they sounded more like lawn equipment than seafaring vessels. But still, a group of British dudes on a bachelor trip—they call them stag parties—had decided to take their chances with one, snuck down to the dock in the middle of the night, and made waves. Folks said they wouldn't get far, that the boats weren't made for the open ocean, and that the tanks didn't hold enough diesel to get them to the next island, wherever that was. That sounded like sour grapes to Dan. He was only angry he hadn't thought of it. Even if a rogue wave swallowed them up or they struck an iceberg or whatever, at least they'd die free men.

Why would they disable the other boats though? That was

the part that didn't make sense. They smashed up the engines and tossed them in the ocean. Dick move.

The Grab 'n' Grow Breakfast on the Great Lawn was less impressive by the day. That morning, it was blueberry mini muffins and pomegranate juice, followed shortly by the Pledge of Allegiance, a new addition to the resort schedule. They weren't even in America, but they had cobbled together a makeshift American flag using pool towels and printer paper and hoisted it. From atop a Jeep, Lilyanna covered her heart and recited the pledge like Reagan was listening. Guests shivered. The temperature had to be in the forties now.

Afterward, staff members, still adorned in black, separated guests based on their pitch-in cards. Dan and Mara received yet another new assignment—group sewing in the Main Building ballroom. Along with fifty or so other guests, their task would be to convert extra comforters and quilts into pants and coats and gloves and hats for the upcoming ice age. Before the morning assembly could break, Pete Collins, dressed again in a full suit, rejoined his wife on top of the Jeep. As usual, he was way too chipper.

"Hold on, folks, hold on just one more second, if you would." He flashed a million-dollar smile. "Gosh, look at y'all, so eager to get to work. This lady over here's trembling with anticipation. Ya love to see it."

Rico appeared from behind the Jeep. He leaned on the hood and stared out into the crowd. Dan stepped sideways to avoid his gaze.

"Hiya, Rico," Pete said. "Okay, now, I know we already had Worship Service this morning—and I don't know about y'all, but I thought it was a pretty darn good one." Pete laughed, then realized he didn't give the punch line. "If I do say so myself!" He laughed again. "But before you go, I just thought—well, Lilyanna and I thought—we can really feel the Lord's presence on the Great Lawn this morning. Would you indulge us in just one more prayer? One more prayer before we start the day, whaddya say?"

There was a smattering of applause from the more delusional among them.

Pete put his arm around his wife, and they bowed their heads. "Heavenly Father, we don't need the sun in the sky to thank You for this beautiful day. We pray that You watch over our hands so we may complete Your work, watch over our mouths so we may only speak of Your glory, and gosh, You know what? Watch over our hearts so that they may only be filled with Your spirit."

Gag. Dan looked around, like, Are you guys hearing this?

"Father, we ask that You help us work together as a team so that we may bring out the best in each other and so we don't have to place anyone on one-tenth rations, which, as of this morning, Lord, is the new lowest level of rations one may be placed on for unsatisfactory work. In Your name we pray, Amen."

Dan's head rolled backward. More bad news delivered by prayer. One-tenth? They would really put someone on *one-tenth*?

Two rows back, a woman fell to her knees, weeping. The guards were immediately on her.

There were only three sewing machines in the whole resort, and even fewer people who knew how to use them, so Dan, Mara, and dozens of others were given cardboard templates to place on top of quilts and cut around so that the more experienced sewers had a head start in completing the winter wear. Mrs. Betty Shannon, an elderly woman from Building A, demonstrated how. Her bony hands shook as she carefully cut through the fabric with a pair of scissors.

"It's like anything else," she said, sounding like that tree in Pocahontas. "Take your time with it. Go at your pace. Don't look at your neighbor's and think, Oh, she's going faster than me, he's already done with that, I have to catch up. No, no. That's how you make a mistake."

After a few minutes, she held up a piece of fabric in the shape of a mitten, and guests passed it around like it was the *Venus of Willendorf.* "Nice and steady now," she said, "and if a few of you will help me pass out templates and scissors? That's a dear. Thank you." Dan was given what looked to be a coat, Mara a pair of pants. They sat across from each other at one of the many rows of tables that lined the ballroom.

Dan slipped into a terrible mood. Maybe it was the lack of sleep, maybe it was the impact this was all having on Mara, maybe it was a week without a hint of natural light. Or maybe— maybe it was these stupid fucking scissors. He couldn't get them to cut right. He clamped down, and they folded sideways, barely leaving a dent. Mara was rounding the crotch of her pants template while Dan hadn't even reached the jacket cuff. What were these, safety scissors? For construction paper? After a maddening few minutes, he tossed the project onto the table.

"I can't do it. My scissors blow."

Mara rolled her eyes. "You have the same scissors as everyone else. Here, you just—" She walked to his side of the table, made a few easy cuts. Slices of blanket slid away like Easter ham. "See? Easy. Just go steady."

Dan scowled as she returned to her seat. His talents were wasted here. Maybe he should be out chopping trees with the men. He snatched the scissors with both hands and squeezed as hard as he could. It wasn't long until he'd lopped off the arm of his template.

"Christ, Danny." Mara shook her head. "You're like a gorilla. Listen to instructions. Slow down."

Dan pushed the materials aside. He glanced around the room, studied the top of people's heads as they toiled away. He'd been able to keep his cool the past few days, but after blowing up on Mara last night, he felt antsy. Uneasy. He became aware of his hand tapping his leg.

After a moment he asked Mara, "Hey, remember that episode of *Disappearance Report* where the couple climbed that mountain in Alaska but the wife disappeared?"

Mara nodded but didn't look up. "I still think the husband had something to do with that."

"Yeah. Maybe." He drummed the table. "How about the one with the navy pilot? In Florida."

"Jane MacCallum. I joined a subreddit about her. I actually think that one's solvable."

Of course Mara joined a subreddit. While Dan was content to just watch the show, shrug his shoulders, and think, Geez, that's a mystery, alright, Mara immediately had to go about solving everything.

Dan studied the ballroom chandeliers. "Hey, remember that one where—"

Mara's head snapped. "Danny. If you're not going to work, don't distract me. What happened to keeping our heads down?"

Right. Heads down. Dan picked up his scissors.

Five days. They hadn't heard from Alan in five days. What if Charles was right—what if they'd hurt him? They wouldn't hurt him, right? He was Lilyanna's only hope of getting off the island too. Well, unless—unless they found another engineer in Building A. Dan's heart pounded. It was feasible that there were two people on the island who could fix a plane. What if...?

Dan clicked off his brain. "I just miss TV," he said. Old Lady Betty hovered behind them like a ghost. Her fingers coiled atop Dan's shoulder. Mara raised her eyebrows at him.

"Oh, dear," Mrs. Betty said, poking Dan's ruined template. "No, no. What happened, hon?"

"Sorry. I went too fast."

Mrs. Betty handed him another. "Remember: *your* pace." She looked at Mara. "My husband is the same way. Can't stand to be outdone by anyone. How long have you two been married?"

Mara smirked, on to another pair of pants already. "He takes his time on *some* things."

"Oh!" Mrs. Betty craned over Dan, looked him in the eyes. He wished she'd go away, he had more templates to ruin.

"How old are you?" she asked.

"Danny's twenty-nine," Mara said. "I'm twenty-seven."

"Hmm," she said, like that was much too old to be unmarried, like she doubted their parts worked anymore. "And how long have you been together?"

Why was this any of her business?

"It was two years in October," Mara said.

"And do you live together?"

Mara slouched. "I moved in at the end of my lease."

What was that tone in her voice? When'd that start? They'd talked about marriage before. Plenty of times, obviously. He explained this to her. He wanted to wait until he found a new job, something that paid more than Marvel Maids, and he wanted to really start writing, maybe, and—

"We were just waiting for the right time," Mara said.

Mrs. Betty touched Dan's shoulder. "Well, are you in love with him?"

This lady had some nerve. When people reach eighty, their filters need changing. Air filters in cars are changed every fifteen thousand miles, so. Way past due.

Mara bit her bottom lip. "Most days."

"And look how pretty you are. I know he must love you."

Mara and Mrs. Betty stared at Dan, like he had to answer, like why hadn't he already leapt on the table Tom Cruise–style and professed his love so that the whole Bahamian sweatshop could hear him.

"Of course," he said.

"Well, then!" Mrs. Betty patted his back. "Sounds to me like the timing is perfect. You know, my husband asked me to marry him after *three dates*." Probably wanted to fuck before you both succumbed to typhoid fever, Dan thought. "And we're here because it's our sixty-fifth wedding anniversary."

"Wow, Mrs. Betty," Mara said. "Congratulations."

"You can just call me Betty, darling." She drifted away from Dan. He hoped she was gone for good, but she materialized on the other side of the table. She wanted to sit, so Mara helped her sit. "I have a wonderful idea. What if you two were married here?"

Mara and Dan laughed, but Mrs. Betty's gaze was steady.

"Now, I'm serious. Pete Collins could do it. He could marry you."

"Right here," Dan said.

"On the island, yes."

"Gonna make a wedding dress out of beach towels?"

"Oh, I'm certain we could figure something out."

Dan waved her off. "You're nuts, lady."

"That's sweet," Mara said, "but I want my mom at my wedding."

Mrs. Betty patted her hand. "The sun's exploded, dear, and you're already twenty-seven. Now's not the time to be picky."

There was a timed restroom break around ten—guards banged on the stall of anyone who didn't poop quickly enough—and then it was back to the ballroom for more garment construction. Dan's technique hadn't improved. Piles of completed templates swelled throughout the room, but his remained embarrassingly small, and the ones he did complete looked less like coats and more like baby ponchos. He was risking some serious rations, here.

Dan had just sliced through the collar of another coat when a man sidled up next to him.

Oh, God.

Beard man.

He was a fidgety type, one of those guys who always has to play with something, part house cat. He juggled a length of thread in his fingers. His eyes protruded from their sockets like someone was squeezing the sides of his head, and, goodness, his breath was less than fresh. That was one thing they didn't touch on in postapocalyptic movies. Human beings turn rank in a matter of days. We don't keep well.

"Remember me?" he said, and he stuck out his hand, and Dan looked at him, blinked, shook the scissors from the indentations in his fingers, and took it. It was moist. "I know we got off to a rough start, dude. But remember, I was the one who played ukulele at Julio's funeral."

"And in the gardens the other night," Dan said. "Sorry about your ukulele."

Heartache flashed briefly across his face. He ran his fingers over the cut on his head. "I didn't get to say anything to you then, but I really liked what you said at the funeral. And, you know, when you were up on the table that first day. Spot on. Thank you for that, dude. I'm a big fan."

Fan?

"They said your name was Dan. Is that it?"

"Yes," Dan confirmed.

"Yeah, that's what they said. Hey, uh, listen, Dan. Is it true what I heard about the other night? 'Bout you gettin' dragged back to your room in handcuffs? What were you doing? Some of the guys think you were trying to take another one of those boats, but I told 'em you wouldn't leave everyone like that."

From the corner of his eye, Dan watched a smirk curl across Mara's face, the first one in days. She loved that he was having to meet this guy again.

"All nonsense," Dan said.

Beard guy nudged Dan's arm and winked. "Yeah, I gotcha. Hush, hush. The DL. Word. But listen." He leaned in closer, whispered. It smelled like a mouse had crawled into his gut and drowned in ammonia. "I see what you're doing. I see the ring around your eye. Fighting the power. Pushing back on the man. The *wo*man, right? A lot of these people are too scared to say something, but know that we're with you, Dan. And... we want in."

In? In what? There was nothing to get in. Dan shouted into a megaphone for a few seconds five days ago and then got caught sneaking out after curfew, that was it, that was the extent of his defiance. Now, unless Alan came through, he was going to freeze to death in the Bahamas with his girlfriend while making baby ponchos.

"I don't know what you mean."

"I mean I want *in*."

"Yeah, my ears work. Nose too, unfortunately. But I don't know what you mean."

"The *resistance*, man. I want *in*."

Resistance? This guy really *was* insane. Dan couldn't have anyone using the *r*-word in his vicinity. Guards near the door of the ballroom noticed the whispered conversation, stepped nearer. Dan subtly looked away from beard man, came up for air.

"I'm cutting a coat from a jizz-stained quilt," he said. "Do I look like I'm resisting anything?"

Beard guy laughed, not getting it. "Yeah. But man, what's *next*? I heard that your neighbor hasn't been here the past few days because—"

"What's next is I'm going to plant these scissors in your

kneecap if you don't take your breath and go fumigate someone else."

Beard man's mouth sealed shut. He opened it again, considered saying something else, but Dan's grip tightened around the scissors. Beard man stood and walked away, and the guards returned to their posts.

Dan wouldn't have done it, of course, he didn't even like stabbing frozen vegetable bags, preferring instead to open them carefully along the perforated edges, but it felt invigorating to threaten someone. His first successful intimidation. The secret was crazy eyes.

He looked at Mara, like, Can you believe that guy? but she was having none of it. Her head shook as though on a swivel, not a good sign. Her cheeks were flushed too, like everything she'd wanted to say for the past few days was stockpiled just inside her mouth.

"That was exceptionally rude," she said. And then, "You're a dick, Danny."

"*I'm* a dick? Did you hear him?"

"He was looking to you for help."

"I'm not in a position to help anybody."

"Everybody's in a position to help somebody."

Oh, come on. Is that the nurse creed, or something? Do they recite that each morning with their hands over their hearts while facing the Rod of Asclepius? Dan turned away. This was actually shaping up to be his best baby poncho yet.

Mara scoffed and got back to work too, but Dan knew better than to think she was done. It was never that easy. After a moment, she tossed her scissors on the table.

"You weren't always this mean to people."

"I'm not—"

"What about that woman at the ice cream place before we left?"

"Oh, come on. She asked for a sample of *vanilla*. She doesn't know what vanilla tastes like?" Ugh. Just recalling that made Dan angry.

"And that guy." She signaled to rejected beard man, who'd returned to his seat. "A week ago, at the amphitheater. He was just making *conversation*."

"Jesus, Mara. His shirt said, WITH GREAT BEARD COMES GREAT RESPONSIBILITY."

"Who *gives* a fuck?" she shouted. Then, because the whole room was staring, more quietly: "*Who gives a fuck?* So if someone doesn't share your sense of humor, that means you treat them like shit? Because they're somehow beneath acclaimed humorist Daniel Foster?"

"I didn't say—" Dan stopped himself. Damn. She was going in.

"I'm super curious which part of your white middle-class life made you hate everything, Danny. Was it your parents' healthy marriage? The car you got on your sixteenth birthday? Oh, I know!" She did a baby voice and twisted her fists under her eyes. "Aw, I was in smawt classes gwowing up, and now I hate my job. Waah."

Okay, that last part just wasn't productive. And when he turned sixteen, Dan received a 2001 Saturn Sport Coupe purchased from a GameStop manager off Craigslist. Not exactly a Range Rover. But he hardly complained about it. Besides—

"You've lived a blessed life, Danny. Why are you so miserable?"

Dan cleared his throat, the question rattling his skull like an overloaded washing machine. "I think the sun exploding has made you a little tense. That's perfectly—"

"You'd think the sun exploding would put things in perspective for you. Aren't you supposed to receive some type of wisdom in your final days? Some clarity? The apocalypse just turned you into more of a miserable dick."

She'd worked herself into a huff. She folded her cardboard template into her completed pieces and stood, blew hot breath from her mouth to push the hair from her face. The guards walked her way to see what the commotion was about.

"Mara," Dan said, standing too, his hand out. "Come on."

She leaned in. "That beard guy—everyone—is just looking for something to believe in, Danny. That's what we need right now."

"I'm not—"

"I know, Danny. I know." She almost lost control of her swaying pile of fabric but recovered. "Story of your life, right? People think you're someone you're not." She walked away, past a dumbfounded Mrs. Betty. "You can forget about that wedding, Mrs. Betty." Then, to the guards who stepped in to stop her from leaving the ballroom: "I'm just working over here now. Jesus, don't get your panties in a twist. I'm just doing my work over here now, thanks."

She sat at the end of the table and got back to cutting, her foot real fidgety, and Dan could tell she was singing "Linger" by the Cranberries softly under her breath.

12

Mara Nichols's father mailed her a gift every year on her birthday, two hundred dollars every Christmas, and child support payments every month—on time. (The child support payments were for her mom, of course, but he always addressed the envelope to his daughters.)

But the last thing he ever sent her was a text message. One word, no punctuation, certainly no gifs or emojis or any of that silliness. Just one word wrapped in green because he never did like Apple phones, he was an Android man through and through, said there was more freedom in the Android platform and that society was constricting enough, he didn't need chains wrapped around his goddamn phone, too. The message just said *happy*, of all words, of every choice he could've made. This in response to the series of messages she'd sent him twelve hours earlier, asking where he was, saying Dad, please respond, please, the police are searching for you, finally saying, At least tell me you're okay, Dad, at least that. Twelve hours later, he sent the word *happy*, and, as far as they knew, that was the last thing he said to anybody. Police found his Jeep Cherokee parked down near the Mississippi River, his body stiff in the back seat from the smack.

Police told her he looked peaceful, but they probably told everyone that.

She was twenty-two when her dad was found, still in nursing school, recently fired from her job at the UPS Store because she refused to charge people two dollars a page for faxes. Dan asked her, when she finally opened up to him about her father, if he mailed all those gifts because he was never around. She laughed and said, "No, that's not it," she saw her dad plenty. He just liked the United States Postal Service and always looked for excuses to use it. Said in over two hundred years, the postal service was the only thing the United States government got right. Less than fifty cents, and you can mail a letter straight through to Alaska, by God, and someone up there'll be reading your handwriting in a few days. Ain't that something. Yet they can't cut me my disability check when I'm standing across the counter at the VA, right there in front of 'em.

No, he was around. A weekend parent, Mara's mom called him. She'd won custody of the kids, but after a few years, on particularly hard days, she wondered aloud over the kitchen sink if she'd won anything at all. She was the week*day* parent, and the weekday parent is the homework parent, and the dinner-after-a-long-day-at-work parent, the clothing-and-water-and-basic-needs and bad-dream and mean-girl parent, the parent who snaps more than they should because it's just easier to snap on a Tuesday than it is on a Saturday.

Mara's love for rare steaks came from the weekend parent. More than rare, actually, the restaurant called them blue steaks, a category of ultra-rare some places won't even do. I want you to take a New York strip, he'd say to the waitress, and walk it past the grill so it simply grasps the concept of heat, and then plate it next to some potatoes. I'll take an Old Fashioned too, but don't put a cherry in there, please, Sarah. Thank you. He also taught her the joys of camping, and how to skip rocks, how to help someone who needed it even if their pride wouldn't let them accept it. How to befriend strangers. Rob—that was his name, Rob—was better with strangers than he was with folks he knew. Mara thought it was because he liked the concept of people more than he liked actual people. People disappointed him. She could see the disinterest in his eyes rise like floodwaters the more someone spoke to him, the more he learned about what was actually going on inside their heads.

It's what led to her mom kicking him out. She said it was the alcohol, and the fact that he didn't want to work anymore, content to live off his meager disability checks and worn-down credit cards. Mara's grandmother said it was because he was white— that their mixed marriage was doomed from the start.

But Mara told Dan it was those eyes. The way they stared straight through her mom when she talked about work, about her family back home in India, about moving to the other side of town someday, to a neighborhood where the city still filled pot-holes. Those weren't the eyes of the man she met at the Memphis State football game all those years ago. Those weren't the eyes she wanted to fall asleep beside for the rest of her life. So she sent them to go look through someone else.

A few years later he was prescribed those pain pills for his back, and—well, everyone knows that story. It ends in the back seat near the Mississippi.

But why the word *happy*? From what Dan ascertained, Rob was far from it. Maybe it was autocorrect. *Help* begins with *H*. So does *hopeless*. And *high* and *habit* and *hurry* and *heroin*.

But he'd sent *happy*, and now that was tattooed on the inside of Mara's left wrist in Helvetica, and it was the first thing she read every morning because she slept on her right with her arms wrapped around the pillow. Then, when she stared through it, she saw Dan. Shirtless and doughy and scratching himself, groaning because he woke up grumpy again.

Lunch was served cafeteria-style at the restaurant on the ground floor of Building B, Tlaloc. Before the sun exploded, Tlaloc offered American and Southwestern comfort food—burgers, popcorn shrimp, cheese quesadillas. Dan and Mara ate there on their first day, too drunk and giddy to notice if it was any good. They were sober now, depressingly so, and the food at Tlaloc was terrible. Fellow guests—like the know-it-all-guy who shared fun sun facts while they ran for their lives days ago—worked the line. Dan handed him his ration card, a repurposed postcard from the gift shop: WISH YOU WERE HERE! The man plopped a spoonful of what seemed to be beans on Dan's tray, and they were runny and got all over his chicken sandwich. Dan hated when his food touched. He thought to say something, but he was already on thin ice with Mara, her eyes hadn't met his since the blowup earlier, so he let it go. They found an empty round table near the back of the place, next to a replica totem pole, and crumpled into some seats.

Dan seized Mara's hand and did his best Pete Collins impression. "Lord, Heavenly Father, big papa in the sky, ya know what?

We just ask that You bless this shitty-looking food to the nourishment of our bodies. We also ask that—"

Mara yanked her hand away. The silent treatment. That's perfect. Fine—two could play silent treatment. Just call him Charlie Chaplin, honey, because Dan Foster could be silent-er than anyone. Yeah. He'd just eat this amorphous mound of food in front of him and think about nothing. His favorite.

The chicken had the consistency of a bike tire, and the beans slipped through the slots in his fork before he could shove them into his mouth. The water tasted like it came from the toilet. After sampling everything, Dan shoved his tray into the center of the table. He wasn't hungry enough to choke down this shit.

"'Ey, look who it is, my fellow escapee." No doubt who that voice belonged to. Lenny Fava plopped into a seat across the table, followed closely by a woman Dan assumed was his wife. She had either absorbed the power of the extinguished sun or spent far too long in the tanning bed. The bags under her eyes were paper, not plastic, and her dirty blond hair fell to her shoulders in tight ringlets like Arby's fries. Oh, man. To have some curly fries right now.

"Yous don't mind if we sit, do you?" Lenny asked, already sitting. "Our lunches never line up like this. Gloria, this is the Dan I told you about. The one who stood—"

"Stood up to Rico," Gloria said, awkwardly reaching across the table to shake his hand. She had the voice of a smoker and the grip of a sailor. "The one with the megaphone a few days ago. Nice to meet you, handsome."

"This is Mara," Dan said, resulting in more awkward handshakes.

"Get a look at you, doll," Gloria said. "Va va voom. Who's

she look like, Len? She looks like—who's that girl on the show we watch?"

"I dunno," Lenny said.

"You know, you know! The girl. I think she's Colombian. The one with the annoying voice but who you like 'cause of those shirts she wears."

"I dunno." He was embarrassed.

Gloria leaned in. "He knows. He definitely knows. Well, she's beautiful, and so are you, honey. What're you? Indian?"

"Half."

"Hear that, Len? Half!"

There was something disarming about Gloria. Like she didn't know any better, like she came from another planet where it was customary to inquire about someone's ethnicity seconds after shaking their hand. There was a light in her eye, too, that said, We're just having fun here, sweetie, lighten up, we're all gonna be dead soon.

Gloria sighed. "Look at you, gonna die young and beautiful, all frozen in time like that. Christ, I'm jealous. They're gonna dig me up a thousand years from now and say, Woo, boy, cover that one back up. Fright night."

Mara opened her mouth to respond, but Gloria hardly took a breath.

"So this fuckin' blows, right? Well, the sun exploding, yeah, obviously, but what is this place now? North Korea? They got me working with the housekeeping, mopping floors in Building A. And you should see these rooms. Hot tubs right in front of the beds, rose petals, balconies overlooking the ocean. I'm collecting silver platters with caviar on 'em. They ain't eatin' *this* shit. And

my husband"—she placed a toasted hand on Lenny's shoulder—
"they got him chopping down woods at his age. He has a heart
murmur. They're gonna kill him."

Lenny patted her hand, like, I'm fine, I'm fine, but he was a
shell of the man Dan had met in the parking lot behind Building
C. His cheeks were sunken, his shoulders narrower.

"It's bullshit," Gloria said. Then louder, so tables nearby
could hear. "It's *bull*shit. I told Lenny, I said to him, 'We gotta do
something about Building A and this Lilyanna twat.'" She waved
her hands and leaned in. "I'm sorry, I'm sorry, we're eating, you
seem like nice people. I don't mean to offend, but my God. We
paid to be here like everyone else. I mean it was a discounted rate
through that ad we got in the mail, but still."

Discounted rate? Dan had paid full rate. Who discounts their
grand opening?

Lenny looked at Dan. He tapped the pocket of his cargo
shorts and whispered. "You remember what I said to you? 'Bout
taking our food back? I been studying those plans we found in
the hangar."

The underground plans. Dan forgot about those. Wait—
those hadn't been seized when they were caught?

Lenny grinned. "They never think to check the interior
pockets of cargo shorts."

Gloria rolled her eyes under her purple eyeshadow. "Again
with the cargo shorts."

"There's a way in, Danny boy. We crawl right up their asses,
bro. I been talking to some of the guys in C, they're coming
around to the idea. They're pissed, man. Hungry. Everyone not
wrapped up in this BeachBod cult is fucking pissed."

Mara glanced over her shoulder and then leaned in. "What about the guards?"

"Half these guards never fired a gun in their lives," Lenny said. "Alan took down one with a single punch. Boom. One shot, goodbye. We just need a diversion. Something big. I'm workin' on that part."

Gloria nudged Lenny's ribs with her elbow. "Get a load of this guy with the plans. Haven't seen him this fired up since the eighties. Back in the Heights? You rememba?"

Lenny sheepishly grinned, shrugged.

"They called him Leonard Layout back in the day, you know that? He always had a plan. Come here, hon." And now they were kissing. Dan and Mara feigned interest in the ceiling, stared at it until the sound of mixed macaroni subsided. Thankfully, another tray soon rattled atop the table.

"Well, I saw him." It was Charles, a frantic mess. He waved his hand, poked Gloria's shoulder so she'd detach from her husband's mouth. "Yoohoo. Stop that, people are dining. You hear me? I saw Alan."

Mara's arm was instantly around Charles. "How is he?"

Dan's chest tightened. "Did he say how the plane's coming?"

"Y'all, he looked...so exhausted." The corners of Charles's eyes glistened. "They let him come back to the room to rest for a few hours, gave me a quick break to go see him. Rico stayed in the room, like it was some sort of...some sort of conjugal visit! Alan could hardly say anything to me with that ugly man breathing down our necks. I hate him so much."

Dan rubbed the side of his face. "Join the club."

"He's horrible," Gloria said. "One of the girls on janitorial accidentally knocked something over in the lobby of Building A. So on the next water break, Rico made her drink from the mop bucket."

"He's awful," Charles said. "So he's following me around the room, making sure Alan doesn't say anything to me, I suppose, or try anything tricky. Alan tells me he just needs sleep more than anything, and that we should keep doing what we're doing. Keep our heads down and work. How am I supposed to work when they have my husband like Tim Robbins in *Shawshank*?" He buried his face in his hands. Mara rubbed his back.

Lenny huffed. "'Ey, Charles, Alan's a tough son of a bitch, alright? You shoulda seen him the other night. He's gonna be fine."

"He is," Mara said. "Did he say anything else, Charles? They're feeding him, right?"

"If you call this food." Charles took a quick bite of his sandwich, threw his hands in the air, and spit it into a napkin. "Good Lord, y'all. I'm so hungry. I've got to eat it. But—"

"It feels intentionally bad," Dan mumbled.

Charles's head whipped to Dan. He rummaged through his pocket and slid out a scrap of paper. "I cannot believe I almost forgot. Rico graciously allowed Alan and me a quick hug before he escorted me back to laundry. And my man must always be thinking, because later I found *this* slipped into my pocket."

Dan unfolded it:

HAVE DAN MEET ME AT THE HANGAR AFTER DARK (HA HA).

Dan, wide-eyed, looked up. "Why didn't you lead with this?"

Charles rubbed his face in his hands as the note made its way around the table.

Lenny said, "Oh, man, he's cookin' up something."

Gloria said, "Ya gotta go. Maybe he got it fixed."

Charles said, "I'll give you some clothes to take."

Mara slid the note away, sat back, and crossed her arms. She idly tapped a finger. Then: "Lenny. What kind of diversion are you thinking?"

Dan flashed her daggers. Why was she encouraging him? That wasn't—

"A fire, maybe." Leonard Layout whispered as much as a loudmouth can whisper. "Propane tank explosion. Something. Just to throw things off a bit, scatter the—"

"What about during entertainment?" Mara asked. "It's so loud."

"See, I thought of that too. But my buddy who's working food service says they start preppin' for breakfast the night before, so the tunnels are—"

"*Guys.*" Dan slapped the table harder than he meant to. A few nearby guests, understandably on edge, spun their heads. Dan took a deep breath and waited for them to look away. "We're losing focus here. You heard Charles. Alan says we should keep our heads down. He's working on the plane. Now is not the time to orchestrate a heist. If we just—"

Lenny's head was shaking. "People are hurtin', bro, they're hurtin' right now. And—"

"We're not even positive Alan's gonna get the plane *fixed*," Mara said. "We might be waiting on nothing. Meanwhile—"

"He'll fix it," Charles said.

"*He'll fix it*," Dan snapped, his tone and eyes very much conveying that Mara should stop speaking. If there was one thing Mara didn't like, it was any suggestion that she stop speaking, ever. The corner of her mouth twitched. Dan softened his voice. "I'm sorry. I'm sorry. I just—I don't want to blow my best chance of getting you out of here." He pleaded with the table. "Of getting us *all* out of here."

Lenny grinned at Dan like he appreciated the concern, but he was clearly unconvinced. "You know. People are looking at you, kid. Talking about you. You might not know it, but people are talking."

Dan scoffed. "What? No, they're not."

"I've heard it too," Gloria said. "I couldn't wait to meet megaphone boy."

Lenny counted his meaty fingers. "The megaphone thing, the funeral, getting dragged back to the room in handcuffs, the black eye. Oh, big-time. You're like Moses or something."

"I didn't ask for that."

"Ask for it, don't ask for it, you're it. People are watching your next move, bro."

Dan scanned the restaurant, felt other guests' eyes dart back to their plates. He wanted to stand on top of another table— this one—and tell them they got the wrong guy, that he was flattered, really, that's nice, but that he worked in digital marketing at Marvel Maids in Memphis, Tennessee, and even there he was a mediocre employee at best. That he wasn't their Moses, he couldn't be their Moses, and he wasn't even totally sure what Moses did. Build an ark? Wait, no, that was Noah. See?

But instead he just sat there, hands in his lap.

Lenny choked down his final bite of chicken. "Come on, Mara. Tell him."

She stood, stacking Dan's uneaten tray of food atop hers. "He doesn't listen." She stormed away. Before exiting the restaurant, she slid Dan's food to a frail woman seated near the door.

"She's upset," Charles said. He popped up from his seat and walked after her.

"Okay," Gloria said, gathering her things. "Yeah. Girl time. Here we go." Then she was gone too.

Lenny came around the table and sat next to Dan.

"What was that, kid? Trouble in paradise?"

Dan folded into himself. His stomach ached. This whole vacation was trouble in paradise.

"Let me tell you somethin'. Can I tell you something? You don't let a girl like that walk away, man. You go after her. Go."

Dan shook his head. Mara needed space, she needed to cool down. She'd understand eventually. He loved her compassion, really, it was one of his favorite things about her. But Dan didn't have the luxury of compassion. He was a man, and that meant he had a job to do.

Lenny nudged him. "What's a matter with you? Make nice. You can't be mad at each other with the sun gone. Don't make sense. Listen, if I had a girl like that, I'd—"

Dan lost his cool. Again. "Lenny, I'm not really after life advice from a Building C Jersey City deli owner. Thanks."

Lenny face froze in a twisted expression of betrayal.

Fuck. Dan didn't mean it. It just spewed out of him. Why'd he do that?

Lenny shook it off and stood, leaving Dan alone with the collective eyes of the restaurant. "You ain't Moses," he said. "You're a fucking prick, 's what you are."

13

Dan's post-lunch coat templates were even worse than his pre-lunch coat templates, and that was saying something. Now, though, he made them completely alone, on the floor, tucked away in a corner of the ballroom behind mountains of cloth like a drifter in an alley outside Jo-Ann Fabrics. His fingers hurt, his head hurt, his stomach gurgled. He should've eaten lunch. That was bravado, pushing away the meal like that. It's the end of the world, Dan, you eat dog food if it's served warm.

Just like at regular work, by midafternoon Dan coasted. He only cut fabric when Mrs. Betty was watching, otherwise he reclined into a completed pile of winter socks and dreamed of Domino's pizza. God. Domino's. That was his childhood pizza place—hey, there weren't many options in Tennessee—and Dan could eat through the entire menu right about now. Consume all these feelings. Missing the sun? That's a large four-cheese pizza. Worried about Alan? Buffalo wings. Regret snapping at Lenny? Spicy meatball, extra sauce.

Nervous your girlfriend realizes she's wasted two years with a man that's done nothing with his life and who will ultimately disappoint her at every conceivable opportunity for the foreseeable future?

Uh... Diet Coke.

Several excruciating hours later, the doors to the ballroom burst open, and in strolled Rico Flores with two lackeys, swaggering like they owned the place. They each held a stack of ration cards, and Rico shuffled through them as he walked, whistling. Dan hid behind one of the larger piles but kept an eye out. Rico wasn't usually the one to distribute ration cards, the enviable task delegated to his men. What changed? And why did he keep looking at Mara?

"Bernie Rinehart!" Rico extended a card above his head.

On the right side of the room, a short man with a bald crown stood and said, "H-here!" like it was roll call. Rico, playfully exasperated, shook the card in his direction. The man waddled over to collect it.

"Nice job, Bernie!" Rico announced. "Three-quarter rations tomorrow. Pick up the pace, and you'll earn yourself a full card next time."

Groans flooded the ballroom, and the guards accompanying Rico instinctively clutched their pistols. Rage shot through Dan's veins like hot marinara sauce. This was his fifth rationing ceremony, they should've been mundane by now, but each one still felt like a scab being picked.

Rico hollered over the crowd, his gold tooth catching the light of the ballroom chandelier. "Ladies and gentlemen, ladies and gentlemen, don't weep for Bernie! Three-fourths isn't bad! A lot of you did a lot worse than that! Omar Williams, come on down!"

He was taking such pleasure in this. Omar received half rations, triggering even more of an uproar. Omar, incensed, rushed headfirst into Rico, who laughed and barely had to brace himself. The guard to Rico's left cracked Omar over the head with the butt of his gun, and Omar collapsed, another pile of fabric on the floor.

Guests fell back in order after that, some weeping gently as they received their cards, others hugging their loved ones and promising we'll share, we'll share, it's okay. Some took another approach completely: thanking Rico for their half rations, their quarter rations, gifts from a benevolent God. The sun may have gone out a week ago, but the last of the light was just now flickering.

"Dan Foster!" Rico called after a while, a trace of amusement in his voice, and Dan crawled from his corner and approached the front, everyone watching because he was megaphone guy, *Mara* watching, waiting, breath held. For the first time since the day Julio was killed, Dan felt their collective expectations atop his shoulders. I'm not Moses, he repeated to himself. Can't be the Moses.

"*Quarter rations,*" Rico said, handing Dan the card and patting his face where he'd slapped it. Dan's stomach somersaulted. His rations had never been cut before. Rico's coffee-colored eyes bore into his, searching every crevice for a hint of fight, a spark of resistance. He found none. "Come on, Foster. You've been avoiding me all week. That all you got? You were such a big man at the hangar."

Dan turned and sulked back toward his corner.

Rico cleared his throat. "*Mara. Nichols.*"

Dan froze.

Mara stood from her seat and shuffled past him.

"One-*tenth* rations," Rico announced.

A collective gasp.

Bullshit. That was total bullshit. No one else had received so few rations. And Mara—Mara had cut more templates than almost anyone. Four times what Dan did. And her templates were quality! Dan trembled with fury, crumpled his own ration card where he stood. He could feel Rico's smirk burning into the back of his neck. He wanted to kick that gold tooth in, he wanted to put him in a headlock, wanted to twist him into a pretzel and ration off bits of *him.*

That's what Rico wanted too. He was practically begging for it.

It's what *everyone* wanted. Something to believe in, Mara had said. Dan stood there a moment, unable to move. He saw flashes of Julio in red, saw Charles weeping on Mara's shoulder, saw the elderly couple she snuck food to. He saw Lenny's hollowed cheeks, the inedible chicken, the broken ukulele, and the man eating off the gym floor. He heard Mara call him a miserable dick, heard her stomach grumbling, felt the rock with waves on it from their first date, which he'd thrown into the ocean in a fit of despair.

People are watching your next move, bro.

Dan spun and faced Rico. The bruise on his face throbbed again.

"Hell yeah, Foster," Rico said, cracking his neck. "What're you gonna do?"

Dan took an unsteady breath, the crowd inched closer. He

couldn't fight. He'd proven that at the hangar. Not against a rifle, not against Rico. He wasn't that type of Moses.

But Mara said he was a good talker.

Dan straightened. "I'm going to speak with your manager."

Rico's face scrunched. "What?"

There was a megaphone on the floor—Mrs. Betty had been using it because her voice hurt from shouting instructions—and Dan snatched it, rolled past the guards, and turned to the room, to all those bewildered faces watching him. "I'm going to talk to Lilyanna!" he shouted, which was overkill, because the megaphone worked fine. One of the guards lunged at him, but Dan sidestepped him, tugged the ration cards from his hand, and threw them in the air like confetti. "You guys," he said, steadying himself, panting. "I think—I think you all should come with me!"

To Dan's immense relief, folks cheered and immediately swarmed his position as if this was something they'd rehearsed. Wow, okay. That was easy. What next? Without thinking, he kicked open a ballroom door and rushed backward into the Main Building lobby, waving for everyone to keep up. Before Rico could process what was happening, he was engulfed in the huddled masses and Dan was carried forward as if caught in a riptide. "Let's go talk to Lilyanna!" Dan hollered as they passed the fitness center, astonished he had made it this far, and there was a collective cry of defiance.

The energy from the ballroom flooded the building, guests filtered in from the gym, Tommy Bahama, the spa. Heavy doors slapped against walls like shutters in a storm. Rico bellowed from somewhere, threatened people's lives, their rations, but Dan shouted over him and pushed on.

"They put my girlfriend on one-tenth rations!" he screamed as the growing assembly passed the gift shop. A guard snatched Dan's collar, but it was a small guard, thankfully, and Dan shook free of him and darted between—and then atop—some furniture. He balanced himself on the arm of a sofa. "*One-tenth!* Why should Building A have any say on how much we eat? We paid for an all-inclusive!"

He pumped his fist in the air and the lobby erupted. Some shouted, "Yeah," and "Hell yeah," and "Me too, brother, you said it." Dan frantically searched for Mara in the tightening crowd, but it was impossible. Several sets of hands caught him as he hopped from the couch. He sprinted though the hallways, banging his fist against doors while others did the same. They exited the Main Building from the south, resort lights casting their shadows against the wall like a parade of phantoms.

Dan didn't have a plan—the thought of Mara going hungry was an invisible force propelling him forward. He just knew he wanted to be loud, he wanted to be disruptive, and he wanted to talk to the lady in charge.

They passed the gardens behind Building B, walking now because there was no need to run. Dozens marched with him. More. He stumbled when his foot caught an in-ground sprinkler, but a woman steadied him. Dan's heart fluttered as he pointed.

"This is where we buried Julio Martinez, the pool boy they murdered!"

Booing, now. Some tore their ration cards and threw them in the air, others yelled about fascism, hunger. Rico's men paced along the outskirts of the crowd, waved their pistols, but they didn't know what to do. One guard attempted to pull a man back, but the crowd insulated him. Dan cackled when the guard ended up on his ass.

"We have to work together," Dan said. "We have to be smart! But does that mean we should accept table scraps from Lilyanna Collins and Building A?" They all screamed no. Dan pumped another fist, chills rolling up his spine. "Right! Then…let's go tell her!"

As they stepped atop the pool deck, Dan felt a familiar hand in his. Mara. She looked proud, she looked impressed, she looked confused. "What are you *doing*?" she asked, laughing.

"I'm Moses," Dan said, and Mara squeezed.

They were one hundred strong now, at least, and people flipped tables and threw chairs into the pools. Tlaloc's windows shattered. The tiki bar where Dan first spoke to Alan was raided, but the booze was all gone, so pint glasses ricocheted off buildings and the ground. A guard was tossed into one of the lazy rivers. Rico shot back into view, running and screaming, making a show of cocking his rifle. He rushed Dan, but even he couldn't break through the horde, and Dan felt emboldened by the hand in his. Someone in the crowd began singing Rachel Platten's "Fight Song," perhaps the lamest song a group of rioters can collectively sing, but it felt good to take something back from Lilyanna. Dan didn't know all the words, but he shouted the ones he did into the megaphone alongside Mara.

Building A was in sight. Rico must've radioed ahead because several of his men were lined up beneath it, shoulder to shoulder, guns raised. Dan shuffled Mara behind him. The crowd swayed in unison, one thunderous voice singing about the fire burning in their bones, about the fight left in them. And there she was,

Lilyanna Collins, on a balcony of Building A, leaning over the railing and shouting into a radio. Pete was beside her, he looked frantic, and Dan stared at them both, singing loudest of all.

Then there was an explosion, as if their singing had broken the sound barrier, and the air shot from Dan's lungs, and he was ripped from Mara's hand, and he crashed onto the pool deck with a sickening thud. He squeezed the ground, gasped desperately for breath. Guests shrieked, scattered, stampeded. Mara screamed for Dan, screamed worse than when the sun exploded, and his hand was back in hers, and she said, "Look at me, baby, look at me, look at me, that was so good, it's okay, you're okay." But he didn't feel okay, he felt like he was dying, and before succumbing he thought maybe he was actually born to die here, and maybe he would just have to live with that.

14

Darkness. Impenetrable black, nothingness, oblivion. Dan floated through it. No—you don't float through darkness. You wade in it, feel it slide through your fingers like oil, squeeze between your toes like mud. Each step agony, every blink eternity. An endless ocean of night.

Welp. Better get used to it, huh?

But there was a voice. Soft at first—then louder.

Danny!

Practically shouting now. Geez. Pipe down. Dan was dead, he'd been shot to death atop the pool deck of Tizoc Grand Islands Resort and Spa while...singing. Ugh. Be quiet, please. The least a man can ask from death is a little quiet.

God, Danny!

Oh, no. That's God's voice? Dan didn't have the energy to meet God right now, he wasn't in the mood to explain everything. His browser history, his general attitude toward others, the time in third grade when he wore blackface for his book report on Booker T. Washington.

Wake up!

Dan's eyes shot open just as Mara walloped the side of his head. She cocked back, ready to throw another.

"Goddamn, Mara, I'm awake, I'm awake." Dan clutched his face. She'd slapped the same side as Rico. A few more and he'd look like Harvey Dent. He tried to shift himself—he was lying on a stone floor, somewhere—but his ribs screamed in agony.

"Danny!" Mara shrieked, wrapping her arms around him, kissing him all over. "Oh, Danny! You wouldn't wake up. I had to slap you. I'm sorry. I couldn't think of anything else."

"You're a nurse." Dan attempted to prop himself against one of the walls—also stone—but he winced and grabbed his midsection. One wrong move and breath shot from his body like someone sitting on a whoopee cushion.

"Oh, babe. Rico shot you right in the stomach."

Dan groaned. "With a cannonball?"

"Beanbag."

Fuck. Dan associated beanbags with comfort. Mara placed her hands under his arms and helped him to the wall. It felt like his top half might detach on the journey. Eventually they made it though, and he rested his cheek against the cool wet rock and felt some relief. Mara carefully slid down beside him, put her head on his shoulder, ran her hand through his hair the way he liked. "Shh," she said. "Shh." Dan wasn't talking, there was nothing to shush, but he appreciated the sentiment.

"Where are we?" he finally asked.

"Jail."

Jail. Of course. His eyes adjusted to the dark. The cell looked to be about six by six, barely enough to lie in either direction, and the wall opposite Dan consisted of rusted iron bars. Water dripped and pooled in some spots, there wasn't a single piece of furniture or a toilet, and it was cold. Christ, it was cold. Dan couldn't see his breath in all that dark, but he felt it escape his mouth and float to the ceiling like an apparition.

"In one of the underground tunnels," Mara added.

"Why does a resort in the Bahamas have an underground jail cell?"

Mara shrugged. "For drunks? Or rabble-rousers? You started a riot."

Dan chuckled. It hurt. "So much for laying low." He shook his head. "I shouldn't have done that. That was stupid. It's just—when Rico cut your rations—something snapped. But I could've found another way to get you food, I could've worked with Charles, or…" His voice trailed, joined their breath somewhere near the ceiling.

"I wasn't expecting the singing," Mara said.

"Hey, I didn't start that."

Mara laughed, nuzzled closer to him. "It wasn't stupid, Danny. It wasn't. You stood up to Building A. You fought back. People need to see they can still fight back."

If Dan really had helped the people of Buildings B and C, if he boosted their resolve at all, he was happy about it. But that wasn't worth jeopardizing Mara's safety. He felt like he was being torn in two, and it wasn't all beanbag.

"What now?" Dan asked. "They just gonna let us rot in here? If I die first, you have permission to eat me." He shifted slightly and took a sharp breath. "I recommend avoiding the torso. Pretty sure there's bone shards in there."

Mara put pressure on the area just above Dan's rib cage. It helped, somehow. "They didn't say anything. Just dragged us from the pool deck and tossed us in. After they shot you, the guards took back control. You *really* pissed off Rico."

"Fuck Rico."

"Yeah," Mara agreed. "Fuck Rico."

They lay quietly for a while, the water from the wall—Dan hoped it was water—dampening their hair. This was the coldest he'd been all week, and it would only get colder from here. Dan always liked the cold, but his idea of cold wasn't real cold. It was Tennessee cold. Real cold—parka cold, long underwear cold— was foreign to him. This was how mankind ended? A species that had moved at a blistering pace since it first emerged from a cave—a species that went from horse-drawn carts to space stations in one hundred years—would be frozen in place for eternity. A cruel joke.

At least let us blow each other up like civilized beings.

"I miss the internet," Mara said.

Dan did too. "Oh, man. The internet. Will we ever get on the internet again?"

"I want to check Instagram so bad."

"God, if Instagram was up, it would be so good right now. Can you imagine the stories? Or YouTube?"

Mara smirked. "Top Five MISTAKES When Trying Not to Freeze to DEATH."

Dan clapped his hands together once. "Hey guys, if you like this video of me slowly starving, make sure to hit like and *slam* that subscribe button for daily starvation videos."

"And giveaways."

"That's right, for my thousand-subscriber special, we're going to be giving one lucky viewer a single grain of rice, mint condition, let me know in the comments below how hungry you are to enter."

They developed the giggles.

"There are so many things we're never going to be able to do again," Mara said. She gasped and her eyes widened. "Danny, we're not going to know who wins this season of *The Bachelor*."

"Or watch any more *Disappearance Report*," he said, his voice a petulant child's.

"Oh, my God." Mara buried her face in her hands. "So many good shows. Do you think I'll ever pet a dog again?"

"What about Auntie Anne's pretzels?"

Mara laughed. "What about them?"

"When you were in the bathroom at the Atlanta airport, I saw an Auntie Anne's. And I wanted one so bad, Mara. It smelled incredible. The line was short, they'd just taken a fresh batch out of the oven. But I didn't do it. I didn't do it because I knew I'd be eating like shit on vacation. I told myself I'd get one on the way back home. Now I'm locked in an underground Bahamian prison."

"There's a lesson there."

Dan nodded. "Always get the pretzel."

They were quiet again, and Mara's fingers fell from Dan's hair, and her breaths were shallow. He thought she'd fallen asleep, which only she could do in this icebox, but after a moment she sighed and said, "I'll never see my mom and sister again."

Dan nestled into her, ignored the searing pain. "Hey, don't say that. Why are you saying that? I know things looks bad right now. But I told you, we're going to figure this—"

"Quit it, Danny."

"Quit what? Listen. We're going to figure—"

"We're probably going to die on this island."

Dan recoiled. "Hold on a minute. You're mixed up. You're the optimist. Remember? Mara, I'm going to get you home."

"I don't need you to save me, Danny. It's okay. Hey, look at me. It's okay. I've accepted it. There are worse places to die."

She meant the island, of course, not the underground dungeon, but the reality of their surroundings in contrast to her statement made them both laugh.

Mara placed a hand on Dan's cheek. "Maybe it's a blessing, Danny. If we accept it, then we can focus on making things better rather than worrying about what comes next."

That lit a fire in Dan. No, no, no. Dan didn't want to die on this island. He didn't want to die at all, actually. But more than that, he didn't want *Mara* to die on this island. He'd made his mind up the day the sun exploded. Mara Nichols wouldn't die in the Bahamas. She'd see her mom again and Raveena, her dumb sister, and the ivy that wrapped around the drainpipe near their front door, if it hadn't shriveled up already.

"When did you give up?" Dan asked, hating the question.

Mara blinked, looked away. "When you did."

What? Dan hadn't given up. Every single decision he'd made since the sun exploded was about saving them. Saving her. And—

"When you stopped fighting," Mara said more quietly. "When you screamed at me for helping people."

"We were laying low," Dan said for the hundredth time. "Our best bet was to hope Alan fixed the plane and rescued us. And these people—you know, who knows—maybe there are other planes coming. Maybe—"

"You can't just do nothing and expect good things to happen, Danny."

Damn. That struck him like another beanbag.

He knocked his head against the stone a few times. "Well. I did start a riot."

Mara held him tighter. "That was good. Let's help these people, Danny. Maybe we can at least make everyone more comfortable before the end. Push back against Building A. Do the right thing with the time we have left."

Dan buried his face in her hair. Hearing her speak like that tore at his eardrums, pulled apart the lining in his chest. This wasn't the end. Not yet. Not if he could help it. But in the meantime... Yeah. He could do more to help people. He could try. For her, he would try.

He sat quietly for a while, pretended they were at home in bed, that the dripping water was from the shower because he hadn't completely closed the tap again.

Finally, he said, "Just promise me that if I find a way for you off this island, you'll take it. Promise me that."

She fidgeted. "Only with you."

"Promise me, Mara."

She squeezed his hand. "I promise."

There'd been other girls throughout Dan's life, of course, but not really. Not like Mara. He enjoyed himself when he was with those other girls—sometimes tremendously—but he always knew something didn't fit quite right. His shoulders were too broad, so she couldn't lay her head comfortably, or her hipbones came to too fine a point, digging into his thighs. When he quit holding the other girls, he still felt the weight of them there, the imprint of their bodies like divots in a mattress. But not Mara. She fit so perfectly into him that when they held each other, he heard the sound of a LEGO clicking into place. And when she left, he didn't feel her absence in his thighs, or his shoulders, his groin. He felt it somewhere else. Deeper down.

That's what love is. The LEGO clicking sound.

"You called me a miserable dick," Dan said after a while.

"I did."

"I don't want to be a miserable dick. I'm working on it."

Mara looked up at him. "You're *my* miserable dick."

"Would you like to have and to hold this dick forever?"

She laughed. "I'm not sure I understand the question."

"I don't have a ring."

Mara propped herself up. "Wait. What are you doing?"

"I've been thinking about what Mrs. Betty said. Obviously this wasn't the setting I had in mind, and I know I said I wanted to wait until I got another job. But—my plan was to get our wedding bands made out of the rock with waves on it. I'm not even sure if that's possible, I've been doing some googling—"

"What rock?"

"Our first date rock. The one you wouldn't let me throw back into the lake. But—"

"You *kept* that rock?"

Dan scratched his head. "Well, I did, yeah. Up until a week ago. Here's the thing. I lost it in the ocean. I'm so sorry. Maybe I can find it. Maybe it washed up."

Mara slapped his shoulder, mouth agape. "You kept the rock from our first date for *two years?*"

Dan was beginning to feel stupid. "Yeah. And I wanted to take you back to the lake, you know, and I was going to bring some carrot cake. And I was going to hold your hands and say something like, I never want to throw you back in the lake either. And I know that line needs some work. I was workshopping it. But that was the idea."

She collapsed on top of him, his ribs on fire. She kissed his neck, his face, his lips. She clutched the sides of his head with both hands and said, "Of course I'll marry you, Danny. I don't want to die without having been your wife. I want to marry you on this island." And Dan felt like he could pry open the bars of their cell, like he could lift the island and carry it home, like he could reignite the sun with a couple of matches.

"Mara Usra Foster," she said proudly, slipping next to Dan. Usra was a family name, one Mara had never been particularly fond of.

"M-U-F," Dan said. "Muff."

They looked at each other.

After a pause, she said, "Mara Nichols Foster."

"M-N-F. *Monday Night Football.*"

"Better."

"Way better."

She squeezed him, and he squeezed back, and her left hand was on his tummy, and on her wrist the word *happy* was tattooed in Helvetica.

15

There are few things worse than waking up in an underground Bahamian jail cell, but one of them is waking up in an underground Bahamian jail cell to the sound of Rico Flores laughing. The lights clicked on in the tunnel. There was shuffling outside. Guards. Carrying something heavy.

Carrying *bodies*.

Dan and Mara stood, Dan feeling unbearably stiff. Had he slept in a puddle of water or superglue?

Rico flashed his twenty-four-karat smile and ran a baton along the bars of their cell. "Rise and shine, shitheads. How those ribs feel? Got something I wanna show ya."

He stopped a couple of the guards as they passed, summoned them closer. Draped between them was a bloated body, a man with pale skin and swollen lips, clothes a tattered mess. It was one of the Brits who'd tried to escape by boat. Rico squished the dead man's cheeks between his fingers, forcing his engorged mouth to move.

A puppet corpse. Quaint.

"*I tried to steal a boat and escape the island, but the boat broke and I drowwwwwned. Maybe I should have followed orders, and I wouldn't have died like a dog!*" Rico laughed, slapped the dead man's cheek. He waved the guards away.

"You're sick," Mara said.

"And you're on my island," Rico snarled, his eyes narrowing. "Sooner you realize that, less chance you got of ending up like Rodney King and his buddies over there."

"Rodney King?" Dan asked.

"Rodney King," Rico repeated.

Dan motioned in the direction the bodies were carried. "You said he drowned. Why would you call him Rodney King?"

"Rodney King drowned."

"He did?" Dan looked to Mara, who shrugged. Dan's face was still healing from the last time he'd teased Rico, but he couldn't help himself. Teasing was the only power he had over the man. He raised his eyebrows at Mara. She grinned.

"I just know he was beat by the police," Mara said.

"That's what I thought too."

Rico sheathed his baton. His face twitched. "Yeah, well, later he drowned."

"Huh," Dan said. "Same incident?"

"What? No. He drowned years later. In his pool. Don't you watch the news?"

Dan's nose wrinkled. "I thought I did."

"But he's famous for the police beating," Mara said.

Steam shot from Rico's nostrils. He spoke through gritted teeth. "I know he's famous for the police beating. The reference was to his *drowning*. It was widely reported."

Dan clicked his tongue. "Super weak reference, bro."

"I agree," Mara said.

"When you reference Rodney King," Dan said, "the assumption is you're referencing some sort of brutality by an authority figure. Like when you slapped me the other night. In that instance, someone could've called *me* Rodney King. See?"

Mara said, "But that guy drowned."

Dan said, "Right."

Mara said, "I would've gone with Whitney Houston."

Dan considered that. "See, now, that's interesting. I associate her death with drugs, not so much the actual drowning in the bathtub."

"I could see that. But would you agree she's a better drowning reference than *Rodney King*?"

"Oh, without question. One hundred and ten percent."

Rico slapped the bars with his hands, his rings reverberating against the metal. "It was a perfect reference, bitch. It's not my fault you don't read the fucking news. You want Rodney King?" He frantically fingered the keys on his belt. "I'll show you Rodney King."

Dan shielded Mara, but before Rico could get the cell open, a slender white hand draped over his shoulder. "Oh, leave it, Rico," Lilyanna said. "They're just fussing with you. You run hotter than a diesel engine, I swear. They're tryin' to get you to open the cell."

Rico locked eyes with Dan, and his expression said, That true? Dan winked at him. Rico stepped away from the cell and nodded at his boss, grumbling.

"Now go make sure everyone gets safely to their morning work assignments," Lilyanna said. "Go on. And be nice to 'em,

like I told you. Whaddya use to catch flies if vinegar ain't working, Rico?"

Rico's chin found his chest, and he muttered something.

"Darling, I can't hear you."

"I couldn't hear him either, actually," Dan said.

"*Honey*," Rico said.

"That's right!" She slapped his butt. "Let's get out there and
use some honey, honey. And bury those British folks quietly, in
the garden near that pool boy. No need to go upsetting everyone."
Her voice became quiet. "Terrible, ain't it? One thing my daddy
taught me growing up is don't tempt the ocean. It'll swallow you
whole and spit out the bones."

Rico walked out of sight. Dan yelled after him, "Keep up
the great work, honey!" and then, more quietly to Mara and
Lilyanna, "I think the poor thing's a little burnt out with his line
of work. We had a heart-to-heart the other night."

Lilyanna let loose a cheerful chuckle. Well, she looked fresh
as a daisy. Hair all done up, pink tracksuit. Zipper strategically
placed so she had just the makings of some cleavage. Looked like
she got a solid eight hours and a warm shower to boot. Were her
nails a different color?

"We could use a toilet," Mara said, getting right to the
point.

"Darling, I imagine you could use a lot of things. I came
down here to apologize for the cell. Make nice."

"And for shooting my fiancé?" Mara asked. Fiancé! It was the
first time she said it. Dan couldn't wait to try it out too.

Lilyanna's grin tightened. "Now, y'all didn't give us much of
a choice. Can't be having folks all riled up like that. You're lucky

I radioed down. Made Rico switch to nonlethal rounds, thank the Lord above."

"Shame you couldn't do the same for Julio," Dan said.

Mara lifted Dan's shirt. His midsection was the color of an eggplant.

Lilyanna gasped. "Oof. Bless your heart. I'm sorry about that, Mr. Foster, truly I am. But you can't be hostin' riots on my pool deck. We lose order on this island, that garden's gonna be gettin' mighty crowded."

"You put my *fiancée* on one-tenth rations," Dan said. Wow, it did feel good.

"Now, that was Rico. Trying to get under your skin, as he's known to do. Appears he was successful. I reviewed Mara's output yesterday, and I don't agree with it. You're on three-fourth rations, darling, and visitants from Building A thank you for your hard work. Those coats are gonna save lives."

Mara scoffed. "How long do you expect to maintain control while rationing people's food?"

"How long do you expect us to have food if we don't?" Lilyanna cocked her head, like, You poor, naïve things. "Let me tell y'all something about business—"

Dan rolled his head. "If you're going over the three *D*s again, Lilyanna, just have Rico come back and finish me off. I swear to God."

She put up her hand. "Fine. We don't have to agree on the way I run this island. But I need y'all's cooperation. The folks in Buildings B and C look to you, for whatever reason. Lord! We slapped you with a little Beanie Baby, and this place almost burned to the ground. Still might if we don't prove you're alive and well."

"Alive, anyway," Mara said.

Lilyanna put her hands on her hips. "I need y'all to make nice. To quit it with this mutiny, call off the dogs. There ain't no reason we can't make this mutually beneficial."

"We don't work with fascists," Mara said.

"You said *mutually beneficial*," Dan said, leaning against the bars.

Lilyanna smirked. "Uh oh, got someone's attention! See, sales ain't about what you can do for me, it's about what *I* can do for *you*! Tell you what. You cooperate with Building A, you make nice publicly, I'll put you on full rations. Both of y'all. No strings attached."

Mara crossed her arms and turned away. "Fuck off."

"Turn our water back on," Dan said. "Permanently."

Mara hit him. Why did everyone keep hitting him?

"I can't turn water back on just to your room, darling. Don't work like that."

"Then move us to Building A."

Mara hit him again. "Dan!"

Lilyanna shook her head, her hoop earrings large enough for a gymnast to dangle from. "We're all full up, hun. Can't do it."

Dan thought hard. "Seats on the plane. Guarantee us seats on that plane once Alan gets it running."

Lilyanna was taken aback by the proposal. "It's a six-seater. And that includes the pilot, son. I can't make any kind of guarantee about two—"

"One, then," Dan said, sticking his hand through the bars. "Guarantee me there will be a seat on that plane for my fiancée, Lilyanna, and we'll play ball. We'll become BeachBod boss babes, for Christ's sake. Whatever you need." He reset his hand to emphasize the point.

"Dan," Mara said. "*No.*" Dan turned to her. He mouthed, *You promised.*

Lilyanna looked through Dan, sized him up, tapped her foot. She took his hand. "Alright, Mr. Foster. That's a deal. You have my guarantee."

Dan kept hold. "Swear on your children."

"I swear on my babies."

"Okay," Dan said. "Tell us what you want us to do."

Lilyanna grinned.

"I had a nice chat with Mrs. Betty this morning. Did I hear y'all say *fiancée?*"

16

MARA USRA NICHOLS AND DANIEL LEWIS FOSTER REQUEST
THE PLEASURE OF YOUR COMPANY AT THEIR WEDDING
CELEBRATION, TOMORROW, TWELVE NOON, LOCATION TO
BE DECIDED, RECEPTION TO FOLLOW.

That was the language they agreed on. The invites would be printed on resort stationery and slid under everyone's door during that evening's entertainment. It was the first step in reuniting the island, Lilyanna said, of making nice and restoring order. Her husband, Pete, would officiate, and Lilyanna would plan the whole thing, pick the flowers, the menu, the music. Make it real elegant. Real special. That way, folks in Buildings B and C would see that the Collinses and soon-to-be Fosters had buried the hatchet. Become friends. More than friends, really—practically family! They were in their wedding, after all.

Dan had never been the type to envision his perfect wedding, but if he had, someone like Pete Collins wouldn't be at the altar, the guests probably wouldn't be half-starved, and the sun would exist. Despite all that, he liked the plan. Their wedding accomplished two things: First, if they completely cooperated with Lilyanna and her ilk, it ensured Mara a seat on the Piper Cherokee six-seater. Second, and this was a nice little bonus, he'd be marrying the love of his life. If everything went belly-up, at least he could call Mara his wife before the end. That wasn't nothing.

Mara seemed uneasy. Not uneasy about marrying Dan, she loved him. Uneasy about getting in bed with the Collinses, uneasy about making pretend nice with Julio's killers, uneasy about boarding that airplane and dooming everyone else to suffer under the oppressive rule of whoever was left. "Plus," she asked Dan, "didn't we also agree to start helping people?" Dan shushed her, told her he had it all under control, that it was part of his master plan, that she should just work on her vows because his were going to be real tearjerkers and she didn't want to look ineloquent by comparison.

In truth, he had no master plan besides marrying her and getting her the hell off this island. But that was enough.

Once released from jail, they went their separate ways— Lilyanna took Mara to see about getting a dress made, and Dan was tasked with meeting Pete Collins because he insisted on chatting with his grooms before the big day. So while guests shuffled atop broken glass in single-file lines adjacent to the lazy rivers on their way to work assignments, Dan strolled toward Building A, which glimmered on the surface of the darkened resort like a polished dime.

Dan shared stoic nods with people in line as he passed. A few brave souls offered fist bumps, handshakes. When a trembling young woman looked him in the eye, Dan's gaze found concrete.

Twelve hours ago, he'd roared back onto the scene as a revolutionary. Now he was on his way to have some snacks and a nice chat with these people's oppressors.

For Mara, he told himself.

Guards too close to ignore freely shared sentiments of dissent roughed people up a bit, a shoulder shove here, a kick in the knee there. One guest practically tackled Dan and begged for more food, said he was starving, that his wife was starving too. The guards pried him off and then disappeared with him somewhere behind Building C.

Most folks, though, were too cold to revolt any more, and the guards too cold to be particularly cruel. There hadn't been enough winter clothing made yet, so only those with acceptable work outputs were bundled up. Others trembled in shorts and tank tops, huddled together as much as you can huddle in a single-file line.

Dan met Pete Collins on the pool side of Building A. He was dressed in a slim navy suit and shoes that reflected the resort lights. Dan hadn't met him up close yet, despite the mandatory worship sessions. He was a pastor, alright, but not like the priests Dan had grown up with. He had a dimple in his chin, and he kept in immaculate shape, and when he smiled you knew immediately this was a guy who flossed. A streak of gray hair spouted from his forehead and was combed back through the rest of his jet-black mane, the spot where he'd been touched by God himself. He was as handsome as his wife was beautiful.

"Well, now, I know you," Pete said, a chuckle in his throat, his grip solid. He playfully wagged his finger at Dan. "Mr. Fight the Power! You got a silver tongue up in there, don't ya, Dan?"

Dan matched Pete's energy, threw his hands in the air with

a good-natured laugh. "Guilty as charged!" Then they laughed together, and Pete put his hand on Dan's shoulder and kneaded it, and Dan could tell already this guy was way too touchy for his taste, but he had to play nice as per the agreement.

"How about this weather, huh?" Pete said, hands on his hips, looking up into the charcoal sky.

"Well, the sun exploded," Dan said.

"Well, yeah, but how about these clouds, Dan? Whaddya think? Rain?"

It did look like rain, come to think of it. Would it still rain without the sun?

"Maybe rain," Dan said with a pleasant nod.

Pete shook his head. "Boy, I tell ya. It's like I tell folks visiting Nashville. I say, 'Hey, don't like the weather? Just wait twenty minutes and it'll change!'" He slapped Dan's chest with his knuckles and laughed as Dan winced.

"Yikes. I'm sorry about that, Dan. Rico tagged ya pretty good, huh? That guy's a crack shot, I tell ya what. Glad he's on our side, right? Just *boom*, you know, no thinking. Line up the shot and *bang*. Meanwhile, I can't even hit my azaleas with the garden hose out back without a step stool and a prayer. Can ya believe it?"

Pete's hand found Dan's shoulder again, squeezed him in real close as they walked toward the entrance of Building A.

"So I hear you're finally taking the plunge, huh? I hope you're practicing your yes, dears—you're gonna need 'em!" He laughed and laughed. "No, no, I'm just foolin'. I like to have fun, keep things light, you've probably noticed. They say I'm not like the other pastors, all buttoned-up. Sterile. No, sir. I think one of the most amazing gifts God gave us was humor, don't you, Dan? So, my thinking is…what better way to use that gift than to spread His word?"

Dan could just feel Pete capitalizing God's pronouns in those sentences.

"Tell me, Dan—is it okay if I call you Dan?"

Dan forced a big smile. "Sure you can, Pete."

"Tell me, Dan, are you religious?"

"No. Catholic."

That got another good chortle out of Pete. "Wuh-oh! Watch out for this one! We got a jokester over here. I love it. Say, what about your bride? She looks very—she looks—what's the deal there, Dan?"

"Her mom's Hindu. But Mara's not real into it."

Pete wiped his forehead theatrically. "Whew! That's a load off. Don't wanna have to do the Allahu Akbar stuff up on the altar if I can help it, ya know? Gives me the willies."

"That's not—"

"Come on inside."

Pete waved at the guards, who eyed Dan with suspicion but then stepped aside. The automatic doors slid open, and they waltzed shoulder to shoulder into Building A, a feeling of incongruence washing over Dan. Building A's lobby felt like it belonged to another resort entirely. It was like the Palace of Versailles, with marble walls, a grand staircase, a three-piece band playing softly in the corner. Dan and Pete stood under one of two twinkling chandeliers. Across the massive atrium was a bar and its bartender, a man in a bow tie shaking drinks like nothing had happened. Building A visitants mulled about the space, laughing, drinking, smoking cigars. There was food everywhere. A buffet stretched along the left side, with a build-your-own hash brown station and fresh-squeezed orange juice and a chef preparing omelets. And were those...? They *were*. Stacks of candy bars— the ones stolen from the resorts' vending machines—were free to take. Dan watched in awe as a woman opened a Crunch bar, took a bite, decided it wasn't what she wanted, and tossed the rest away.

Brody Sheridan, his man bun rattier than ever, lay passed out on one of the deep leather sectionals, his shirt open and a girl comatose atop him, breasts spilling from her bikini. Dan's fists clenched. A woman near the doors to the beach was literally receiving a massage.

A staff member offered a silver platter of Bellinis to Dan and Pete. Pete waved her off, but Dan snatched one, took a big gulp, swallowed his anger.

For Mara.

Pete ushered him quickly through the lobby and past two pairs of doors off a side hallway. Dan recognized the room from Tizoc's website. The movie theater, an exclusive amenity for vis-itants of Building A. Ten descending rows of luxurious leather recliners before a stage and fifty-foot-wide screen, better than any of the theaters back home. The stage glowed, basked in the light of dozens of candles of various heights, and a glass pulpit had been erected in the center. Pete hopped onstage—he sure was spry for his age—and held his arms out.

"Well? Whaddya think, Dan?"

Dan looked around, feigned his approval. "Can we watch *Dunston Checks In?*"

"*Dunston Checks In?* What? No! Can't you see it? We're

converting this into the island's church!" Pete sprung from the platform, put his hand on Dan's back, led him forward. "Can't keep using the Great Lawn as it gets colder. Don't you just think people need the Word of God now more than ever? We've got guys from Building C using some of the fresh lumber for crosses, those should be installed this afternoon. Over here is where we'll put the choir, I think." He punched Dan's shoulder. Ow. "And here's where we've been accepting donations, which are just *pouring* in. People are so generous in times of need, wouldn't you say, Dan?"

Pete signaled to a dark corner on the right side of the stage. There sat piles of food, toiletries, stacks of cash and jewelry. A man appeared and dumped another haul—gently used clothing.

Pete shook his head, like, Can ya believe it, put his hands on his hips and smiled. "More where that came from, Wally?"

"Way more," Wally grunted, disappearing again.

"You're actually collecting donations," Dan said.

"Well, sure, Dan. A church only runs on the generosity of its flock. And it seems that God graced this island with the charitable sort, praise be. Not everyone on the island is mutinous, you know." He sifted through some of the donations. "Folks in Building C, especially, which I gotta say, really chokes me up when I think about it. Those who have the least, giving the most. If that doesn't tell you everything you need to know right there, boy, I don't know. When's the last time you went to church, Dan?"

"Been a while." For this reason exactly. Dan's façade was fading, his smile morphing into gritted teeth.

Pete wagged his finger, laughed. "Your generation, Dan. I tell ya. It's your generation. We need to bring the youth back to the church. That's our role. It's why I try to talk to these kids in their language, you know? At their level. I got a group of kids that skateboard in the parking lot of our church back home in Nashville, right, and they're vaping, and they're listening to their Wiz Caliphate, and security wants to chase 'em off. And I say no, Dan, right, I say, No, let me go talk to them. And I talk to 'em, and I say, I get what you boys are doing. You're just hangin' with your homies. And I say, Actually, I'm inside the church and I'm just hangin' with my homie too. And their eyes get real big like, Wow, okay, this guy is speaking our language. No adult has ever talked to us like this. And I say, Wanna know my homie's name? *JC.* And they're thinking, Who's JC? Who's this JC guy? And I tell 'em, Dan, I tell 'em: *Jesus Christ.* That's *my* homie. And suddenly they get it. And they wanna be a part of it. It's about talking to them on their level, Dan."

Dan wondered if he killed Pete if anyone would think to search for his body in the donation pile. Wally appeared and dumped another pallet.

"Guess you didn't come here to listen to me drone on about the state of the church, did ya, Dan? Let's find a quieter place to chat, give Wally some space to work."

Pete shuffled Dan from the chapel, back into the hallway, and then inside a corner office that overlooked the black beach. It was Brody's, no doubt about that. Antique pistols were framed near the window and a massive sound system hung from the back wall. Photos of Brody and that girl from the atrium, must've been his girlfriend, littered every surface. They were in exotic locations around the world, clearly drunk, high, whatever. In more than half the pictures, Brody made a *V* with his fingers and licked the space between.

"Sorry about the mess, Dan, sheesh," Pete said, wading through piles of paperwork stacked on the floor. "If cleanliness is next to godliness, we need to baptize this Brody fella, pronto." He chuckled. "I'm just kidding, he's a good kid. Little over his head, here, but that's why we're helping. Take a seat."

Dan pulled the chair next to Pete. There was another stack of paper on it. He plopped it on the desk.

"Yikes, that one's my fault," Pete said, wetting his finger and sliding the top page from the pile. "This one's a head-scratcher. You know anything about energy, Dan?"

He knew this building was zapping all of his, but beyond that, not really, no. He somehow produced a curious grin. "Why do you ask?"

Pete waved it off. "Ah, it's nothing. Just says here this island runs off eight *megawatts* of power. I read that and I said, you know what I said? Mega-*what*? No, it's just unusual because boy, that is a lot of power. I know they got the observatory up there, but geez Louise. It's enough for a small city. Tell that to your folks who are upset about the rationing."

That was kind of weird, maybe, but Dan had no reference point. And besides—

"You're here because you're getting married!" Pete said, slapping his knees and leaning forward. "How wonderful. Now, tell me a little bit about your bride."

Dan didn't wish to talk to this man about Mara. Dan didn't wish to talk to this man about anything. His mind returned to the chapel. That pile of donations was really big, and the people outside were really cold.

"Mara is—" Dan paused, felt his words collide into each other.

"Oh, come on now," Pete said. "It's just guy talk. Just a couple of guys here. Tell me about Mara, Dan. Why do you want to marry her?"

"I'm in love with her."

"Well, now, that's a good start!" He crossed his legs, tilted his head. "What do you love about her?"

Dan rubbed his neck.

"Let me start," Pete said. "I love my wife, Lilyanna, because she is kind and ambitious and an amazing mother to our two children. I love her because she is a leader of people. Women see my wife, and they see someone they can look up to, someone they can trust, someone who wants the best for them." A mischievous smile crept across his face. He tapped Dan's outer thigh. "And she can wear the heck out of a tracksuit!" He laughed. "See, Dan? Just guys here. All good."

Dan drained the remainder of his Bellini. Play nice, he said to himself. Play nice, play nice, play nice.

"I love Mara because she's Mara."

Pete pursed his lips. "Come on, mister, that's a cop-out."

"No. What I mean—what I mean is, she's *always* Mara. I change depending on who I'm talking to, where I am, how self-conscious I'm feeling moment to moment. But Mara is always... Mara. She's unafraid to be herself, to express exactly how she's feeling, all the time. She's authentic, I guess." Dan scratched the top of his head. "And...she cares about people. So, yeah, I admire that. I love that about her."

Pete received this with a knowing nod. "She's Mara," he echoed.

"She's Mara."

Pete smiled, tapped Dan's thigh again. "And I bet she can wear the heck out of a bikini!" Dan imagined breaking this guy's fingers one by one so he could never playfully tap anyone again. "Y'all want kids?"

Kids? The sun exploded. Who's thinking about having kids?

"Boy, you should have kids. It can be challenging, you betcha. But I tell ya, there's no greater blessing. No greater blessing."

"Okay."

Pete was testing Dan's patience, you betcha, and if he didn't get out of here soon, he'd say something that would ruin Mara's spot on that plane.

"You know, I feel really bad about not finishing my coat templates yesterday," Dan said, standing. "Really bad. Think I'm gonna get back to it."

"Oh, gosh, already?" Pete said, standing himself. "But I like that, a man who knows the value of a hard day's work. Okay." He balled his fists and boxed the air. "Hope you don't feel like you just went twelve rounds with the champ." He laughed, coiled his arm around Dan and led him to the door. "I just like to get to know my grooms, you know, helps me craft the ceremony. We'll let the girls work out the finer details. And I wanted you to see the venue! Pretty slick, huh?"

Dan couldn't get married inside Building A. It was opulent and cold and smelled of self-tanner and greed. Mara would hate it. Plus—and he couldn't believe he was admitting this to himself—an idea was tugging at the back of his head. A dumb idea, probably, definitely, but boy, it had itself a good grip, and it was tugging like a son of a bitch. For it to work, though, they would need to get married somewhere else. They'd need some distance between the ceremony and Building A, they'd need to be somewhere like—

"The beach," Dan said.

"What's that?"

"We want to get married on the beach."

"The beach?" Pete laughed. "It's forty degrees, Dan my man. And who knows what tomorrow'll be? By the way, so much for global warming, huh? Those liberal pundits on PBS must be pulling their hair out."

"So we do a couple of bonfires. Mara always wanted to get married on the beach, Pete."

Pete placed his hands on his hips. "Gosh, Dan, I don't know. You sure you don't wanna see the crosses first? They're gonna be big, boy. Jesus could've been four hundred pounds and still fit on one of these things."

Dan stripped all pretense from his voice. This time, it was he who squeezed Pete's shoulder. "We're working with you, Pete. We're working with you. But you need to work a little with us too. Mara's always wanted the beach."

Pete wriggled under Dan's grip, choked on a smile. "Geez then. We'd better give her the beach then, don't you think? Happy wife, happy life, I always say."

17

Dan needed to see Lenny Fava.

The idea tugging at his brain had now completely consumed it, swallowed it whole like a snake ingesting its own tail. Lenny Fava was the man for the job, Dan just had to pitch it to him. He needed to apologize too, for what he said last time they spoke.

Maybe he'd start with that.

Wind caught the canopy over the tiki bar against Building B, and Dan felt the first drops of rain since before the sun exploded splash against his face. God, they were cold, like condensation on a soda. He pulled closed his ill-fitting coat made from a duvet cover and dug his head into the wind, continuing his march toward the Main Building. It was lunchtime, and meals were being served in the ballroom since the riot destroyed Tlaloc. Maybe he could catch Lenny there.

From the corner of his eye, he caught movement in the darkness. Through the increasingly dense swirls of rain, Dan made out a figure at the base of Building C, hopping and waving and wriggling like an eel in a fish tank. As he got closer, he realized it was a woman, and she was wriggling for him, and he shouted at her, but rain snatched the words and drove them into the ground.

He groaned—What now?—and veered from his path, walked along the edge of the lazy river, past a storm grate that bellowed because, like everyone else, it didn't want to work. He skipped over a puddle forming where one of the walkways to Building C met the courtyard.

"Lenny's looking for you," the woman said, standing aside as Dan entered the breezeway to shake off.

"*I'm* looking for *him*," Dan said.

She glanced around—for guards, probably—and then said, "Follow me."

There was no arguing with the woman, she was back in the rain before Dan could object. He followed her because she reminded him of a cafeteria lunch lady, the type with hollow cheeks and hard eyes who were usually very kind but who would also look at you in a way that suggested they'd feed your bones to their pit bulls if you didn't start acting right.

She led him around Building C, to the east side, Dan was pretty sure, past some naked palm trees, and through an unlocked gate surrounding humming generators. There was a set of cement stairs leading down to a steel door marked BASEMENT, and the woman stopped before reaching them, pointed down, signaled for Dan to go on without her. Dan just stared at the woman because this is how horror movies start, but she pointed again, harder this time, a real forceful point indicating she wanted out of the rain, and Dan said, "Alright, alright, sheesh."

"Inside and to the right," the woman said, her voice the timbre of nicotine patches and vodka, and Dan waved over his shoulder.

The door screamed open and, yup, this was a basement, alright, a dimly lit hallway wrapped in cement and exposed wiring and adorned with Coke cans and cigarette packs and Frito bags. Dan considered turning back, considered telling the lady, No, thanks, have Lenny text me, or something, but the door slammed shut behind him. He sighed, found a drop of resolve, and inched forward, his fingers running along the wall to his right.

FUCK THE COLLINSES was spray-painted in black on the opposite side, and a little further down, another poet had written **GREED KILLED THE SUN** but they dotted the *i* with a heart, an interesting choice.

A streak of black shot over the ground and past Dan's left foot, and he screamed, hugged the wall like it was his mother. When his vision refocused, he saw that it was just a rat, just a stinking little rat, and he was thankful he was alone.

"Yo, who is that?" Lenny's voice. Growing louder from around the corner. "Oh! Danny boy! I thought I heard a little girl!"

Lenny barreled forward, his shoulders scraping opposite walls simultaneously. He tussled Dan's hair. "How was your night in the slammer? Cold as shit today, huh? My balls are like ice cubes."

"Hey, Lenny. I've been looking for you. First of all, about lunch yesterday—"

Lenny waved the apology away. "Forget it, forget it."

"No. It was out of line. I shouldn't have—"

"Ancient history, kid." He yelled down the hallway. "Hey, guys, I got him!"

He led Dan around the corner and through an unmarked door. Oh. *This* is where they do laundry. Teal washing machines and dryers the size of hot tubs lined the walls, and in the center of the tiled room was a massive table for folding. Around that table stood more familiar faces: Charles and Lenny's wife, Gloria.

"There's our freedom fighter!" Gloria said, cigarette dancing in her mouth. "Look at him, my God. They put him in one of the tropical duvets. He looks like Freddie Mercury, ha. Hey, Dan, how's your tummy?"

Dan lifted his shirt.

"Oh, honey," Charles said. "You're the color of Barney. Look what they did to you. Is Mara—"

"She's okay. It was just—it was a long night."

"Yeah, well, those assholes are gonna get theirs," Lenny said, approaching a dry-erase board. It was covered in resort blueprints and Lenny's insane scribbles.

"What are you guys doing here?" Dan asked. "How'd you break away from the guards?"

"They hardly check at lunch hour," Gloria said. "Stuffing their faces, big pigs. But we gotta hurry this up, Len, because this room's gonna be filled with the laundry crew again in about twenty."

Lenny cleared his throat. "Right. Okay. Now that Dan's here we can really dig in. Dan, man of the hour. Listen. I got a lead on some supplies for Molotov cocktails. We're gonna burn 'em out, bro. My buddy in food service, he helped me steal—"

Dan waved his hands. "Whoa, whoa. Wait. No fires." He took off his dripping coat. "Sorry. But—I've got news."

Lenny capped his marker and folded his hands.

"Mara and I are getting married."

There was an explosion of confused congratulations.

Charles hugged him, careful around the torso. Gloria said, "Mazel tov," Lenny said, "Get a load of this guy." Dan sat down and explained everything—what Mrs. Betty said, the agreement with Lilyanna, his tour of Building A. He explained where Mara was too, and that they could expect invitations later that night.

"I know the deal I struck was selfish," Dan said. "I know—I just—I saw an opportunity to save Mara. I had to."

Charles shook his head. "Stop, stop. It's fine. No one blames you. We'd all do the same."

"She's your girl," Gloria said.

"This is all great, kid," Lenny said. "No bullshit, I'm happy for you. But it doesn't solve our problem."

Dan rubbed his face. He was actually going to say it. "Yesterday. At lunch. You said you needed a diversion to steal back the supplies, right?"

Lenny grunted.

"You do it during the wedding."

Charles gasped. Lenny's eyes widened. He instinctively uncapped his marker.

"Everyone's invited to this wedding," Dan said. "The whole island's going to be there. If there was ever a time to do it, it's then. And I convinced them to have it out on the beach, away from the building, the tunnels. It's risky, I know." God, it was risky. Dan's throat was dry talking about it. "But there's something very important—"

He'd lost the attention of the room, everyone's eyes shifted to the door. Dan turned. It was Mara, dressed in an insulated terrycloth coverall, and she was soaked. She dropped the food she was carrying and pounced on Dan, kissing the side of his face and neck.

"Oh, I'm sorry, your ribs," she said, pulling away. She squeezed his head, looked deep into his eyes. "You really did have a plan."

Dan said, "Yeah, of course I did," because that sounded way better than "I needed yet another reminder of Building A's avarice and wanton disregard for humanity before I considered inconveniencing my personal interests."

"I love it," Mara emphasized, kissing him one more time. "I love you."

"Aw, see, now that's nice," Gloria said, ashing her cigarette. "It's a good idea, Dan. Hey, Len, who do they remind you of at that age? I never looked that good soaking wet, but who do you see?"

Lenny held a fist to his mouth and leaned backward, giddy. "Oh, it's a beautiful thing." He turned back to the board and wrote furiously. "The beach is beautiful." He went on, mumbling to himself.

Dan could get used to not feeling like a disappointment, that part was great, but Mara and Lenny's enthusiasm rattled him. Was it a stupid idea? It *was* a stupid idea. He'd just made an agreement with Lilyanna about Mara—this wasn't exactly toeing the line. But could Lilyanna even be trusted to make good on their agreement? And, actually, if the whole plane thing fell through, stealing back food *was* protecting Mara. His heart raced, he wished he could turn back time two minutes, he needed a quiet room to think this all through.

"How would you do it?" Dan asked.

Lenny turned. "What's that?"

"The food," Dan said. "There's got to be hundreds of pounds of it."

"Not just food," Charles offered. "They took all the medicine on the island too. People are getting sick. The lady working that machine"—he pointed to one in the corner—"spit up something green this morning."

"Food, medicine, whatever," Dan said. "How would you take it?"

Lenny sniffed. "I got a crew."

"He's got a crew!" Gloria said with a laugh. "Listen to him. You sound like such a badass, Len. It's so hot. Come here."

"Is it the Avengers?" Dan asked. "Because you'll need the Avengers."

Lenny's forehead creased. He looked around the room. "Kid, this is your idea."

"I know. I just—"

"Danny," Mara said. "Hey. It's a good idea. Don't doubt yourself."

Oh, don't doubt yourself. Why hadn't Dan ever thought of that? Let me just turn off the doubt switch in the ol' noggin. Ahh, that's better.

"Look, bro," Lenny said. "You just focus on gettin' hitched. Look at this girl. Tomorrow's the happiest day of your life, man, you don't worry about nothing else. The Building C Jersey City deli owner's got it under control. Okay?"

No, not okay. What was Dan thinking? There were so many problems here that he didn't know where to start, but the most pressing among them was that Lenny and his band of merry men were connected to Dan and Mara, meaning Mara would almost certainly lose her seat on that airplane. Come to think of it, a seat on the airplane wouldn't even matter, because Rico would make sure bullets had seats in each of their heads.

"They can't know it was us," Dan said, leaning across the table. "Lenny, I really need you to hear me on that. They cannot connect it back. Lilyanna caught us together at the hangar. I have to hedge my bets here, I need to stay in Lilyanna's good graces, because Mara—"

"I don't need you to save me," Mara reiterated.

"We all need saving, honey," Gloria said.

Lenny shot a finger gun at Dan. "It's good to have someone on the inside, bro. What you got goin' with Lilyanna, see, that's good. I ain't gonna mess that up. Like I said, I got a crew. I get dressed up real nice, got my girl on my arm, and I go to your wedding while's they execute the plan. Ya see? Lenny's got it under control. No problem."

Dan sat back. "And if Rico decides to just open fire on everybody?"

Lenny tapped the side of his head. "I got it under control, boss."

18

There was still the matter of Alan's note.

It was just a slip of paper, barely larger than the ones they fold into fortune cookies, but it'd felt heavy in Dan's pocket since yesterday. In the late afternoon while sitting on the can, Dan rummaged through his pants and found it. He was used to browsing his cell phone on the toilet—sometimes for half an hour, long after he couldn't feel his legs—but without internet, this would have to do.

HAVE DAN MEET ME AT THE HANGAR AFTER DARK (HA HA).

Dan had missed that first appointment, of course, but Alan would understand. He'd been in prison. Now, though, on the evening before his wedding, Dan's schedule was free. The smart thing to do would be to forget about the note, go to bed, marry the woman of his dreams tomorrow, and hope Lenny didn't get them all killed.

But—Alan.

Alan had promised that he and Charles would have Dan and Mara's backs if they'd have theirs. Dan rubbed his eyes with his palms.

He should've washed first. That's how pink eye gets you.

He finished up—had to push the handle four times to get the water he needed—and opened the bathroom door. He was so startled by Charles that he almost fell back onto the toilet.

"You're going tonight. Right?" Charles's arms were folded, and he looked on the verge of tears.

Over the next half hour, Dan, Charles, and Mara paced the room, weighing the pros and cons of the situation, cradling their faces in thought, and combating hopelessness, and pounding their feet in collective childish frustration. Mara didn't want Dan to go, obviously, not because she was worried about losing her seat on the plane, but because she was worried about losing her husband before he officially earned the title. And Charles understood that, really, he did, and he didn't want anything to happen to Dan either, but *his* husband was somewhere out on this terrible island, in the rain, and he'd taken a big risk sending that note, and what if they weren't feeding him, or if they were abusing him, or, Jesus—what if he just couldn't get the plane to fly and was no longer useful to them? Charles worked himself into such a tizzy that he snatched his rain slicker and proclaimed he would go himself, but Dan and Mara blocked the door.

"I'll go," Dan said. Then, more quietly, "I'll go."

Mara said, "Me too."

Dan scoffed. "Like hell."

"Danny, you can't go al—"

"I won't have my bride looking less than fresh on the day of our wedding. You know how you get when you don't sleep. The puffy eyes. God, imagine the photos." He grinned. "I'll be fine, babe. Let me do this."

Mara closed her eyes and squeezed his arm, a wordless surrender.

"Think of it like a bachelor party," he said.

"No strippers."

"No promises."

Charles hugged them both at once, his arms like a teddy bear's, and they stayed like that a moment, stewing quietly in the decision they'd made together.

"You didn't pack your raincoat," Mara said.

Charles found Dan's awkward duvet coat, wrapped him in it. "It's alright," he said. "You'll wear your duvet cover. And then over that, you'll wear my raincoat. Now, this is a Stutterheim from Bloomingdale's. Do try to take care of it." Charles clutched the lapels, shook Dan. "But most importantly, you find my Alan and make sure he's alright."

"I will."

"I know you will."

Dan kissed Mara. When he pulled away, her eyes were glassy. She smiled and said, "This isn't something a miserable dick would do."

Rain blanketed everything. Sheets of it cut across the courtyard like God was trying to wipe the world clean, start over. They shattered against the resort buildings in a steady roar. It was miserable—Dan already felt his boxers taking on water—but he also felt insulated by it. The guards wouldn't be out in this. Nobody with any sense would be out in this. Once the cold seeped into his bones, which happened very quickly, he was able to turn his mind from it. Like jumping into a swimming pool in February, he waded through the water until he became numb.

He followed the murky resort lamps toward Building C, tripped over a cabana that had been destroyed in the riot. The resort stunk. Had it always smelled this bad? It was like a mixture of sewage and body odor, stale air and recycled water. Not even the rain smelled fresh.

Dan made it to the parking lot, past the bus where he, Lenny, and Alan had handcuffed that young guard. Dan sidled up to the bus, tried to pull Charles's coat further shut. Heavy branches had been blown in by the storm, a golf cart turned over. He had a choice to make now—take the road to the west where they'd bussed guests from the airstrip and risk getting caught by a patrol, or head back into those damn woods. They loomed like a black hole at the north end of the lot.

His choice was made for him though, when from the western road, a pair of headlights sliced open the rain. The hood was blown from his head as Dan rushed forward into the woods, but branches from the trees grabbed hold and shoved him back out. He landed on his ass in the mud and groaned because, you know, fuck this, but then was back on his feet and trudging again. He broke through the forest barrier just as the Jeep lights scanned the parking lot, and the trees closed up behind him, swallowing him inside.

It was pitch-black.

He didn't use his cell phone light, not yet, he was too close to the resort, and he needed to conserve battery, so he walked like a blind man with his hands in front of him, attempting desperately to stay in a straight line while zigzagging around trees. The airstrip was straight north, that much he knew. Any variation from the path, and he'd end up God knows where, probably off the edge of one of those rocky cliffs that insulated the island.

When he felt adequately deep into the black hole, Dan turned on his cell phone light, but it hardly helped. He watched his tennis shoes sink into the earth with each step, could barely make out the bark of a tree before he slammed nose-first into it. He felt horribly ill-equipped to navigate this maze. He needed a real man, someone with a sense of direction built in, he needed an Alan or a Lenny, because he already felt turned around. He walked for thirty straight minutes—or maybe forty-five—before panic set in. Twice he decided to go back to where he came from, recalibrate, but he didn't even know where that was anymore, and then he tripped over a fallen tree and he landed hard in a puddle and his ribs hollered and his phone skipped ahead like a lightning bug and then extinguished. He was plunged into nothingness, his mouth and eyes filling with rain, Charles's Bloomingdale's coat definitely ruined. He scampered forward on his hands and knees into a tree, then into something that felt like a rock, and then into another one.

He desperately patted the ground for his phone. His heart threatened to tunnel through his chest like a freight train, his hands trembled like pebbles against the track. What was he thinking, coming out here alone? *Fake it till you make it* works up until the point you don't make it, up until the point you inexplicably drown in the woods of a Bahamian island several days after the sun explodes.

He closed his eyes—not that it made much of a difference—took two deep breaths, straightened the raincoat, and willed his shit together. It was just rain. They were just trees. "I'm a grown-ass man," he said aloud to the darkness. I'm a man. I got this. I got this. I got this. I got—

My phone!

Dan dove for a sliver of light inside a patch of slick growth. He collided with another rock—Jesus, had he walked to Stonehenge?—and snatched his phone from the ground, hugged it, kissed it, apologized to it. He turned the flashlight away from him, to get a better look at these rocks, but they weren't rocks. They were tombstones, and Dan—or the wind—had knocked one over. He ran his light and his fingers over the inscription.

JANE

1986

What? It made no sense. Dan scurried backward, his back slammed into a tree at the edge of the clearing, and he took in the scene as best he could under all that water. Seven graves in two uneven rows, three of the tombstones upended, ripped from the earth, a graveyard in the middle of the woods. Why a graveyard in the middle of the woods? Deaths in 1986? The resort only opened a week ago.

For a split second, the sun reignited in Dan's world, he could see everything as if it were daytime, but then his insides shook like a paint mixer, and there was a sickening crack above him, the tree he was against had been struck by lightning, and shards of it poured down as he tried desperately to shield himself. He stumbled forward, over the graves, faintly aware of the warm urine on his leg mixed with all that cold rain. Then there was another light, from a more permanent source though, and Dan fell face-first into it, washed himself in it.

A hand was under his arm now, it hoisted him to his feet, and a voice navigated the wind.

"Sir. Sir! We must leave these woods at once!"

Dan nodded—he would've followed Mussolini if he knew the route out of here—and he shined his cell phone up at the man. He had dimpled skin and tiny black eyes, and he carried himself like a man who knew things, like it was his job to know things.

It was Dr. Terry Shae, the man who lived in the island's observatory, and Dan could've kissed him.

19

_

"A fire, I think, would be nice. No?"

Dan nodded through his shivers. He was under a blanket and atop a leather armchair inside Dr. Terry Shae's dimly lit study, the front room of a modest cabin nestled at the base of the island's observatory. Shae had given him a fresh set of clothes to change into and had popped a box of Bagel Bites in the oven. Three Cheese, objectively the worst Bagel Bite flavor, but Dan was in no position to complain. His mouth watered as the smell wafted over the hardwood and up the paneled walls. Rain slapped against the window as if it wanted in too, and who could blame it. Dan sipped his bourbon, his phone charging on a table nearby. Sure was cozy in here.

Shae stood from the fire, and Dan scooted closer to it.

"Who thought to equip a cabin in the Bahamas with a fireplace?" Shae said, clapping his hands together to remove the dirt. "Never thought I would find occasion to use this thing. Funny, funny."

He sat in a thin wooden rocking chair across from Dan, crossed his squat legs, and packed a pipe with tobacco.

"Thank you again," Dan said. "Really."

Shae waved that off as smoke billowed from his lips. "What were you doing out there?" He nodded toward the window. "In this?"

"I got lost." That wasn't a *total* fabrication.

Shae received Dan's response with a rise of his brow. It was clear there was no use lying to him, there was a certainty to his expression that collected in his irises, saw through nonsense like X-ray vision.

"I was heading to the airstrip," Dan admitted. "I have a friend there that I need to check on."

"Alan Ferris."

"You know Alan?"

"They certainly talk about him a lot."

Shae pulled himself from the chair and walked to a bookshelf near the fireplace. He clicked on a small radio. Static at first, but then a muffled voice, Rico Flores's voice, and it said, "Need team Charlie at Building C. Reports of activity on second floor, southeast corner room. Keep an eye out for the missing pistol. Still at hangar, over."

Then, after a second: "Roger."

Shae switched it off. "No, I would not recommend visiting the airstrip tonight. Along with Mr. Flores, that brute of a man, Mrs. Collins is there."

"Why? Is Alan okay?"

"Inspecting the plane, I believe. From what I gather, your friend has almost completed the repairs. And ahead of schedule, sounds like."

Dan felt as though his heart has been stabbed with a frozen knife. "Holy shit."

"Holy shit, indeed." The oven dinged. "Oh. The Bagel Bites."

Dan shook off the blanket and followed Shae into the small kitchen. There was a table in there, past the cabinets, with one lonely chair and an ashtray at its center.

"Did they say when they're taking off?" he asked. "It's really important that I know that."

"You have a seat reserved, Mister...?"

"Foster. Dan Foster."

Shae nodded with a smile, pulled the tray from the oven, and shook its contents loose before placing it on the counter. "Thought that was you."

How'd this guy know everything?

Shae plated a few of the bagels, offered the plate to Dan. He chuckled. "Your code name is 'Shitlicker.'"

Shitlicker? That's the best they could do?

Shae hummed as he walked back to the study, back to his chair, placed his pipe on the table and his plate of trans fats on his lap. Dan sat again too and thoughtlessly stuffed a bagel into his mouth. Fuck. Hot! Hot, hot, hot. He inhaled sharply, waved at his mouth, tried to cool it down. He was going to freeze to death with a burn on the roof of his mouth.

"You should let them cool," Shae said.

Dan smirked. Ya think? He put the plate down. "My fiancée has a seat on that plane," he said, his tongue resting against the burn.

"Does she?"

"Yes. Did they say when it was leaving?"

"Just that it was almost complete, I am afraid."

Dan peered out the window, at the vegetation turned sideways past the porch lights, at the flashes of lightning.

"Again, I would advise against that," Shae said, reading Dan's mind. "Even if the plane was ready to fly, it would be suicide in this weather."

Dan shook away the impulse, stuffed another Bagel Bite in his mouth. Jesus, still really hot. What the hell was wrong with him? "How do you know so much?" Dan asked, though with his mouth full it sounded more like, "'Ow you knof so muff?"

Shae blew on a Bagel Bite, looked deeply into its molten yellow center. "If the past few days have taught me anything, Mr. Foster, it is in fact how little I know."

"I mean about the resort, the plane, me, and my friends. How come I haven't seen you at Sunrise Yoga? Or on work assignments?" Dan paused. "How the hell do you have *Bagel Bites*?"

"Mrs. Collins and her men certainly paid me a visit, if that is what you are asking."

"And then left you alone."

Shae shrugged, took a pull from his pipe. "Mr. Sheridan helped there. They determined my work too important to disrupt."

Must be nice, Dan thought. "And how's that work going, Doc? You find the sun yet? You'd really help me out of a couple of jams if you found the sun."

Shae chuckled. "No, I am afraid not."

Dan waited for more. There must be more. He leaned forward, elbows against his knees, opened his hands to Shae. Shae just ate another Bagel Bite.

"That's it? One week alone with frozen dinners and a big-ass telescope, and you've got *nothing*?"

"I know that the sun no longer exists."

"That much I gathered."

"But I still see Mars." Shae pointed to a spot on the ceiling. Dan would have to trust that's where Mars was. Shae pointed to another spot, then another. "I still see Mercury and Ceres and the rings of Saturn and Hyperion. And they are all precisely where they should be, Mr. Foster, as though our sun was still here, as though its gravitational pull still existed." He ran a hand through what remained of his hair. There was a glint in his eye, the same one he'd had onstage that first day. Leave it to an egghead to be fascinated by all of this. "None of it makes any sense."

"Maybe...maybe it just extinguished, Doc. But, like, the core of the sun is still there. The rock part. And that still has the gravitational pull."

Dan was caught off guard by Shae's brief unhinged laughter. This guy was just having a grand time, wasn't he? "There is no *rock part*. The sun is made of gas and plasma."

"Okay. Right." Dan knew that. "So—when you point your big fucking telescope at the part of the sky where the sun's supposed to be, what do you see?"

"Nothing."

"Nothing?"

"Nothing."

"Do you see stars and things that would've been, like, previously *blocked* by the sun? But that are visible now it's gone?"

"No. I see nothing. I see black."

"A black hole then."

"No." Shae ate another Bagel Bite, nearly swallowed it whole. "A black hole is different. This is just…black."

Dan fell deeper into the armchair. If Dr. Shae didn't know what the hell was going on, what hope was there for the rest of them?

Shae said, "I have studied space for over forty-five years, Mr. Foster. Undergraduate at Purdue. Master's from UCLA. Doctorate in astronomy from Northwestern. I worked for my father's aeronautics firm for more than thirty years, and now I provide data to the Space Telescope Science Institute. There is an asteroid named after me."

"Oh, yeah?" Badass.

"829 Shae." He puffed the pipe, lost himself in the smoke as though it were space dust. "All that time. All that *knowledge*. Decades of research—but there are still many things I wish I knew."

Dan was stress eating now, two Bagel Bites at a time until his plate was clear, and then he eyed Shae's. Shae said, "Oh, go on," and handed it to him.

"You sure?" Dan said, already tearing through them. "It's just, the food back at the resort, man. You wouldn't—it's disgusting."

Shae nodded. "Well, it is hard to match the smooth cheese and subtle tomato notes of the humble Bagel Bite."

"You said it." Dan licked his fingers, tasting a tinge of guilt when imagining Mara's grumbling stomach. Then he perked up. "You got anything sweet?"

Shae stood. "Ice cream?"

"Fuck yeah, ice cream." This guy was living like a king!

After a moment, Shae returned with two bowls of rocky road.

Once it hit Dan's tongue, he closed his eyes and looked to the heavens. It was the best thing he'd ever had.

"Good, right?"

"Dude."

Shae laughed. "I always keep rocky road in the freezer when I can get it. It was my father's favorite."

"You said your dad owned an aeronautics firm? So you grew up rich as shit, then, right?" Dan felt talkative under the influence of ice cream and Bagel Bites and bourbon and warmth.

Shae laughed again, waved his spoon in the air. "It sounds more impressive than it was. ShaeTech, he named it. Our bread and butter were ballutes."

"Ballutes?"

Dan recognized Shae's trivializing tone as the one he used when describing his job at Marvel Maids. "Ever see something released from an aircraft at a high velocity with a little parachute attached? A bomb or supplies?"

"Sure."

"That little parachute is a ballute."

"Huh."

"Captivating, I know. But there was also a small research division of ShaeTech." He took a mouthful of rocky road. "I led that. The company bought this island, built the telescope. This location has incredible astronomical benefits, you know. Over the years, ShaeTech fell on hard times. The research team dwindled until I was the only one left. Knowledge isn't as lucrative as it should be." He stirred his spoon in his bowl. "Before the company went under, my father gifted the island to me. Then a few years ago, I sold most of it to Mr. Sheridan, who built the resort you and your friends are enjoying. On and on, you know how things go."

What type of "small research division" purchases an *island*? "What were you researching?"

"Exoplanets." Shae's tiny eyes filled with wonder at the sound of the word on his tongue.

"Exoplanets," Dan repeated.

"Planets outside our solar system. Planets similar to ours— planets that could potentially support life. Potentially even human life in the future."

"Find any?"

"Oh, yes, we have discovered thousands."

"Find life on any of 'em?"

"You would have heard."

"So we're alone," Dan said.

"Of course not. What would ever give you that idea?"

Dan churned the question in his head for a second, considered whether he cared enough to dig any deeper.

"There were graves out there," he said. "In the woods."

Shae paused, the spoon still in his mouth, rocky road just hitting the back of his throat. The wonder in his eyes dissipated. Dan could sense his sadness, feel it enter the room as if it'd pulled up a chair and scooped some ice cream for itself.

"I was wondering if you saw those," he said.

"Smacked my head on half of them."

Shae sighed. "Robert's buried out there. Jane too. Mr. Houser. That man was so big they had to construct a custom casket for him."

"Who were they? Why are they buried *here*?"

"They wished to be. Felt so strongly about the island, about the research we had done together. That's the misery of growing old, Mr. Foster. It's not the creaky knees or the hangovers or the"—he shook his belly—"the way your body betrays you. It's slowly watching everyone you love die." He blinked. "Though I suppose that will not be a concern much longer."

Dan had two thoughts. First, Shae wasn't *that* old. No older than Dan's father, but he talked like he was days away from keeling over. Well, he *was* days away from keeling over—they all were—but not from old age. Second, how could anyone love a job so much that they'd request to be buried there? If Dan was buried under his cubicle at Marvel Maids, he'd haunt the ever-living shit out of that place.

Actually, wait a minute, there was a third thought now, and it barreled over the others and knocked against the front of his skull.

"Easy to speak of misery from your warm cabin filled with nonperishables and overstuffed footrests," Dan said, placing his feet firmly on the ground in protest. "You're worried about people dying? Do you have any idea what's going on just down the hill?"

Shae was unstirred. "I have some notion."

"Six people dead. That I *know* of. One shot right in front of me, Doc. Bled to death in my fiancée's arms. Others are starving, forced to work all day with little to eat. They don't have access to medicine, to plumbing, to the spa packages they paid for…and you're up here burning the roof of your mouth on Bagel Bites!"

"That was you."

Dan paced. "And guests are looking to *me* for help because they're stupid—really they just need a leader—but I've fallen in with the autocracy because I want to provide my fiancée with just the *slightest* chance at living. *Then* I come up with an idea that maybe walks the tightrope between both, and immediately after I pitch it, I start backtracking because I'm scared of everything. Fuck me, right? I'm a terrible guy. That's what you're saying. Wow, Doc, give it to me straight. You don't pull any punches, do you? I sold these people down the river for my own interests, and I can't even commit to making it right. I get it."

Shae blinked at Dan.

He placed his bowl of ice cream on the table beside him and slowly puffed his pipe. "Have you ever heard of the Gaia hypothesis, Mr. Foster?"

"Of course," Dan said, returning to his seat, and then, "No," because of course he hadn't.

"It is the theory that all of life on Earth actually exists as a single living organism. That Earth itself is alive and capable of regulating the environment for its own well-being, similar to how a dog regulates its body temperature through panting or we regulate ours through sweat."

"Okay."

"Much of the scientific community rejects the idea. Too teleological, too neat. A plant releases oxygen into the air not because other species on Earth need oxygen to survive, they say, but simply because that is what plants must do in order to survive *themselves*. The benefits to other organisms are simply good luck, or evolutionary in nature."

"Okay…"

"But the Gaia hypothesis makes compelling arguments about the peculiar feedback loops that keep our planet in balance. Our oceans should be far too salty to support life due to river runoff. But the cracks in the ocean floors act as filters. If Earth's oxygen values were to reach 30 percent, every flash of lightning would result in devastating fires, dooming us all. What keeps that oxygen in check? The biological production of methane by bacteria! On and on, countless examples of Earth regulating itself like the thermostat in your home."

"Why are you telling me this?"

"Ethically, I do not agree with the actions of Building A. As a scientist, though, and researcher, I am *fascinated* by life's response to such devastating stimuli. And Tizoc is only a small sample. Imagine this happening throughout the world, Mr. Foster, species dividing back into tribes, purging each other to consolidate Earth's resources, thus lessening humanity's demand on a planet that can suddenly support so little life! Is this not the Gaia hypothesis playing out in real time?"

He was practically giddy, kneading his hands and trembling like a boy at a pet store. Dan didn't understand a lot of what was just said, and the speed at which he said it, but he knew he didn't like it.

"This isn't a science experiment. People are dying, Doc."

Shae shook out of it, composed himself. "Of course. Of course. I know that. One glass of bourbon and some time with my pipe, and science gets the better of me. Happens most evenings, but rarely do I have an audience. It's just..." His voice trailed off, up in smoke with the tobacco.

"It's just what?"

"Perhaps I've been pointing my telescope in the wrong direction."

A loose beam of light flashed past the southern window, and Dan shot Shae a panicked look. He snatched his phone. Shae jumped up, rushed to the radio, and turned the dial. The voice was muffled, but someone whispered on the other end, "Approaching observatory now. Will report back, over."

"Quickly!" Shae said, waving Dan toward a closet door just past a coatrack. Dan opened it. It wasn't a closet at all, but a small room with a ladder inside. "Up! Up! Keep quiet and do not touch anything. Understand?"

Dan opened his mouth to say yes, he did understand, but Shae slammed the door in his face. Dan turned and ascended the ladder as the front door of the cabin burst open.

20

"You go out tonight, Dr. Shae?"

Rico's voice. Dan climbed the short closet ladder to a cold tile floor at the precipice of a pitch-black room. A cavernous room, if his breath was any indication. It floated past his nose and over his head and somewhere up into the ether. He dared not proceed any farther. He knew where he was. Sensed it. The base of Dr. Shae's massive telescope lay somewhere in all that darkness. It was unnerving, the same unnerving feeling you get in the ocean when you swear something's looming below you, just out of sight.

"In all this rain?" Shae asked with a laugh. "No, Mr. Flores, I have had a quiet night in, thank you very much. Though I see you cannot say the same. Your boots are quite muddy. If you would not mind…oh."

Rico's jewelry rattled as he shook clean like a dog. "Got reports of a light coming from the woods near your place 'bout an hour ago," he said. "And none of my men have been over this way."

"A light?" There was a wobble in Shae's voice. "O-oh, yes! Of course. I did go out."

"You did."

"Yes. Apologies, Rico, this bourbon. I was out earlier, see, checking on the generator. Had a momentary lapse in power, damned thing. But then again, I just had momentary lapse in memory, so who am I to criticize?"

Rico's boots crept across the wooden floors. Dan leaned down over the ladder, held a rung for support, tried to get a view of the men in the strips of light that poked through the splintered walls. His heart ricocheted off the tile floor.

"Two bowls of ice cream," Rico said.

"I should probably get better about washing my dishes when I'm through," Shae said. The confident timbre returned to his voice. "One is from last night. A thousand pardons, Rico, but what is this concerning? If it is the same to you, I would like to get some sleep. Even without the sun, I feel it important to retain circadian rhythm, I—"

Dan winced as the cabin shook. Shae gasped and kicked. Rico had lifted and pinned him against the wall.

Rico spoke through gritted teeth. "Don't fuck with me, Doctor."

"What? R-Rico, I—"

"The ice cream ain't melted, hombre. Think I'm fucking stupid?"

"No, no, of course n—ah!"

Rico slammed him against the wall again. A picture—or something—fell to the floor and shattered.

"I know Brody's got a soft spot for you. I don't have soft spots. There are rules on my island."

Dan's ears burned. Again with the *my island* stuff.

"Who was here?" Rico demanded.

"Rico, I told you, I—"

Slam.

"Who. Was. *Here?*"

"Please, Rico. I-I just—"

Shae shrieked and a shadow shot across the slats in the closet walls. The doctor collided with a credenza—part of him went through it—and papers and knickknacks rained down on him. Dan flinched, furious, and his foot hit something in all that dark, a desk or a table or a heavy chair, and whatever it was scraped across the tile and made enough racket to pause the scene below. Rico's hunter instincts kicked in. He took a deep whiff, like Dan was something he could sniff out, and his heavy boots approached the closet door. Dan scrambled backward into the dark, hit his head on something, his wrist on something else, toppled over another something.

He pinned his back against what felt like a large filing cabinet, prayed that when the lights clicked on, he was out of view, not casually sitting in the open like some sort of snared rabbit. He slammed the back of his head on the cabinet in frustration, which was a dumb move because something dislodged from up top, and somehow all of his muted senses worked together in a perfect moment of human reflexive harmony, and he caught the falling object in the dark. It was heavy and cool and round but who cares—he'd just done something super impressive and not a soul had seen it.

The blue lights of the observatory clicked on in pieces, illuminated the room quadrant by quadrant. Dan's quadrant was last, and when he peeked one eye open, he indeed was hidden, tucked between a filing cabinet and a steel desk against the room's round metal walls. He was holding a snow globe, of all things.

"I'm gonna put a bullet in anything breathing up here," Rico announced, his voice echoing.

That isn't much incentive to reveal oneself, so Dan balled up as tight as he could and held his breath.

Shae was up the ladder now, panting.

"Lilyanna agreed my observatory was off-limits!" Dan was impressed with the spunkiness of the old man who'd just been yeeted through a credenza.

"Well, Lilyanna ain't here," Rico said. Something turned over on the other side of the room, a resounding crash that caused Shae to cry out.

"You absolute oaf! What gives you the right to raid my—"

That next sound was a slap, no doubt about it. A Rico slap—those sucked. Big-time. Shae was on the floor now, sniveling, weeping, crawling, and Dan felt terrible because this was all his fault, so terrible that he almost popped up, but not so terrible that he wanted to get shot over it. His quivering hands upset the contents of the snow globe. Look at that glitter fly.

"You find where the sun went with this thing?" Rico asked, ignoring Shae's sobs. He flicked the telescope, it bonged like a drum. "I got a theory that it didn't explode. That something just knocked into it, sent it flying like a pool ball."

No response.

"Don't like that one? I got others," Rico roared as he upended a desk, sent papers flying into the air. Some of the documents floated down atop Dan. A Polaroid photo appeared from under the filing cabinet, like it was looking for a place to hide too. It bounced off Dan's foot.

Any fear of being discovered was temporarily pushed aside by his immediate fascination with the photograph—it was yellowed and nearly out of focus, but Dan recognized Dr. Shae. He was younger though, with a full head of hair, and he stood near seven others in the woods. Nobody in the photo smiled—the largest man, the one next to Shae, practically scowled. Something about the photo was perverse, it felt dirty in Dan's hand, his instinct was to fling it back under the cabinet and forget it existed. He almost did, but then...

The woman in it—the one standing in front with bushy black hair and unsure eyes and freckles peppered over her nose and cheeks like stars in the night sky—that woman...why did she look so *familiar?* Dan flicked through the Rolodex of faces in his brain, then back again, and she was there, she was somewhere in there, her file just out of reach, calling out to him, her cries fainter with each pass...

The steel desk beside Dan flipped, almost crushing his fingers, and Dan buried his head in his arms, wanted to think of Mara in his final seconds, but instead was stuck thinking about this woman, this stranger—or was she?

"Another thought is the sun's still there, right?" Rico said. "But we just can't see it, 'cause aliens wrapped the planet up in something, like how you wrap food and put it in the freezer till you want it."

Rico's seized the filing cabinet. Dan tucked the photo into his pants and braced himself. He'd rush Rico. His best chance was to surprise him. Rico was much bigger than Dan—like if they were

Russian dolls, Rico would be the outside layer and Dan would be the nougaty center—but big boys startle easy, Dan's father had taught him that, something about them never expecting to be rushed because of their size, just look at elephants and mice. Maybe that's part of why he attacked him in the hangar. Dan was ready to go balls to the wall, to go out swinging, but just before Rico turned the cabinet, his radio buzzed like in the movies.

"Uh, Chief Rico. Come in, Chief Rico."

Dan rolled his eyes. They were calling him *chief* now?

Rico sighed. "Yeah. Go ahead."

"Uh, sir, Mama Bear's real upset. Asking for you."

"This fucking lady," Rico said under his breath. "Tell her the K-Cups are in the cabinet in room three fifty-two. I moved them because—"

"No, sir, it's not that. We're still at the hangar." And then, in the background, Lilyanna Collins's voice. "Is that Rico? Is that Rico? Give me that. Rico?"

Rico murmured, "Fuck," and then, "Yes, ma'am."

"Rico, you told me you'd be five minutes. Where are you? Where'd you go, son?"

"Mrs. Collins, I—"

"Listen. I don't like the way this Alan fella's looking at me over here. So, I ain't feeling so secure. Am I crazy for thinking that should concern my chief of *security*? Am I paying you well?"

"Yes, ma'am."

"Then do your job, son, and come on back to the hangar."

Rico's frustration radiated through the filing cabinet. "Yes, ma'am."

"Thanks, hun." Lilyanna pulled away from the radio and

hollered. "Pete. Pete! Baby. What'd I tell you about standing so close to the propeller? Lord almighty, these men…" The radio cut off.

No one moved. The metal on the telescope groaned. Rico took a deep breath, gathered himself, and spun toward Shae, still a heap on the ground. He walked over him, his boots like hooves against the tile floor, and descended the ladder without a word. Dan didn't emerge until he heard the Jeep outside drive away.

The observatory was a mess. Papers everywhere, film reels unspun, computers shattered. The telescope was impressive though. It was the first time Dan got a good look at the thing. There was a striking contrast between the telescope and its operator: one stood proudly in the center of the room, searching diligently for other worlds, and the other slunk against the floor, sifting through the ashes of his.

"Saved your snow globe," Dan said, helping Shae to his feet and placing it softly in his quaking hands.

Shae barely saw it. "Yes. Yes, thank you."

"Look, Doc, this is my fault. I'm sorry, man. Rico is such a prick. Let me help you clean up. Christ, look at this place." Dan bent to collect some papers—gotta start somewhere—but Shae's hand appeared on his shoulder.

"No. No. We must get you back before he returns."

"What? No. I wanna hel—"

"You can help me by leaving."

There was finality to that, Dan knew better than to push it. Plus, Shae looked like he might cry again, and there's nothing more depressing than watching a man in his sixties cry.

"Okay," Dan said. But first, he had to know. "Doc. Why'd

you bring me back here? Why'd you help me? They're clearly keeping a close eye on you."

Shae briefly looked up, considered that. "It can get lonely in outer space. Now go."

"I don't know the way back," Dan said. The words felt even more pitiful leaving his mouth than they were inside his head. "And these patrols..."

The color returned to Shae's face. "You think Mr. Sheridan's the only one on this island who thought to build a tunnel?" He winked.

"ShaeTech had a tunnel?"

He ushered Dan toward the ladder. "And now, as a result of this conversation, two people on Earth know about it."

"What do people studying space need with a tunnel?"

Shae wiped a tear from his eye. He must not have heard the question.

21

Dan had the morning of the wedding to himself.

Mara was off with Charles somewhere preparing the final touches, finding something borrowed and something blue and something frumpy and something glued, or whatever the saying is. She'd been in a rush to leave, a whirlwind of eager chaos like most mornings, a vigor in her that Dan never understood. His mornings were slow, morose little things, but hers were set afire, from the bed to the shower to the sink to the coffee maker to the closet to the car, all one unstoppable bolt of activity, God help whatever's in the way. Dan barely had a chance to tell her about his detour with Dr. Shae other than to confirm again that yes, he was alive, as was Alan, and yes, he would still very much like to get married if she would.

Dan sat quietly under a quilt on the balcony, breath rising from him like train exhaust. He didn't feel the cold after a while, instead focused on Julio's plot in the dark garden below and the five others dug alongside it. Someone had whittled crosses from driftwood for each of them, stabbed them in the dirt almost like a proper cemetery. Others had laid flowers, though those were beginning to show their age after a week without the sun. Whole island was, really. Every so often there'd be a thud on the roof, another bird fallen from the sky. Fish washed ashore too, according to the guy who delivered Dan's finished tux. Dan wasn't exactly sure how the sun impacted fish, but it made sense that they needed it somewhere along the chain.

Everything did.

Despite death washing ashore and raining from the sky, people seemed in good spirits, relatively speaking. Lilyanna announced mandatory work assignments were canceled for the day and that everyone would receive full rations in celebration of the upcoming nuptials. She made this announcement while straddled between the seat backs of a Jeep driven aggressively through the resort by Rico. Behind the Jeep, empty cans tied with string popped against the pool deck. Her plan was working. There was a buzz about Tizoc like vacation was back on, even if just for a few hours, and Dan heard laughter from the surrounding rooms for the first time in days, watched as others indulged from the beer cart making rounds. No talks of mutiny, or rebellion, or 1776. Someone, somewhere, was singing the theme song from *The Jeffersons* while folks clapped. She sounded great.

Dan should've been happy too. Well—part of him was, obviously. It wasn't an ideal scenario, but in a few hours he'd marry the love of his life, a woman so far out of his league she was playing a different sport altogether.

What was she thinking?

He was charming, for sure, and funny, and that alone can get you really far with a girl. But he couldn't coast on charm forever.

He was almost thirty, for God's sake, and at some point it's not cute to be poor or aimless or sad. Was she only marrying him because he was the guy around at the end of the world? And if they did somehow survive this thing, if there was some sort of postsun civilization developing back in the States, an underground society of mole people or something, what then? Would Mara expect Dan to reach his full potential under those circumstances? And what if his potential had been a lie the whole time, or a mistake at least, and she was stuck forever with the man she married today, this lump of self-doubt, this near-empty bank account, this Marvel Maids marketing specialist? What if, in a few years, she realized her mistake because Dan never started writing, and he couldn't afford an underground mole person mortgage, and they stop texting on their lunch breaks or drinking wine with ice in it or watching *Disappearance Report* on Netflix together? What then?

Yeah. Best-case scenario: they get married, she gets on the plane, and he dies alone on the island, a memory of untapped potential. That'll have to do.

Dan tried to shake the miserable thoughts loose, to fling them from his ears like drops of water, but they clung. Okay. Screw you, brain. He'd think of something else instead. Dan pulled the Polaroid from his pant pocket, the one he'd found in Dr. Shae's lab after Rico wrecked the place. Her. There she was again—the woman with bushy black hair. Who *was* she? Dan was positive he knew that face, the rise of the tip of her nose, the small scar on her chin. He focused hard on her. The rest of the world melted away.

She said, You know me.

I *know* you.

Then who am I?

Tell me. Just tell me. I'm getting married today.

I was married too.

Yes! You were. Who were you married to?

She said, Getting married today, and already looking at other women? Christ.

Except she didn't say that last part. That sounded like Alan's voice, and Dan pulled himself from his haze and spun around on the balcony, and sure enough, there was Alan Ferris, by God, and he was dressed in a suit made from beach towels, and he smirked. Dan rushed to hug him, forgot how he wanted Alan to think of him as a man, as a tough guy, forgot all that because sometimes you just need to wrap your arms around a person to make sure they really are there.

"Whoa-ho, now," Alan said, patting Dan's back. "Good to see you too, kid."

Dan pulled back. "I'm so sorry I didn't come to the hangar, man. Really, I am. I tried. The first night I was in jail for inciting a riot. And then last night I got turned around in the storm— ended up at Dr. Shae's place and—"

Alan lit a cigarette, shook his head. "Charles told me everything. Don't sweat it. He's pissed about that Bloomingdale's coat though."

God, Dan almost forgot how effortlessly cool Alan was. Every little flick of his hand, every steady footstep, every subtle crease in his face. Big Tobacco's wet dream. When he smoked, smoking was *cool*, man, didn't matter how many after-school programs told you otherwise. Alan strolled to the balcony railing, peered down at the gardens.

"Those the Brits next to Julio?"

Dan nodded.

Alan took a long pull. "Fuck this place."

Dan wasn't sure where to start. It'd been a week, and there'd been so many times he'd needed Alan for guidance, or advice, or a reassuring nod—*something*—and here he was. He started with the obvious.

"Is the plane ready?"

Alan grinned. "Maybe."

Hold up.

"What do you mean, maybe? Don't play with me right now, Alan. If it's ready, then what are you—"

"Lilyanna wanted me here. Said it'd mean a lot to you."

It did, actually. For a homicidal empress, Lilyanna could sometimes be downright thoughtful.

"Hold on. Are you telling me the plane can fly right now? Is that what you're telling me?"

"Keep your voice down."

Dan whispered, "Alan. Is that what you're saying?"

Alan peered over his back into the empty room, then scanned the garden. He leaned a bit closer to Dan. "*Yes.*"

Dan laughed, clutched Alan's terry cloth lapels, and shook him. "*What?* Then what the hell are we doing? I've got Mara a guaranteed seat on that plane, dude. You have to go! Right now! What time is it? You could be to Florida in, like, what? A few hours? Right? Clear skies too. Holy shit."

"You're being loud again." Alan seized Dan's wrists and removed them, the hot end of his cigarette almost a relief in all this cold. "Lilyanna thinks I need another day. At least."

Dan's eyes widened.

Alan nodded. "We need to be smart about this. We get you married this afternoon, get everyone feeling real nice and boozed up, then sneak the fuck out of here. They've got one guard on the plane—Hunter. He's a moron. We're in Florida by midnight."

Dan could've wept. "All of us?"

"Me and Charles, you and Mara, Lenny and Gloria. It's a six-seater, kid. Works out perfect."

Dan was flabbergasted. They could *all* go! Maybe Dan could see his parents again. Maybe he was overreacting on the mole people thing, maybe they had things under control on the mainland, had warming stations, and food supplies, and some sort of infrastructure to maintain the—

Wait.

"Wait. Alan, shit. Lenny's planning something today. It was my idea, it was stupid. I tried to backtrack, but he kept calling me *boss* and saying he's got everything under control. Had these elaborate plans drawn up. If he does that, then—"

Alan blew smoke from the side of his mouth. "Yeah. Charles mentioned it. I'll talk to Lenny. He's a good guy to have around in a scrap, but he's not the thinker he thinks he is. Where is he?"

Dan shrugged. Burrowing under Building A, for all he knew.

"Okay. Well, get changed. We'll find him."

Dan turned to enter the room—he'd literally follow any directions Alan gave him right now—but someone hollered from below, in the garden. Others joined.

"Is that Alan?"

"Hey, Alan Ferris! Where you been, man?"

"We thought you were dead!"

Five or six guys from Buildings B and C, dressed in winter clothing and holding Frisbees, on their way to the Great Lawn. Who plays frisbee in the dark?

"Hey, fellas," Alan said with a nod. "I've had a wonderful vacation, how's yours?"

Laughter.

Dan popped his head over the railing.

Cheers.

"The man of the hour!"

"You lucky son of a bitch, you!"

"Drinks are on you tonight!"

Alan waved at the men. "Drink up tonight, boys!"

More cheers. Dan watched them saunter away until they were swallowed by the dark.

Dressing up is just the absolute worst. Dan tugged at the collar against his neck, tried to breathe. He'd asked Mrs. Betty to loosen it a bit, but it felt tighter than ever. A noose.

"Hey, looking sharp."

Alan leaned against the doorframe separating their rooms. "Just—hang on." He approached Dan, brushed his shoulders off, fixed the jacket so it would line up properly with the shirt in the back. "What'd she make yours out of?"

"I know it features elements of a shower curtain."

"You have to admit, the old girl has talent."

Whatever. Dan smelled a little like mildew.

"Alright. Clean up nice, Dan. You ready to do this?"

Dan sat on the edge of the bed.

Alan signaled toward the door. "Party's that way."

"I don't know."

"You don't know?"

"I don't know."

"Kind of late for *I don't knows*, kid."

How could it be late for *I don't knows*? Dan had been saying *I don't know* his entire life, and when he wasn't saying it, he was thinking it, because he never knew anything. He buried his face in his hands.

Alan sighed, took off his coat, sat on the bed next to Dan. "What is it?"

Dan waved his hand over his entire body, like, Isn't that obvious?

Alan grew quiet, uncomfortable. He wasn't the guy for pep talks, for relationship advice. He was the get-shit-done guy, the take-action guy, not the cross-your-legs-and-reflect-on-how-that-makes-you-feel guy. But he was the only one there.

"Well…hm." Alan cleared his throat. "She loves you."

Dan considered that. "Yeah?"

"Definitely. It's obvious."

"Okay."

"You love her?"

"Yes."

"Alright. How do you know?"

Dan remembered the answer he gave Pete Collins. "Mara is just always…Mara. She's so unafraid to be herself, to express exactly—"

Alan shook his head. "Didn't ask what you loved *about* her. Any idiot could see that. I asked how do you *know* you love her?"

"How do I *know*?"

"Yeah."

Dan thought about it. "I want her to be happy."

"Bet you want most people to be happy. You want a dog on the street to be happy. How do you know you love *her*?"

What kind of riddle was this? "I don't know. I just know."

"You don't know but you just know," Alan repeated.

"Yeah."

He stood. "Well, there you go. You'll be fine."

Dan raised an eyebrow. What? That was it? He wasn't expecting a heart-to-heart with Mr. Rogers or anything, but Alan really sucked at this.

"That's all you got? How do you know you love Charles?"

Alan turned, placed his hands in his pockets.

Yeah. I went there, old man.

Alan licked his teeth, shuffled a foot. Looked at the ceiling like his answer might be written there. It was a wonder that a guy like Alan could make it work with Charles, a man whose every flamboyant thought sat only a breath away.

His eyes fell. "I didn't come out till I was your age."

"Oh." Then, after a pause, "That must've been hard."

"I come from a Mormon family out of Idaho. Dad was really involved in the church. His dad too. Generations of LDS. That's not the point. Point is, my brothers, my dad, my mom...they weren't the progressive type. Weren't marching in any parades. So I buried that part of me. For a long time. I was already on thin ice with the church when I 'abandoned my mission' and enlisted instead. A closet queer in the United States Air Force in the 1980s. That was a lot of fun." He rubbed his neck. "After

Desert Shield came 'Don't Ask, Don't Tell.' Wasn't long before I met Charles."

Dan leaned in.

"And now I got a choice to make. My family wasn't going to change. I wasn't either, as much as I fought it sometimes. I could be open about the man I love, but I risk losing my career, my family, my childhood home, the only people I ever had."

"They'd disown you?" Dan asked. "It was that bad?"

Alan laughed. "Couldn't exactly bring Charles home for Sunday dinner. And the Air Force—back then, they were serious about that shit."

"So what'd you do?"

"Told 'em."

"You told them?"

"My family, yeah. Went about as well as you'd expect."

"And the Air Force?"

"That took a few years. Word got around though, and one day I get the call from my company commander. Discharged under 'Don't Ask, Don't Tell.' Nothing I can do."

"Fuck," Dan said. Because what else do you say to that?

"Yeah. Moved to Michigan with Charles, started my career up there, haven't spoken to most of my family in twenty-five years."

"*Twenty-five* years? They haven't gotten over the fact that you're gay in twenty-five *years*?"

Dan thought he should hug him again, pat his back, at least, but he didn't. They stayed quiet for a minute.

Mara was right. Dan had no reason to be so miserable.

"That's how I know I love Charles," Alan finally said. "I

set fire to my entire life to be with him. I'm willing to sacrifice everything—everyone—to do what's best for him, what's best for us and our boys." He stuck an arm in his coat. "You willing to do that for Mara?"

Dan didn't think. Didn't need to. "Yes."

"Then fix your collar. Let's go find Lenny before he fucks it all up."

22

B oy, you look sharp. That Betty is a real wiz, isn't she?
Wouldn't you say she's a real wiz, Dan?"

Pete led Dan and Alan through the lobby of Building A and into the large beachside bathroom that would serve as Dan's dressing room before the ceremony.

"So we got snacks out here if you're hungry, but I bet you've got a bit of a bellyache, huh? When I married Lilyanna, boy, I couldn't eat for weeks. Passed out on our honeymoon while doing a ropes course if you believe it, smacked my noggin something fierce on the way down. Good gosh, that was scary. But I guess I don't need to talk to the pilot about heights! Aye, aye, Captain!" Pete laughed, placed his hand on Alan's shoulder, and squeezed.

"Geez, you fellas look great. Speaking of looking great, how about this resort, huh? Pretty snazzy for your big day! So we've got these two big bonfires on the beach. I was out there earlier, and I gotta say, Dan, you'd never know the sun exploded. You wouldn't. I turn to one of the guys, I turn to one of the guys, and I say, 'Hey, can someone click on the AC?' I swear I did! Also, you probably noticed on the way over, we drained the pools, drained the lazy rivers. Couple reasons. First, one of the older folks got in last night, and the poor guy almost froze to death. He was blue when our boys found him, good gosh. The other reason is, and I don't wanna be crude about this..." He ducked his head, whispered, "Some *Building C* folks were using the pools like... well, like the little boys' room. It was contributing to the smell, actually, so we took care of that."

"Might be because the water's off in their rooms," Dan said.

Pete threw his hands in the air. "Gosh, I don't know. Lord knows I can't run a resort. I can barely run my car! No, no, thank goodness for Lilyanna, she's keeping things in check. And I gotta tell ya, Dan, I think today's gonna be something special. I saw your bride earlier!" He jabbed Dan's chest, Dan flinched. "Oh, gosh! Are you still sore from the beanbag?"

"It's getting better."

"Well, praise God for that. 'Cause you're gonna need those chest muscles to keep your heart from beating out once you see Mara! Goodness gracious, what a vision. Alan, you should see this woman. I know, well, I know you don't—I know that's not your taste. But actually, once you see Mara today, good gosh, you might rethink—"

Alan glared at him.

"Right," Pete said, "okay, I'll leave you two to it. Say, Dan, real quick. For the ceremony, are you more of a Corinthians 13:13 guy or a Peter 4:8?"

Dan didn't know either of them. "Uh. Peter."

"Peter!" Pete said. "Love that. Obviously. Good choice. Welp, fellas, I'll catch ya later."

Just as Pete *finally* seemed to be leaving, he turned around at the door and said, "Hope not!"

It confused Dan. "What?"

Pete laughed, slapped his knee. "Oh, that's just what my kids say when I'm leaving, got it stuck in my head. I say to my teenage girl, I say to her, 'Okay, love you honey, see you later!' and that little rascal says, 'Hope not,' and doesn't even look up from her phone. I tell ya, they get their dark sense of humor from their mother. They do."

Then he was gone.

Alan scoffed. "Jesus, that guy is touched."

Dan checked himself in the mirror. "Incidentally, Jesus was the one who touched him. Where are the others?"

No sooner had the words left his mouth than the bathroom door swung open again and there she was.

Dan had seen countless videos of grooms crying when they first saw their brides. But he always thought it was put on—by obligation or the presence of cameras or decades of social constructs—not genuine emotion. Like most things, he was wrong about that. The sight of Mara Usra Nichols, soon-to-be Mara Nichols Foster, took his breath away, turned his knees to spaghetti. He didn't cry—he couldn't, Alan was right there—but he understood now. Her dress was fashioned from some sort of white quilt, and it was beautiful. Mrs. Betty really *was* talented. Her hair was done up in a way Dan had never seen it before. She looked like the royal duchess of the bedding department.

She looked…perfect.

"You look gorgeous," he said, hugging her.

Mara plucked a piece of goose down from the dress and

flicked it away. "I better look gorgeous. I've had feathers poking my tits all morning. Alan!"

She embraced him.

"You look beautiful," he said. "Charles told me you were having a hard time deciding between a dress and a saree."

Mara laughed. "Mrs. Betty's good, but when I asked her about making a saree, she said I had nothing to apologize for. I've got another idea for how to bring my Indian half to the wedding."

The door popped open again, and in came Charles, Lenny, and Gloria, none of them looking too shabby themselves.

"Whoa-ho," Gloria said, her false eyelashes curled like rib cages. "The men's bathroom. Zip it up, boys, momma ain't covering her eyes. Ha! Oh, God, would you look at Danny? He looks so handsome!"

"He really does," Mara said, clutching Dan's lapels and pulling him in for another kiss. Dan beamed. Dan could remember, like, four physical compliments he'd received in his lifetime, and he held on to each of them like trophies, looked at them when he was feeling down. Now he had five.

"Beautiful couple," Lenny said.

Charles put his arm around Alan, held him close. "Well, shit. I'm gonna cry, honey, aren't I? I always say I'm not gonna cry, but then I do."

"Aw, my Lenny cries too," Gloria said. "He does!"

Lenny shrugged that off, fixed the cuffs of his shirt. He was all business today. He folded his hands in front of his belly, a marble statue against the porcelain wall. This wasn't the bombastic, loudmouth Lenny Fava that Dan knew. No, this was Leonard, Leonard Layout, the man with the plan. Leonard demanded respect. Leonard got shit done. Leonard's shoes were untied.

"I'm actually glad everyone's here," Dan said.

"Me, too," Gloria said. "This is nice."

"No, we need to discuss something. Alan told me—"

Alan held his hand up to quiet Dan. He broke away from Charles, peeked inside the three toilet stalls, and then ran his fingers behind the edge of the large mirror. He carefully scanned the ceiling. Satisfied, he nodded at Dan. "Alright."

"Okay," Dan said. "Lenny, I know I pitched you an idea, and I'm sure you'd do a great job pulling it off. But Alan has another one, one that could get us all back home. Together. They don't know this, but"—he looked around, bent forward and whispered—"*the plane's ready.*"

Mara and Gloria gasped. Dan gasped too, but only for dramatic effect.

"Yeah. He thinks we can be in Florida by *midnight*."

"Home, guys," Charles said, having already known. "We could all go home."

"If we leave now?" Gloria said.

Dan clutched Mara's hand. "Gotta marry my girl first. It's perfect though. Everyone'll be drunk off their asses tonight. Everyone except the six of us. We take it easy...but act the part. When they're all plastered, Alan'll give the signal. Then we break off in pairs and get to the plane."

Lenny used his shoulder to push himself from the wall. "Yeah. And what about the stuff? The food? The medicine."

Dan said, "We won't need it, man."

Lenny grunted. "They still will."

They being the remainder of Buildings B and C, of course, those who had no idea a plane even existed outside the ones originally scheduled to arrive later that week. Dan felt a tinge of something—shame—but he shelved it.

"It sucks, Lenny, but—"

"They're not our problem," Alan said, undeterred. "We're on our own. That's not our battle."

Lenny scoffed. "I got my guys positioned, trained, ready to go the second I give 'em word. They're ready to die for this if they gotta. Feels kinda like my battle, bro."

Alan said, "No one has to die. Call it off, Lenny. You pull any shit today, and you can count the plane out of the equation. They'll beef up security. We'll lose our shot."

"That wasn't part of the plan."

"There's a new plan. A better one."

"And what am I supposed to tell my guys?"

"Fuck your guys. Tell them to come to the wedding."

This wasn't going well.

"Fuck my guys? Fuck you, pal. I'm trying to do the right thing, here."

"What you *think* is the right thing is going to get your wife killed."

Lenny was breathing heavy now. Leonard had left the building, and here was the guy Dan knew all along, passionate and flustered, face a shade of strawberry.

"You don't ever let someone take something of yours that don't belong to 'em," he said, like he was reciting a poem, a tagline graffitied onto the walls of his brain. "Nevah. You gonna let those pricks in Building A get away with this, Alan? That sit okay with you?"

Alan didn't budge. "Not my problem."

Lenny punched the wall. Gloria tried to calm him, but that was like trying to calm a buffalo who'd been speared. He thrashed about the bathroom, saying things under this breath, and Dan could only make out every third or fourth word, things like *fuckin'* and *bullshit* and *psh.*

"Is there a way we can do both?" Mara asked. Her hand was sweaty. "Lenny's guys get the supplies. We sneak off during the chaos. Maybe both can work."

Lenny stopped. "Yeah. Both can work."

"Both can't work," Alan said. "It's too risky." He laughed, but it wasn't a real one. "I wasn't expecting such a fight here, guys. I'm telling you a way we can get back *home.* You can see your families again. How's this even up for discussion?"

"Because there's more to it than just us, Alan," Mara said. She slipped her hand from Dan's. "Charles, I know you see that. You have to."

Charles looked like he was being torn in two. "I—"

"Things aren't *that* bad here," Alan said. "Look at the food they're prepping for today. Dan and I saw ice sculptures on the way over. Everyone's invited to the party. These people will be fine."

Mara shook her head, like, Are you kidding? "That's *today,* Alan. And it's a mirage to keep us from rioting. I know you've been at the hangar, but people are starving here. They're filthy. Sick. Some women are having to decide whether to use the rationed toilet paper to wipe their asses or make tampons. The man sewing beside me yesterday afternoon has arthritis. He wasn't producing. Think Rico and his thugs reassigned him? He got hit with the butt of a rifle and spent the night in the same holding cell they threw me and Danny."

"And you think starting a war will fix all that," Alan said. "Because that's what you'd be doing if you try to take those supplies: starting a war. Listen. I've seen oppression firsthand. Somalia. Bosnia. It's not like the movies. What do you think happens, nine times out of ten, when civilians fight back?"

Nobody wanted to know. They already knew.

"The streets run red. You pull some shit today, Lenny, it'll be a bloodbath. You banking on Rico Flores placing his rifle down, realizing the error of his ways? Come on. Come the fuck on."

"So fuck 'em all," Gloria said, her hand on her man's shoulder. "Long as you and yours are safe. That right?"

Alan nodded. "That's right."

Charles scolded his husband, but Alan recoiled.

"What? *What?* Guys, the fuckin' *sun* exploded. If you think I'm missing a chance to get home to my boys because an old man has arthritis or because some women can't wipe their asses, you're insane. In-sane. Anyone else on this island would take that plane. Wouldn't even think about it. But we gotta be the A-Team?" He realized he was shouting. He closed his eyes, collected himself. "Heroics died with the sun. Here's all that's left: people who survive, and people who don't. Charles is going to survive. I am too. So will our boys. I'm inviting each of you to survive. To not die on this fucking island like the rest of them. It's hard, I know. But it's reality."

No one said anything for a while. They stared at the floor, at the ceiling, at their shallow reflections in the mirror. When Mara broke the silence, she rubbed her left wrist.

"Despite the risks—I still vote we help the people here." Mara turned to Dan. She practically whispered, "Come on, Danny. You'd really leave them?"

Dan's eyes found hers. That tinge of shame, a little thing at first, a warm tickle on the inside of his ear, spread until it rattled his insides. He couldn't do it. He couldn't put her at risk to save people he hardly knew. He wasn't like her, like Lenny. He wasn't like Alan either, for that matter, because they were all strong people with convictions, and belief systems, and a firm sense of who they were and where they stood in the world. They were solid. He was liquid, contorting to fit any container in which he was poured, a glass half-full one day, a puddle on the sidewalk the next.

He saw an easy way out. He had to take it.

"I stand by what I said. We leave."

Lenny and Gloria hugged each other, like, Jesus, he really means it, and Alan and Charles nodded. There was a finality to Dan's decision, somehow, like he held the deciding vote, even though the group was clearly split down the middle. Mara hugged herself, leaned back against the sink. She felt smaller now, and her eyes avoided Dan's.

This is me, he wanted to say. This is the man you've chosen to marry. Are you sure?

Instead he placed a hand on Lenny's shoulder. "You've got a heart of gold, man. But we gotta get you home to your nephew. To your deli. Think how much good you can do in Jersey City."

That seemed to resonate. Lenny wordlessly tapped Dan's hand.

"It's the right thing," Alan said.

"The right thing," Dan repeated.

23

Dan had to hand it to Lilyanna and Pete—the beach looked fabulous.

Two generous sections for seating, split down the middle by a large aisle of dark sand adorned with rose petals. A couple of massive bonfires on either side. Pete was right. It *was* warm. The light of the fire danced against guests' faces and made everyone feel more alive, more kinetic, like their skulls were lanterns for the flames they carried inside. Through the wedding arch, the black ocean crashed against the shore.

Lilyanna's plan had worked. Seemed everyone was here. Standing room only in the back, where throngs of guests jostled and swayed to get a better look.

It was perfect, actually. Dan couldn't imagine his wedding to Mara under normal circumstances being as beautiful as this. He wished his mom was there, his dad, his sister. Some friends. Of course. But new friends were here. Alan stood behind him, a calming presence. Behind Alan, Lenny. And across the way, past Pete with his open bible, stood Charles and Gloria. Charles wanted to be on Mara's side. In Dan's new world, the one the size of this island, everyone was here. Everyone except—

A string quartet began, and guests rose from their seats. Dan caught Charles's eyes, and, as promised, they shimmered. At the end of the aisle, past dozens of rows of turned heads, Mara appeared as though she was God's replacement for the sun, his condolence gift, because she shined almost as bright, hurt so much to look at that Dan almost shielded his eyes. Guests gasped when they saw her, and for a moment, shame bubbled in Dan's belly again. He popped it.

She walked down the aisle unaccompanied, bouquet in hand, thinking of her dad, Dan was sure, thinking of her mom, her sister, her friends. She smiled at Dan, and Dan smiled back, and everything else faded away.

When she reached the altar, Charles fixed her dress behind her.

"Well, now, aren't these two just a sight?" Pete said, signaling for those with seats to sit. The crowd voiced their consensus. "Now, I gotta say, I've married a few couples in my day, and of course I say all the brides are beautiful, because gosh, all brides are beautiful on their wedding day, aren't they? But I ask you folks, I really ask ya, have you ever seen a bride as beautiful this?"

Cheers from the crowd, laughter from Charles, a *woo* from Gloria. Dan almost *woo*ed himself. Mara blushed. Dan mouthed *I love you* to her, and she mouthed it back. She was nervous, a little jittery, but so was he.

"Friends, guests, Building A visitants, we're gathered here before God to witness and bless the joining together of two souls in holy matrimony on this day. *Day.* That's a funny word, now, isn't it? Dayyy. How can there be days without the sun? God says in Deuteronomy 4:19, He says, when you look up at the sun, the moon, and stars—all the forces of Heaven—don't be seduced into worshipping them. The Lord your God gave them to all the peoples of the Earth. Say—what's He mean by that? What's He gettin' at? Well, friends, what God's saying is that while the sun may be the center of our physical universe, each of us gets to choose what's the center of our *own* universe, the universe inside our..."

Pete droned on for a while, and Dan stared lovingly at his bride. He was doing something with his life. Finally. He was marrying Mara! And he'd get her home today. To the mainland, at least, but then home home. He was going too, which was better than he'd even hoped for.

She'd forgive him, right?

Pete called Lilyanna up to read from Peter 4:8, and, oh my God, she was wearing white.

Dan didn't know much about weddings, or about women, obviously, but he knew you didn't wear white to someone else's wedding. And this wasn't like an off-white, or an eggshell, or a functional beige, this was *white*, like, look-at-me white, like, pure-as-the-driven-snow white. And there was cleavage and the slit on the side of the dress stretched all the way to Milwaukee, and she walked to the altar like this was her show, her big day. Dan looked at Mara, like, Can you believe this lady, but Mara just smiled at him and rolled her eyes, unbothered.

There was a mic on the side of the stage, and when Lilyanna reached it, she put both fists in the air and said, "Okay, y'all, this one's for all my prayer warriors out there. Give me an amen if prayer's the most powerful weapon on this planet!" There were a lot of amens. A spooky amount of amens.

"Now I'm about to read from Peter 4:8, y'all, which is one of my favorites, but before I do, can I just borrow your ears for a moment?"

Translation: Do you mind if I make this about me?

"Just a quick second, y'all, and then I'll get back to my seat because I know I'm going to cry when I see this beautiful couple say 'I do,' and I can't have y'all seeing my makeup run. I can't! I just wanted to say, y'all, real quick: Look around. Look at your neighbor, look across the aisle, look in front of you, and look behind you. This is the power of gathering with a grateful heart, y'all. I tell my ladies, my BeachBod by Lilyanna ladies, I tell them that when women gather, great things happen. But that applies to our men too. Hey—shout-out to all our men on this island, ladies, because Lord knows we wouldn't be starting any fires without them."

She laughed, some women from the crowd cheered. Dan heard Alan grunt. After everything Lilyanna had put this place through, there were still people in this crowd who bought in?

"And I just want to say—we've had some tussles over the past week. Some growing pains, y'all. No one said this was going to be easy, but hey, no one said it was gonna be this hard either! I laugh with Pete at night, we visit and laugh, because I say, 'Well, no matter how hard things get on this island, it ain't as bad as raising two teenagers back home!' And in some ways, I mean it. I think I speak for all of us when I say thank you, Brody Sheridan, for making Tizoc an adults-only resort. But seriously, y'all. I just wanted to say tonight that we appreciate some of the feedback y'all are giving us about how things are running around here. That's why we threw this party tonight, invited everyone, not only because it's so easy to celebrate special friends like Dan and Mara, because it is. But we're also here to celebrate each of you, each of us."

If Dan wasn't dressed in his best shower curtain, he might've puked.

"Now, okay, Lilyanna's gonna get off her soapbox. Lord knows I can talk. My momma used to say, Lilyanna, if you ran like your mouth does, you'd lose that baby fat. Anyway, so let's hear from Peter 4:8…"

She read from Peter, and it was nice, because she had a real nice reading voice despite everything. Dan was annoyed she stole the spotlight from Mara, wearing white and talking on and on like that, but whatever. Let her have her moment. *Little does she know…*

"Okay," Pete said, a few minutes later. "Dan, would you take Mara's hands in yours?"

Gladly, he thought, and Mara passed her bouquet to Charles, and Dan reached out and clutched his bride. His heart pounded. He'd written some killer vows. Like, he was glad most folks were sitting, because these would knock them off their feet. Dan wasn't usually so good at saying how he felt, but this was his chance, before God and man, to profess his love for this woman, to shout it over the crashing of the ocean, to scream back into the void, "Universe, there are some things you can't extinguish."

Oh, damn. *There are some things you can't extinguish.* That's a good line. Dan thought through his vows. Maybe he could slip it in there…or there…or after that part, yeah, hit them with the ol' razzle-dazzle…

The texture on the back of Mara's hand felt different. Dan looked down at it. What were those black streaks? What were those—oh. *Oh*. How had he not noticed?

He looked up at Mara, she smiled, and a tear had started in the corner of her eye. She'd used henna to draw the rock pattern on her hand. The rock with waves on it, the one from their first date, the one Dan threw into the ocean last week like an idiot. That rock. She'd applied the pattern to her hand from memory, and suddenly Dan's vows felt inadequate.

"Gloria helped," she whispered. "We used coffee powder."

Dan shook his head at her, like, What did I do to deserve you?

She winked.

"We will now begin the reading of the vows, my absolute favorite part," Pete said. "Dan, if you'd do us the honors. Oh, man, I bet these will be good, folks, because he may not look it, but this guy's a romantic. He's a romantic, alright. I know that from my private conversations with him. He—"

Mara ripped her hands from Dan's and slammed one of them right into Pete's mouth, totally catching the guy off guard, sending him stumbling through the arch and toward the ocean. Before Dan could even grunt his confusion, even calculate what just happened, she tore from the altar and pounced on Lilyanna in the front row, tugged her up by her extensions. And Dan thought, Wow, women really *don't* like it when you wear white to their wedding, but this actually seemed bigger than that, and now there were fabric scissors in Mara's hand, and she held them to Lilyanna's throat and dragged her screaming to the altar. Alan shouted something, like What the fuck? and then Lenny was shouting, and he had a gun—a pistol—and he said, "Stay the fuck back, stay the fuck back, everyone stay calm," and he pointed the gun at Rico and his guards as they approached. They raised their hands in the air, because they didn't want Mara to hurt Lilyanna, and Mara screamed, "Stay back," and she sounded more intimidating than Dan had ever heard her. Rico looked like he could tear the head off a horse. Dan wasn't sure what to do with his hands, wasn't sure if he should help or what, but Charles had dropped the bouquet in the confusion, so he picked it up. So now Lenny had a pistol, Mara had scissors, and Dan had a bouquet of flowers, but he held it as threateningly as he could.

No one was sitting anymore, everyone stood in place, gasped, screamed.

"This is a hostile takeover!" Lenny shouted, brandishing the gun like Dirty Harry. Dan had never seen Dirty Harry, but he was pretty sure that's how he brandished a gun. "Put your guns in the sand! Guns on the beach!"

The guards hesitated. Mara spoke next. "I swear to God, I'll cut her throat!"

Dan almost laughed at that, because there was a 0.0 percent chance Mara was cutting anyone's throat, even Lilyanna's, because Mara was the type to put spiders in a paper towel and escort them outside, and she could barely open a box from Amazon if they double-taped it. But she did her best to sound menacing, and it actually must've worked because Lilyanna really looked scared, eyes wide and rabid. Rico told his men to hold steady.

"Lenny, what the fuck are you doing?" Alan asked, a genuinely good question.

"The right thing, bro."

Dan's trembling free hand found Mara's bare shoulder. "Was this the plan all along? Mara, you were in on it? You weren't supposed—"

"I love you, Danny," she said. "But I told you. I don't need you to save me."

"Honey," Lilyanna pleaded, "I got babies. A sweet thing like you don't want to—"

The crowd gasped as Pete came stumbling back through the arch, his mouth a bloody mess. Mara had some power behind those fists. He made a half-hearted lunge toward Lilyanna, but Alan saw him coming a mile away. He sighed, seized Pete, and buckled him with one blow. Lights out. Alan spun Pete's limp body in the sand so he wouldn't suffocate.

"What now?" Charles said, frantic. "What now?"

"Yeah," Rico echoed, his gun on Lenny. "What now?"

Gloria appeared behind Lenny. She held a walkie-talkie. Was there a hostile takeover depot on the island Dan didn't know about?

"Roger," she said into it. She tapped Lenny's shoulder, her voice high and fast like air escaping a balloon. "We did it! We did it, Len! Oh my God. I'm gonna faint, I swear. They didn't get everything, but they got a lot."

Lenny smirked, real cocksure. "Guests of Buildings B and C!" he announced. "Tizoc Grand Islands Resort and Spa has been liberated!"

Dan could tell he was expecting an ovation or something, like in the movies, but folks just stood around, dumbfounded, scared. Alan rubbed his face with his hands. Charles looked like he might pass out.

"It ain't too late," Lilyanna said, the scissors carving a dimple into her throat. "This was stupid, y'all, it was real stupid, but we all do stupid things sometimes. You let me go, darling, and you put down that gun, Mr. Fava, and we can move on from this. We ain't gonna be friends, but—"

"Shut up," Mara said. "Do you ever shut up?"

"Guests of Buildings B and C!" Lenny said again. "We have this situation under control!"

Sure didn't feel like it.

"We will regroup in the lobby of Building C! Please! Walk calmly toward Building C, do not make any stops, and await further instruction! Thank you!"

No one moved. Rico laughed. He motioned toward Mara.

"Whaddya bet I can tag her forehead over Lilyanna's shoulder? One shot. Easy."

Dan, still not used to staring down the barrel of a gun, slid in front of Mara and Lilyanna. Lenny's resolve was beginning to rupture. He wasn't holding the pistol with the same authority anymore.

"Dan, you tell 'em," Lenny said.

"What?"

"They'll listen to you. Tell 'em to go to C."

"Lenny, what's our endgame here? What are—"

"Do it, Danny!" Mara shouted.

Dan raised his hands in the air. "Everyone!" His voice cracked. Damn it. He cleared his throat and started over. "Everyone! Thank you for coming! We have everything under control here. A few days ago, we demanded change. Well, as of tonight"—he glanced backward—"*everything* has changed. But we still need your help. Please, guests of Buildings B and C. Walk to the lobby of Building C, and we'll meet you there soon." He paused. "Consider it a reception!"

At first, no one moved. Dan's heart sank. But then someone stepped into the aisle—it was the guy whose beard was his whole personality—and he shouted back at Dan. "Hell, yeah!" he said gleefully. "I knew you were planning something, Foster! We'll meet you there!" Others murmured their agreement, and the back rows slowly emptied. They marched north through the sand, hundreds of them, a procession from a dream. No one looked back, no one hesitated any longer, they strolled past Building A, along the pools, and toward Building C, their new future.

"Get Building A guests outta here too," Lenny said.

They didn't need to be told twice. The front rows—the rows full of those much better dressed, those who looked more insulted than terrified—brushed off their pants and gowns, shuffled politely into nearby Building A. Brody Sheridan tried to lose himself among them, but Lenny called him out.

"Not you, Sheridan. Stay. You hear this too."

The only people who remained on the beach were the guards, the wedding party, Lilyanna, Sheridan, and Pete's crumpled body.

"Okay," Rico said, the corner of his mouth curled into a tight smile. He was enjoying this. "All alone. What's stopping us from wasting all you right now?"

"I-If I die," Lilyanna stammered, "y'all don't get paid, Rico. How's that for starters? Hun, could you loosen your grip? No? Okay. Okay. Now, let's just talk through this. What do y'all want? Where we goin' here, 'cause I'm having trouble with the plot."

Dan was too.

Gloria said, "Tell 'em, honey."

Lenny's swagger returned. "We took back what was ours. You think you can just take and take from the working man and we ain't ever gonna take back? No more. Alright? No more. Now *we* got the goods. *We* got the power. You understand that? *We* got the numbers."

"You hit the supply room," Rico said.

"Sharp as a tack, this one," Gloria said.

Rico snarled.

"We only took back what was ours," Lenny said. "Left the caviar for you. People don't deserve to suffer in their final days. They deserve some comfort. Full bellies. Medicine. Maybe a couple of drinks to remember their families back home. If they're gonna die on this island, least I can do is make them comfortable. Right? It's the least we can do. We're gonna go back there, and you're gonna stay here, and that's the end of it." He signaled toward Lilyanna. "And to make sure you don't pull nothing, we're taking BeachBod with us."

"No," Lilyanna said. "No."

Rico laughed. "You didn't answer my question. What's stopping us from taking everything back, big guy? You might have the numbers. We got the guns."

Lenny cocked an eyebrow and nodded at the pistol grasped in his beefy hands. "You sure about that?"

Another guard spoke up. "Rico, they hit the security room too. Gomez isn't responding. We had—"

"Shut up," Rico said. "Alright. There were three extra pistols in the security room. Some ammo. And I'm guessing the pistol in your hand is the one that went missing two days ago. Safe bet? Let's also assume Gomez is dead, and your men got his gun too."

Dead? Had Lenny's men killed someone?

"So, at most, you've got five Glock nineteens. Okay. I've got eleven trained men with guns. Ten, if Gomez is dead. You like those odds, fat boy? I like mine."

This sure was a long conversation to have at gunpoint. Gunpoint conversations are supposed to be snappy, full of one-liners. This was like Thanksgiving dinner and a math problem.

"While you're here running your mouth," Lenny said, "my men are fortifying Building C. We got balconies, we got a roof-top, we got sniper nests in the windows along the third floor. We got tradesmen, nurses, contractors. Ex-military. People who know how to use their hands. Look at what Mara and my boy Alan did to soft Pete over there. Made a fool of him. And you sure you got your math right about those guns? You better be sure, bro. You real good at math? Inventory management? I ain't real good at math, Rico, but you asked me about odds. Odds are my people at B and C could wipe the floor with the wealth managers and politicians you got holed up in A. Those are good odds, you ask me."

Leonard fuckin' Layout.

"Plus, you try anything, we open up Lilyanna."

"*Yeah*," Mara said.

Dan wished he had something cool to say, but it's hard to say something cool while also feeling violently ill. The reality of the situation was catching up to him. He felt emasculated, betrayed, sick with worry. A little turned on too. He'd never seen Mara like this.

"We got the plane," Rico said, flustered.

"We got the pilot," Lenny said.

Well, that was that. An impasse. No one spoke for several moments. It was awkward, almost, like lining up behind an old classmate at the grocery store checkout. What else was there to talk about...? Dan glanced around. Had they really done it? Seized back control of the resort? *They* being everyone else besides Dan, obviously. He had done absolutely nothing. He loosened his tie, undid his top button.

Breathed.

"Okay," Dan said, tossing the bouquet to the sand. "Well, it really meant a lot to us that you came, Rico. Fellas. See ya later." He placed his hand on the small of Mara's back, prodding her to walk. Team B and C shimmied clockwise, dragging a deflated Lilyanna with them. Then they walked backward down the aisle, a wedding tape on rewind.

"This isn't over," Rico called.

"Okay, thanks again," Dan said. "Drive safe."

Rico and his thunderstruck men remained at the altar. Brody Sheridan bent to retrieve Pete. Dan and the others eventually stepped from the sand, onto the wooden beach access ramp, then onto the textured cement of the resort. When there was adequate distance, they spun on their heels and ran. The warmth of the bonfires slipped away, cold sunk back into their bones.

"That was an incredibly stupid move, y'all," Lilyanna said near the pools. Mara removed the scissors and shoved her at Lenny. With Alan's help, he hoisted Lilyanna onto his shoulder and carried her like King Kong.

"Building C really as fortified as you said?" Alan asked, checking over his shoulder.

Lenny shrugged, bouncing Lilyanna. "Got a few guns."

"Enough to make a run on the plane? They'll be sending more guards to the hangar now."

Lenny huffed. "Probably not."

"Then she's right," Alan said, disgusted. "That was an incredibly stupid move."

24

Were they even married, technically? They hadn't said *I do*. This question did not hang heavy in the lobby of Tizoc Grand Islands Resort and Spa's Building C, where a party was underway. Dan flinched as the first champagne bottle popped. Someone had swiped the sound system from the Maize Pool, and the mariachi band was performing Montell Jordan's "This is How We Do It" at an ear-piercing volume. Lenny manned a sandwich table, made reproductions of his famous subs from the deli back home in Jersey City, called out orders like he was conducting an auction. Gloria led guests in resituating furniture so there was a dance floor, and she currently had her hands in the air, waving them like she just didn't care, singing and bobbing her head off beat. Dan and Mara, legs weak, sat at a table in the corner. Mara drank from a champagne flute and pulled Dan in for a big kiss.

"We did it," she said, still ravishing in her wedding gown. And not an ounce of blood on it!

"We did it," Dan repeated, though not as enthusiastically. Then, after a moment, he whispered, "You could've told me."

Mara's face dropped. She looked away. "I couldn't, Danny."

"Why?"

"You wouldn't've let me."

"*Let* you? Like I can stop you from doing any—"

"You would've told Alan. You would've blown it."

Dan didn't want his first conversation with his maybe-wife to be an argument, so he let that fester. But then someone knocked over a table of drinks while attempting to moonwalk. He turned back to her.

"Maybe someone *should* have blown it." He paused. "Clear something up for me. Did the plan always have you brandishing scissors? What the hell was that? I thought Lenny was going to make it look like we weren't involved. I thought—"

"You said it yourself. Rico would've killed us." She smiled at someone as they passed, and then her head snapped back to Dan. "I did what I thought was right."

"I had a seat for you on that plane, Mara. Then we *all* had seats. What about your mom? Or Raveena? I'm glad everyone here is better off, really, but what about—"

Someone slammed a bottle on their table, beer shooting from the spout like a geyser. A woman and her husband. Dan recognized her—she'd been at his riot, she'd steadied him when he tripped on a sprinkler. She bent down and pulled Dan into a hug.

"Thank you. Thank you, thank you, thank you. When I heard about the wedding, and I heard that Lilyanna and Building A were throwing it, I knew there was no way—no way—I knew you had to be up to something, Dan Foster. You did it!"

She pulled back, shook Dan's hand. Her husband hugged

Mara tearfully. His bottom lip quivered. "We just—I know things aren't perfect now, I know we might still… But we have food and guards of our own and—maybe we can hang on, you know, maybe—" He lost it, hugged Mara again, hugged Dan.

"We're with you all the way," the wife said. Then she laughed. "The look on Lilyanna's face! Girl, you have a mean right hook. Hey, what's that design on your hand?"

Gloria appeared, seized Dan and Mara, pulled them onto the dance floor. Lenny snatched the mic from the mariachi band and introduced them as Mr. and Mrs. Foster, and the place just erupted. Dan was swept up in the spirit of it all—it was impossible not to be—and he had some drinks and Mara had some drinks and he was still mad and his stomach hurt, but soon they were on a table leading the crowd in a rollicking rendition of "Livin' on a Prayer."

When that was over, someone yelled out, "Speech!" then another person echoed that, then the whole room chanted, "Speech, speech, speech," and Lenny chanted it too as he ran the microphone to Dan. Dan shook his head emphatically—he didn't do this. He wasn't even *consulted* on this. "This one's yours," he said to Mara, his voice completely drowned out.

Mara nodded, understood. She grasped the microphone in one hand, grasped Dan with the other. She took an uneasy breath as the room quieted down.

"Hi." Her voice trembled. Gloria hollered from somewhere, which made Mara laugh, and then she tucked a delinquent hair behind her ear and swallowed her nerves. "Hi. I guess most of you know me by now, but for those who don't, my name is Mara N—" She paused and looked at Dan. He shrugged, because despite how Lenny introduced them, he didn't know either. "My name is Mara. And this is Dan. I think you know him."

Massive cheers. Someone threw part of a sub sandwich in the air while Dan squirmed. After everything, they still had the wrong guy. Their savior was standing on the table, but it wasn't him.

If it were up to him, they'd be halfway to Florida by now.

"Yeah," Mara said, rubbing Dan's shoulder. She grinned. "He's pretty great. Okay. I won't take long because I want to dance. But—" She closed her eyes a second, chewed her bottom lip. "I *have* been thinking about something this week. Growing up, my mom hung a wooden sign above our kitchen door. It was a Hindu saying—my mom's Hindu."

She had them. They were hanging on every word. Dan had to scream to get the attention of a room like this, Mara spoke as if she was sipping coffee across from a friend.

"*Aap bhale to jag bhala*," Mara said, her head bouncing as she recalled each syllable. "I'm sorry to anyone who speaks Hindi—I probably butchered it. But what it means is, *If you are good, then the world is good*." She lingered on that a moment. "Do good, *find* good. When the sun exploded—or whatever—I wasn't thinking about others. I wasn't thinking about how I could help. My only thought was getting home to my mom. My sister." She pumped Dan's hand. "I know you'd love to see your families too."

Her eyes glistened. Dan looked out. The room was chock-full of glistening eyes. Lenny sniffled, kissed his girl on the forehead. Even Charles, who'd been off trying to calm Alan down, was in the crowd now, entranced by it all. He hugged the stranger next to him, wrapped her up in all his folds.

"And while I'm sad about that"—Mara wiped her face with

the inside of her wrist—"I also know why Mom hung that sign where she did. She wanted it to be the last thing we saw before we left the house every day, before we each went out into the world. She wanted me—she wanted us—to remember that we always have a choice. Well, today we made that choice. We chose to do good." Applause. "And because of that, I think we proved that even if this is the end...the world is good too."

The place shattered. Dan was in awe. He clapped too, though he didn't deserve it. He hadn't made that choice. Not like Mara. The choice was made for him.

"Having said that," Mara said with a laugh, cutting through the ovation. "I have to admit, it felt really good to punch that man." They roared. The building shook, ceiling tiles bounced in place. Dan and Mara suddenly had drinks in their hands, and when Mara raised hers, everyone followed suit. *"Aap bhale to jag bhala!"* she said, and they all did their best to say it back. The mariachi band was *on it*. The choice of "Walking on Sunshine" was a little cheeky, admittedly, but something about it felt good, and Dan and Mara hopped from the table, and the crowd parted for Mara like the sea parted for Moses, and they waltzed hand in hand to the middle of the dance floor and got their boogie on, Dan pretending everything was fine. Then Lenny was there, he danced exactly like you'd expect a deli owner from Jersey City to dance, and Gloria smelled like smoke, but she was hilarious, she was always hilarious, and Charles grabbed Mara's hands and shimmied with her and then did a twirl and told Dan how lucky he was, and Dan said he knew. And they danced for what felt like forever and no time at all, danced because they didn't know if they'd ever dance again, danced like if they danced hard enough the sun might come back just to watch.

25

Dan was feeling particularly charitable as he strolled up the outdoor staircase to the third-story room where Lenny and his men had stored Lilyanna Collins. He had a cold beer in one hand and a sandwich in the other. Lilyanna had to eat, at least—the Geneva Conventions were strict on that point. The guard outside her room was the same woman who ushered Dan into the basement yesterday morning, the one who looked like a lunch lady, and she had a pistol holstered at her hip and she stared straight ahead as Dan approached.

"Hey again," Dan said. "Lenny radioed, right? Bringing dinner to Lilyanna."

The woman nodded.

Dan closed one eye and peeked through the peephole before realizing he was on the wrong side of it. "How's she been in there?" he asked, playing it off.

"Been screaming a lot."

"Any screams stand out?"

"Something about an airplane. Gibberish, mostly."

Dan nodded. "Okay. You'll be out here?"

"Just holler if you need me."

Dan knocked. Seemed like an appropriate thing to do, even for a prisoner. No response. He knocked again. Nothing. He cracked open the door.

Lilyanna sat on the bed closest to the bathroom, eyes pinned open, hair extensions on the floor beside her, frozen in place.

Yeesh. Building C rooms really *were* a downgrade, even worse than the pictures. No private balcony, no minifridge, TV like a postage stamp. It was a small step up from a roadside motel. Some of the cold from outside had seeped in too. Go figure—they hadn't installed heat at a resort in the Bahamas.

"Hi," Dan said. He shut the door softly behind him, shuffled over to the desk. "Brought you dinner. Lenny actually makes an amazing Italian sub, you've gotta give it to him. And there's a beer here. We didn't have dessert—Building A still has our wedding cake—but one of the boxes we took back was from the vending machines, so there's a Butterfinger for you. And a Crunch bar for myself."

He sat on the bed across from Lilyanna's, opened the Crunch bar, got a better look at her. She hadn't budged. She looked different in cheap light, like someone was tired of playing with her and removed the batteries. Her makeup was running a bit, her white dress stained with something.

"You gonna eat?" Dan asked. He took a bite of his Crunch bar. Delicious. "I mean, it's whatever, but if you are—the bread'll get soggy from all the oil if you leave it sitting too long."

"Y'all sure are loud down there," she said.

"Oh, good, you're still speaking. Yeah, well, we have

electricity tonight. Running water too. Guess your people want to make your stay more comfortable."

"That was some move Lenny and your girl pulled."

"It was all of us."

That got a laugh out of her, returned some color to her cheeks. She scooted forward on the bed and over to the desk. She took the sandwich and stripped off the bread, ate the deli meat from her hand like an animal.

"The sun exploded, Lilyanna," Dan said. "Have some carbs."

"You had nothing to do with what happened," she said, licking oil from her thumb. "That ain't your style. You were as surprised as I was." She looked at him for the first time. "Tell me I'm wrong."

He didn't.

She chuckled, twisted open the beer bottle, and took a swig. "Y'all could've at least put me in Building B, I swear. It's cold, but I won't use these sheets. Gonna have to use my dress like a blanket."

"You shot me and put me *under* the resort."

She hopped back on the bed. "So. What's the plan, Mr. Foster? Do you even know?"

"I know."

"Do you?"

He didn't. Plan? He thought they'd already done the plan. He improvised a new one. "The plan is to keep Building A from ruining any more lives. The plan is to let these people live in peace." He paused. "Even if it's only a few more days."

"Oh, you think that's what's gonna happen? We're gonna live in peace now? Join hands 'round the island and sing kumbaya?"

"Partial to 'Lean On Me,' myself."

She laughed.

"What's funny?"

"Y'all have no idea how good you had it."

"Tell that to Julio."

"How long you gonna hang that over my head?"

"Long as he's dead. There are other things I can hang over your head if you'd like. You put a psychopath in charge of security."

"That was Brody. He was head of security before—"

"You had me shot. Ordered old men and women beaten for not meeting *production*. Switched off water, electricity. Cut rations. Hey, Lilyanna, remember when me and Lenny were almost *executed* at the hangar? If it hadn't been for Alan, I'd be in the garden right now. Jesus, saying all these things at once is bizarre. You're insane, you know that? Did you just say something about how *good* we had it?"

She rolled her eyes. "Calm down, hun. Take a deep breath. You're gettin' all red in the face." She sipped her beer, focused on the space in front of her nose. "I didn't make all the right calls. Suppose you would though, if you were in charge."

"I'm, like, 95 percent sure I wouldn't kill anyone."

"You look back on any of the great leaders, son, and you list their mistakes one after another like that, you'd probably think they were awful, too. Abraham Lincoln, Churchill—even Mary Kay Ash, God rest her soul. No one's perfect. But I *know* this island would've been worse off without me. Without some order. These people would've torn each other to pieces."

Dan took another large bite of Crunch bar, envisioned it was Lilyanna's head. "We could've worked together. We could've—"

"You know how Building A came into possession of all that food and medicine, Mr. Foster? That first night after the sun exploded. You know how we got all that?"

"You paid off the guards and they helped you steal it."

"Half-right. I paid off the guards, sure. But that's because folks from Building C, led by your Lenny, got caught trying to take everything. Didn't tell you that, did he? Left that part out, I reckon."

They *what*? That—that wasn't true. Lenny wouldn't do that. Would he? Dan put on his best poker face, pretended it didn't get to him, but Lilyanna saw through it.

"If I hadn't stepped in, Building C would've been in charge. How you think that would've gone? Think they'd've shared? What kind of rules do the uneducated put in place? Lord. We wouldn't have to worry about the cold because this resort would be on fire."

Dan shook his head. "You're lying."

Lilyanna shrugged. "You go on believing what you want. Honestly, I don't care." She tossed her bottle cap across the room. "Alright. So the plan's to live in peace for a few days. That's darling. And what about me? What do y'all plan to do with me? Firing squad?"

Dan could hardly concentrate. Had Lenny and his people really tried to take everything that first night? Is that what put everything in motion?

"Shut up," he blurted. "Eat your Butterfinger. It was lovely seeing you, Lilyanna, as always, but—"

Lilyanna's face curled around a mischievous grin. "Come on, Mr. Foster, you just got here. You're the shepherd of this flock, ain't ya? You're the name they shout, the man they look to. You call the shots. I wanna know what's next."

"If it were up to me, we'd bury you next to Julio."

"Aw. That's not true. We both know that's not true. Why ain't it up to you, Danny?" It was the first time she'd called him Danny. He didn't like it. "Ain't you in charge? Ain't you head honcho?"

She leaned into the gap between the beds, peered into Dan's eyes. Dan had to scoot back to avoid their noses touching.

"No," she said, and she rolled her eyes again, sat back up straight. "You ain't in charge of nothin'. A scared little man."

She stood, went back to her dinner on the desk. She unwrapped the Butterfinger. "I never eat candy." She bit off a piece, chewed it a while. "Is this what y'all eat?"

"It has a new and improved taste."

She spit it out. "Well, sometimes the old ways are best."

They both fell silent. Lilyanna's words ricocheted between Dan's ears. *Little man.* I'm not a little man. I'm just a man. A fucking *man.* Then he accidentally said one of his thoughts aloud: "You don't know anything about me."

Lilyanna gave that a chuckle, took another swig of beer. "Know you? I practically married you." She had his attention. "Let's see here. Bet you're a mama's boy too. And you got trouble relating to people, and you're confused because you thought you'd do something great when you grew up, make something more of yourself." She raised her eyebrows, like, Am I close? She doubled down. "Bet you can't sleep some nights because going to sleep would mean putting a pin in another day of just being plain ol' you." She paused. "Did I just nail that or what?"

"No." Dan tossed the rest of his Crunch bar on the night-stand. He stood. "That Pinterest board philosophy might work on the hillbillies who buy into BeachBod, Lilyanna, but I—"

"I know you 'cause I *married* you." Her eyes fogged like a shower door. "Pete was the same way at your age, I swear. Couldn't understand why he wasn't more successful, working some little job in finance, taking orders from people he was smarter than, funnier than, better than. He'd had all this poten-tial, see. Grew up in a good family. Been told from the time he could lift a pencil that he was God's gift to the world. A real special boy." She clicked her tongue. "Does something to a man, finally facing who he truly is. To look in the mirror and see that first gray beard hair, having done nothin'. Woof."

Dan found his first gray beard hair six months ago when he let it grow out for the holidays. He plucked it with a pair of twee-zers when Mara wasn't home, and that night, under the oppres-sive glow of his cell phone light, he scoured his face for others.

But what did Lilyanna know? He was nothing like Pete.

Please, God, don't let me be *anything* like Pete.

"But you married him," Dan said, returning to the bed.

"And Mara married you. It's amazing the anchors women chain to their ships when they're in love. I was engaged to Pete before I realized he was as useless as a price scanner at the dollar store. By the time I came to my senses, it was too late. Couldn't live without him. So, I did what women do. Set out to fix him."

"This is the fixed version?"

"Congregation of over a thousand. Brought in more than two hundred thousand dollars last year. He don't wear the pants in the relationship, but I don't have to change his diaper anymore either.

I'd say I wrung just about everything I could out of that stupid man."
Lilyanna considered Dan. "I wonder what Mara's got planned for
you." She made a box with her fingers, peered at him through it. "I'm
thinking local office. You're a decent public speaker. Alderman?"

Dan shifted his head so it wouldn't fit in her box. "You don't
know me," he repeated.

"Oh, hun. You think she's happy with this current version of
you? She invested in a fixer-upper. Hey, don't take it personal.
You got good bones. Curb appeal needs a little work. How's your
plumbing?" She laughed at herself. "I mean, if Mara was younger,
okay, maybe she could be a bit more particular, try on someone
else for a while—"

"She's twenty-seven."

"And bless her heart for finally settling down. Whether she
admits it to you or not, son, she's got a timeline in her head. And
you happened to be there around the deadline for gettin' hitched.
Doesn't hurt that it's the end of the world either. Right place,
right time. Ain't that the story of men?" She took another drink.
"Look at you. Fists clenched, foot tapping a hole in the carpet.
Why you in such a huff? This can't be coming as a surprise.
You've seen a photograph of the two of you together, right?"

Dan looked down.

"Oh, Danny. You ain't the main character of this story. Bet
you think you are, don't ya? This is all happening to you, right,
and Mara's an important part, sure, but she's just part. The real
star is Danny Foster. That right?"

"Okay," Dan said, getting up again—again. "This has been
fun. I've always wanted to be psychoanalyzed by someone at the
tip-top of a pyramid scheme, so thanks. I'll see you—"

"You're the *boyfriend*, Dan," Lilyanna said, undeterred. "Character actor. Second billing. Quick recap. Who rushed off to try and save Julio's life the second he was shot?"

He tried to resist, but Dan still answered her inside his head. That was Mara.

"Who's been pushing you to be a mouthpiece for the resistance from the beginning?"

Mara.

"Who actually planned and executed the revolt?"

...Yeah.

"You're around, Mr. Foster, but you're a pawn. A planet stuck in her orbit." She smiled, proud of that one. "Mara, though, gosh. She's a disrupter. Grabs life by the throat. I'd kill to have a few more like her on my executive sales team." She tilted her head, real sweet-like. "It's actually lucky she's got a husband like you. Capable men can't stand being outshined by their partners. Eats 'em up inside, turns 'em resentful. Little men like you though—ideal for women like Mara. You fit right into her pocket, something to carry around and look at when she's bored. Pocket lint in the shape of a man."

Dan was at the door. "You done?"

Lilyanna shrugged, like, I guess so. Then she got a real pensive look on her face. She put a finger to her chin. "Unless..."

Dan should have just opened the door, obviously. Why hadn't he opened the door? His fingers wrapped around the handle, a simple twist would do it. What was the inescapable pull of this woman? She was belittling him, making him feel smaller than the sand caked to his flip-flops, but he had to listen, to hear her out. Maybe he *had* spent his whole life stuck in orbit around powerful women.

He dropped his hand. "Unless what?"

"You could take back control," she said.

"Take back control."

"Take back control! How come you weren't in on that wedding spectacle, Danny? Why didn't you wanna do it?"

"I—"

"You didn't think it was the right move, did you? I told you—Mara gets shit done. Here's the thing about people who get shit done though. They're so focused on getting shit done that they don't take two seconds to consider whether it's the right shit. Lord, forgive me. I haven't said *shit* this many times in years. This building brings out the slum in me. Shit, shit, shit. It's fun. I get the appeal."

"Wait till you try *fuck*."

Lilyanna laughed, maybe the first real laugh Dan had ever heard from her. It was disarming, somehow, like a snake shedding its skin. She sat back on the bed, rested against the headboard, looked to the ceiling. "You *are* funny, Danny. I get what Mara sees in you. Really, I do."

That was nice to hear, Dan needed a confidence boost today, but he considered the source. "Okay," he said, turning back to the door. "Well, it's been a day. So—"

"This is your chance, Danny," she said. Her eyes again met his. She sounded...sincere? She never sounded sincere. And was it Dan's imagination, or had she lost some of the Southern twang? "This is your chance to be the man. Take back the power. Do what you know is right."

"Or I could walk through this door," Dan said.

She nodded, threw up her hand. "Or you could walk through

that door." She spun, planted her feet back on the carpet. She put her hands on her knees. "I was too harsh. It's not easy being a man. Y'all have societal pressures too. Being a man means making the call."

"I didn't make the call today," Dan said, slumping against the wall.

"You still got time." She stood, walked toward him. "Sneak me out of here, Danny. We'll get Alan. There'll be a seat for you *and* Mara on the plane. I promise. Pete could never be the man for me. He didn't have it in him. But you—"

She clutched his hand.

"You have it in you, Danny. I know it. I can *feel* it. Do the right thing. Be the man. Save her life."

He *could* do it. He really could. There was one guard outside, the lunch lady, Dan was pretty sure he could take her. Come out alone, act all casual, then wallop her with an alarm clock. And he could sneak Lilyanna back to Building A or the hangar, then he could sneak back again and tell Alan, who would be thrilled, and he could grab Mara, throw her over his shoulder like a man, tell her he has to do what's best for her, and he'd ignore her kicking and screaming, because she wouldn't get it. She'd be mad at first, like, really mad—but eventually she'd understand. She'd understand when they got home, when they saw their families again. She'd eventually realize what he did was right.

Lilyanna grasped Dan's hand with both of hers now, and she said, "You can do it, you can do it," and she looked at him with big soulful eyes. He smiled at her, and she laughed, like, That's it, come on, and sparks shot across her eyes like the tail end of a firecracker.

Dan ripped his hand from hers and pulled back, but she

seized him again, so this time he pushed her away, not a hard push, just a little one, but she exaggerated and fell on the bed, screaming. When she popped back up, the sparks in her eyes turned to fire.

Dan said, "You really thought that would work on me, didn't you?" And he sounded really confident, really self-assured for a guy that definitely almost worked on. The door to the room swung open, and the lunch lady's head popped in.

"What the hell is going on?"

"You little fucking man," Lilyanna cried. She grabbed the clothing iron from the bedside table and hurled it across the room. It shattered against the wall. Lunch lady barreled in, pistol drawn, but Dan pushed its aim to the floor and said, "Whoa, whoa, it's fine. Leave her. Come on."

"He attacked me!" Lilyanna screamed as they shuffled outside. "That little fucking man attacked me! You fucking white-trash pieces of—"

Dan and the lunch lady slammed the door shut behind them, hardly muffling Lilyanna's screams. The door throbbed as she collided with the other side.

"I will kill *everyone* on this island to get home to my babies, do you understand me? I will make a *raft* out of your *bodies* if it means getting home to my babies!"

Wow, okay. Dark. Definitely not on brand.

Dan stepped away from the door as she continued shrieking.

"I didn't—" Dan said, struggling to find words. "I wasn't trying to—I did not attack her."

The woman lit a cigarette, returned her back to the door, shrugged. "Whatever, man. Not my business."

Dan stared blankly at her.

Dan found Lenny and Alan in the parking lot, next to the bus where they'd locked that kid to the steering wheel over week ago.

Over a week ago. Christ.

They were, of course, arguing. Whisper-arguing, which was kind of funny, like an old couple having a spat during church. They'd both been drinking and were different types of drunks. Lenny was touchy, used *bro* every other word, pulled from a cigar like a cartoon bulldog. Alan was angry, his manic eyes searching for something to hit, something to rip apart with his hands.

"Dinner with Mrs. Collins went as well as could be expected," Dan said.

Lenny nodded profusely like it was all going according to plan. He glanced up at the room where Lilyanna was held. "So she's good?"

"Well, Lenny, *good* is subjective. Shit, it's cold." Dan buttoned his jacket, hugged himself. He decided against asking Lenny about what Lilyanna revealed. Best not to make another enemy right now. "What are you two doing out here?"

Lenny laughed, like, heh, heh, and elbowed Dan. "Bro, you're asking what *we're* doing out here? It's your wedding night. Party's over. Don't you have somewhere to be?"

"It's not too late," Alan said, shaking, from cold or anger or both. "We take her now, Dan, and carry her straight to the hangar. Use her as leverage to get to the plane."

Alan's plan sure sounded familiar.

Lenny took a puff. "They'll just shoot us and take her. Simple. Least here we got some protection, some cover. Shut up about it already. Besides, we take her from here, no reason Building A won't overrun the place. Take back the supplies, screw all these people again. That what you want?"

"I want off this island, Lenny. Thought that's what you wanted too. They won't shoot me. I'm the only pilot on the resort."

"Oh, right, so they'll just shoot me, Dan, and our wives. Yeah, real good. Beautiful. Good thinking."

Sarcasm didn't suit Lenny.

"I can negotiate with them."

"She's staying here. I don't wanna hear about it anymore."

Alan turned to Dan. His eyes pleaded with him.

Desperation didn't suit Alan.

"You're okay with this?" Alan asked. "You really think this is the right play?"

The wind picked up, and something dull but persistent flecked past the lights of Building C.

No way. Was this…?

"Snow," Lenny said, holding his hand out. "Whoa. Get a load of that. It's snowing. I gotta get Gloria. She's gonna freak. Hey, maybe if it sticks, we can line this place with trenches or something, for more cover. In Hackensack we used to—"

Dan tuned him out.

Up on the walkways, a few doors opened, and out popped curious heads.

"Snow!" someone called, like school might get canceled.

"*Snow*," another said, like it was a death sentence. This wasn't something to celebrate. This was the manifestation of everyone's worst fears in delicate, floating crystals. This was perpetual winter. This was freezing to death in the dark.

Dan asked Alan, "Could you fly in this?"

"I can fly in anything."

Lenny didn't love that exchange. He called up to the lunch lady guarding Lilyanna's door. "Hey, Madge, you got enough ammo for tonight?"

Madge. Of course her name was Madge. Dan had never seen a more Madgey Madge in his entire life.

Lenny stared straight into Alan when he said the next part: "Anyone comes near Lilyanna, you know what to do."

26

Dan brushed snow from his pants as he entered the room for the night. They were lucky to have their own—most of the other couples had doubled up to accommodate Building B refugees.

"It's snowing," he announced, and Mara's silhouette appeared in the bathroom doorway. She was brushing her teeth. She walked past him, smelling of booze and peppermint. She cut the vertical blinds with a finger.

"That's terrifying," she said, mouth full. "And…kind of pretty."

Dan clicked on a lamp. "It's dark in here."

"Guess I've gotten used to it." Mara disappeared inside the bathroom and spit. "Using water that hasn't been sitting in a tub for a week—now that, I missed." She reappeared, wrapped in a Tizoc robe. Her hair was still up from the wedding. She joined Dan on the edge of the bed, an arm's length between them. Dan slid off his jacket, threw it somewhere.

"How was she?" Mara asked quietly. She massaged her punching hand.

Dan scoffed, furious that Lilyanna had gotten to him. "She was...Lilyanna."

Mara nodded. "Yeah."

Dan considered undressing completely, going straight to bed. He was the definition of weary, and tomorrow promised to be another humdinger. But it was his first time alone with Mara since the wedding. He yanked his tie loose. What was it they said about going to bed angry?

"We should talk," Mara said.

"We should," Dan said.

They started at the same time, each talking over the other.

"Sorry," they said in unison.

Mara wordlessly gave him permission to go first.

Dan closed his eyes. "You promised me."

"What?"

"In jail. You promised me if there was a way off this island, you'd take it."

"Yeah." She blinked. "And you promised we'd help people."

They slowly turned from each other. Neither spoke awhile. Wind rattled the window, slid under the door. The blinds danced. Outside, resort lights were fuzzy with falling snow.

"It was a good speech," Dan offered. "Hindi was a nice touch."

"I'm pretty sure I said it wrong."

Dan buried his face in his hands.

After a minute—or an hour, Dan was so tired—Mara scooted closer.

"Penny for your thoughts."

He came up for air. "'Penny for my thoughts?'"

"My dad used to say it."

"Yeah, well. You'd be overpaying."

"Probably." She poked him, which felt like a peace treaty. "But if we're married now, what's yours is mine. If we get divorced, I get half your thoughts."

"I knew I should've put thoughts in the prenup."

"Too late now, dude."

He glanced at her. Her hair was still lightly bleached from the sun, the freckles on her cheeks unearthed. She'd never look like this again. Dan took a deep breath.

"Do you think I'm a little man?"

That took her by surprise. Sometimes she giggled when she was surprised. "What are you talking about? Who called you a little—oh."

Yeah.

"Come on, Danny. She got in your head? Really?"

Dan fiddled with the bedsheet. "I don't know." He sighed. "I probably haven't been completely forthcoming with how I've felt lately. I—" He paused.

"What?" Mara was beside him now, her hand on his shoulder. "Hey, it's okay. Tell me."

"It feels pretty stupid to worry about if we're going to freeze to death." It actually always felt stupid to worry about—just especially now. Dan may have lacked every other facet of traditional masculinity, but he had one in spades: it was hard to discuss feelings. Especially with Mara, for whom he should be a rock. Strong, steady, unwavering.

Mara voice softened. "If we're going to freeze to death, now's the perfect time to tell me."

"I just—it's stupid."

"It's not stupid."

It spilled out. "I feel like maybe I haven't made anything of my life, and I'll never make anything of it because I'm not who everyone expects me to be and I'm a failure, you know, or at best I'm average, and I was never supposed to be average."

Mara waited. She sensed more coming. Dan stood and paced.

"And I don't want to let you down, and I don't want to let my parents down—or my sister or my old teachers, friends, anyone who's believed in me over the years. And sometimes when I sit down, and things are quiet, and you've gone to bed, and I don't have my phone to distract me or the TV or PlayStation, and I really just sit, just sit and think, you know, I remember all these times growing up when people said I was going to be something. My dad once said I was going to be rich, because I was smart, and good-looking, and charming, and now some months I barely make rent. And Mrs. Humbolt. I never told you about her, but she was my creative writing teacher sophomore year. She said I had it, that I was special, that she was going to read my books someday. Well, she hasn't, and she won't, because I haven't done shit. And even you, you know. I know you think I'm capable of more. You don't say it, because you're really considerate of my feelings, but I know you're hoping I'll…do something. Something. Even on this island—even when I finally had a chance to prove myself to you, to show you I can be the person you need me to be, I let you down. I'm never going to be the guy. And now that's especially true. I'm going to die a Marvel Maids marketing specialist."

He was practically panting. They were quiet a moment, and neither moved, and Dan thought maybe Mara was regretting ever going on this vacation with him, ever going to Chili's or wherever their first date was two years ago, ever associating with this doughy lump of feelings. But then she stood from the bed, stripped off her robe, stood naked. She pulled on Dan's fart pants, which were in a pile in the corner, tied the elastic band real tight to her waist.

"What are you doing?" Dan asked.

"I'm going to punch another Collins. For whatever she said to you." She pulled on a bra, clasped it in front, and then awkwardly shuffled it around her body. She grumbled. "Little man? He's not a little man. Your husband—your douchebag husband—that's the little man. If she thinks for one second she can—"

She was pulling on a shirt now. Dan seized her wrist as she reached for the door.

"Mara. What are you doing? It's freezing."

"I told you."

Dan laughed. "No," he said. "No. Stay here."

Mara took a step back, blew hot breath from her mouth to push a hair out of her face. She crossed her arms. "You are *not* a little man."

"Okay."

"You are not." She fell into Dan, wrapped her arms around him. "Listen to me. Okay? I have loved two men in my entire life. My dad. And then you. People used to say he was worthless too."

Dan didn't remember using the word *worthless*, but he let her roll with it.

"I was at this cheer practice once. Like, third grade. And my mom was there to pick me up, and one of the girls asked why my dad never came to practice, and another girl said it was because he was a deadbeat. And I knew, even then, that that wasn't her word, you know? Kids don't say *deadbeat*. She heard it from her mom or another adult, and I asked my mom on the way home what it meant, and it took her a second, but then she said a deadbeat was someone who didn't meet expectations."

Mara broke the hug and sat in one of the cheap chairs next to the bed, tucking one foot under her butt. "And from then on, you know, I started to realize that's what everyone thought of him. My grandparents, my friends, even Raveena said it once. But to me, he was just my dad. He didn't make a lot of money—hardly any money—and he didn't always have gas in his car to make it to cheer, and he could never move my mom to the neighborhood she wanted. But he was a good person, and he loved me and Raveena so much, and he took us camping and taught us to fish and was so, so funny and knew the right things to say all the time. But people like my grandma..."

She shook her head, tapped her finger on the table.

"It's like society thinks there's something broken about a person who's just living. Like there's no inherent worth to people unless they've accomplished something."

Dan returned to the edge of the bed. Mara, who always had a flair for dramatics, collapsed to her knees and scooted closer to Dan till she was between his legs. She collected his hands in hers and looked up into his eyes.

"You could never let me down, Danny. Because you're Danny. You're enough. No qualifiers."

"But you hid things from me. You went behind my back because I disappointed you."

Mara recoiled like it was the silliest thing she'd ever heard.

"I went behind your back because I knew you would sacrifice everything—even yourself—for me. Do you know how loved that makes me feel? How safe? I couldn't let you do it. But you didn't *disappoint* me, Danny. Is that really what you think?"

Dan needed a moment with that. Mara crawled on top of him, and they flattened into the bed. She held his head in her arms, kissed the side of it. You didn't disappoint me, Danny. It played in his head, over and over. You didn't disappoint me.

"And about your job," Mara said.

Dan groaned.

"If you work at Marvel Maids till the day you die—"

"So tomorrow?"

"Till the day you *die*, I'll be proud of you. Because when people ask me about you, Danny, I don't tell them what you do."

"I don't blame you."

"I tell them you're funny and charming, and that you donate to that random elephant sanctuary in Tennessee, and you return shopping carts in the parking lot that aren't even yours because you don't want them to scratch someone's car. I tell them you would be my phone-a-friend on *Who Wants to Be a Millionaire?* because you always know things, even if you don't think you do, and I tell them about that time I caught you crying at *How to Train Your Dragon* when you thought I was in the shower."

"You tell people that?"

"You're my best friend, Danny. You're a wonderful person. You don't have to worry about making it." She paused. "You already have."

Dan felt something well up inside of his chest, something he would normally shove back down into his gut, but he didn't this time because of the way Mara looked at him. And then his eyes became moist, and his throat clogged, and he tried to break free from Mara's grasp, but she only held him tighter.

And then Dan Foster cried.

A lot. Not because he'd held it in all week, but because he'd held it in for years, and he wiped his face with his wrists, and Mara wiped his face too, and the coffee-powder henna smeared everywhere, but they didn't care.

When Dan finally composed himself, Mara clutched his hands in hers. "We never made it official, Danny."

He felt short of breath. "You're sure?"

She smiled. "Bet your ass, I'm sure."

Dan grabbed her waist, pulled her in. "Mara Usra Nichols. You're the best thing that's ever happened to me. *I do.*"

Their noses touched. "Daniel Lewis Foster. There's nothing I want more than to be your wife. *I do too.*"

They kissed deeply and stayed up another hour together, and when sleep finally washed over Dan, he dreamt of being frozen in place for all of eternity with Mara Nichols Foster, and he didn't feel like a little man anymore.

27

Dan knew what Mara said about people was right—they do have inherent worth. But people also have problems, big ones, and one of those problems is that they'll often make decisions counter to self-interest just to be part of a winning team. Overnight, nearly a dozen denizens of Buildings B and C broke ranks, crossed no man's land, and joined up with Building A. Some left notes. A few were BeachBod boss babes and disagreed with the treatment of their dear leader. Some were religious and felt Building A was more closely aligned with the church. Others just felt like Building A was better equipped to win the war, and they wanted to be on the right side of the pool deck when the smoke cleared.

They had a point.

Despite the hiccup, Dan was feeling better when the Fosters, Favas, and Ferrises met for breakfast in the lobby of Building C. Not great, because, you know, still trapped on an island during Armageddon. But he was definitely married to the love of his life now, no ambiguity there, and Mara's pep talk—combined with the incredible make-up sex afterward—really helped. There was still the matter of what came next though, and on that, Dan was conflicted. The plane remained a factor, Alan brought it up as soon as they sat down. But the choice Mara made yesterday was paying off. There was applause when they entered the room. Plates were full, folks lined up for seconds. Stories and memories were being shared over coffee, laughter bounced from the rafters. The Hindi phrase from Mara's speech was spray-painted above one of the exit doors.

Maybe Mara was right about that too. Maybe just doing good for the next few days was enough. Maybe—

A guard stumbled into the lobby, tripping over chairs, causing a ruckus. The entire room—a hundred people, at least—stopped to watch. He hollered for Lenny.

"Lenny! S-sir." He was breathless, awkward, even less intimidating than some of Rico's men.

Lenny stood, Gloria's hand grasped his forearm. "What is it?"

"Outside. I was on the roof using the binoculars you gave me? They're not very good, but—in front of Building A, they're lining up those people who defected, man. They're lining them up, and they're on their knees. Looks like they're…"

Alan buried his face in his hands.

"What?" Charles asked.

The guard leaned in and hissed. "It looks like—like they're going to shoot them."

"Oh, God," Charles said. Mara stood, pulled Dan up with her. She locked eyes with Lenny.

"The roof," they said.

Minutes later, the six of them stood above Building C, Dan

wishing he had thought to stuff his quilted pockets with mini muffins. He was hungry. And cold, Jesus. It hadn't snowed all night, but long enough to cover the darkened resort in about three inches of the stuff. Palm trees look funny in the snow. Multiple bonfires lined the bases of Buildings A and C, but the long stretch of pools, lazy rivers, and tiki bars in between lay undisturbed, coated in a layer of peaceful, unspoiled white, illuminated from beneath by path lighting.

It *was* kind of pretty.

They took turns with the binoculars. Just beyond the Sola Pool were twelve blurry people spaced six or so feet apart. They were on their knees in the snow, hands laced behind their heads, trembling.

"What is this?" Lenny asked no one in particular.

"Your bloodbath," Alan said.

Dan thought about what Lilyanna said last night. About Lenny, about Building C. Was this all his fault?

It was still Dan's turn with the binoculars when Rico marched from the base of Building A, theatrically warmed his hands next to one of the bonfires, and then waved. Rico wasn't using binoculars but somehow saw Dan perfectly, like his eyes had a pinch-to-zoom feature. Dan turned away, unnerved by the sight of him. Rico always looked crazy, but now he looked like he had been dipped in crazy and marinated overnight. There was a spring in his step, a giddiness Dan didn't associate with darkness, or cold, or executions. Rico looked like he was right at home, like he'd just returned from a long trip and he was ready to pop off his shoes, pop open a beer, pop some heads. This dude was evil personified, and he was dancing at the end of the world.

"We have to do something," Mara said.

"Do somethin'?" Lenny asked. "They left us."

"So we just let Rico *shoot* them? Lenny."

Lenny shrugged, but Dan could feel his confliction, feel him struggling within himself. Lenny dug his foot in the snow. "Choose the side with assholes, and you're gonna step in some shit."

"Beautiful," Dan said. "Thank you, Lenny."

Mara tugged Dan's arm. "Maybe we can talk to Rico."

Dan opened his mouth to speak, unsure himself what would come out, but he was interrupted. Charles gasped and shoved the binoculars in Alan's face.

"Oh, y'all, something's coming this way!" Charles said, clutching the sides of his head. "It is!"

Alan stepped closer to the edge of the roof, leaned into the dark. He was tracking something. "A golf cart," he said, confused. "Heading straight toward us. Who's that driving it?"

Lenny snatched the binoculars. "Holy shit. Holy shit. Gloria, radio down. Golf cart kamikaze! Golf cart kamikaze!"

"Oh, God!" Gloria said, and she clutched the radio on her waist and shrieked into it: "Come in, downstairs! Come in!"

A voice sputtered from the other end. "Go ahead."

"We got a golf cart approaching at rapid speed! Wouldn't you say so, Len? It's coming from—what direction we facing? Without the sun, I don't ever know. You know, I nevah knew even with the sun!"

"South," Alan said.

"Coming from the south!" Gloria screamed. "It's coming from the south, it's approaching the Maize Pool and on a collision course for Building C!"

"We see it," the voice said.

Dan saw it too, growing larger every second. It was definitely a golf cart, and whoever was driving was *booking* it. Well, as much as a golf cart *can* book it, anyway. Maybe fifteen miles per hour.

"Shoot it!" Lenny screamed into the radio. "This is Lenny! Your orders are to open fire! Put down that golf cart!"

There were pops of gunfire from all corners of Building C, unsteady shots, unfocused. This wasn't the well-trained tactical assault of a competent force. It sounded more like someone skipping on bubble wrap. Pockets of snow around the approaching golf cart erupted and sizzled. But nothing could stop it. The golf cart was inevitable.

"It's gonna crash!" Lenny screamed. "HIT THE DECK!"

He seized Gloria and dove into the roof. Dan, caught up in the moment, held Mara tightly to his chest, like that would do anything, and Charles screamed, but Alan barely flinched. The golf cart puttered out of view below and crashed.

Kind of anticlimactic, really. It wasn't even loud, just the sound of plastic scraping against concrete, a kid dragging his toys home after dark.

Lenny stood, brushed himself off like it was nothing, like he knew that would happen. He radioed down, having shaken the panic from his voice. "Come in, this is Lenny. Please report. Who was driving the golf cart? They alive?"

"They are very much not alive, sir."

"We hit them?"

"Uh—" The radio cut out.

"Come again. Did we hit them?"

"No. Uh, no. It looks like—yeah, we missed."

Missed every time? They must've fired two dozen bullets.

The six of them shared baffled glances and then rushed downstairs to see for themselves. There was no elevator in Building C, so the stairs had to do. The wind nipped their cheeks and sliced through their makeshift winter clothing.

When they reached the ground floor, they saw it. The cart was overturned, the back wheels still spinning.

Charles screamed. The driver was...beheaded.

The driver was also a mannequin, the one from Tommy Bahama that Dan had folded into inappropriate positions last week. The poor guy was a mess. His right arm was cracked in two places, his Mojito Bay Palm Row IslandZone® Camp Shirt (available in sizes XS to XXXL) barely recognizable. No use checking for a pulse. DOA.

A brick was tied to the accelerator.

Lenny snorted. "What's his game?"

"Sir!"

It was the same breathless guard who'd alerted Lenny at breakfast. He found a room service menu taped to the back of the cart. Written across the menu, in thick, black letters: CHANEL FIVE.

"Chanel Number Five?" Charles said. "The perfume? What sort of message is he sending?"

"He's an idiot," Dan said. He motioned for Lenny to pass him the radio. "He means channel five. The asshole wants to talk."

Back on the roof with the others, Dan clicked on the radio, tuned it to channel five, and waited. He peered through the binoculars at the hostages shivering in the snow.

They were right to be scared. Dan's stomach bubbled. He tried to shake away the feeling.

Mara gasped as the radio sputtered. Dan spotted Rico standing over an old woman. Real tough, aren't you? Rifle to an old lady's head. Fucking coward.

"Danny boy," Rico said, as if greeting an old friend. "That you? Y'all sure wasted a lot of ammo on an empty golf cart."

Dan looked to Mara. You can do this, she mouthed.

"Heya, Rico, yeah, it's me. Listen, I've been thinking. I want to change my answer. I'm gonna go with...mixologist."

A moment of silence, then: "What the fuck are you talking about?"

"Still trying to guess what you wanted to be when you grew up. That's clearly not it. Okay. Final answer: misunderstood neighborhood recluse with a heart of gold."

"You talk a lot, Foster."

"I've heard that."

"I'm going to kill this lady now."

That shut Dan up, at least for a minute. He turned to his crew. His *crew*. A couple of over-the-hill deli owners, a drunk pilot, a nurse and—what did Charles even do?

"What do I do?" Dan asked.

Lenny said, "Uh—"

Alan said, "Ask him what he wants."

Lenny said, "Yeah, right. Ask him what he wants."

But Dan already knew what he wanted. He pivoted, tried to stall.

"It doesn't have to be like this," Dan said. "It's unnecessary, Rico, it's—"

"Three seconds," Rico said. The woman in front of Rico tried to stand, but he kicked her legs out from under her and laughed. She collapsed back into the snow.

"*Okay*," Dan said. "Okay. What do you want?"

"You know what I want, faggot."

"Oh, come on, Rico," Dan said. "In this day and age? The f-word? You're better than that." He turned to the others and whispered, "I don't actually think he's better than that."

Charles waved it off, like, No worries, I've heard worse.

"Turn over Lilyanna, I let them go," Rico said. "You don't… well—"

"Can you give us a moment?"

"What?"

"Just a moment, Rico. Thank you. Be right with you."

Dan turned his back to him.

"So, he's lying, right? He'll kill them even if we turn her over."

"What if he's not?" Mara asked. "We can't gamble with their lives."

Lenny huffed. "We don't negotiate with assholes."

"Since when?" Charles asked. "Did you slide a Building C mutiny booklet under our doors that I missed? Because Lenny, darling, it feels like you're making this up as you go."

"*They* defected," Lenny said. "*They* chose to join up with Building A after everything they've done. They signed up for this. We don't owe them nothin', far as I see it, and that's all I'll say about that." He crossed his arms, having won the argument with himself.

"You're a real man of the people, Lenny," Dan said.

Gloria brushed her husband's arm. "Len, are you sure? That's Bobby and Angie Cavallari over there, the ones we met at the swim-up bar. From Philly."

Lenny didn't respond, the cement drying on his decision with each passing second.

Dan turned to Alan. "Want to jump in here?"

Alan shrugged. "It won't matter."

"It won't matter," Dan repeated.

"You can't trust the word of a man like Rico. It means nothing. Listen, I counted seven guards earlier. That means, at most, he's got three guards on the plane. We could head there now, we could—"

"Fuck's sake," Lenny said, and he snatched the radio and binoculars from Dan's hands.

"Listen up, motherfucker. You piece of shit. You don't scare me, pal. Think you're a real big man because you took some old people hostage, that it? You're nothing. Trash. Bet you ain't such a big man without that rifle."

"Lenny!" Dan dove for the radio, but Lenny shoved him away.

"And you ain't getting Lilyanna. She's ours, okay? Get that through your skull. You failed your job, asshole. 'Less you wanna come get her yourself, come on down here yourself, *Rico*, because we got something real nice for your ass. Quit the bullshit. You ain't scaring anyone today, hombre."

Lenny wheezed when he finished, glanced around for validation. Mara's chin quivered. Dan didn't breathe.

Rico snorted into the radio. "That it?"

"That's it," Lenny said.

They saw the flash before they heard it. Mara screamed, Gloria screamed, Charles gasped and said, "No, no, Lord, no." Dan held Mara, clutched her tightly to keep from hitting Lenny in the face, to keep from hurdling over the side of the building and rushing Rico himself.

Lenny approached the edge of the roof, his mouth agape, muttering, "I didn't think—I didn't think he would really—you gotta believe me, I didn't think for one second—"

"Which part of your experience with Rico Flores made you think he wasn't capable of that?" Alan asked. "That woman's blood is on *your* hands, Lenny, you—"

Lenny let loose a primordial roar and rushed Alan, tackled him to the surface of the roof, his fists like missiles. Alan caught him with an elbow to the nose, and then Charles joined in, shrieking and clawing at Lenny like a cat in heat. Mara screamed, "Dan, do something," and Dan jumped in, pulled at someone, pushed at someone else, yelled something like "You assholes, we're adults, we're adults." Gloria screamed Len, "That's enough," and that distracted him long enough for Dan to yank him onto his back and off Alan. Dan lay on top of Lenny for a moment, rising and falling with the weight of his breath, like Sam Neill on that sick triceratops in *Jurassic Park*.

Rico laughed through the radio. And that was a dick move too, because he had to intentionally hold down the button for them to hear.

Alan climbed to his feet with Charles's help and ran his forearm over his mouth. He spit. "You're going to get us all killed, Lenny. We're all going to die because of you."

Dan shifted off Lenny, gave him space. Blood dripped from his nose, and Gloria came down to cradle his head. He let out a great big sigh, like he was exhaling everything that'd happened in the last week, all of his rage, all of his fire. He traced a sad *L* in the snow with his finger.

For *Lenny* or *loser*?

"He executed an old lady, bro. Just shot her, no hesitation." He sat up, and Gloria used a scarf to wipe his eyes. "Ah, shit. I didn't think people like that really existed."

"They've always existed," Alan said. "There just aren't shadows to hide in anymore."

The radio buzzed.

"Every half hour," Rico said, "until she's back. Ticktock."

Dan opened the door to find Lilyanna with her legs crossed on the edge of the bed. She applied lipstick, making faces in the vanity mirror.

"Who gave you lipstick?" he asked.

She smacked her lips together and shut a clamshell case in her lap. "Big day today, Mr. Foster. A girl wants to look her best."

28

They negotiated the terms of the exchange.

Lenny would escort Lilyanna across the wooden bridge that stretched over the lazy river and onto the Maize Pool deck. When his spotters on the roof confirmed the hostages were released, then, and *only* then, would he let Lilyanna go. But above all else, there was one condition that absolutely, positively had to be met, or the whole thing would be called off: Rico Flores would stay inside Building A, and he'd keep that damn rifle with him.

Rico accepted. Which meant nothing, of course.

But Leonard Layout, still sullen from earlier, planned for that.

"I got it," he said to everyone, hunched over a map of the resort in the Building C lobby. He held a rag to his nose. "Look at this. We send someone behind enemy lines." He pressed a gloved finger into the map and slid it along the eastern edge. "We use the tree line to sneak them over there, get 'em near A. Stall till they get eyes on Rico. If that size-fourteen boot takes one step outside the front door, they tell us, we bail."

Dan's eyes flicked to Alan's. It was a bad plan, had more holes in it than Rico's latest victim, but there was a scheduled execution in fifteen minutes—what choice did they have? God, Rico had them scrambling, right where he wanted them, and Dan's dread was so heavy that it threatened to sink him into the earth.

Lenny sat back and sighed. "It'll work. It's got to. Only question is—who we sendin'?"

Mara wrapped around Dan's arm like a sloth. Charles clutched Alan's shoulder.

"I'll do it," Dan said, ignoring Mara's sharp tug. She wanted him to help, right?

"Can't be any of us," Lenny said. "If we're spotted—he knows us."

"Let me do it." It was Madge. She had retrieved Lilyanna from the third floor and shoved her into a chair beside Lenny, gun still trained on her. "I've been listening to this one all night. Let me do it."

"Are you sure?" Mara asked. "This seems so dangerous, Lenny. What if—"

"That's perfect." Lenny stood, took hold of Madge, gave her a little shake. "He don't know you. Even if he spotted you, he don't know, you could be from Building A."

No one knew Madge, not really, but one look at her, and it was obvious she wasn't from Building A.

"I like the idea of Danny doing it," Lilyanna said, and she winked at him.

Madge slapped the back of her head. "If I get the drop on Rico, why don't I just shoot him?"

"If you shoot him, his men shoot the hostages," Alan explained. He was still agitated. Restless.

"What about after the handoff? I could shoot him then."

"Have you ever shot anyone before?"

Madge's bottom lip swallowed her upper one. "I stabbed my ex-husband once."

The snow had picked back up. Residents of Building C congregated outside the lobby door, far enough back to be safe, probably, but close enough to satisfy morbid curiosity. The bonfires at the base of Building A roared in the distance, candles beckoning Lilyanna home.

Dan hated this. All of this. The recently drained pools and lazy rivers were dark, eerie voids. They offered too many opportunities for ambush, too many places to hide. They'd have eyes on Rico, yeah, but what about his men? Dan took a deep breath through his nose and out his mouth. Mara sang softly.

Lenny radioed upstairs. "This is Lenny. We in position?"

"Position one checking in."

"Position two checking in."

Then, after a moment, Madge crackled through. She whispered, "Position three. I've got eyes on Rico. He just reentered A."

Lenny put his gun to Lilyanna's back. He turned to the others and shrugged, like, Here goes nothin'. The lines on his forehead cut deep. He set his eyes forward, grunted, but before he could take that crucial first step, Gloria was on him. She snatched his wrist and laced her fingers with his.

"No, Glor, you're stayin'," Lenny said. He tried to shake free of her, but she held on.

"I'm coming, Len, I'm coming. Don't waste your breath."

That was that, they all knew it was settled, and Lenny quit fighting, and Lilyanna mockingly said, "Aw." Gloria was going with her man. Obviously.

"Be right back," Lenny said to Dan. "With the others."

"Okay."

Lenny switched the radio to channel five. "Rico."

"Yup."

"We doin' this?"

"Waiting on you, tubs."

Lenny turned his radio back to Building C's channel, lowered his shoulders, and they walked. Well, Lenny and Gloria walked—Lilyanna strolled. She may as well have been shopping on Rodeo Drive with the way her arms swung, the way her head bobbed playfully. By the time they reached the arched wooden bridge that crossed the lazy river, Dan's insides were rioting. They were out of reach now, on their own.

Lenny's voice crackled through the radio. "How we lookin'?"

We're lookin' pretty damn exposed, Dan wanted to say, but as he brought his radio to his mouth, one of the other guards buzzed through.

"All clear. It's hard to see in this snow."

"Our people are walkin'?"

"Yes. They have them grouped real tight. Guard on either side. They just reached—uh—they just reached the loungers south of the Sola Pool."

"Why'd you hesitate?"

"One of them tripped over a pool noodle. They're up, walking, we're good."

"Eyes on Rico?"

Madge chimed in. "Followed him inside. He's still here."

Dan and Mara shared a glance. *Followed him inside?* How the hell did she do that? She was talking into a radio, for Christ's sake. They'd spot her in two seconds.

"Do you still have those binoculars?" Mara found Alan and Charles in the crowd at the base of the building. "Something seems weird, we just want to—"

"I heard," Alan said. He pulled the binoculars from his coat, scanned the resort. "I don't see him. But I can hardly see anything, these things are shit."

"Yeah, well," Dan said, "they're for bird-watching."

Alan gave up. "Lenny's going to get us all killed."

"You've mentioned that," Mara said.

"It's fucking true." Alan tossed the binoculars to Dan.

"Stop bickering, y'all, please," Charles said. "God, I'm so nervous, I could scream. They wouldn't risk Lilyanna like that, right? They wouldn't do that."

Dan couldn't find Rico with the binoculars either, so maybe he really was inside. Instead he focused on Lenny and the others. They'd reached the edge of the Maize Pool, stood frozen on its lip. Gloria tried to stand beside her man, but Lenny repeatedly pushed her behind.

"Where they at?" Lenny asked. He held the radio button down too long though, so in the background Dan could hear Lilyanna saying, "Let me go, y'all, we're here, let me walk."

A spotter weighed in. "They've come to a stop just west of the Sola Pool. They're just...standing there."

Dan couldn't help himself. He buzzed in. "Madge. Where's Rico?"

Silence.

"I repeat, *Madge. Where. Is. Rico?*"

"Do I let her go?" Lenny asked. "Feeling pretty vulnerable here. No, Gloria, stay behind me. Behind me, babe."

"Madge, report in!" Dan pleaded. "Do you have eyes on Rico? Is he still in Building A?"

Nothing.

Mara's hands were clammy. "Danny," she said. "Why isn't she responding?"

Dan tried again. "Madge?"

Nothing.

"Fuck," Alan said.

"What?" Charles's voice was a dog whistle.

"*Fuck*," Alan repeated.

The crowd buzzed like a hornet's nest. Some split off and scrambled back into Building C. "Double cross," someone screamed, "Get out there," another yelled, and another babbled, "Something's wrong, something's wrong, something's wrong."

"Madge." Lenny's voice over the radio. "Talk to me." But he held the radio button down too long again, and Lilyanna was speaking now, and it sounded like she'd been laughing.

"Y'all really left me alone with a single mother for twelve hours."

Dan thought Lenny exploded after the first shot. He hadn't, of course, there were no cannons on the island, no grenade launchers or bombs, anything like that. But part of him disappeared, a chunk from near the center, and what remained fell limp in Gloria's arms. A lot happened at once after that, so much that Dan could hardly process it all, but he knew for sure that Lilyanna screamed, and ran, and was gone. Then there were some other shots, and Mara screamed too, and she disconnected from Dan's arm to sprint toward the pool, but he snatched her and pulled her back.

"We have to help them, Danny!" she pleaded, struggling to escape his grasp, but Dan wouldn't listen. More gunfire. His eyes shot to Alan.

"The plane," Alan shouted, his voice clear and steady. He tugged Charles and Dan away from the pool. "We go for the plane right now. Right fucking now! It's our shot!"

Dan could do it. He could throw Mara over his shoulder, kicking and screaming, he could get her on that plane. They could escape in all this chaos. He could do what a man would do, do what he never had the guts to do before, do what Alan would do. She'd eventually understand. Eventually, she'd—

Mara's nails dug into his face. She yanked his head to the side, forced him to stare into her terrified eyes. *"We can't leave them, Danny,"* she said, and Dan heard her this time.

Why hadn't he heard her before?

He jerked free of Alan's grasp, and together he and Mara sprinted toward the pool. They went up over the wooden bridge and down the other side, and there were more flashes of light on the opposite end of the resort, near the hostages, and Dan and Mara collided with Lenny and Gloria, and they all tumbled into the snow in the deep end of the Maize Pool, a tangled pile of limbs and sweat and blood.

Dan ripped himself from the pile and tore Mara away, pinned her against the side of the pool, and checked her for injuries, for holes, for any disappeared parts. Her eyes were wild, and she had blood on her face, but Dan was pretty sure it wasn't hers. She looked him over briefly and then shoved through him toward Gloria, who was hovering over her husband screaming, "Len, no, no, no, Len. Len. Len!"

"Fuck," Mara said. She undid Lenny's coat, ripped open his shirt. Gloria gasped when she saw what Rico had done to him.

"What do I do?" Dan asked. *"What do I do?"*

Dan flinched as more gunshots erupted, but they were coming from both sides of the resort now, bullets flying just above the pool.

Mara tossed a torn segment of Lenny's shirt to Dan. "Apply pressure. Here. And here!" But she'd only given him one small piece of fabric, barely enough to cover the first hole, so Dan used his hand, but it was no use, poor Lenny was all shot up, all shot to hell.

"Use snow!" Mara commanded. "Pack the wounds with snow, Danny, come on. Quick."

Dan frantically did as he was told. But this was just a show, he realized, Mara was putting on a show for Lenny, and for Gloria, and probably for him too.

Gloria cradled Lenny's head, she pleaded with him, and she said, "Len, please. I love you. Please, don't do this, don't do this. Don't you do this, Len. Please."

Lenny held her hand. His eyes were like glass, and he smiled at her, one more self-assured smirk from Leonard Layout. There was a finality to his next breath, a short, shallow gasp, and he was gone.

29

Eventually Gloria fell silent.

Over the next few hours, Dan and Mara did their best to comfort her. They covered Lenny's body with his coat, took turns putting their arms around Gloria. They whispered sweet things about Lenny, said he was a hero and, "He was larger than life, Gloria, truly an incredible man." Even if what Lilyanna said was true, Dan meant most of it. He disagreed with just about every move Lenny Fava had made in the past week, but at least the guy stood for something. Believed in…something.

A lot of good that did him. Betrayed by a woman he trusted. Shot to death. Drowned in his own blood at the bottom of an empty swimming pool.

Mara signaled that they should leave Gloria alone for a while, and Dan followed her advice emphatically. She would know. Mara worked in death, in grief, knew the nasty shapes it took, knew the sight and smell of it. This was all new for Dan.

The gunshots fell silent too. A stalemate. Dan had dropped

his radio in the mad dash to keep up with Mara, and Lenny's radio had shattered under their synchronized cannonball into the pool. They were trapped in these trenches alone, with no means of communication with the base. And it was cold, God, it was cold. Dan and Mara huddled, backs against the south edge of the pool, shivering together. His ass was damp from snow, Mara's fingers were like popsicles.

"Maybe we could sneak b-back," Mara said after a while. "Maybe he won't see us."

Dan rubbed her arms, her legs, tried to get some friction going. "He could be anywhere."

Literally, anywhere. Rico's head could pop over the edge of the pool any second now. Fish in a barrel. Humans in a bathtub. Mara's nose was white.

"We can't just stay here, Danny. We'll freeze."

Dan spotted a pool skimmer in the snow. They must've tripped over it earlier. He crawled over and retrieved it—the metal pole was so cold that it burned—and then he hoisted the net into the air, waved it above the pool line, made it dance in the dark. A gunshot splintered the silence and Dan dropped the skimmer from fright.

"Damn," he said.

A gaping hole right through the middle of the net. Dead center. A beautiful shot, really. Dan couldn't help but admire it.

"Rico," Mara said.

"Rico," Dan confirmed.

He collapsed back into the snow, knocked his head against the pool wall a few times. "Fuckin' *Madge*. What do we do?" He repeated, "He could be anywhere."

Mara huddled up to him again. "We could try shouting, 'Marco.'"

Gloria stirred for the first time in a while. She cuddled up next to her husband in the snow, pulled his limp arm from under the coat and rubbed her cheek with it. She whispered to him, something soft, and then lay still, her head against his enormous chest. They looked like one of those embracing couples unearthed in the ashes of Pompeii.

"M-maybe they'll send people," Mara said.

"Who?"

"Alan and Charles. They wouldn't leave us here."

"Yeah."

"You think they would?"

Dan didn't know. He clamped his teeth shut to keep them from chattering. Mara kicked some snow from her sneaker.

"Lilyanna got away."

"We don't know that. She could be tangled up in a pool chair up there, full of bullet holes."

Mara liked the sound of that. "Say more things."

"Maybe she fell in the l-lazy river on top of Madge, and they both broke their necks. Maybe Lilyanna's extensions got sucked into one of the pool pumps and scalped her."

Mara's lips were nearly transparent. "M-maybe she fell and one of her boobs popped."

"We have to hold on to hope."

Mara placed an ear to Dan's chest. "People like Lilyanna always get away."

"What about people like us?" Dan asked.

"People like us f-freeze to death in the Bahamas."

They sat silently for a while, and even though Dan was suddenly very tired, he knew they shouldn't sleep. But man, a nap would be nice... Just, you know, a little shut-eye... Twenty minutes, give or take, recharge a bit... Dan stiffened his back. No. *No.* He had to fight it. Mara too. Sleep was the enemy. Fuck sleep. Super overrated. If he could just talk, if he could just keep her talking...

"I wanted to tell you something," he said.

Mara stared up at him.

"You know—you know how I make all those smart and, like, really thoughtful comments about movies or TV shows after we watch them?"

"Mm-hm."

"I read them on the internet."

"What?"

"I read them on the internet, and I just r-repeat what other people figured out. And I make it sound like I thought of it, like I'm really good at noticing things. I'm not."

"Why do you do that?"

"I want you to think that I'm smart."

She laughed. Some color returned to her cheeks. "What? Danny, that's the most pathetic thing I've ever heard."

"Just w-wait a while. I've got worse."

"Can I tell *you* something?"

Dan nodded. "Yeah."

"I really don't want to die wearing your fart pants."

She *was* wearing Dan's fart pants. She'd pulled them on last night and never took them off.

"You should be honored to wear my fart pants. They're the most comf-comfortable pants in the world."

"They're really comfortable."

"Have you tried farting in them?"

"No. Should I?"

"Make yourself at home."

"I like how they have pockets. My pajama pants don't have pockets, which is the stupidest—what's this?"

She pulled a creased Polaroid from the pocket. It was the photo from Dr. Shae's observatory, the group photo with the woman with the bushy black hair Dan was sure he knew, sure he recognized. He'd forgotten all about her. Dr. Shae's cabin was a lifetime ago.

Mara studied the picture and laughed at the absurdity of it. "Why do you have a picture of *Jane MacCallum* in your pocket? And who are these other people?"

Dan's heart stopped. "Wait. What did you just say?"

"That's Jane MacCallum. The woman we saw on *Disappearance Report*. I told you I joined her subreddit."

Dan sat straight up. JANE MACCALLUM. *That's who it was!* Jane MacCallum. They had just watched her episode of *Disappearance Report* a few weeks ago. Dan had even brought it up while they were cutting templates in the ballroom.

It was a good episode. Jane was a Navy pilot in the '80s, top of her class or something, some real *Top Gun* shit. Her plane went down during a training exercise off the south coast of Florida. Well, that was one theory anyway, because no wreckage was recovered. Some thought she defected. Others said she was abducted by aliens, because the last thing she said over the radio was something about bright lights... Either way, another unsolved mystery. Add it to the pile, pass the popcorn.

Damn. Jane MacCallum. Mara got it immediately.

Wait though. Why did—

"Why do you have a Polaroid of Jane MacCallum in your pocket?"

Dan blinked at her. "I found it. I—it was in Dr. Shae's observatory."

"Why would *he* have a Polaroid of Jane MacCallum?"

"I don't know."

"Wait. Is that Shae in the picture? He's younger, but…"

"I thought so too."

Now Mara sat up, and the two of them searched each other's eyes for an answer. Mara looked at the Polaroid again, and then back at Dan.

"Was this taken on the island?"

"I don't know. How would I know?" He felt accused somehow. "It kind of looks like the woods north of here."

Mara clicked her tongue. "Is this weird?"

"You know, it feels pretty fucking weird."

"She disappeared off the south coast of Florida, Danny."

"I know."

"Where's Dr. Shae been, anyway?"

"Lilyanna asked her people to leave him alone, but—" A thought smacked Dan so hard that he recoiled. He used the side of the pool to stand, shattering the ice in his joints. He paced and mumbled, "*Could we make it? It'd be risky. Yeah, right, but staying here is risky too. I could go alone. And leave them? That's not right. What if I—hm. No, no. Hm.*"

Mara used Danny's arm to pull herself up. "Danny, what is it?"

"There's a tunnel."

"I know," she said.

"No, another tunnel."

"Another tunnel?"

"Another tunnel. That Rico and his men don't know about."

Mara scoffed. "What the hell is up with this island?"

"It leads to Dr. Shae's cabin. Right to it. Shae may be able to help us. He helped me before. It would at least get us away from"—he threw his hands in the air—"this."

"Where's the entrance?"

Dan pointed. "Behind B. The garden. There's a boulder with a false bottom. I used it to get back here the night of the storm."

"You didn't find that strange at the time, Danny? Why are you just now telling me about a *second* tunnel? And there's a picture of *Jane MacCallum* in your pants!"

"It's been a chaotic few days!" He glanced at Gloria and lowered his voice. "It's our only shot."

"They'll pick us off on the way."

Dan conceded the point. It was risky. "Yeah. But there's more cover than if we were to run for C."

"Less cover than if we were to stay here."

"We can't stay here. We're dead here."

Mara bit her thumbnail. "Danny, I don't know."

"It's okay. I do."

He wasn't sure where this calcification of confidence was coming from, maybe it was the frostbite, maybe it was what Mara said to him last night, but something scraping the inside of his gut told him this was the right move, the only move, the only way he could possibly protect himself, and his wife, and even Gloria. They'd have to run like hell though.

"Danny, if we leave this pool, there's no coming—"

Dan seized her shoulders. "You made the call with the wedding ambush. I make this one."

Confidence must be contagious. Mara's eyes narrowed, she nodded. "Okay," she said. "Your call."

"My call," Dan repeated. He turned to Gloria to help her up, to tell her the plan, but she was already stirring.

They carefully brought her to her feet. She was like a bag of frozen peas. She softly placed Lenny's arm back under the coat, tucked him in like he was just going down for the night. There was snot hardened to her face, her false eyelashes dangled by a thread.

"We have to go, Gloria," Mara said softly. "We'll come back for Lenny. We will. But we have to get ourselves out of here, we're shooting for—"

"I heard," Gloria said. She sniffed. "I heard, doll." She put a hand on each of their cheeks. They were cold—so cold—but somehow warm too. Dan leaned into it, thought of his mom back home.

"We'll have to run," he said. "Can you run?"

"Tramps like us were born to run," Gloria said, gazing down at her Lenny. She smiled and wiped her eye. "But I'm runnin' the other way."

"What?"

"I'll run the other way, handsome. You two run toward the tunnel, the boulder, whatever it is. You two go, and you go fast, okay? That Rico, with the shooting, he's too good. He's too good.

But if I go first, in the other direction, that'll give yous a chance. He's focused on me, right, and *boom*, the two lovebirds slip right out from under him. Oh, it's romantic, if you think about it."

Protests from Mara and Dan were jumbled. You can't— Gloria, no—we have to go together—don't be crazy—

She just smiled again, pulled them both in for a hug. "Not another word, okay? I made up my mind. It's what my Lenny would've done."

"He'll kill you," Dan said.

She shrugged. "Would that be so bad? So I'm back with Lenny again. I don't know. I like it."

"Gloria," Mara said. "You can't do this."

She was doing it. She gave Lenny one last kiss, brushed through Dan and Mara, and crawled her way up to the shallow end and over to the pool steps. Dan and Mara followed. Once there, they all sat crisscross applesauce, out of sight.

Gloria touched their cheeks again. "Look at you two," she said. The pain in her eyes could fill the pool, fill it right back up to the brim and drown them all. "It's the most beautiful thing in the world, what you got. Okay?" She peered up the steps. "So I'll go first, and I'm going to break right, okay? Toward C. And you wait a second, but only a second, and then you rush toward the garden. Hold each other's hands. Come on. There you go."

"Gloria," Mara said, "please. You don't have to do this."

Gloria clung to the first step. Her head was dangerously close to the pool line. "You know, it's weird. The dark didn't really bother me till now." She took a deep breath. "You two be careful, okay? And hold hands. Okay."

Dan thought to grab her, thought to pin her down and

convince her not to do it, thought of what Lenny might say, how he was somewhere in the sky cursing Dan out, saying, How the fuck could you let her do this? That's my girl there, how could you not protect my girl?

Gloria almost leapt forward but caught herself. "Oh. Almost forgot." She tugged a pistol from the waist of her jeans and handed it to Dan. "That was Lenny's. You keep it."

It was heavy. He turned it over. "I've never shot a gun in my life."

A wry smile stretched across Gloria's face. She leaned in. "Let you in on a secret. Neither had Lenny. Ha!"

She took another deep breath, nodded once more at Dan and Mara, and was gone. As promised, she broke right at the top of the stairs. She lost her footing on an icy patch, almost rejoined them in the pool, but she recovered and was off. Dan clutched Mara's hand, said, "Ready?" but didn't wait for a response. As their feet left the final step and landed on textured cement, the first gunshot cracked like a whip. Mara screamed, but they didn't stop, they didn't look back, Dan was laser focused on Building B, on the garden behind it, on the tunnel to salvation. His heart ripped against his chest, the cold disappeared.

Another gunshot. Then many more, but coming from Building C. They were firing back! Dan and Mara hurdled a lounge chair, darted through half a dozen palm trees, and burst through a frozen canopy. They hit an ice patch too and lost their balance completely, ended up on their asses behind a pile of inflatable pool rings. As Dan scrambled to lift himself and then Mara, the pool rings exploded, one by one, a sickening pop each time. Mara shoved him.

"*Go! Keep going!*"

They sound like wasps. That was the best way Dan could think to describe the bullets, like wasps shooting past his ear, pissed-off wasps, wasps on a mission to finish some wasp-related business. They passed a row of ceramic planters that shattered in succession, like in Indiana Jones, and then they dove for safety behind the stucco siding of Building B. The gunshots ceased. They were safe here—momentarily, anyway—out of the line of fire. Dan gathered his breath, wheezed, and he and Mara gave each other another once over, checking feverishly for wasp holes.

"I'm good," Dan said breathlessly, patting her hand.

"I think I am too." Mara squinted, tried to see Building C. "I can't see. Do you think she made it? I can't see her."

Dan didn't answer.

Mara bent over, hugged her knees. "Jesus, Danny, how did it get this bad?"

"I think things turned a corner when they emptied the vending machines." He stood straight. "Come on. We have to move."

30

"Oh baby, that feels good."

Mara warmed her hands over Dr. Shae's fireplace. Dan kicked off his shoes and peeled the wet socks from his feet. His toes danced next to the flames. "Ahh."

Dr. Shae wasn't there, which was odd, because who lights a fire and leaves? His radio was gone too. Dan didn't put much thought into it. The heat was too good. Wrap me in heat, he thought. Roll me in it like it's a warm tortilla and I'm spicy chorizo.

They sat on the splintered wood floor awhile, the flames doing most of the talking. Mara propped her head on Dan's shoulder. When they had warmed up completely, she said, "Tell me she made it."

Dan scoffed without thinking, the way he instinctively did when someone said something absurd. There was no way Gloria made it. No way. She was slower than them. Older. She smoked like wildfire. And she was heading in a direction with virtually no cover. Dan hated it, he hated everything that'd happened in the past week, but there was no point lying about it. She hadn't made it.

Mara blinked up at him.

"She made it," Dan said. "Definitely."

Her head returned to his shoulder. "Okay. Now what?"

"Well," Dan said, glancing into the kitchen, "he had Bagel Bites last time."

"I'm talking about this," Mara said, digging around for the Polaroid. "Where did you find this?"

Dan helped Mara off the last rung of the ladder and into the stagnant pitch-black observatory. He inched along the metal walls and felt for a light switch.

"Last time I was here, this place was a wreck," he said. "Hurricane Rico. Shit. My phone's dead."

"I've got an idea," Mara said, and she disconnected from Dan and scampered down the ladder in the dark. She returned with a candle.

"Ooh, old school," Dan said. "Nice."

They found the switch in no time, and soon the sterile lights of the observatory snapped on in quadrants. The room looked nothing like the conclusion of Dan's previous visit—Shae had put everything back in its place, filed every loose sheet of paper, computers humming again. This was a proper observatory. The pearl white ceiling stretched dozens of feet into the air and was rounded on top, like being inside R2-D2. Dan spun in place with his hands out because the room was alive with the sound of science.

Mara knocked on the telescope. It bonged like a church bell. "It's incredible," she said. "Random, but incredible."

"Right here," Dan said. "I was behind this filing cabinet. The picture slid underneath as Rico tore the place apart." He ran his finger down the cabinet that saved his life. Its drawers were labeled by decade: 1960–1970, 1971–1980, 1981–1990. And so on, all the way to present day.

"What do you think these monitors are for?" Mara asked. They were CRT box monitors, nine of them, stacked in a three-by-three grid. Mara searched for a console, some way to turn them on.

"*Mario Kart* would be incredible in here," Dan said. Mara stared at him. She wanted a real answer. "I don't know. Maybe to record cool space shit. Exoplanets."

"Exoplanets?"

"Planets orbiting stars or something. Hey, what year did Jane MacCallum go missing? Eighties, right?"

"Early eighties." Mara joined Dan at the filing cabinet. "Dude. I'm so nervous. Are we about to solve a *Disappearance Report*? What if she secretly left her husband to come work for Dr. Shae? What if they were in love? Oh my God, Danny, what if it was a torrid love affair?" She squealed and squeezed Dan's love handles.

Dan took one last look at the photograph. At Jane. "We're sure this is her?"

"One hundred percent."

"Because I'm about to open this cabinet. And Shae was actually pretty cool to me. He saved my life." His hand fell from the drawer handle. "Maybe we shouldn't."

"What? Hey, maybe we'll get arrested and extradited back to the states." She pushed past Dan and yanked the drawer herself. The files were so tightly packed that some sprung out like dough from a biscuit can.

"MacCallum…" Mara said, fingering through. "MacCallum…MacCallum…" She gasped and looked up. "Oh my God, Danny. She has a file."

"You're lying."

"I'm not."

Dan's heart pounded. This is actually happening?

Mara tugged it free. "I hold in my hand the fate of Jane MacCallum, *Disappearance Report* season two, episode four." She lowered her voice, imitated the show's histrionic narrator. "It was an overcast, some might say contemplative April day when Jane MacCallum, thirty-one, took off from Homestead Air Reserve on the southern tip of Florida. But did those cloudy skies warn of something more sinister? Something perhaps more—"

"Get to it!" Dan snatched the file from her. "Christ, this thing is thick." He placed it on the nearby desk and began flipping. "Shit. And detailed. Medical records, education, her time in the Navy… Hey, look, she received a medal. Good for her." There were photographs and test scores…a report card from the sixth grade…scanned pages from a teenage diary.

What the hell?

"She was beautiful," Mara said. "But this is creepy. This is way more than an employee file."

It *was* creepy. Dental records, fingerprints, phone logs, credit card receipts. Information about a…miscarriage? She'd miscarried in '79. Dan felt gross reading it. This wasn't his business.

Why was it *Dr. Shae's* business?

"What about her time here?" Mara asked. "Anything about her time here?"

Dan flicked to the end. "Nothing. It stops in '82."

Mara returned to the cabinet, scanned a few more folders. "Danny. There's a second file." It was even thicker than the first. Mara plopped it on the desk, and a giant thud echoed through the dome.

Dan read aloud from the first page, some kind of report. *"Jane MacCallum, test subject NA-31220, acquired on April twenty-third, 1982—"*

"Test subject?"

"—recovered from plane wreckage incited by optical amplification interference." Dan slammed the folder shut and stared up at Mara, his eyes saucers. His stomach barrel-rolled as he pushed the file away. "Fuck this."

"No, Danny, we can't stop now. What's optical amplification?" Mara leaned over his shoulder, read further. *"Subject is recovering in medical ward, wounds superficial...* Yeah, yeah, okay... *Upon recovery, subject will be released... Will assess mental, emotional, metabolic response to controlled stimuli on ongoing basis...* What the hell is this? What was he doing to her?"

"I don't know. I have no idea." He had some idea, an insane idea, but saying that idea aloud would mean introducing it to the universe. Better to keep that thought inside, in his brain's filing cabinet, for all of eternity.

We should leave, he thought, forget all this. Crawl back to the fireplace where things made sense. Fire good. Flame warm. Feel nice.

But Mara, never wary of introducing her thoughts to the universe, flipped through a few more pages and then declared what they both knew. "Jane wasn't an employee. She was an *experiment*."

Dan paced the observatory, squeezed his temples. How could the sun exploding be the second-weirdest thing to happen this vacation? He suddenly stopped in his tracks, a thought struck him like a bolt of lightning. He spun to Mara. "I think she's buried here," he said.

"What?"

"There's a small graveyard in the woods not far from here. I found it the night of the storm. I asked Shae about it, he made it sound like employees of ShaeTech were buried here. Like, really devoted employees who loved…exoplanet work or whatever. I read some names on the headstones. One of them might've said"—Dan racked his brain, knocked against his skull to wake it up—"I think one of them might've said *Jane*."

"What the hell is ShaeTech?"

"Shae's father's company. Aerospace. They made bonnets."

"Bonnets?"

"Ballutes? Something. I don't know. A parachute thing. But they had a research division too that was on this island, this observatory, and Dr. Shae ran that."

"And studied exoplanets."

"Right."

Mara, still nose-deep in the file, gasped. She held a new Polaroid in her quivering hand. It was a photo of a cabin and observatory—the very structure they were inside—nestled in a thick bed of snow. Underneath, a caption.

July 14, 1983—our first snow!

"Snow," Mara said. "In the Bahamas. In *July*."

"What the fuck?" Dan said. He paused, really put some oomph into the next one: "What the *fuck*?"

His brain was melting, dripping down his throat, evaporating against his heart like water on a hot pan. He closed his eyes for a moment, made fists, clenched his teeth. "The file cabinet. Check this year."

Mara was on her knees in a flash, tearing open the bottom drawer. It was packed with files too, smaller files, but hundreds of them. Dan couldn't believe what he was about to say.

"Check for our names."

Mara glared at him. "What?"

"Check for our names."

Mara gasped. Again. She was a great gasper. If Fitzgerald wrote a book about her, it'd be titled *The Great Gaspy*, because there was something very haunting about a Mara gasp, something bone-chilling. She held a hand to her mouth and pulled out a file.

"*Foster, Dan*," she read. She flicked the file across the floor to him, dove back into the cabinet. She screeched, tugged out another. "*Nichols, Mara*. Danny. What is this?"

Dan sat on the floor, took a deep breath, and opened his file. His passport photo. Screenshots of his Facebook, his Instagram, his LinkedIn. God, he really needed to update his LinkedIn—it still listed him as a busboy at Longhorn Steakhouse. The next page was a Google Earth photo of his apartment.

Mara scooched backward across the floor till she was next to him. "Danny. He's got—oh my God. He's got my mom's name and Raveena's and pictures of her house. He's got—this is my old *MySpace*, Danny. *I* don't even know how to get on this!"

Dan glanced over. "You had pink highlights? Is that a lip ring?"

"There was a Hot Topic phase in high school. Danny, he knows where I work. Look at this form. *ER nurse, St. Francis Hospital, Memphis, Tennessee.* My car's registration. My degree, my masters, the award I got from AACN. This is everything, Danny. This—it's everything." Mara returned to the cabinet.

Dan's file was noticeably thinner than hers. "Well," he said, "it's not all accurate. Says here I'm five foot ten."

"Babe. You are five ten."

"What? I'm six foot even."

"No, you're not. I told Dr. Wallace to say you were six foot because I knew what it meant to you."

"*Excuse me?*"

"You didn't think it was strange you hit a growth spurt at twenty-seven?"

Dan scratched his head. "A little, but we took that yoga class at the Y. And I told you I felt something pop, remember? I thought—"

"Hey, Rico's got a file too."

Dan made a face like, *Ooh, gimme,* and Mara slid it over. Dan dove right in.

Mara stood, marched over to the table. "Jane's file is different than ours. Observations of her time on the island, relationships, how she fed herself. He *caught* her, Danny, he kept her here, and he observed her. He studied her every move." She shuffled through more pages. "It was before the resort, when the island was mostly wilderness. There were others too. He studied them like rats."

That was interesting, but Dan was absolutely *loving* Rico's file. "He's from Albuquerque. He's been to prison. Shocker. His full name's Federico. I guess that makes sense, but I hadn't thought about it. Damn, there's some really good stuff in here. Mara—oh, my God." Dan laughed victoriously and slapped the paper. "You're not going to believe this. He—"

Mara snatched the file from Dan and tossed it away. "Forget Rico. What the hell was going on on this island?"

Dan spotted a remote control on another desk near the telescope. He aimed it at the grid of monitors. They clicked on one by one.

"You get all those gasps out of your system?" he asked, swiveling Mara's head to the screens. She hadn't.

The monitors showed every conceivable angle of the resort on rotation. Building A lobby. B. C. Each of the pool decks, where guests sporadically exchanged fire with guards. Four views of the beach. The garden. The Great Lawn, its amphitheater. Dan pressed the channel-up button. Jesus. Rooms now. Guests' *private* rooms. There was a couple cowering in the corner behind their bed in Building C. A man frantically packing a bag in Building A. In another A room, an old man nonchalantly eating grapes from the vine, butt naked.

"I'm going to be sick," Mara said.

"There must be hundreds of cameras here," Dan whispered.

"That means…" Something caught her throat. "That means he saw us…"

"There are so many rooms," Dan said. "You don't know that

he was watching ours. Or when." It was hardly reassuring. If a lonely old man wanted to watch anyone in the shower, or in bed, or in her bikini, it was Mara. Rage twisted Dan's face. Blood pooled in his cheeks. Exoplanets, my ass. I'm going to make him an ex...o...person. Dan couldn't think of any good threats. He was too furious.

Mara shrieked as a cabin door slammed open below them. She slinked behind Dan, who snatched the remote and clicked off the monitors. Together he and Mara walked backward, positioning themselves as far from the observatory ladder as possible. Mara tapped Dan's shoulder and pointed to his waistband.

Right. The gun.

He aimed it at the ladder the same way he'd seen people in movies aim guns. He waited. As each metallic rung of the ladder cried out, Mara's grip on his back strengthened. Dan realized too late that he didn't know if the gun had a safety.

He was the lowest form of man. Truly.

Dr. Shae's bald head popped into view like a gopher's. He smiled warmly at them, smiled at the gun, waved it off like, Oh, of course you're upset, but this is a big misunderstanding, and either way I'm happy to see you. He pulled himself into the room. He was wearing a lab coat, which wasn't helping the mad scientist vibe, and he looked less groomed than usual. The hair on the sides of his head poked out like it was trying to escape from his brain, and his beady little eyes had grown three sizes.

"The tunnel?" Shae asked.

"The tunnel," Dan confirmed.

"Well, I believe congratulations are in order." Shae brushed snow from his coat. He raised his hands and clapped them together above his head. "Marriage! That is wonderful. I have good bourbon downstairs. A drink, perhaps?"

Mara, who must've sensed Shae was physically harmless, stomped out from behind Dan. She pointed at him, and words spewed from her like lava. "You've got a lot to answer for."

Shae nodded at Dan. "She is lovely. Truly. Congratulations again."

"But you knew that," Dan said, the gun steady.

Mara said, "We've seen the files. We've seen the cameras. You've been spying on us!"

Shae sighed and considered Mara like he would an approaching rain cloud, an inconvenience. He glanced at the piles of loose paper on the ground, noted the new location of the television remote. He put his hands up like, You got me. There was no use lying anymore.

"Not *you*," he said. "Not specifically. And *spying* is such a sharp word, no?" He tapped the tips of his fingers together. "*Studying* is softer. More appropriate too, in this case. But—yes. Still upsetting, judging by your faces. To be fair, you were not supposed to find out like this."

"*Talk*," Dan said. "ShaeTech. The truth this time." He was beginning to understand the appeal of guns. He felt powerful. Felt like he could take on the world with this thing.

"Please, Mr. Foster, could you lower that? We can talk, but please. No need for that. You are not Rico Flores."

"You gonna tell us the truth?"

"Yes."

Dan placed the gun in his waistband but kept a cautious hand on it. "Go. You weren't looking for exoplanets, were you?"

Shae inhaled deeply. "We were at first, absolutely. The research division of ShaeTech. See, my father never cared for my research. He was more interested in profitable ventures. I think he was ecstatic when I told him we should purchase the island. If it would keep me out of his office every day, away from the board, his shareholder meetings, he would pay any price."

"Oh, boo-hoo," Mara said.

"Background, Mrs. Foster, not for sympathy."

"Okay," Dan said. "Don't need your life story, Doc. Jane MacCallum."

At mention of her name, Shae's face turned the color of milk.

"Yeah," Mara said. "We know about Jane."

"Can I sit?" Shae asked. He looked like he might faint. "Please. I would just like to—if I could sit. This is quite a lot for me, you see, it's been decades."

Mara scoffed. "Quite a lot for *you*?"

Dan kicked Shae a desk chair. He sat.

"It started with exoplanets, Mr. Foster. Truly." He unrolled a chart on the wall. There were planets—some more detailed than others—in various colors, purples and greens and reds and blues. "There are thousands of them. Thousands of planets that could potentially harbor life. Correction: thousands *confirmed*. There are millions more. We spent years searching for them, discovering them, naming them."

"Okay," Dan said.

"But it was akin to stamp collecting, Mr. Foster. What good does mere discovery do? Who cares if we can proclaim that a distant speck of light in an endless universe may support life somehow, someday?"

"Sounds important to me," Dan said.

"Me too," Mara said.

"That is because you have been programmed to ask the wrong questions."

"I didn't ask a question," Dan said.

"Me either," Mara said.

"As human beings, we want to look up—no—we *need* to look up, to see what lies beyond, to gaze into the great unknown and turn it into the known. It is our ego, Mr. Foster, our great hubris, to seek understanding of the universe when we have yet to even truly understand our own planet—to understand ourselves."

"Feel like we're a bit off track here," Dan said.

"It is a wonder our species still exists. Do you know how close we have come to the brink of extinction? From famine? Disease? War? We are but a cosmic blip on the windshield of time, and one day she will turn on her wipers and there will nary be a trace of us. Do you understand?"

Shae stood, his strength returning. He paced. "And we talk of inhabiting other planets." He chuckled. "Talk of sending groups of people to populate a point in the sky. To farm the land, to build shelter, construct a society. It's poppycock."

Who says *poppycock*?

"We've fought wars for thousands of years over claims on mountains of sand. We brutalize one another over books of fables!"

He waltzed toward them, buttoned the front of his coat like he was receiving the Nobel Prize. "So, yes, Mr. Foster. One day I stopped looking out, and I looked down. At my feet. My island. I knew if humans were ever to take that first step onto a distant planet—and hope to survive—we must have more data. Data unsoiled by the passage of time or geopolitical influence. Data about *ourselves*. Can a group of human beings ripped from their homes, their lives, really rebuild civilization on alien land? Or will human nature—as it often does—get in the way?"

"This is starting to feel like a villain monologue," Dan said. He looked at Mara. "Are we in a villain monologue right now?"

"So you kidnapped people," Mara said. "Set them loose on the island. Studied them like they weren't even human."

"Studied them *precisely* as humans," Shae said. He sat back down, rested his cheek in his hand. "My father, for all his faults, finally recognized the value of my research. He funded improvements to the island for my study. The tunnel. Additional hangars, equipment. Other things."

"Other things?" Mara asked.

"We secured nine wonderful subjects…fascinating subjects. I grew to love each of them. I think they loved me too, in a way."

"Surely," Dan said.

"Why take them against their will?" Mara asked. "I'm sure there are plenty of people who'd volunteer a few years of their life for something stupid like this."

"Yes. But how many would volunteer the *remainder* of their life?"

That certainly sent a chill through the room.

"I didn't want those who would volunteer. I wanted a sampling of the everyman—those who would actually be called upon should our species be forced to inhabit another planet." He twisted in the seat. "Oh, you should have seen what they accomplished. Farms, fisheries, medicine. They developed their own customs, their own traditions. Romances blossomed. They even had holidays! Every nine months or so, when the first of the new coconuts fell from the trees, that was Coconut Day."

Dan remembered the handmade farming tools that Lenny found in one of the hangars. Were those—

Shae rolled backward across the observatory, seized the remote. The monitors clicked on, but it wasn't a live feed of the resort anymore. Dan recognized the muted colors and graininess of eighties home videos. Each screen featured a person performing tasks on the island. Chopping wood, gathering berries, fishing, constructing some sort of shelter.

"That is Robert, there, in the top left," Shae said. "He would sing sometimes when the team was homesick. A baritone. And Mr. Houser, the Black gentleman in the center. Big as a house, that one. Would you believe he was a Somali pirate before we intercepted him?"

"I'd believe just about anything at this point," Dan said.

"Not one word of English. By the end, he was conversing in full sentences with Jane. There's our sweet Jane, right of center." He sighed like a schoolboy whose crush had asked to borrow a pencil. "Truly magnificent. Intelligent, kind, could work a hammer as good as any of the men. And beautiful."

"She had a husband," Mara said. "A life. You took that from her."

"No scientific endeavor has ever been achieved without sacrifice."

"Can I hold the gun a minute?" Mara asked.

"You know," Dan said, "we learned about your girl on Netflix. *Disappearance Report*. People are asking questions about her. It's only a matter of time."

"Oh, yes," Shae said. "I meant to watch it."

"You didn't even watch it?"

"I tried. It asked for my Apple ID. I entered my password, but it would not work."

Dan scratched his cheek. "You shouldn't need your Apple ID for Netflix. Those are different things."

"I know. I had to download the app."

"Did you hit *forgot password*?"

"I tried. It said it would send me an email. It did not."

"That's impossible. It always sends the email."

Mara put her hand on Dan's shoulder and glared.

"I—sorry," Dan said. "It's just—he's an astrophysicist and he can't work Netflix."

"What happened to them?" Mara asked.

Shae blinked. "What?"

Mara motioned to the monitors, repeated herself slowly. "What happened to them?"

"Oh." Shae straightened his coat. "Terrible. Terrible, though informative. A potent strain of flu swept through. Wiped them out. Mr. Houser held out the longest, simply a beast of a man, but alone and hungry, eventually he succumbed too."

"The flu," Dan said.

"The fucking *flu*," Mara emphasized.

"The flu can be quite deadly without proper medical care, especially in a malnourished host. Despite several years of island development, our band of survivors was unprepared. One nasty winter, and that was that." He closed his eyes, cupped his hands in his lap. "Invaluable data."

Dan wanted to strangle the guy, to pop his little head from

his body like a particularly ugly Ken doll. How'd they get the *flu*? Why didn't they treat them? And—

"Winter," Mara said.

"Yeah," Dan said.

Mara shuffled through the folder on the desk, found the Polaroid of the cabin in the snow. "Explain this."

Shae lit up when he saw it, held it at arm's length. "Oh, now, this was a momentous day. Where did you find this? I have been searching for it."

"Explain it," Mara said.

"Why, this is the day we knew the dome worked!"

All sense of feeling left Dan's extremities. He could barely form his mouth around the words he said next. "The what?" He gripped Mara. "Say—say that again."

"The snow, Mr. Foster," Shae said, pointing to the photograph. "That's how we knew the dome worked."

The dome? Dome? The word hit Dan's ear, exploded inside his skull, and sent him and Mara spiraling. No way. No fucking way. A *dome*? Like—a dome, dome?

"Would you two like to sit?" Shae asked, standing. "You appear frazzled. I apologize. Had I not mentioned that?"

"A fucking dome," Dan said breathlessly.

"A dome." Mara pulled on Dan's clothing, clung to him like he was the last shred of reality.

Over the…over the island? There was a *dome* over the island? What kind of cheap-ass…science-fiction…Stephen King Pauly Shore bullshit was this?

"Yes, a dome." Shae made the shape of it with his hands. "You know, think like a football stadium, but quite a bit larger.

We knew if we really wanted to conduct this experiment, we had to stretch the test beyond the Bahamian climate. Beyond Earth's climate even! So, we built the dome at considerable expense. The gift of a lifetime from my father, truly. Well, besides the island itself. It retracts into the ocean, see. And with it we could control the weather, the temperature, create storms, project sky patterns. It was like—well, it was like—"

"A snow globe," Dan said. He retrieved the one he'd caught in the dark from atop the filing cabinet.

"Precisely! A snow globe!"

Mara lunged forward, seized Shae by the lapels of his lab coat. "Did the sun explode?"

"My dear, please unhand me—"

She shook him. "Did the sun explode?"

"Mr. Foster, please retrieve your—"

"Answer her," Dan demanded through gritted teeth.

"Look at me," Mara said. "Look at me, you fucking psycho. Did. The sun. Explode?"

"Well…" Shae chuckled and patted her shoulder. "Well, no, dear. No. Of course not."

31

There's this random YouTube video. It features a kid—in swim trunks—rinsing off after a day at the pool.

The boy is minding his own business, like one generally does in a public shower, and he's shampooing his hair. But when he goes to rinse out the shampoo, more suds appear. Confused, he rinses again—more suds. Then more. *More.* On and on. This stuff won't rinse out no matter how hard he scrubs. In fact, it's reproducing. Taking over his scalp. He gets increasingly frustrated, right, because shampooing is a simple process. Rinse, maybe repeat if you have the time, that's it. Done. But these suds keep coming back, multiplying, and after a while the kid begins to lose sanity. He rubs his scalp like a madman, throttles the showerhead in a vain attempt to choke reality into submission. He calls for help. His very existence is fracturing at the seams, his grasp of the physical world torn asunder by a bottle of Head & Shoulders.

Why aren't things the way they're supposed to be?

It's his friends, of course. They're behind him, discreetly

squirting additional shampoo onto his scalp after each scrub. They own up to the prank. The kid's relieved. But a part of him is also broken, his brain dented in the section where the immutable laws of nature are stored.

That's how Dan felt.

Mara must've felt similarly because she clocked Shae so hard that he spun. She shook the pain from her hand as she retreated into Dan's arms.

"My mom," she said, and she was weeping.

"Yeah," Dan said. "Yeah."

Dan pegged the snow globe at Shae's feet. He meant for it to shatter in an intimidating way, but it just kind of bounced off the floor and rolled away.

Instead Dan cocked the gun—cocking a gun is harder than it looks in movies—and he aimed it at Shae's bloodied face.

"*What's real?*" Dan screamed.

Shae wiped the blood from his nose with his wrist. "Mr. Foster, please—"

"If you don't tell me what's going on right fucking now, I'm going to *lose* it. Is Tizoc real? Lilyanna? Are you telling me the fucking sun is shining outside"—he couldn't even say it—"outside the *dome?*"

"This response," Shae said, "is—is fascinating. I thought perhaps you would react in anger, but the violence, this outburst of violence, it is fascinating."

"Stop talking to us like we're experiments!"

"It's real," Shae said, his hands in the air. "All of it."

"Except the sun exploding," Mara said.

Shae nodded, conceded the point. "Except that. Yes."

"Talk."

"I—please. Okay. Yes. After the experiment with Jane and the others, I had wonderful data. Wonderful. But it was incomplete. We had so much more planned with the dome of course, so much we had yet to learn. But my father, you see—my father. He was always risk averse. He became even more so in old age. Please, Mr. Foster, is the gun absolutely necessary?"

"Keep talking."

"He shut down the experiment after their deaths. People began poking around. It worried him. He lined the correct pockets—he was always good at that—but he forbade me from further experiments, cut the ShaeTech research budget down to nothing. I was to stay in my observatory like a good boy and continue my search for exoplanets. That was it.

"When he passed, the company soon went under. But he had gifted the island to me. I partnered with the Space Telescope Science Institute. The institute, of course, had no notion of the important work done here. No idea of the dome that lay just below the ocean's surface. They only knew of the observatory. So, for decades, Mr. Foster, that was it—I was a lowly astronomer, and I was content to die a lowly astronomer, buried with my unfinished research. I made peace. Until one day, four years ago, while standing atop the rocky cliffs just east of here, a thought occurred."

"Tizoc," Mara said.

"Precisely." Shae soaked his nose on the sleeve of his lab coat. "So much of my island lay untouched. Besides the astronomical benefits, I think you will agree—it is quite beautiful here. Certainly an attractive destination. The answer was right in front of me the entire time. A *resort!*

"What would a resort bring exactly, besides bright lights, loud music, and drunken tourists? I'll tell you. Hundreds of new subjects, delivered directly to me, served on a platter like hors d'oeuvres. This was a revelation—an epiphany. I pored over the idea for weeks. I just needed the right buyer."

"Where's the button, asshole?" Mara said. She broke from Dan and combed the room for a control panel, a lever, something. "Where's the button to retract the dome?"

"Before they both died, my father did business with a Cassandra Sheridan," Shae said. "Brody's mother. I knew the family, knew the boy, though not well. A California trust-fund baby with more money than sense and a lifelong dream of opening a party destination somewhere tropical. Somewhere remote. The perfect candidate. I used my father's connections to schedule a meeting."

Mara tore posters from the wall as he rattled on.

"Mr. Sheridan, of course, was thrilled. We shook hands. He was to acquire nearly 90 percent of the island at an incredible price, I would keep my observatory and the airstrip. The hangars. But Brody and I quickly became more than business partners—I think if you asked, he would call me a friend—and the boy was in over his head. I offered to help him develop the resort, handle the particulars, under the guise of wanting what was best for the island. A silent partner, if you will. He would remain the figurehead, the name associated with Tizoc Grand Islands Resort and Spa. I would stay behind the scenes. I'm only an astronomer after all."

"You manipulated him," Dan said.

Shae grinned. "Mr. Sheridan certainly fits the definition of a *polezny dura*." He read the confusion on Dan's face. "A useful idiot. Soon, I had my hands in all aspects of planning Tizoc. Room layouts, building amenities. I proved my worth to Brody time and time again. It was *my* idea to cater to three distinct socioeconomic populations. *My* idea to offer deep discounts to Building C guests, target Building B guests through self-worth comparisons on social media, attract Building A visitants by going overboard on luxury. I wanted a diverse subject pool, you see, and—"

"The sun," Dan growled. "Get to the sun."

"The experiment itself had to be short," Shae said. "Tizoc's grand opening package was only two weeks long. For two weeks, I could be assured no one would attempt to come or go from the island. But what would I test?

"I knew it was essential I quickly provoke my subjects—to test the limits of what humans are capable of under duress. How humans react to something like, say, their sun dying—well, Mr. Foster, that could help inform decisions made in the event of an actual cosmic disaster. Data like that could help humanity react in the face of certain doom. This research was for the good of humanity. You must understand that."

Shae began to laugh, the same unhinged laughter from the night he and Dan shared Bagel Bites. "I convinced him—I convinced that boy—to theme the entire resort on the Aztecs, a people who famously worshipped the sun. Tizoc? The Sola Pool? *Maize?*" Shae slapped his knee. "We're in the Caribbean! It makes no sense!" He was dying. "There's a mariachi band!"

"You're insane," Dan said.

Shae wiped a tear, composing himself. "Well, Mr. Foster, there's a thin li—"

Dan shook the gun. "Do *not* say there's a thin line between insanity and genius. They always say that. There's a big line! It's a thick fucking line!"

"I can see you are upset. But think of what I have observed in just over a week, Mr. Foster! All the data gathered. Tribalism, idol worship, a developing class system. A government in its infancy. Murder, mutiny. And love! We had a *wedding*, Mr. Foster. Then a war. In fact, that's where I was before joining you. Observing the skirmish between Buildings A and C. Stupendous. Imagine having a front row seat to the Battle of Megiddo."

"The fighting on the pool deck wasn't exactly the Battle of Megiddo."

"I've captured so much of the human experience. More than I could have hoped for. And soon that data will be uploaded for the world to see. You must understand the value of that, Mr. Foster. You must understand how it will benefit future generations. Our small sacrifice—"

"Those British guys," Mara said, abandoning her search. "The ones who stole the boat."

Shae stopped. "Oh, yes, that gave me a scare. I had forgotten about the boats. Imagine those chaps' confusion when they crashed into what looked to be open sea."

"It was *you* who disabled the remaining boats," Mara said.

"I had no choice."

Dan pressed the sides of his head, tried to keep his brain from rebooting. "The cameras in our rooms."

"Brody protested, at first. But I told him they would only operate in an emergency. A safety investment. He's a bit of a prepper, that one, and so easily convinced."

Shae had done the impossible. Was Dan actually pitying Brody Sheridan?

"I must admit though," Shae continued, "not everything was my idea. Some of Mr. Sheridan's contributions, while coincidental, have been immense. Hiring that Rico character, equipping him with a rifle. Incredible. If *he* wasn't plucked right from the Normanist theory of Scandinavian conquest. And Lilyanna Collins!" Shae closed his eyes, pumped his fist. "Could there exist a better analogy for de facto military leaders created in the midst of power vacuums?"

Shae looked at them both like he was actually expecting a response.

"Have I answered all your questions?" he said, blood on his teeth now. "Can we put down the gun?"

"We saw the sun explode," Mara said. "It shattered. Cracked like an egg."

"Mixture of projections, pyrotechnics, and screens built into the dome itself. Convincing, no? I tell you, when this dome was constructed, it was ahead of its time. Father often floated the idea of licensing the technology to Disney World."

Dan thought of the island's power requirements—what Pete said in Brody's office. *The dome.*

He didn't want to pose any more questions, he really didn't, because it was clearly only feeding this demented man's ego. Shae puffed his chest out like he was a real genius, like his brain was wrinklier than anyone else's in the room.

But God, Dan had so many questions.

"We *flew* here," Dan said. "The dome couldn't've been up then."

"Very good, Mr. Foster. Remember the brief power outage your first night? You were likely asleep. Well, it was overcast, and the island lights went dark for half an hour or so, and voilà, the next morning you awoke beneath the dome."

"It's quiet," Dan said.

"Oh, state-of-the-art."

"But Alan's got the plane fixed," Mara said. "And there are other planes from Nassau scheduled to arrive in a few days…"

Something wicked flashed across Shae's eyes. "Oh," he said, "this will all be over tomorrow."

"What the hell does that mean?" Dan asked.

"When the data upload is complete, the experiment will be concluded."

"Okay. One more time: What the hell does that mean?"

Shae sneered. "Remember what I said about sacrifice? A couple of deaths make headlines—but a thousand deaths make the history books, make the annals of scientific discovery. This will be my final contribution to our species, Mr. Foster. The dome was constructed with a self—"

Dan had heard enough. It was the perfect time for some heroics, the perfect chance to impress his new wife.

He aimed the gun at Shae's leg and fired.

Couple things. First, guns are really loud in confined spaces. Like, upsettingly loud. Each of them clutched their ears, even Shae, which Dan thought was odd because he should've been clutching his freshly shot leg. Which brought Dan to his second realization—he'd missed. A near point-blank shot and he'd missed. Just immeasurably embarrassing, made even worse by the fact that they were essentially inside a metal tube, so the bullet ricocheted off the floor, up the wall, and over their heads like Tinkerbell on fire. It sparked off a few more surfaces before coming to a sizzling halt somewhere behind them. Mara shoved Dan in the shoulder, one hand still on her ear.

"What'd you do that for?"

"I was trying to take charge," Dan said meekly.

Shae bent over one of his consoles, clutched his heart, panted. "Mr. Foster. What—what on Earth were you hoping to—to accomp—"

The cabin door slammed open below, like it'd been kicked in, and footsteps rumbled across the timber floor. Shae and Dan shared a quick desperate glance, but before either could move, Rico Flores had scaled the ladder to the observatory and was screaming for them to get on their knees, rifle against his shoulder. Mara screamed something back, and Dan lifted the pistol, but Rico made quick work of that, slapping Dan across the face, one of Rico's signature slaps that sent the whole room spinning, and he snatched the pistol from Dan like he was snatching a baby's rattle. He slid it into his belt. Shae did something—Dan's vision was kind of fuzzy, he was pretty sure he clicked off the monitors—and then he approached Rico, finger wagging. Rico must not have liked that, because he hit Shae with the butt of his rifle, and Shae crumpled to the floor like a collapsing star.

Mara steadied Dan, said, "Shh, shh, hey, look at me. Look at me." And eventually his dueling visions converged, and there was his bride, as wonderful as ever, and just behind her was Rico, as big and sweaty and pissed off as ever. Dan stepped between them, held his hand toward the barrel of the rifle.

Rico seethed. His trigger finger twitched. "I've been waiting all week for this."

"Listen, though, listen," Dan pleaded. "There's something you should know. Okay? Dr. Shae—he just told us that the—"

Mara hugged Dan from behind to shut him up, nuzzled her face between his shoulder blades. They held hands, which was nice, and nobody said anything for a moment.

Then Mara whispered something loud enough for Rico to hear. "I'm surprised he's being such a little bitch about it."

Dan gasped.

"The fuck you just say?" Rico asked.

Mara dug the top of her head into Dan's back. "Oh, Rico, did you hear that? I didn't think you'd hear that. I'm sorry."

"Say it again, bitch."

"That's what I said, actually." Her face poked from behind Dan's shoulder. She spoke loudly, clearly. "I said I was surprised you were being such a little *bitch*."

Dan squeezed Mara's hand, desperately hoping it would convey that she should stop what she was doing immediately, but she only squeezed back. What was she thinking? If they just told Rico about the sun—if they just made him understand, maybe he—oh. He'd just kill them anyway, wouldn't he? Then *he'd* be the only one who knew.

"Oh, yeah?" Rico said. "How am I being a bitch?"

"I mean—after everything—you're just going to mow us down with your rifle?" She did that degrading baby voice of hers. *"My name's Wico, and I pwull this widdle piece of metal with my fingey and all my pwoblems go away. I'm a weal tough man. Waah."*

It was unclear why Rico would cry at the end of that sentence, even if in this scenario he was an infant, but Mara always ended her baby talk with *waah*.

"The fuck?" Rico said.

Dan joined in. "If you think about it, it *is* kind of pussy move." He turned to Mara. "No offense."

"None taken. Total puss move."

"Rico is Puss in Boots."

Mara laughed. "He's a Pussycat Doll!"

Breath shot from Rico's nostrils like a teased bull. He stared down the sights of the rifle. "Wonder if I could open both your skulls with one bullet?"

"That's what we're saying," Dan said. "Literally *any*body could do that." He turned to Mara. "When did guns become associated with tough guys? Is there anything more emasculating than a gun?"

"I can't think of anything," Mara said.

"For real," Dan said. "*I'm in a confrontation, let me go get my big boy toy. Then all I gotta do is point it at anyone who's mean to me, move my finger like this, and then I'll be safe.*" Dan curled his trigger finger, over and over, and Mara joined him, both curling their fingers effeminately and laughing.

"*Hey, those people said not nice things to me,*" Mara said, and she curled her finger three times.

"*Let me run down to Walmart real quick,*" Dan said, "*and after I get back, I'll show you who's boss.*"

They were in hysterics.

Rico said, "Oh, yeah? Fucking yeah?" He loosened the rifle strap, pulled the gun from his shoulder, and unloaded it, pocketing the magazine. He tossed the rifle down the ladder, it smashed against the cabin floor below. Unloaded and tossed Lenny's pistol down there too. "Think I'm a bitch? Think I can't handle you fuckers myself?"

Huh. It worked. Never underestimate the fragility of a man's ego, especially one wearing camouflage pants. Dan and Mara straightened up, regained control of themselves. Rico raised his fists, boxed with the air.

"You wanna fucking go?" he asked. "You're right, Foster. You're right. It's gonna feel much better to cave your skull in with my hands." His jabs were pretty fast, actually. And his fists were like cannonballs. And his footwork—okay, yikes, pretty impressive footwork.

"Okay, Rico," Dan said. He raised his fists. They looked like golf balls in comparison, but, you know, fake it till you make it. "You want a taste of the Foster Fury? Huh? Want me to finish what I started in the hangar?"

Dan rolled his head, sniffed real loud. Tough guys always sniff real loud before a fight.

"Kick his ass, baby," Mara said.

"Oh, he's fucking toast," Dan said. "Put some butter and jam on him, babe, because this dude's toast."

"Come on," Rico said.

"You come on," Dan said.

Dan just needed to tie Rico up for a few seconds, a precious few seconds, so Mara could slip away. Then she could tell everyone on the island what was really going on. Stop the war. Get home. Yeah. Okay. Dan could survive a few rounds with Rico. He was fucking huge, looked even bigger right now for some reason, but *okay. No problem.* David and Goliath.

Macchio vs. Cobra Kai. *Sniff.* He just needed to keep him busy for—

Rico swung left, a haymaker, but Dan saw it coming and ducked.

"Woo!" Rico screamed, and he slapped himself in the face. "That was a test, boy."

Dan motioned Mara toward the ladder, but she didn't budge. She held up her fists as a reminder for Dan to raise his.

What was she doing? *Go!*

Rico charged again, but this time he went low, his fist connecting with Dan's ribs where he'd been shot. Dan buckled, almost collapsed, but he used his last gasp of breath to hook his arm around Rico's neck and hold on for dear life. Rico's muscles spasmed. Dan was wrestling a python. Dan slapped Rico in his face with his free hand, gouged at his eyes.

He never agreed to fight clean.

Rico bellowed and employed his entire body weight to launch Dan and himself at the nine monitors on the opposite end of the observatory. They came crashing down atop them, and Dan lost his grip on Rico, lost sight of him in the avalanche of broken glass and twisted metal.

Dan groaned and pushed a monitor off his chest. His bones felt shattered like the bottom of a pretzel bag. He wheezed. "We'll—we'll call round one a draw."

Rico wasn't as slow getting up. He towered over Dan, chest heaving, and he held a broken monitor above his head, poised to strike. He was bleeding at least. Dan had made Rico Flores bleed. Something positive to reflect on as he was beaten to death with a television. Ironic, Dan thought, that his end would come beneath a television, something he adored. Like being smothered in hospice by a loved one.

Rico released a battle cry, Dan braced, but then Mara was on Rico from behind, climbing his body like a squirrel up a tree, and she dug her nails into his face, tearing at the flesh. He howled and dropped the monitor, flailed backward into the center of the observatory. He slammed her into the telescope, which let out a great big *bong*, then pried her from his back, and flung her across the room. Dan was with her in a flash, helping her up, furious, absolutely furious, mostly with Rico but with Mara a little bit too.

"You were supposed to *run*," Dan said, panting. His insides were on fire.

"He was about to replace your head with a monitor," she said, clutching her foot.

"You need your woman to fight for you, Foster?" Rico laughed, smeared the blood on his cheeks. "That's fine. That's good. You know what *mi madre* taught me about hitting women?"

Mara's eyes narrowed on something.

"You had a *mother*?" Dan shouted back, ignoring good sense because he'd thought of something funny to say. "I just assumed a moose fucked a Monster Energy drink and nine months later you crawled out!"

Mara seized Dan's collar, pressed his nose into hers. "We can't beat him like this, Danny."

Dan began to say, "Any bright ideas?" but he miraculously took flight halfway through the sentence. Rico, apparently none too fond of comments about his mother, had covered the room in 0.2 seconds flat, seized Dan, and tossed him like a discus. Dan landed on his back, but his breath had scheduled a later flight, and he gasped and kicked, and soon Rico was on top of him, eyes bloodshot, mouth frothing. Rico raised a trembling clenched fist in the air.

Dan closed his eyes and screamed, "You wanted to be a stuntman!"

This sudden proclamation bewildered Rico, which gave Dan just enough leverage to scramble out from under him. Dan stood, panting, and signaled for a time-out. "That's what you wanted to be when you grew up. Hollywood—Hollywood stuntman."

Rico lumbered to his feet, fists clenched. "I'm gonna fucking kill you."

"Wait. Wait! Hold on. I'm right, aren't I?"

Rico's eyes answered for him. Dan watched as his boorish face ping-ponged between unbridled rage and confusion.

"Hold on," Dan said, wheezing. "Hold on. Don't kill me yet. Just listen." Mara, still on the floor, slinked out of sight. "That's why you moved to LA, and that's where you met Brody. Right? You wanted to be a stuntman. Since you were a little boy."

Rico growled. "What's your fucking point?"

What *was* Dan's point? He didn't have one yet.

"My point is—my *point,* man, is that—you're being played."

Rico's face twitched. Okay, that did something. Keep going, keep going.

"Hear me out. Hear me out. You met Brody in LA, right? At the gun range. And then you started going up there together. He told you about Tizoc, and you eventually told him about your dream of being a stuntman. And how studios wouldn't even consider you because of your background."

Rico lunged forward, but Dan sidestepped him.

"How do you know," Rico said between clenched teeth. It was more statement than question.

"Brody promised he'd help you, right? He said if you'd come be head of security at Tizoc for one year, develop a security team, that he had connections in the business and could help you get stunt work. Right?"

Rico squinted at Dan.

Dan pointed at him. "I'm not wrong. Well, listen. They're, uh—they're laughing at you, man. They think you're a joke. Brody was never going to help you get a job, even before the sun exploded. He doesn't think you'd *be* a good stuntman. He thinks—and these are his words, not mine—he said your acrobatics are questionable. That you couldn't—uh—you wouldn't hit your marks in a high-pressure studio environment."

Rico snarled. "My timing is fucking impeccable."

"They said—and listen, I don't even like repeating this, but you deserve to know—they said you couldn't even *read* a script and that you had"—Dan scanned Rico's body—"feminine calves."

Rico clutched his leg, fuming. "My calves are proportionate to my overall leg shape." He rolled his pants. "I guess they think I should get implants like every other asshole in that city?" He shook his head, like, Unbelievable. "My fucking stunt reel has over six hundred views on YouTube."

Dan threw his hands in the air. "Hey, hey, you don't have to tell me. I look at you, and I see—I *see* a stuntman. Like, you've got *stunt double* written all over you. It's those guys—it's Brody, and Lilyanna, and other Building A people—"

"You're lying."

"No! If I'm lying, then tell me, Rico, tell me. How would I know? How would I know all that about you? Huh?"

Rico's eyes darted from side to side as he considered the question.

"I know all this," Dan said, "because I've heard them. I've heard them laughing. They're *playing* you. You think you're one of *them*? No way. You're Building C to them. *Less* than Building C, Rico. There's a reason the barracks are underground. You and I have *way* more in common than you and them. Come on. Think about it."

Rico's lowered his fists. He gazed past Dan, at nothing. For a second—like, a split teeny-tiny second—Dan almost felt for him. Lilyanna looked at Rico the same way she looked at Dan, as if she was confused that someone so beneath her had evolved to stand at eye level.

"You know, I wanted to write when I was younger," Dan offered.

Some color returned to Rico's cheeks. He flashed a mocking gold-toothed smile. "I bet you're a shitty fucking writer."

Okay. That didn't last long.

Rico cracked his neck with a twitch of his head. "I'll kill you first. I'll deal with them when I get home."

He didn't make it one step. Mara had found the snow globe, and she brought it down with such force that it shattered against the back of Rico's skull. His body swayed like a poorly animated cartoon before folding in on itself and hitting the floor, just a big heaping pile of man next to Shae.

He groaned.

Mara hopped over him and clutched Dan's wrist, tugging. "Good job," she said. "Come on. Quick. Before he wakes up."

Dan followed her to the ladder. "Me good job? *You* good job. How'd you shatter it? I must've—I must've knocked it loose when I threw it earlier."

"For sure," Mara assured him. "Definitely."

Just as they reached the exit hatch, the cabin door below slammed open again. Dan and Mara scrambled backward, tripping over Rico and onto their asses.

Three of Rico's guards—one of them Madge—piled up the ladder, pistols drawn. Dan scurried to shield Mara from the inevitable hail of bullets.

"Whoa," Madge said, pointing at Rico.

"*Whoa*," said another. "Shit. Is that Rico?"

Rico groaned again.

"Holy shit. Rico. Did you get beat up?" There was a tinge of awe in his voice.

The other guard gasped. "Dude. I think he did. Hey. Hey, Rico!" He nudged Rico with his boot. "Yo, Rico! You okay, man?"

Rico shifted. He pulled himself up, every tendon, every bone of his body straining as if strapped to the floor. The guards helped him, one under each shoulder.

"Geez, Rico," a guard said. "They did a number on ya. These two? *They* did this?"

"Shut up." Rico seized the pistol from the guard and aimed it, trembling, at Dan and Mara.

"I love you," Mara whispered.

"I love you too," Dan said.

Rico let the gun fall to his side. He wiped the blood from under his nose. "No. Too easy. Gag them. They talk too fucking much."

32

The car ride immediately following an argument is always awkward, and it turns out that's especially true if the argument is concluded by someone being pummeled over the head with a snow globe. Rico and his guards hardly said a word the entire ride, and actually neither did Dan and Mara, but that was due in large part to the fact they'd been gagged with sweaty bandanas.

After a few minutes, they arrived at the tarmac in front of the hangars. Rico lifted them both—one over each shoulder—and slammed them face-first into the snow. Dan's whole body ached as Rico bound his hands behind his back, and he heard Mara grunt as another guard worked on her. When they were finished, Rico yanked each of their faces from the snow and forced them onto their knees.

There was the plane, the one Alan had been working on, the one with the red stripe. And there was Lilyanna and Pete Collins, and Brody Sheridan, and Brody's girlfriend, and they were loading luggage onto the plane and laughing with each other.

Rico hobbled between Dan and Mara. He bent over, smacked Dan lightly on the cheek, and then seized his jaw.

"I was gonna kill you, Foster," he said. He pushed his finger into Dan's forehead. "Was gonna put a bullet right here. But, nah. I'm gonna make you watch. Gonna make you watch as we fly away. My guards back here? They got orders to make sure you don't move. You're gonna freeze to death on this island."

Dan laughed. He couldn't help it. Fly away? They'd hit the dome. Just like the Brits, they'd crash into the dome, and that would be it.

"Laugh it up," Rico said, and he gave Dan one more good smack. Then Rico bent over Mara. "Maybe I should take you with me. You got a lot of fight in you, girl, I like that."

Dan's laughs turned to screams, and he launched himself toward his wife, landing shoulder-deep in the snow. Rico snorted. "Damn, son," he said. "Selfish much? At least she'd *live*. Nah. I'mma leave her here with you. Too much mouth on her."

Near the plane, Lilyanna caught Dan's eye and she grinned at him, like, How'd you think this would end? And then she and Pete strolled over, and she helped Dan back onto his knees. She brushed the snow off his face and pinched his cheek.

"Bless your heart. I hate that it's come to this, y'all, I really do, but what choice did you leave us with? Really?"

"Yeah," Pete said, scratching his head. "Gee. This isn't what we had in mind, I can tell ya that. Just, you know, the plane's only so big, and I doubt you can hang on to the wings! And then ya punched me and stole my wife during the wedding, and that just...well, that wasn't real chill with us, if we're keeping it one hundred. Whaddya think, though, Lily, do we leave 'em in the snow like this? Maybe ask Rico to cut 'em free. Gosh, I don't know."

Lilyanna ignored him. She caressed Mara's face. "Oh, honey. Maybe you could've fixed him if you had more time. Ya just—ya can't bet on the wrong horse so close to the finish line."

Lilyanna glanced up at Madge, who stood behind Dan and Mara with the other guards. "Remember what I said now, Madge: executive earning potential, working part-time from home. Once we get the rest of these planes back for y'all, you're joining team boss babe."

"And you'll waive that fee for the starter kit?"

Lilyanna winked at her. "We'll talk about it."

The Collinses returned to the plane, loaded the last of their luggage. Look at them. Completely oblivious. Those stupid assholes. Those selfish, stupid, *greedy* assholes. Lead the island into chaos and then escape by dark of night—dark of day— whatever. Well, they'd get theirs. In a decadent pageant of cosmic irony, they'd get theirs. And Dan was going to enjoy the fireworks.

Wait. Parts of Dan's brain were still clicking on.

Wait.

Who was the pilot? There was only one pilot on the—

Oh, no. No, no, no.

The door to the cabin sprung open, and out stepped Alan Ferris, some paper rolled in his hand.

"These charts are ancient," he said, "but I can get us there. Wheels up as soon as possible. Looks like it might storm again, and we can't—" He stopped dead when he saw Dan and Mara. "Who brought them here?"

"Rico," Brody said.

Alan tapped the map in his palm. "Fuck." He hung his head, trudged through the snow to them. "Why are they gagged? Who gagged them?" Alan reached to undo Dan's restraints, but Rico stepped in.

"They stay gagged. These two talk too much. They get in your head."

"Rico, come on. Let me talk to them and—"

"So talk," Rico said. "They can listen."

Alan glanced at the grotesque bruise spreading across the dome of Rico's head and nodded. He stepped back. *Why did he step back?* He'd really leave them gagged like this? In the snow? The dread in Dan's belly sidled against the rage in his chest. He twisted in his restraints, snarled like a muzzled dog.

After everything—*everything*—you're flying *them* out of here? The Collinses? And Sheridan? *Rico?* You were the best man at my wedding! You only found this plane because me and Lenny risked our necks to help you. Remember Lenny? He's dead, by the way. The thug you're about to private charter shot him to death. I can't even look at you. Don't do this, man, don't do this. You don't even know what you're doing. Look at my eyes, Alan. You're usually the one who knows what to do, but I need you to look into my eyes this time, man, please.

"Look, kid." Alan got eye level with Dan, placed a hand on his shoulder. "This, ah…" He paused. "I'm sorry about this. It's a tough deal."

A tough deal? Accidentally liking an ex-girlfriend's photo on Instagram is a tough deal. Realizing too late a public bathroom has no toilet paper in a tough deal. This…this was betrayal.

And *stupid* betrayal too, because—Alan, please, you don't know everything.

Alan made like he was about to stand, like that was all he had to say, but something occurred to him. "Listen. You realize when you get older—there are things that're bigger than right and wrong. Okay? There just are. Family. Your people. They come first. They have to come first. It's all we have."

There was a dramatic gasp from somewhere near the plane. No doubt who that belonged to. God, Charles. Sweet Charles. Mara shrieked for him, pleaded with him, pointed her chin to the sky like, Look, dummy, look, you're gonna experience some turbulence. Charles fell to his knees and hugged her.

"Alan," Charles said, his voice shattered. "Alan. We can't leave them. We just can't. Maybe—could they sit on our laps?"

"It's a weight thing, Charles."

"Then dump my bags. Leave the bags. All my clothes, honey, I don't care. But please. I thought I could do it, but I can't. We can't—oh, how can we live with ourselves?"

Alan clutched Charles's shoulders and stood him up. "We have to get home to our boys."

"Alan—"

"*We have to get home to our boys.*"

Charles returned to his knees, ran his fingers through Mara's bloodied hair. "I am so, so sorry. Mara, honey. I…we have to get home to our boys." Charles and Mara sobbed into each other. "I love you." He turned to Dan. "We'll send help—as soon as we get back to the States, we'll send help. I swear to God."

"Come on, Charles," Alan said. "The storm's coming."

And that was it. Lilyanna, Pete, Alan, Charles, Brody, and

his girlfriend looked out from the tarmac one last time, into the woods and at the island beyond. They were leaving Tizoc. Really leaving.

Kind of.

Dan didn't want to throw up, not with a bandana in his mouth, but he—

Wait a minute.

Dan cycled through the passengers again. The plane's a six-seater. Lilyanna, Pete, Alan, Charles, Brody, and his girlfriend. Dan was no mathematician, but what about—

Rico cleared his throat. "Lilyanna." He staggered between Dan and Mara, closer to the plane, closer to its passengers. "Hold on a minute. I didn't know the fat one was coming. This math don't add up. I count seven."

Lilyanna smiled at him, a big fake smile, a smile that was meant to disarm him but had the opposite effect. "Well, now, Rico, I've been meaning to talk to you."

He recoiled. "Don't do it, lady."

She held up her hands. "Listen, Rico, hun, listen to me now. We're gonna come right back for y'all, okay? Right back."

Rico spit in the snow. It was red. "You fuckin' kidding me? We had a deal."

"Yes, we did. Yes, we did. And the deal's still on, son. You'll get paid. We'll send a plane for you. Lord as my witness. And for your men too. I swear on my babies. Alan refused to fly without his husband, okay? And it's only six seats, Rico. Simon Cowell didn't even make it."

"Only six seats," Rico repeated.

"That's right. Only six seats."

"Okay," Rico said, and he pulled Lenny's pistol from his pants and shot Pete Collins in the face. Lilyanna caught her husband's limp body as it folded into the tarmac, dead before he hit the ground. Dan could hardly look. Rich crimson stained the snow. Lilyanna screamed, begged. Everyone screamed actually, besides Alan, who shook his head in disgust. Rico holstered the gun.

"Guess we got room now." Rico approached the plane, but Brody and his girlfriend retreated, shielded themselves behind Alan and Charles. Rico laughed. "Anyone else got a problem with me catching this flight? No? Okay." He turned around. "Lilyanna. Come on. Leave it. You heard the man. Storm's coming."

Lilyanna was draped over her husband. "My love," she said. "My love, my love, my love. I'm so sorry, Pete. Please, please." She burrowed her face into his chest, probably listening for a pulse, listening for anything, but there was only wind.

Rico approached her. "Lilyanna. You coming? Last call."

She didn't budge.

"Okay," Rico said. "Up to you, ma'am. Well, now we got an extra seat. Do we—" He put his hands on his hips. "We could take the girl. I know I said she talks too much, but—" He smiled. "You know, she's growing on me."

"No," Dan screamed, and his mouth was still muffled, but it was very clearly the word *no*. He was shoulder to shoulder with Mara now, and he wanted to chew through these restraints, wanted to smother Rico and his gold tooth in the snow.

Charles wiped the snot from his nose and refused to look at Rico. He spoke softly. "Mara, honey. Do you want to come with us? We could take you. We'll send help for Dan, for everyone, but in the meantime, you can get home to your mom."

Rico shrugged. "Let's take her."

Mara scrambled to get away, and Dan threw himself atop her, but Rico kicked him in the gut, snatched Mara, and tossed her over his shoulder in one swift motion. Dan could hardly breathe, but Mara's screams lifted him from the ground. She thrashed and kicked in Rico's arms, and Dan tried to tackle him, but he was backhanded.

One of Mara's kicks connected. Rico dropped her, and she scrambled to Dan.

"Fuck," Rico said with a laugh. "You can't pry these two apart. Bitch, you'd rather die with him than go back home? I really like her. I'm keeping her."

"Leave her," Alan said.

Rico glared at him, raised an eyebrow. "What's that?"

"Leave her."

"I want her. I'm taking her."

"You're leaving her with her husband, or I'm not flying this plane."

"Alan…" Charles said.

"She wants to be with her husband. Rico, if you're coming, get in. We're leaving now."

Rico spit. "Fine. Fucking freeze here." He considered his guards. "'Ey, Madge. You want a ride?"

"Hell, yeah," Madge said.

She broke from the others and climbed onto the plane. Brody and his girlfriend attempted to board next, but Rico seized Brody by the collar. His eyes shifted between his two remaining guards and Brody.

Brody stammered. "I-I can pay you double."

"Tell me I'm a good stuntman," Rico demanded.

"Dude. What? You're an amazing stuntman. The—the best."

"Now tell me you'll pay me triple."

"Yeah—bet. Bet. Triple."

Rico's bloody grin touched both ears. "All aboard then." He turned to the others. "Sorry, boys, we'll send help if we can. Just make sure these pieces of shit are frozen to the tarmac when it gets here."

"What did he say?" Charles asked. Alan shoved Charles into the plane. "What did he say? He can't do that. He can't make them stay out there. Alan. Alan, I'll never forgive you. Alan—"

"Get *in*," Alan said.

The plane door slammed shut. Charles's face was plastered against one of the windows, and he was shouting something and banging on the frame, but Dan couldn't hear it over the wind, over Lilyanna's cries, over the engines. The plane had started up, by God, it started right up because Alan knew what he was doing, he really was a capable man even if he couldn't always see what was right in front of him. The propeller spun faster and faster until it vanished, and Mara wept into Dan's shoulder because she couldn't bear to watch. The plane turned, straightened itself on the tarmac, and then was off, leaving dual tracks in the snow. Maybe it won't lift off, Dan thought, maybe it won't fly. But it reached the end of the runway and took to the sky, its taillights like stars in all that black.

It flew higher and higher until it could hardly be heard anymore. A bead of doubt formed in Dan's mind, because gosh, they were getting high up there now, surely they should've hit the dome. What if everything Shae said was a lie? The new stuff anyway. What if the sun really had exploded, and the experiment wasn't actually a dome, but it was lying to people about a dome and seeing how they reacted? What if…? Of course there wasn't a dome. A *dome*. A fucking *dome*? Over an entire island? How stupid could he be? Dan was beginning to feel really silly, really—

Oh.

There it is.

Mara screamed as the plane exploded, the flaming wreckage falling from the sky like comets. The nauseating sound of twisted metal and the flash of light momentarily pulled Lilyanna from her grief.

"What the fuck?" one of the guards said.

"Dude," said the other.

Dan screamed for Lilyanna, slapped the restraints against his ass. Dazed, she scurried across the pavement to him, made quick work of the knots. Super quick. It would have been impressive, actually, had Dan had time to reflect on it.

"Hey," one guard said, his heart barely in it. "Hey, don't—"

The entire sky flashed royal blue—the color blue like when a computer crashes—and then immediately gave way to a disorienting static, a crack fracturing from the plane's impact site. For a few seconds, Tizoc Grand Islands Resort and Spa existed inside a TV with poor signal, the X-rated channel no one paid for, and the convulsive locomotion of the universe made Dan feel lost in time and space.

"*Is this it?*" asked one of the guards frantically. "Is this the end of the world?"

Lilyanna undid the bandana from Dan's mouth.

"It's a dome!" he screamed. He dove for Mara, pulled helplessly at her restraints. "Undo hers! Undo hers!"

Lilyanna did as she was told, yanked wildly at Mara.

"There's a dome over the whole island!" Dan said.

"*What?*" Lilyanna freed her.

"A dome!" Mara said.

The static ceased and the island was plunged into a sickening darkness. Electricity had been severed—the lights along the runway faded like memories. Dan clutched the shape of Mara to his chest. Not like this. *Not like this.*

There was rumbling, the sound of a thousand drums pounded upon in Heaven, and a large chunk of dome near the crash site crumbled. It broke off in pieces, one by one, monstrous fragments of distorted metal and rebar falling thousands of feet in seconds and crashing into the ocean below. Through the hole, as if it'd been trying to push its way through this whole time, was something Dan and Mara were sure they'd never see again.

Sunlight.

It poured through the opening like a spotlight, pristine, and blinding, and probably warm—so warm. Dan wanted to swim out there and wrap himself in it, strip off his clothes and bathe in it, run it through his hair like shampoo and make love to his wife in it, melanoma and sunspots and SPF 30 be damned.

That one swatch of light gave Dan a sense of things, helped him calibrate the world around him. He could see the dome for what it was now. A grid of dark ribbed metal. LCD screens, tinted glass. He could see the seams where it was welded together, where repairs had been made, its curvature against the horizon. It was like being inside a theme park ride with the

lights switched on. How could they have been fooled by something so ridiculous?

Everyone, even Lilyanna, sauntered toward the light like
zombies, like moths. Lilyanna whispered quiet, bewildered gibberish, the guards said the f-word a lot, and Mara pushed Dan in
the shoulder, like, You seeing this?

It was over. There was light up ahead—*light!*—a way out.

Something to crawl toward.

Then more rumbling. Ground-shaking, earth-shattering,
eardrum-pulverizing rumbling. Cracks from the crash site splintered over the dome, light poking through the fissures. Another
piece of dome broke off, this one nearer the airport. It landed like
a lost spaceship, creating a smoldering crater. Mara shrieked and
spun Dan just in time to see yet another piece fall, past the woods
where the resort stood. Wind carried guests' screams.

Dan and Mara shared a panicked glance. "The tunnels," they
said in unison. They sprinted for the guards' Jeep, yelling for the
others to follow, but the guards blocked their path and shoved
them backward. One cocked his pistol.

"Rico said you stay put!" he said, resolute.

"You've got to be shitting me," Dan said. "The sky is *literally*
falling!"

"Yeah, well, an order's an ord—"

A chunk of dome obliterated both guards. It was so close that
Dan felt a draft as it passed.

"Fuck," Mara screeched. "Fuck!"

Dan seized her wrist and swung her over the hole containing
guard compote and pointed toward the waiting Jeep. "Get in!
Find the keys!" He turned back for Lilyanna, who hadn't moved,

her head off-kilter and makeup running. "Lilyanna. Come on!" Dan grabbed her, but she resisted, pulling for her husband.

"I can't—Pete—I can't—"

Dan twirled her toward him, shook her frail body. "Look at me! Hey, Lilyanna, *look at me!* Your kids. This means they're alive. They're back home in Tennessee! You get that, right?"

Mara screamed at Dan as another mass of metal landed feet away, showering them in earth and snow. At the mention of her kids, Lilyanna snapped back to reality—whatever this version of it was—and she nodded. She took one last longing gaze at her husband before sprinting toward the Jeep, her hand in Dan's.

Mara tossed Dan the keys from the passenger side, Lilyanna climbed in back, and Dan took off, the Jeep spinning out before catching the remains of the runway.

"Seat belts!" Dan screamed as he veered left and then back right. Another missile hit just outside the Jeep, catching the edge of the rear passenger wheel and sending them careening. Dan regained control, prayed the wheel hadn't popped, and slammed the gas. He swung off the airstrip and onto the wooded road leading to Tizoc.

Lilyanna, even in mourning, was just the *worst* backseat driver. She dug her nails into Dan's shoulder. He repeatedly shook her off, but seconds later she'd reattach. "Look out," she screeched, "up ahead, up ahead, left, left—right! Go right, Dan, there's a big one. Y'all!"

"You're not helping!" Dan swerved to narrowly avoid a fracture that split part of the road in two.

Mara slapped Lilyanna's hands. "Get off him!"

"I'm tryin' to help!"

"You're not helping!"

"Will you two *shut up*?" Dan curved left to avoid a flaming hollow. The Jeep's side mirror collided with a tree and snapped off.

Mara's knuckles were white as she gripped the passenger handrest. "Shut up, Lilyanna. He doesn't perform well under pressure!"

Dan scoffed. "What? Sure I d—"

"Look!"

The manicured entrance of the resort rose in the distance, and Mara opened the center console and found a radio. She clicked it on: static. "Whoever can hear this—guests of Tizoc! Get underground! Underground now! It's a dome! I know it sounds crazy, but I swear to you, it's a dome! Get underground n—"

Everyone screamed as debris the size of a Buick pulverized the earth directly in front of them. There was no avoiding it. Dan turned too quickly to the right and felt the Jeep's tires leave the pavement. His stomach entered his mouth, and the airbags deployed—he was sure of that—but then he briefly lost consciousness. When he awoke, he was upside down in the Jeep. He saw Mara outside through the open passenger door, and she was all cut up but okay, and she cried his name and scraped her knees on the broken glass. She reached in, seized his arm, tried to tug him free.

Dan groaned as he stretched for her. "My…my leg." His left leg was lodged somewhere in the bent metal frame. He couldn't free it. And he smelled…he smelled gasoline. Oh, shit. Smoke. Dan smelled smoke. A fire had started in the engine. Flames licked up the windshield.

"Come on!" Mara said. Her eyes were panicked, feral. "Danny! Danny! Pull, baby, pull! Fuck. I can't—I can't get you out!"

The heat was quickly becoming a factor. Dan's body was slick with sweat. If his heart pounded any harder against the steering wheel, the horn would honk. He tried to wrench himself free using the hand brake, anything to leverage himself, but he was stuck.

This is how I go? *Fire?* During the fake apocalypse?

Dan quit struggling. He winced as another sliver of dome landed somewhere nearby. "Go," he said to Mara, waving her off. "Go! Get underground!"

Mara shook her head. "I'm not leaving you."

Lilyanna Collins limped into view.

"Help me!" Mara shouted. "Lilyanna. Lilyanna. Danny's stuck. Help me get him out!"

Lilyanna ignored her.

"Don't you *dare*," Mara said, furious, but then she pleaded. "Lilyanna. Please. He's my husband. Please."

Lilyanna stopped. Her fists clenched, her head shook as if in an imaginary argument. She took a deep breath and turned.

"Come on," she said. "Grab the other arm, girl." They each seized one of Dan's clammy hands. "Okay. Put your back into it now. Pull! One more. Pull!"

Dan used his loose foot to apply pressure. Somehow, the three of them working together did it, and Dan was pulled from the wreckage as flames overtook the cabin. Mara pulled him into her, kissed his face a thousand times.

"Come on," he said, unsteady in the melting snow. "We have to—"

A deafening roar. The dome wasn't breaking off in pieces anymore. What remained was collapsing, the entire thing, thousands of tons of metal returning to the earth in violent black sheets. It started from the north, flattening the airstrip and working its way over the dense woods, bringing the trees to their knees, snapping them like toothpicks. They no longer had minutes, they had seconds, and Lilyanna signaled toward a service door next to the resort entrance wall. Without a word—they wouldn't have heard each other anyway—they sprinted for it. Please be open, please be open, please be—

Dan burst through the steel door and immediately toppled down a flight of cement stairs, his leg screaming through the adrenaline. Mara and Lilyanna joined him in a flash. They yanked him to his feet, and together they bolted down another flight and then another, before a wave of incomprehensible destruction swallowed them whole.

33

⌐∿⌐

I 'm just saying, you overplayed your hand when you emptied the vending machines." Dan shimmied his shoulders, tried to make his Dan-shaped hole a little roomier. "That's what did you in. It was the vending machines and the plumbing. At the end of a long day, Lilyanna, people just want some trans fat and a quiet place to shit. That's it. Everything else is window dressing."

Lilyanna's dusty accent called back from somewhere in the dark. "Quit talking to me."

"And then there was the electricity. I actually think you could've pulled that off. People understand the need to conserve energy, that's a simple concept. But lighting up Building A like a goddamn Christmas tree every night—what were you thinking? How'd you think they'd—"

"Danny," Mara said from below. Or above? It was impossible to tell. "Maybe let's be quiet for a while."

Dan *had* been talking a long time, though it's worth noting that time, famously an abstract concept, only becomes more nebulous once entombed. He'd been talking for two or three hours straight at least, and actually, you know what, it had probably been the better part of a day because he'd already explained the intricacies of Dr. Terry Shae's evil plan, recited the wedding vows he memorized but never delivered, and pondered aloud why the latest *Die Hard* movies were both thematic and structural disappointments.

He'd now shifted his monologue to cover Lilyanna's toxic leadership style and how it had directly led to everyone's demise.

"I'm just warming up," he said, because it was true. When he was talking, he wasn't thinking about what happened to Alan and Charles. He wasn't thinking about all the guests at Tizoc. He wasn't thinking about what was going to happen to him and Mara either.

He used his fingernail to pry loose a small rock he'd been picking at for hours. Once dislodged, a larger pile of debris shifted, further compressing their graves.

Lilyanna shrieked as the ground settled around them. And then: "Gracious Lord, we pray that You would be with us today in mind, body, and spirit, to remind us that You made plans for each of us long ago, that we—"

"What's this *we* stuff?" Dan asked. "Lilyanna Collins is not authorized to speak on my behalf, Lord. Actually, I've got some things of my own to say to you once I'm finished with her. I—"

"Danny," Mara said. "That's enough."

"We're trapped beneath thousands of tons of LCD screens because of her, Mara."

Lilyanna said, "That's Shae's fault."

Dan lifted his head, whacking it against something. "Well, you certainly didn't help the situ—"

"*Danny.*" Mara was stern, as stern as one can be from the fetal position. "Fuck. She just lost her husband."

Dan scoffed at that, which was a pretty mean thing to scoff at, but come *on*. Yeah, she'd lost Pete, but how many people on Tizoc had lost their Petes? Gloria's Pete was shot to death. Alan and Charles, they were each other's Petes, and they exploded. Mara's Pete was two soliloquies away from succumbing to dehydration. Shae was the root cause, sure, but Lilyanna and her ilk were just as culpable, just as—

"Did you scoff, son? Did you just scoff at my husband's death?"

"Whatever," Dan shot back. "I know how you felt about Pete."

Mara gasped so hard that she probably inhaled two tablespoons of sediment.

"No, really," Dan said. "You should've heard her in the hotel room, she—"

"You have *no* idea what you're talking about. You need to—"

"—called him useless, stupid, said he was an anchor to her ship. Said he could never—"

Lilyanna snapped. "And I loved that stupid, useless man with every fiber of my being. I was a prisoner of war, son, you caught me at a weak moment. Stay married for nineteen years, and tell me if you don't once criticize your wife."

Now she was weeping again, and Dan felt Mara's glare through the earth, felt those dual lasers slice clean through the wreckage and flambé his still-beating heart.

"Of course you loved him," Mara said softly.

"Pete was the father of my children. He *was* the anchor of

our ship. I—gave up my last chance to see my babies again just for another moment with him. So don't you tell me I didn't love him. How *dare* you."

No one talked for a while, not even Dan, until there was finally a break in Lilyanna's tears.

Mara said, "That's why you helped me save Danny."

Lilyanna sniffed. She took a long breath. "Oh, hun. I put so much work into that man. You know what that's like. You should've seen him when we got married. In worse shape than yours. Just a complete blank canvas. I spent years fixing that—"

"*Fixing*," Mara emphasized.

"Fixing, hun. Fixin' him into the man I—"

"You're so full of shit." Woah. The empathy had abruptly drained from Mara's voice. Dan knew that tone. That was the Mara's-thinking-about-tearing-your-ass-up tone.

"Don't act like you didn't have similar plans for Dan," Lilyanna said.

Mara laughed. "Everyone needs fixin' till you come along, right, Lilyanna?"

"It don't say *life coach* on my Instagram for nothing."

"Right. You coach the hell out of those BeachBod boss babes. And this island," Mara slapped some wreckage, "certainly would've been lost without you."

"That's right."

Mara shifted. Oh, boy. She was settling into this one. Dan chewed one of his fingernails, pretended it was popcorn.

"So let's take a look at your scorecard, Coach. Those BeachBod women—all million of them or whatever—the vast majority of them *lose* money, don't they?"

"Now, that ain't true. Income potential is based on individual output and any earning claims are—"

"We're buried alive, Lilyanna. The FTC can't get you here." Mara clicked her tongue. "Okay, crappy start. Let's talk about the island. You're right that Shae started all this. But do you think that maybe—*maybe*—if we had all worked together, we could've figured out what was going on before it came crashing down on our heads? All anyone's been focused on for over a week is class warfare, so we completely missed the real threat staring us in the face. That's because of *you*."

Lilyanna began to protest, but Mara rolled on.

"And Pete. I'm sorry what happened to him, Lilyanna, truly. He didn't deserve that. But *you* empowered the monster that took his life. And now you have the gall to say you *fixed* him? You know what Pete said to me before the wedding? He said your daughter wouldn't even talk to him. For *years*. He saw me in my wedding dress, and he almost cried because he was convinced his own daughter wouldn't want him at her wedding. Said he wished he'd made different choices." Mara scoffed. "Despite appearances, that dude was broken."

Dan remembered Pete saying something weird about their daughter that day too.

Mara gave Lilyanna a moment to respond, but she didn't take it.

"You don't fix people—you bring out the worst in them. Life coach, my ass. Anyone who claims to have mastered life to the point that they're qualified to coach others' is full of shit. Each of us is just figuring this out as we go. There's no playbook, or secret to success, or even one definition of what the hell success *is*. So don't tell me, Lilyanna, about plans to *fix* my husband. Dan doesn't need fixing—he just needs what we all need: nonjudgmental love and support. Maybe if *you'd* had some of that, you wouldn't have turned into such a colossal uppity bitch."

God*damn*. Dan would've pumped his fist in the air if there was any nearby. Instead he just mumbled, "Mm-hm," like that added anything, and for the first time since he'd met her, Lilyanna was speechless.

The three of them lay silent for hours.

Mara was a master at dressing people down, and she certainly had a flair for dramatics, but she inevitably felt guilty afterward. Dan imagined what she'd text him right now if their phones worked. She'd say, *Was I too harsh*, without any punctuation, followed immediately by *I'm starting to feel bad lol*. And Dan would say, *no, no way, Lilyanna needed to hear that*, and then he'd say, *it was actually kind of hot* with the eggplant emoji. And Mara would just say, *haha*, and nothing else, which Dan would take as a sign that she wanted him to be serious, so he'd say, *OK maybe we can soften it the next time we talk to her. SLIGHTLY*.

"Hey, Lilyanna," Mara eventually said. "About before. I—"

Lilyanna sniffed. "No, you were right, hun." She paused. "I think there's something wrong with me, y'all." She laughed, but it wasn't a real laugh, no way, and she became quiet again.

"We were going to steal the plane," Dan admitted, feeling like maybe he should be reflective too. "We were going to leave everyone behind to fend for themselves. I was okay with that. Maybe there's something wrong with me too."

"I shouldn't have ruined our wedding," Mara said.

"You didn't do anything wrong," Dan said.

"It was awful of me to wear white, hun. It's not even in my top three colors."

"If I hadn't gone along with Lenny's plan…" Mara's voice trailed. "I just got so caught up in winning, you know, being the person I thought my parents would want me to be. Maybe the war wouldn't have happened. Lenny. Gloria. *Charles*. So many people would—"

"I made up that stuff about Lenny stealing the food on the first night," Lilyanna said. This enraged Dan, but he didn't express it. Their grave had suddenly morphed into a safe space. "My whole life, I've always said anything I needed to get my way."

"I threatened to stab scissors into the guy whose beard is his whole personality," Dan said. "The one who sang 'Bubble Toes' at Julio's funeral. I was really mean to him."

"I tried to manipulate your husband on y'all's wedding night," Lilyanna said.

"I know," Mara said.

"It didn't work," Lilyanna said.

"It kind of almost did," Dan said.

Lilyanna prayed. "I know I don't deserve a second chance, Heavenly Father, I know it. But if You see fit to get us through this trial, Lord, things'll be different. *I'll* be different. I'm not gonna try to fix people, Lord, I'm just gonna help them. I have the money and power to do so much good in Your name, Lord, I do, and I can make a difference. I'm gonna be better."

She stopped. "I'm gonna be better, y'all."

The ground shifted but no one cried out. As debris again settled around him, something wriggled down near where Dan's hand was folded. A rat, he thought, which was perfect. Plague was the only postapocalyptic box they hadn't yet checked on their vacation.

But it was Mara's hand. She'd found him in the dark, and he squeezed it and she squeezed back.

Space and time collapsed. The sun circled Earth, not the other way around, fish climbed trees and chimpanzees swam the Pacific. Dan's entire world was flipped upside down, pulled inside out, and the ringing in his ears had softened to a dull, mournful hum.

He was awake or dead. Definitely one of those, but also maybe neither.

No one had spoken in what felt like years. Dan was afraid to speak, terrified Mara wouldn't speak back. Did his legs work? He wiggled a toe. Yeah. What about—what about your hands, Dan? His left pinky twitched. Hey, that's something! Okay.

He summoned the last of his strength—that got him up on an elbow—and he inched toward a side wall, disconnecting from Mara. He brushed his hand over it. Pebbles skipped away, dust filled his nose. He swatted the wall again. Again. A thousand years from now, when they found their tattered clothes down here, there'd be evidence. Evidence that Daniel Lewis Foster hadn't given up completely, that he'd left some sort of mark, that he tried. Even if he never made it out, even if he didn't get any-where, he hadn't gone gentle into the night either.

He'd done something.

A larger chunk of rock gave way, and the ground shook from above. Oh, God. The biggest landslide yet. Nice, Danny. They'd be—wait.

Hold on.

Dan listened intently, every hair in his ears at attention.

Were those?

"MARA! Mara!" He shook her hand.

"Hm?" She hardly stirred.

"Voices!"

"What?"

"Voices, Mara! Voices!" Danny tried to scream but mostly spat out dirt. "Down here! DOWN HERE!"

Lilyanna was moving now, somewhere out there. She screamed too. "YOU FOUND ME! I'm right here! It's Lilyanna! IT'S BEACHBOD BY LILYANNA!"

That dull, mournful hum didn't belong to the space between Dan's ears, it belonged to a backhoe, and it loosened the earth and debris above their heads, so close that Dan thought it might crush them. Dan and Lilyanna screamed some more, and Mara joined in, and Dan's vocal cords scraped like sandpaper against stucco. The backhoe puttered to a stop, and there was a moment of silence, but then someone hollered back, said, "We can hear you, we can hear you. We're from the United States, and we're here to help."

Dan, Mara, and Lilyanna cried from joy.

Dan could've delivered ten more monologues in the time it took them to clear a path out. It was careful work, removing all that rubble, like sweeping fossils with a seven-ton brush. But eventually a gloved finger poked through the ceiling, and then another, and when they retracted, light filtered through the holes.

The rescue team lifted Mara out first because she couldn't stand on her own. They covered her eyes with a bandana so they wouldn't be damaged by the sun, and she floated into the light like an alien abduction, her hand glued to Dan's until they were forced to part. Then they freed Lilyanna.

Finally they seized Dan, exhumed him with one mighty pull, and placed him on a stretcher, six men wearing clothes with Red Cross emblems, and they said, "You're a tough son of a bitch, man. We got you, we got you, here, cover your eyes."

But Dan pushed away the bandana, and he gazed into the endless blue sky, because for the first time in a long time, there wasn't anything hanging over him.

34

The joke was that the medical tents—the dingy, crowded, sweltering medical tents erected on the remnants of the airstrip—were still better accommodations than Building C.

Once they had the strength, Dan and Mara pushed their cots together to form one mega-cot, and for days—there were real days again—neither left each other's side except to visit the porta-potty. Mara's right foot was shattered in two places. Dan had swallowed so much debris that they temporarily placed him on oxygen.

They were the lucky ones.

Beyond the airstrip, Tizoc was unrecognizable. Piles of rubble stretched above Dan's head, four stories high in some areas. House-sized craters had been burrowed into the ground to reach the tunnels where most survivors were located. There were no birds, no insects, even the breeze had found another island to haunt.

Within days, the number of FBI agents coming and going from the tent rivaled the number of Red Cross workers.

Lilyanna Collins chartered a private flight home at the first opportunity.

Dan and Mara caught her late one night on a small section of cleared tarmac. There was a flurry of ass-kissing surrounding her jet—photographers and stylists, influencers and bag handlers—and in the middle of it all was the woman herself, holding court and smiling real big, the bruising on her face hidden beneath a layer of bronzer. She was wrapped in a brace for a broken clavicle, but it was hot pink and had *BEACHBODY BY LILYANNA* emblazoned on it.

Dan pushed through the horde of underlings to reach her, his frail body knocked off balance more than once. Mara limped atop crutches just behind.

"Danny," she called out. Then, more forcefully: "Danny." Mara seized Dan's shirt. "Leave her."

"She's running away," Dan said, flabbergasted. A camera flashed. "After everything—she's still running away."

Mara coaxed him backward, away from the crowd.

Dan's fists were clenched, but he was too weak to hold them long. Rage exploded from him in a violent coughing fit. Mara patted his back, a signal for him to not get worked up, but he pulled away. "There are people here in critical condition, Mara. The hospital ships won't arrive for days. She said she wanted to help people, and she's—"

"Not worth it, Danny. Hey." Mara held Dan's face. She was mad too, Dan could see it in her eyes, but she wasn't disappointed like he was. "Just let her go. The FBI knows what she did."

Dan nearly buckled from exhaustion. He fell into his wife. Before hobbling back to the tent, Dan took one last glance at the crowd, and by some miracle, he caught Lilyanna's eye. She looked scared of him at first, like a drifter had stumbled into her dinner party, but she quickly ascertained that his fight was gone. She tilted her head and winked. She didn't say it, but Dan heard it: *Bless your heart.*

She turned away.

Dan thought he might puke up more island. Lilyanna Collins would be recording new workout videos in a month. Remarried in a year. What happened on Tizoc wouldn't stick to Lilyanna like it was going to stick to Dan. At a certain tax bracket, trauma is deductible.

The squealing crowd reentered its orbit around Lilyanna, swallowing her whole.

She was one of the last to board. Dan thought she'd pause at the top step maybe, that maybe what Mara had said to her underground had made some sort of dent, planted some sort of seed, and Lilyanna would remember—even for a second—how many people had actually lost the center of their universe on that island.

But she didn't.

35

They hadn't found Dr. Terry Shae—not yet anyway—but his life's work escaped Tizoc unscathed.

Emergency crews restored cellular to the island on the same day Shae's data hit the web. Dan's shattered phone was bombarded with the images and videos of himself and fellow guests across news sites and social media. He sat on the edge of the mega-cot, hands trembling. There he was, inciting a riot on TikTok. And there was Rico Flores on Fox News, executing an old woman in a pixelated video. Then there was Lilyanna Collins—it must've been that first night—rallying visitants of Building A to commandeer the island's supplies.

Dan grinned for the first time in days. She couldn't run from that.

There were terabytes of data—or gigabytes, whichever's larger—and next came the text messages and the phone calls and the emails, and now the president was commenting on Tizoc, the disaster had its own Wikipedia page, and Marvel Maids let Dan know he was out of PTO and wouldn't be paid for any additional time away.

In a press conference, the Space Telescope Science Institute condemned Shae's actions in the clearest possible terms, but then a hot mic caught the director whispering, "The data *is* invaluable. You've gotta admit that."

36

Gloria Fava was weepy.

A woman had just announced through a megaphone that flights to the Northeast were boarding, and Gloria fanned her eyes with her free hand as she stood from her messy cot. A man in an AC/DC shirt, who didn't even stop to mutter an apology, bumped her left arm as he hustled to get in line. It remained rigid in its sling.

Dan hooked a Red Cross bag around Gloria's good shoulder. Mara fought her way up, waddled over with her crutches clicking beneath her. It was early morning. Outside the tent, the sun hadn't risen, but massive floodlights cast shadows on hundreds of aid workers in reflective vests scurrying along the airstrip. They pushed handcarts and wheelchairs, signaled box trucks and bulldozers. Broken families and friends huddled in tight circles, while many guests stood alone, their hands at least half as full as when they arrived.

Mixed with the smell of jet fuel and antiseptic was the smell of eggs, and peppers, and sausage. Simon Cowell, who actually *was* at the resort the whole time, believe it or not, had stayed behind even after most of Building A was gone. He announced one morning that he was using his private jet to fly down some of the best chefs in Los Angeles, and they were here now, preparing breakfast burritos, and making jokes, and hugging people because maybe not everyone in Building A was that bad.

They reached the line for Gloria's plane. Mara wordlessly hugged her, a long, heavy hug, and when they detached, her shoulder sleeve was damp. Dan hugged Gloria next. He could feel the weight of loss on her, feel Lenny's spirit leaning against her shrunken frame, just out of sight.

She cupped Dan's face as he pulled away. "So handsome," she whispered.

The three of them just stood there a moment, Dan unsure of what to do with his hands or eyes or anything else. They shared a weak chuckle, because, you know, now what?

A Jeep rumbled onto the airstrip and screeched to a halt, seizing everyone's attention. It was the crew from *Disappearance Report*, Netflix had flown them down, and Jane MacCallum's husband was there too. He was in his seventies but in great shape, and he hopped from the Jeep with the vigor of a man on the trail of something long ago lost. He had a hurried, hushed conversation with an FBI agent while the *Disappearance Report* cameras rolled, and then the FBI woman signaled to more FBI people, and several of them spoke into their radios as they rushed to their SUVs. They sped off together, the Jeep leading the pack, and murmurs swept over the tarmac like wildfire.

The general consensus was that they'd found Shae's body.

People began to cheer, to embrace, guests from A, B, and

C celebrated with one another because nothing brings people together like something to collectively hate.

"Oh, I hope it's true," Gloria said with a sniff. "Look what that man did to all of us."

Dan hoped it wasn't. It seemed too simple an end for Shae, too convenient, tidy. Crushed to death by the weight of his own sick experiment, how poetic, how trite. Dan wanted to see him in handcuffs, wanted to see him answer for Alan, for Charles, for Lenny, for *Jane*, for everyone.

But Dan could feel in his gut Shae was gone. It was up to them to pick up the pieces he left behind.

They made a final boarding call for Gloria's plane.

"Okay, well." Gloria took a deep breath. "Guess I don't have much to carry on. Ha."

"You get home safe, Gloria," Mara said. She reached out and grasped her hand. "Keep in touch. Really."

"What will you do?" Gloria asked. That's what she said, anyway, but it sounded more like What should *I* do? which no one knew the answer to. She was going back to Jersey and her family and the deli, of course, but only part of her.

"We're just going to do the best we can," Mara said. "And we're going to make sure Alan and Charles's boys are okay. We owe that to them."

"Yeah." Gloria nodded. That seemed to be enough for her, at least for the flight home. "Do good, find good. Okay. I better go before the waterworks start again. Look, I've got your numbers, I'm gonna call you when I get a new phone, I'm gonna keep in touch because we went through something together, okay? I'm gonna be in touch. Maybe we go see those boys together."

"We should," Dan said.

"Okay. Sounds great, doll. Love you guys. I'm gonna go."

Flights to the Southeast wouldn't take off until later in the morning.

Mara was helping pass out meals, and Dan had been too, but he needed a break, so he sat alone on a pallet of bagged rice, away from everything. Marvel Maids emailed him again. Using Shae's data, someone had uploaded to YouTube a supercut of every instance where Dan bitched about his job to Dolly Parton's "9 to 5." Marvel Maids wanted him to know it was making its way around the office, and they weren't mad, not really, but maybe he could say something to the troops when he got back.

The bag beside Dan deflated.

Dan didn't recognize him at first, but then realized it was the guy whose beard was his whole personality, but his head was shaved because of a nasty gash that had been stitched up. His facial hair was still intact, thank God, and he was wearing the same Red Cross–issued, gently used clothing as Dan.

He had two beers. He handed one to Dan. The sun hadn't risen yet, but Dan had grown accustomed to not waiting for the sun.

Neither said anything for a bit. They quietly sipped and watched planes come and go.

"I owe you an apology," Dan finally said, not breaking his gaze.

"Nah, man."

"I do though." Dan turned to him. "I was really shitty to you, like, several times under the dome. I shouldn't have been like that." He saw Mara across the airstrip, smiling and handing a stranger breakfast wrapped in foil. He sighed. "I'm not sure why I was."

"I'm Tim," beard guy said, and he offered his hand and Dan took it.

"I'm Dan."

"Yes, you are," Tim said. "You're going viral, man. I rewatched the wedding on Facebook last night."

A forklift carrying boxes of computer equipment lumbered by. Tim said, "Did Shae really have to upload, you know, *everything*? My girlfriend's tits were on a message board."

He'd violated them all. Most websites were doing their best to remove anything private that popped up, but the creeps already had it. One final *fuck you* from Shae.

"One of the gossip websites posted a picture of me getting out of the shower," Dan said. "The headline was, *Love Handle Dandle: Five Fast Facts about Dan Foster.*"

"Did they pixelate it at least?"

"Yeah. But it only took, like, one or two pixels."

They laughed.

A thought occurred to Dan. He took a panicked glance around the airstrip and then back at Tim. "Your girlfriend. She—"

"She's okay," Tim assured him. "Traumatized, you know, but okay. She's around here somewhere. Said she needed to walk." He tore at the label of his beer, considered the tarmac awhile. "We lost some friends though."

Dan grunted. "Us too."

A plane to the West Coast was boarding. Dan and Tim watched as they lined up. A woman wrapped in a blanket wept. Another nearby was on a video call, and she said, "Mommy's coming home, I'm coming home," and then a little voice asked if Aunt Sharon was coming too, but the woman just repeated that she'd see them soon.

Tim took a gulp of his beer and pushed back further into the rice.

"You know," he said, his voice steady, "my first job was working for this kids' birthday party company." The shadow from a taxiing jet stretched across his face. "I've been thinking about it a lot since the dome fell."

"Oh, yeah?"

"I was fifteen, couldn't even drive yet. The lady had to pick me up, take me to these places all over. Wilmette. Lake Forest. Glenview, sometimes. They dressed me up like Batman, you know, or SpongeBob SquarePants." He chewed on that for a second. "That's actually where I learned ukulele."

Dan laughed but Tim didn't.

"I was Spider-Man a lot. The tights, you know, the mask. Costume was legit too, man, movie-quality stuff. Kids loved it, right, I'd swing into the party on a zipline that their dads hooked from the treehouse to like a tractor or whatever. Music playing. They went nuts."

"Sounds fun," Dan said, though it didn't sound like fun at all.

"It was alright. Paid cash. Only had to work weekends. Free food, usually." He shook his head, smirked. "But at every party, dude, at every party there were always the older kids, you know?" He pointed his beer at no one. "The older brothers who were too cool for this, you know, older than me a lot of times. And they'd always try to ruin it, right, prove to everyone they knew better. They'd be off to the side, shouting at me while I was playing with the kids. Saying, 'Spider-Man, do a flip! Jump on the roof, Spider-Man!' Shit like that. Man, I couldn't do flips. I was just trying to make some money so I could take girls out."

Dan sipped his beer. "Yeah. Assholes."

"That's what I thought," Tim said. He finished the last of his bottle, eyes lost in the rubble beyond the airstrip. "Now I think back on it, and I'm just like, who can blame them? I was the one who kept putting on the mask, you know?"

Before Dan could even consider a response, Tim's girlfriend appeared, and she wrapped herself around his shoulders.

"We're boarding soon, babe."

Tim stood, and Dan stood along with him. Dan offered his hand this time.

"I wish I could say it's been fun," Dan said with a wry grin.

"Oh, my review is going to be *scathing*."

It made Dan laugh.

37

That familiar fog floated between Dan Foster's ears, and the hair on his head felt heavy. It was the perfect predawn temperature, he pegged it around seventy-two degrees, give or take, and the waves were big enough that he wished the ocean would cough back up that rock he'd thrown in so long ago.

"You weren't supposed to leave the airstrip."

Mara Foster. She was behind him now, struggling with her crutches on the beach because she was holding more beers. Dan was there in a flash. His strength was returning, so he lifted her off her feet like he was carrying her across the threshold or something, and Mara giggled as they fell into the sand.

"Know what I'm doing when we get to the airport?" Dan asked.

"Auntie Anne's."

"Fucking right, Auntie Anne's." He shook his head. "Always get the pretzel."

"Always get the pretzel," Mara repeated.

They watched the water awhile.

"I just called my sister again." Mara used her left foot to brush some sand off her cast. She opened a beer. "They're all going to be there when we get back. I'm going to freak out when I see them, Danny. Your family's coming too. They want to throw us a big party for our wedding, but I told her to wait until my foot heals because I want to dance. Oh, and she said my work sent over a huge care package, it's at the apartment for us. How nice is that?"

Dan unlocked his phone, having only digested half of what Mara said. His head throbbed with thoughts of Tim's stupid Spider-Man story. He was thinking of Lenny too, and Alan and Charles and Gloria. The halo of red snow around Pete Collins's head. Julio under the garden. Rico as a stuntman. What Lilyanna said underground. He heard the deafening roar of the collapsing dome, but he shook it away.

"Did my work send anything?" he asked.

Mara took a swig. "Marvel Maids?"

"Yeah." Dan opened the mail app.

"Raveena didn't say anything." She touched his leg and quickly followed up: "But that doesn't mean they won't."

"Uh-huh."

Mara rested her head on Dan's shoulder. "Don't do that, Danny. Don't start worrying about that stuff right now. I've been thinking about what you said to me on our wedding night. I know Marvel Maids isn't where you'd thought you'd be. I know it's not your passion. I think you should write. Or whatever. Whatever you want to do. I mean, you're right, I do think you're capable of more than that place, but if nothing ever changed that would be okay too. But, hey, let's not even think about it right now. Let's get home. I just want you to be happy, Danny, even if—"

The *mail sent* chime rang from Dan's phone.

Mara lifted her head and scowled. "Did you seriously not listen to anything I just said? You're sending *email*? Wow, Danny, I—"

"I just quit." Dan dropped his phone into the sand like it was white-hot.

Mara pushed off him, beer leaking from her mouth. "You *what*?"

Dan tried to keep a straight face, but a smile broke through the surface, and he repeated himself because he needed to hear it again too. "I just quit."

Dan laughed as Mara lunged for his phone. He sipped his beer, watched her navigate to his sent folder. She found and quickly scanned the email. Her mouth agape, she looked from the phone to her husband, from her husband to the phone, back again.

"You just fucking quit," she uttered.

"I did." *I did!*

Mara shrieked and launched at him, hugging and kissing Dan and knocking him over. He cackled and pushed her away, but she clung on, and Dan said, "Careful with your foot, careful with your foot," and she finally settled down atop him but still excitedly slapped his chest.

"You're not mad?" Dan asked.

"No! Are you kidding? Danny!" She squeezed the sides of his head. "This is what I've *wanted* you to do! Screw Marvel Maids! This is so good. Wait. Does this make me a sugar mama?"

"I don't know what came over me. I just—I had to, Mara. No more bullshit. Okay? No more feeling sorry for myself. After everything that's happened..." He stopped. That wasn't just Mara he was feeling on his chest anymore. "Christ. Okay. That was impulsive. Was that too impulsive? You just married a man with no source of income."

"My mom will have questions."

Dan found her eyes, stared deeply into them. "I'm really going to try to do something. Write something. I could write about what happened here, or—I don't know. And even if it doesn't work out, you know—it's fine. I'll get another job. I'm going to figure it out, Mara. I promise."

"*We're* going to figure it out," Mara said, curling into him.

Mara and Dan Foster were on their second Miller Lites when the sun rose.

READING GROUP GUIDE

1. At the beginning of the story, our main characters find themselves witnessing the start of the apocalypse on the island
   resort of Tizoc. What were the reactions of the vacationers
   when the sun suddenly disappeared? How do you think you
   would react if something like this happened to you while you
   were on vacation?

2. How does Dan and Mara's relationship evolve throughout
   the short time that they are stuck on the island? How did the
   situations they were put in bring them together in the end?

3. Dan faces a major choice in the story: save himself or help his
   fellow resortgoers. How does Dan grow as a character and
   eventually come to help the people on the island of Tizoc?
   Then, think about if you were in his situation. What would
   your survival plan be?

4. If you were stranded on an island during the (maybe) apocalypse and only allowed three items, what would they be and why?

5. As the island of Tizoc plunges into darkness, the inhabitants start to show a dark side of their own. Discuss the tensions that rise as the resortgoers fight over resources. How do the buildings represent a certain class? Though this might be an extreme example, do you think this kind of divide is possible in a situation such as this? Explain why.

6. Discuss the role each character has on the island and how they contribute to the satirical nature of the novel. Who were your favorite characters and why?

7. By the end of the story, it's revealed that this apocalypse isn't all that it seems. What role does Dr. Shae and his laboratory have in the disappearance of the sun on Tizoc, and how do Dan and Mara find out? Were you surprised by the twist? If so, what did you think was going to happen in the end?

8. This novel might be considered a satire as it explores timely themes and concepts through humor and outlandish situations. Why is satire an important form of storytelling? What parallels were you able to draw between the characters of the story, the events that occur on Tizoc, and our current, real-life world?

A CONVERSATION
WITH THE AUTHOR

This is a hilarious satire that has so many twists and turns. What was your inspiration for this story?

Thank you! Turning thirty was my personal apocalypse. Like Dan, I spent my twenties cubicle surfing, too lazy—or scared—to pursue my dream of writing. It's easy to dismiss your dreams in your twenties. You have all the time in the world! But then thirty hit, and I was bald and had gray beard hair and my knees began making a Velcro sound when I stood up. I was officially getting old, and I hadn't accomplished anything professionally I was proud of.

Zero Stars was my way of working through those feelings. I thought an end-of-the-world scenario—a scenario where an underachieving character was *literally* out of time—would make a decent canvas to explore themes of inherent worth, modern restlessness, and toxic masculinity.

The reveal at the end is shocking and changes everything we

thought we knew was happening in the story. What was it like to write this twist?

Pretty fun. I'm not usually a big twist guy, but I am a mostly-happy-ending guy, so I knew from the beginning I wanted to provide Dan and Mara an off-ramp. Developing Shea's motivation was a blast. Who doesn't love playing mad scientist?

The trickiest part, for me, is leaving enough breadcrumbs throughout the story for a reveal to feel obvious in retrospect but not so many that the characters seem dumb for not figuring it out sooner.

If you were stranded on an island during what you thought was the apocalypse, which of your own characters do you think you'd be most like and why?

In the first chapter, there's a throwaway line about old people sipping on mai tais at the swim-up bar as the world falls to chaos around them. I aspire to be like that.

What does your writing process look like? Are there any ways you like to find creative inspiration?

I'm a firm believer that the writing process never really begins or ends, which sounds more self-important than I mean it. I've written some of my favorite sentences while hungover in the back seat of an Uber. I've written some absolute drivel while attempting to hit a word count at a weekend writing retreat.

You can't control when inspiration will strike, but you can build a lightning rod and hope for the best. My lightning rod is built from things like folk rock music, showers in the dark, and eavesdropping on strangers' conversations—but everyone's is different.

What do you hope readers experience while reading this book?

More than anything, I hope folks who read *Zero Stars* have fun. My primary goal is always to entertain—anything else is icing.

What are some books you've read that have influenced your writing?

Lonesome Dove is the book that made me want to be a writer. I also love Kurt Vonnegut, Douglas Adams, and more recently, I've been on a Barbara Kingsolver kick.

What are you working on nowadays?

I bought an Ooni Pizza Oven, so that's been a whole thing. The secret to a successful launch is sprinkling some Semolina flour on the peel before you assemble the pie.

Work has also begun on another silly novel.

ACKNOWLEDGMENTS

Unending thanks to:

My parents, siblings, and friends, who never let me take anything too seriously.

My agent, Brady McReynolds, for believing in this book and
pushing me to find the perfect ending.

My editors—MJ Johnston, Kelly Smith, and Liv Turner.
Y'all were right about the golf cart scene (among many
other things).

My rock with waves on it, Leslie.

Thanks as well to James Farner, Christina Zobel, Stevie
Finegan, and the team at JABberwocky Literary; the teams at
Sourcebooks and Bonnier Books; the Tennessee Young Writers'
Workshop; public education; the Reddit writing commu-
nity; Valerie Middleton, Kelly Medley, Allison Barney, David
Kumbroch, Sharon Pelletier, Sean Berard, Shivani Doraiswami,
Olivia Marzella, Brooklyn Wassmer, Matthew Marzella,
William Wassmer, Eliza Johnson, and Auntie Anne's pretzels.

ABOUT THE AUTHOR

MJ Wassmer is an author of speculative fiction who lives with his wife in Tennessee. *Zero Stars, Do Not Recommend* is his first novel.